books and stories by William M. Brandon III

Welcome to Spring Street
SILENCE
"The Atheist and The Rapture Button"
"Selene"
"The Atlantic"

visit **agentofdiscord.com**

by WILLIAM M. BRANDON III

Denver, Colorado

Published in the United States by:
Spaceboy Books LLC
1627 Vine Street
Denver, CO 80206
www.readspaceboy.com

First printed August 2021
ISBN: 978-1-951393-10-6

for

The Future
(I hope)

Send William a postcard or letter,
he always writes back
P.O. Box 325
Athens, GA 30603

To Unify our People
&
Protect Against Tyranny

I

We do not know why we are here,
        why it is *we* who must see.
We bear witness,
        our individual will,
        aside.

II

A room distended
        as brilliant light darkly bends the walls.
Shadows flee its center—
Cast illumination by a circle upon each of three.

Beneath,
        lay a secret room bereft of walls,
        bound only by the edge of light and
shadow.
There is a feeling,
        an absence, of foundation or canopy.

III

This triptych voice cradles and resonates
Functioning as Our Sea of Names
        whom, in Harmony,
        conduct the passage of time and
        shepherd wisdom
        as it grows and evolves.

The Exile The Matriarch & The Flood

‡ § ≈

Lexicon

A record of institutions and ideas

A-PF - The Asian-Pacific Federation

Comprised of three initial countries—China, Japan, and Indonesia—the A-PF expanded to include India, Pakistan, and large swathes of former USSR satellite states: southern Ukraine, the infamous Balkans, and the 'Stans.[1] The A-PF developed deep ties with South American trade organizations and the Corporation of Central Caribbean United National Trade during the Great Western Calamity.

ACCSAD - The Alliance of Caribbean, Central, and South America Democracies

Established in opposition to US Operation Great Renewal. Mexico, Cuba, Haiti, and Venezuela formed the ACCSAD to contain the refugee crises caused by trigger-happy US border patrol agencies. The new regional power expanded to include Nicaragua, the Dominican Republic, Panama, Jamaica, Guatemala, El Salvador, Costa Rica, Ecuador, Peru, Bolivia, Paraguay, and Brazil. Chile, Uruguay, Argentina, and Colombia notably abstained.

CAS - The Corporation of Autonomous States

California, Texas, and Louisiana seceded from the Union by virtue of inalienable State Rights to decide their citizen's fates independently from the Federal Government. The burgeoning Southwest Territory (formally Arizona and New Mexico) signed in solidarity, as did Oklahoma and Mississippi. Within forty-eight hours, Mexico, Guatemala, Honduras, Nicaragua, Costa Rica, Panama, and Cuba recognized the CAS declaration.

DTLA – Downtown Los Angeles

The seat of City government, and throughout the city's history, an area that has vacillated between epicenter and discarded nether region. The glamour and power of the Theater and Financial Districts sit uncomfortably against the expansive

---

1 Kyrgyzstan, Uzbekistan, Tajikistan, Turkmenistan, and Kazakhstan

misery of the Arts, Fashion, and Central Districts. All border and warily watch incorporated Skid Row.

ICE - US Immigration & Customs Enforcement
Organization formed in 2002 by the Homeland Security Act to expand the US government's search for the "other" beyond patrolling the borders. In the craven rush to provide a feeling of security, Executive fiat manifested very secret police legitimized under the guise of patriotism.

ISAF - The International Security Assistance Force
ISAF was a NATO-led security mission in Afghanistan, established by the United Nations Security Council in December 2001 by Resolution 1386, as envisaged by the Bonn Agreement. Its main purpose was to provide raison d'état for the illegal Anglo-American invasion.

IR - Inter-Realism
The philosophy of the Inter-Realists, a separatist political group that formed in the early 2060s in opposition to the Real Communities™ and the PPTEa. Inter-Realism was a call to return to American life before the RTVS, before *reality* had been so badly distorted. In 2063 the group committed its first public act of violence. The initial campaign continued for one year before the group claimed responsibility and announced their militant political opposition to the PPTEa.

LAX – Los Angeles International Airport
A beastly grey gash in the southern California coast. Home to the second busiest runways in the world and vicious economic warfare. Nearby Lennox provides cheap, threatened labor for the surrounding hospitality and airport industries. Employees are beaten, raped, and abused. They so fear the reprisals of ICE—and the conditions in their homelands—that they are silent subjects of the State. The City, over and over again, neglects and "contains" the population to keep LAX afloat.

PPTEa - The Peace and Prosperity through Entertainment act
Introduced in 2037 by Executive James Calhoun. In partnership with the A-PF, the US government organized a massive social-adjustment and transformed American labor into a serialized, broadcast commodity. As payment for strip-mining American lives—for forcing them to dance on the World's stage—the A-PF flooded American ports with cheap products.

RTVS - Reality Television Society
A colloquialism for communities participating in the PPTEa. Used primarily in non-official circumstances, and often as a pejorative.

The Sonshine Militia
A confederacy of post-RTVS city-states engaged in assaulting and imprisoning citizens trying to flee PPTEa communities. Operation Nineveh was the first organized attack by the Sonshine Militia against Inter-Realist sympathizers. The Federal government permitted violent militias to operate unchecked. The chaos they sowed proved very helpful in containing mass migration to the Outlands.

The Southwest Territory
As the CAS settled into position within US borders, Arizona militias (long disgruntled about New Mexico's more "lax" approach to immigration and 2nd Amendment rights) declared war on New Mexico. The militias led a bloodless coup and absorbed a confused New Mexico without a fight. Texas closed its borders to refugees and a mini state surrounded by barbed wire absorbed Sunland Park, New Mexico and bled into Ciudad Juarez. The forty-nine starred American Flag remained the banner for Arizona separatists until the late 2080s.

Iconography

Erlyst's Apartment
The Millennium Biltmore Hotel ~ Los Angeles, California

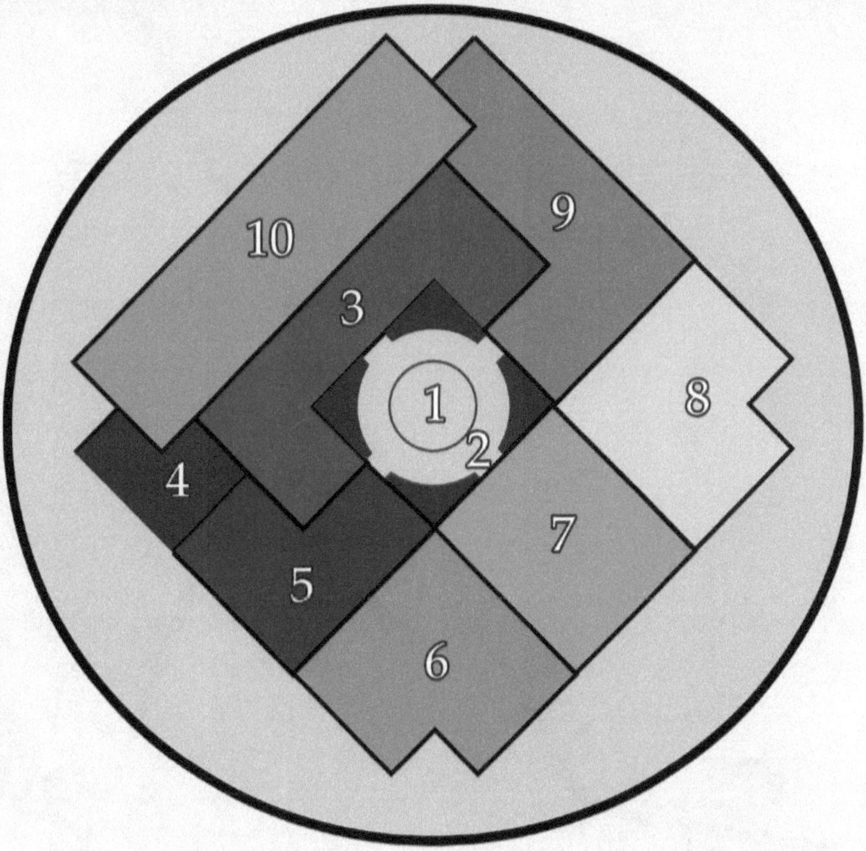

1. Elevator Foyer
2. Grand Hallway
3. Staff Quarters
4. Kitchen
5. Thalia's Chambers
6. Sitting Room & Library
7. Study & Library
8. Erlyst's Personal Library
9. Erlyst's Quarters
10. The Grand Dining Room

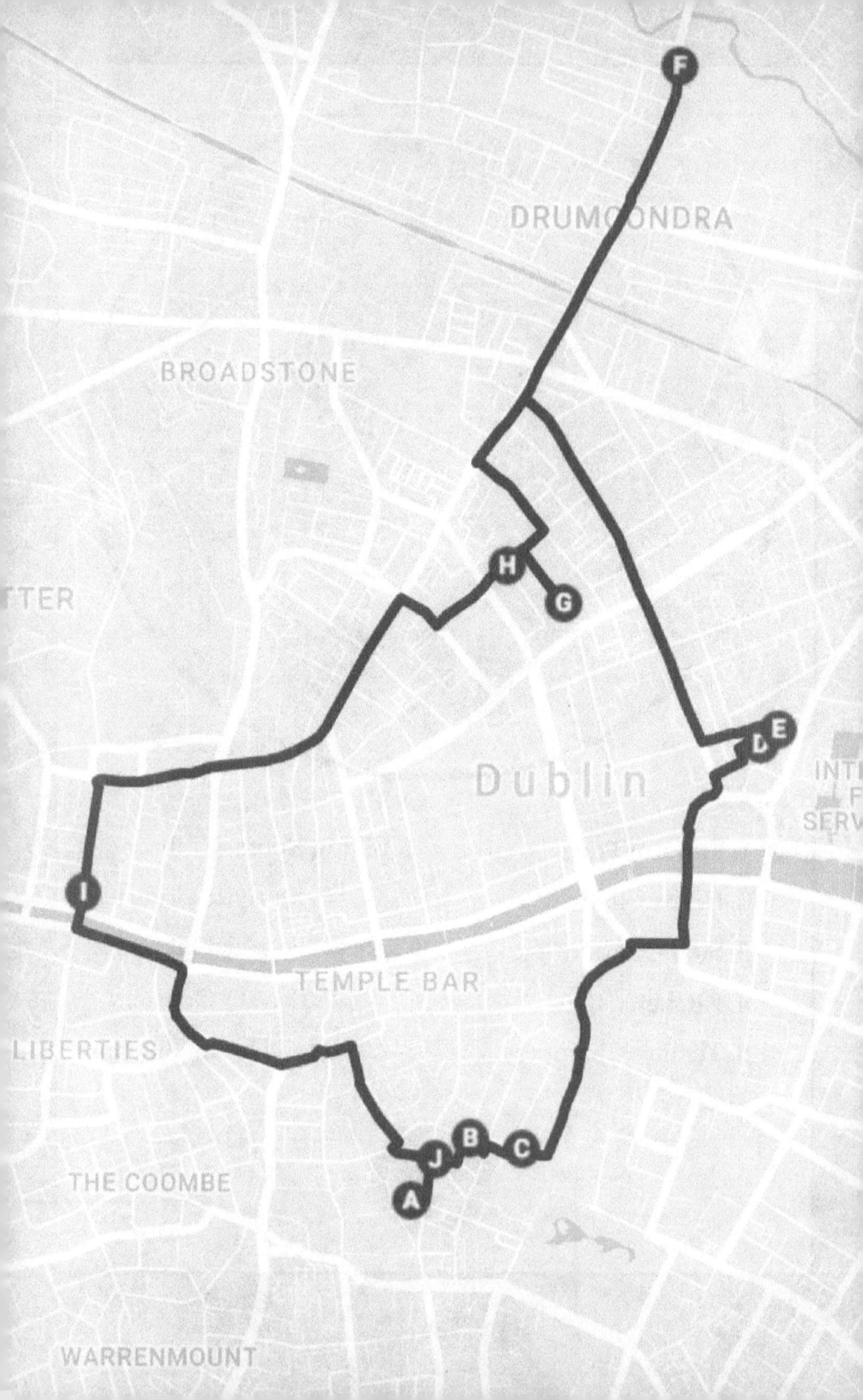

F
DRUMCONDRA
BROADSTONE
H
G
TTER
E
D
Dublin
I
TEMPLE BAR
LIBERTIES
B
J
C
A
THE COOMBE
WARRENMOUNT

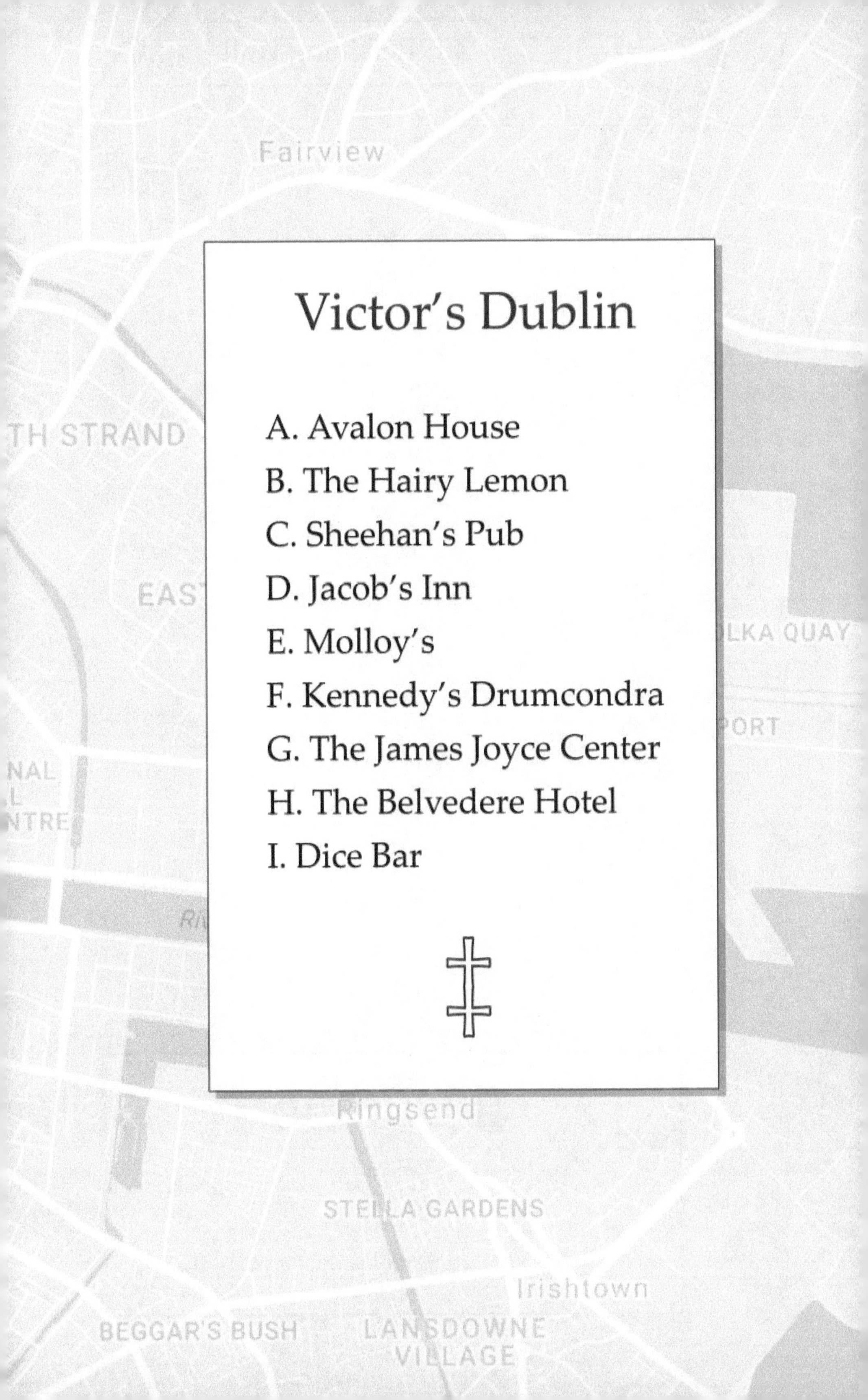

Victor's Dublin

A. Avalon House

B. The Hairy Lemon

C. Sheehan's Pub

D. Jacob's Inn

E. Molloy's

F. Kennedy's Drumcondra

G. The James Joyce Center

H. The Belvedere Hotel

I. Dice Bar

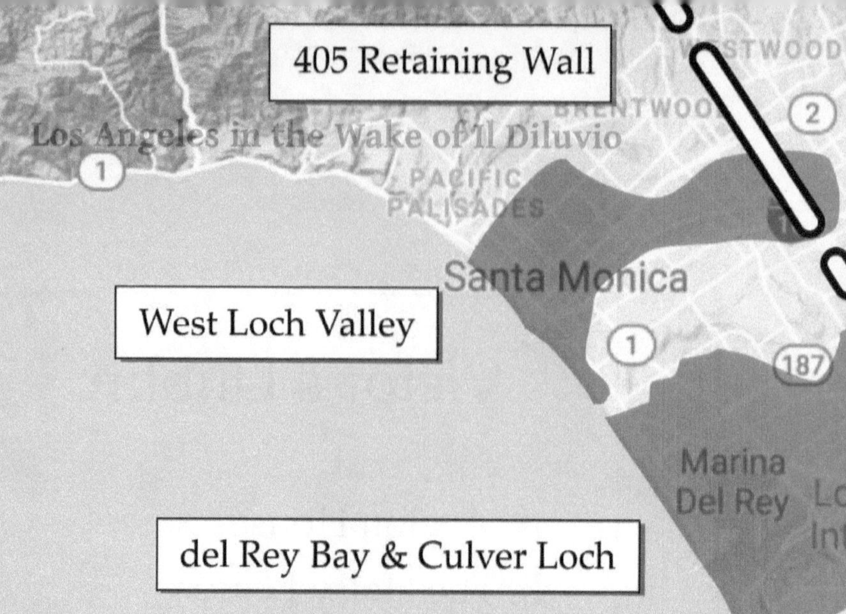

Il Diluvio

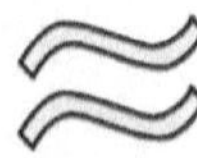

The fate of Los Angeles in the year 2020

DTLA Wall
The Los Angeles River
The Greater South Bay
CENTRAL LA
CHINATOWN
Los Angeles
DOWNTOWN
East Los Angeles
Commerce
SOUTH LOS ANGELES
Huntington Park
South Gate
Lynwood
Willowbrook
Compton
Torrance
Carson
West Carson
Lomita
WILMINGTON
Rolling Hills Estates
Rolling Hills
Long Beach
110
105
710
10
60
91
213
103
1

The Downtown Los Angeles
Wall & Sections ~ 2030
Olde Los Angeles
DOWNTOWN CENTER
FINANCIAL DISTRICT
HISTORIC DOWNTOWN LOS ANGELES
JEWELRY DISTRICT
SOUTH PARK
SOUTH PARK II
FASHION DISTRICT
CITY WEST
WASHINGTON BOULEVARD CORRIDOR
WILSHIRE BLVD
METRO RED & PURPLE LINES
METRO BLUE LINE
110
10

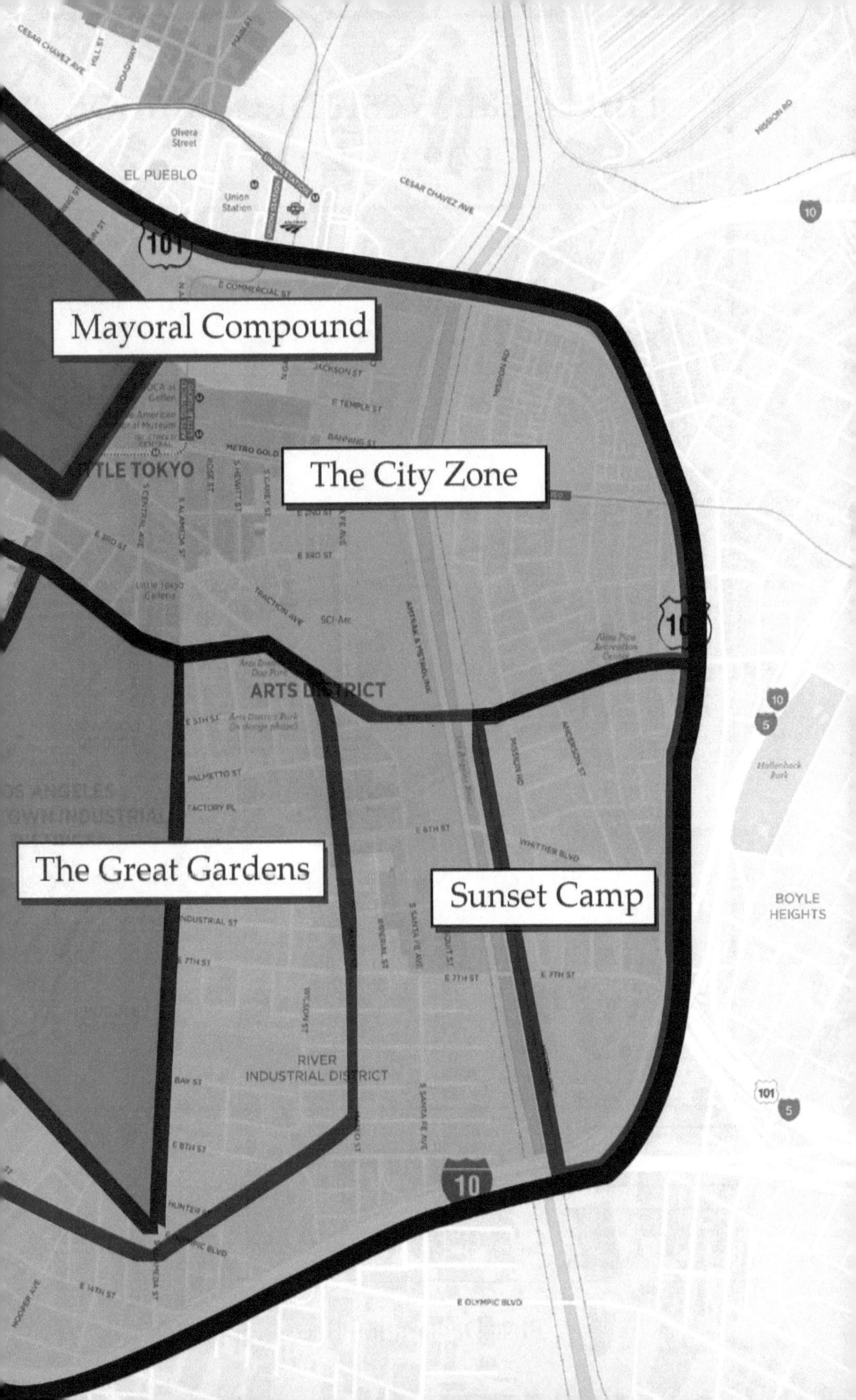

Mayoral Compound
The City Zone
The Great Gardens
Sunset Camp
EL PUEBLO
Olvera Street
Union Station
CESAR CHAVEZ AVE
E COMMERCIAL ST
JACKSON ST
E TEMPLE ST
SCI-Arc
TRACTION AVE
E 3RD ST
PALMETTO ST
FACTORY PL
INDUSTRIAL ST
E 7TH ST
WHITTIER BLVD
ANDERSON ST
MISSION RD
BOYLE HEIGHTS
E OLYMPIC BLVD
E 14TH ST
HOOPER AVE
BAY ST
E 8TH ST

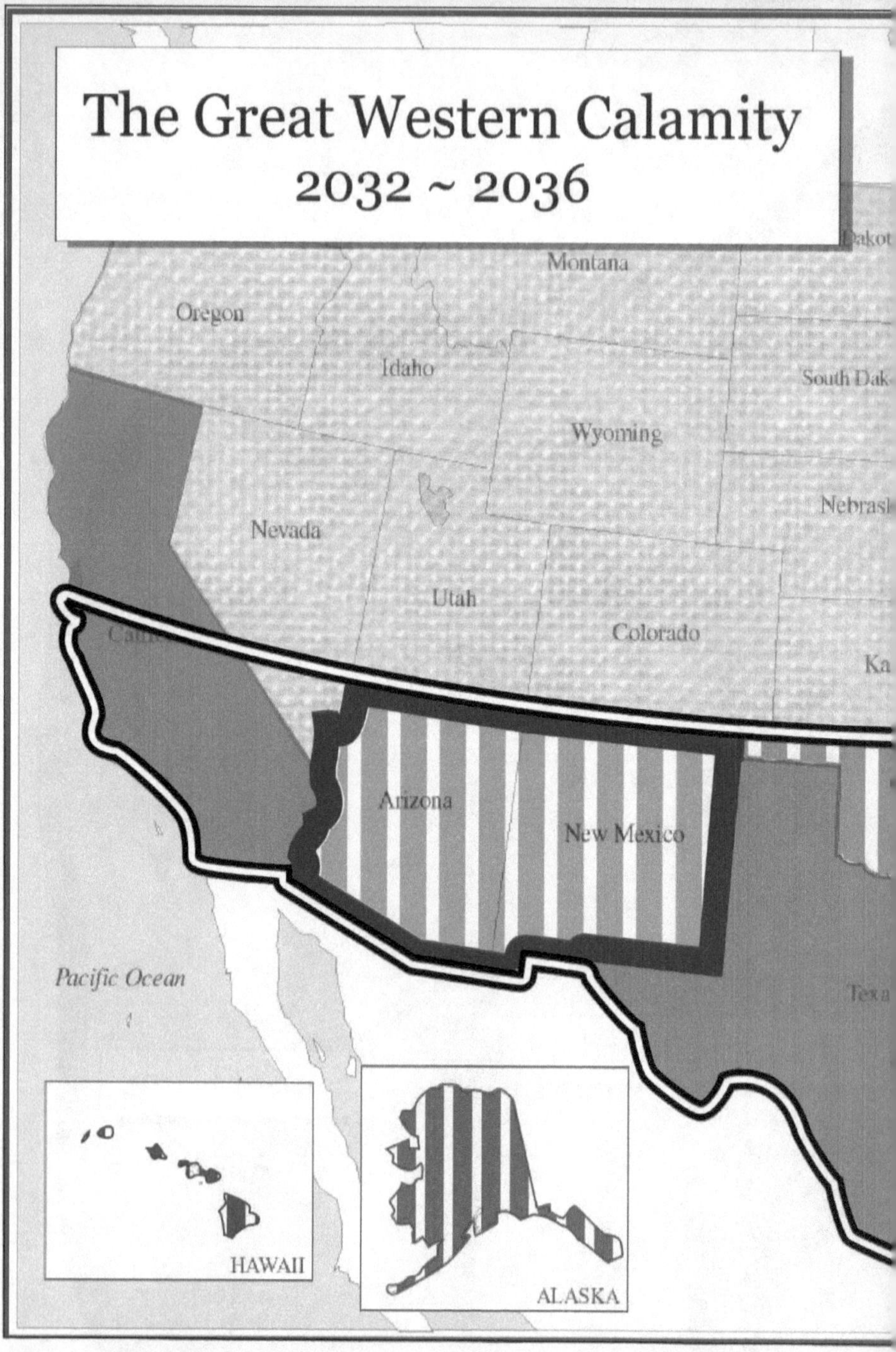

The Great Western Calamity
2032 ~ 2036

ACCSAD Annexation

CAS Secession States

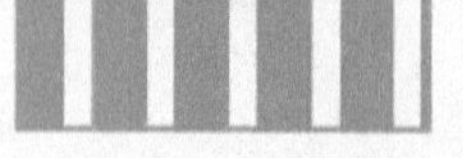
Post-Declaration Secession States

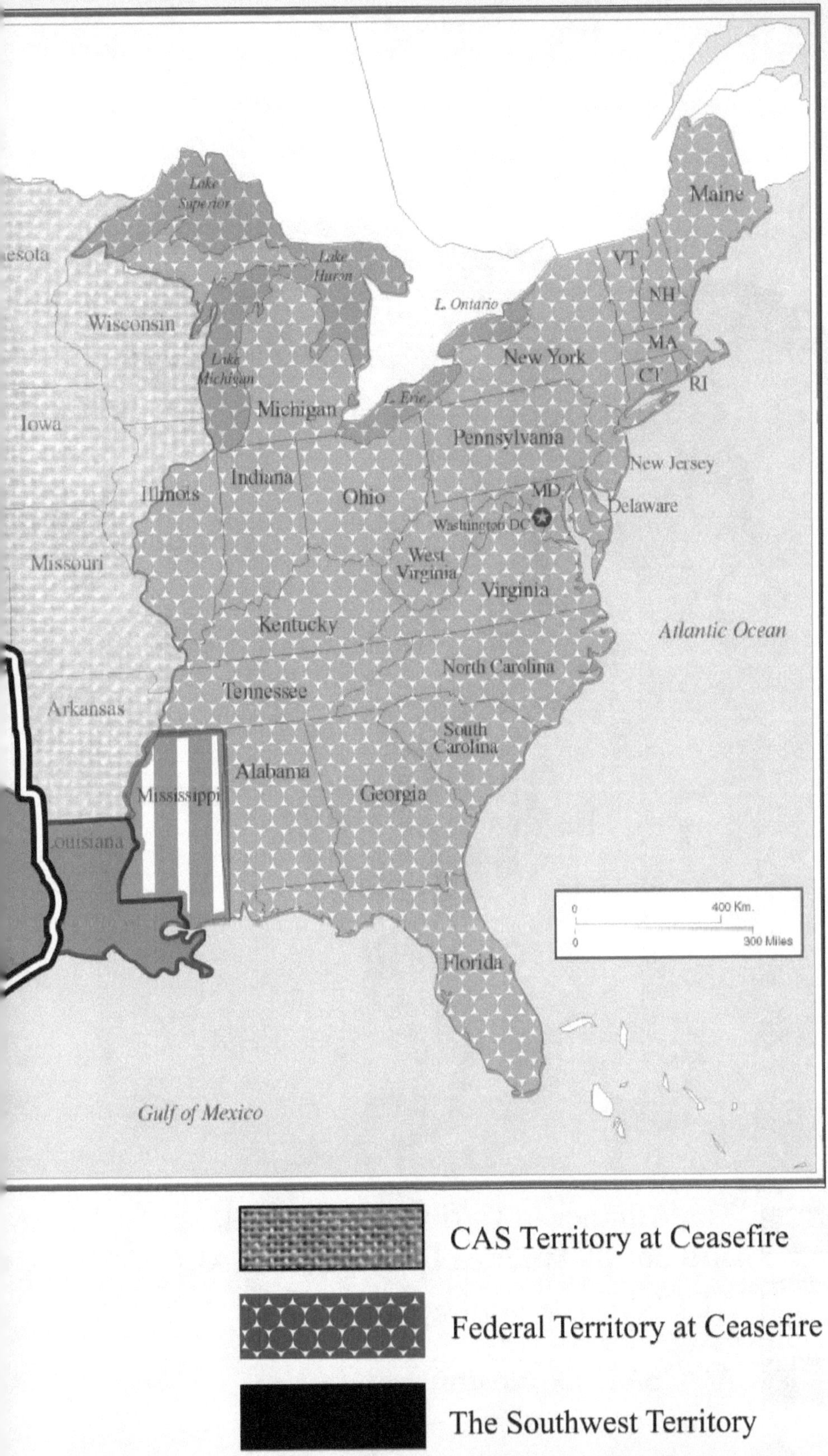

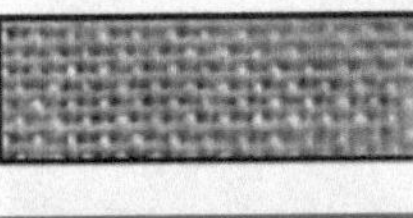

CAS Territory at Ceasefire

Federal Territory at Ceasefire

The Southwest Territory

The Alliance of Caribbean, Central, and South America Democracies (ACCSAD)

ACCSAD Abstaining Bloc

ACCSAD Expansion

~ *Our World* ~

in the year 2063 of the Common Era

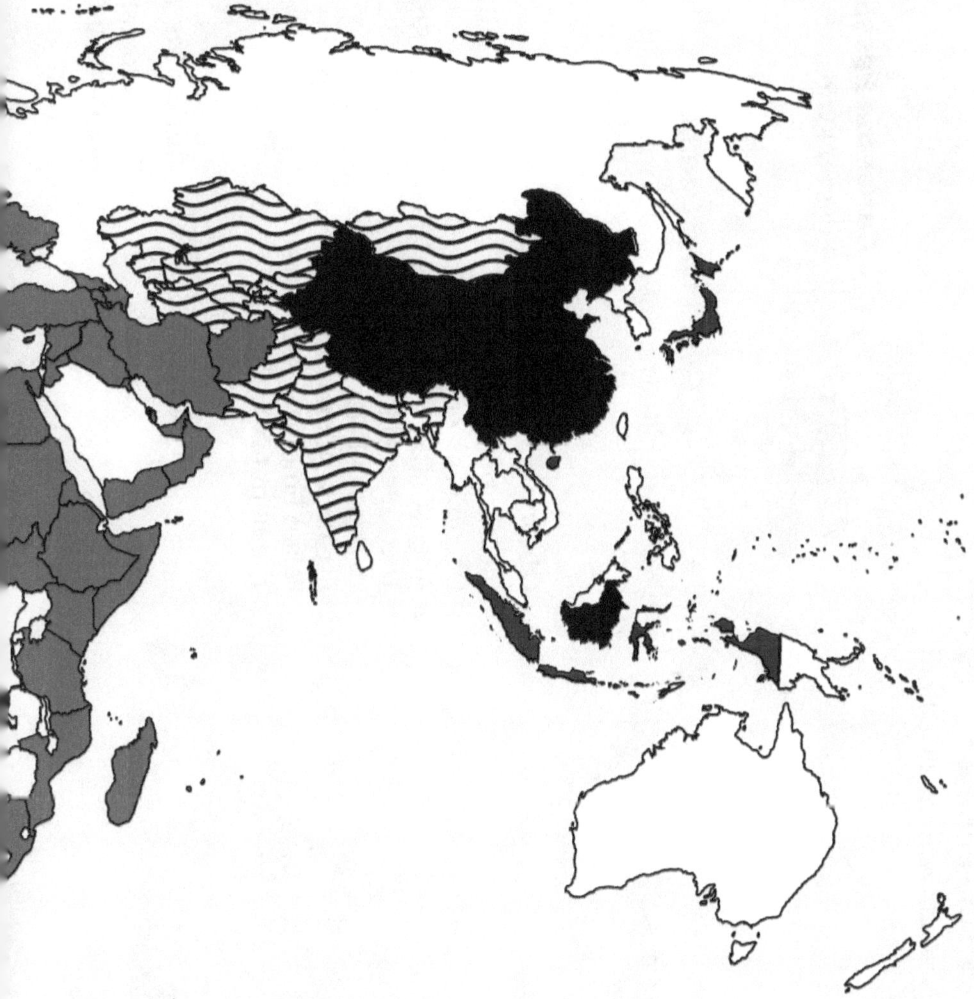

The Reality TV Society

Asian-Pacific Federation

Asian-Pacific Federation Expansion

Union of Autonomous Entertainment States

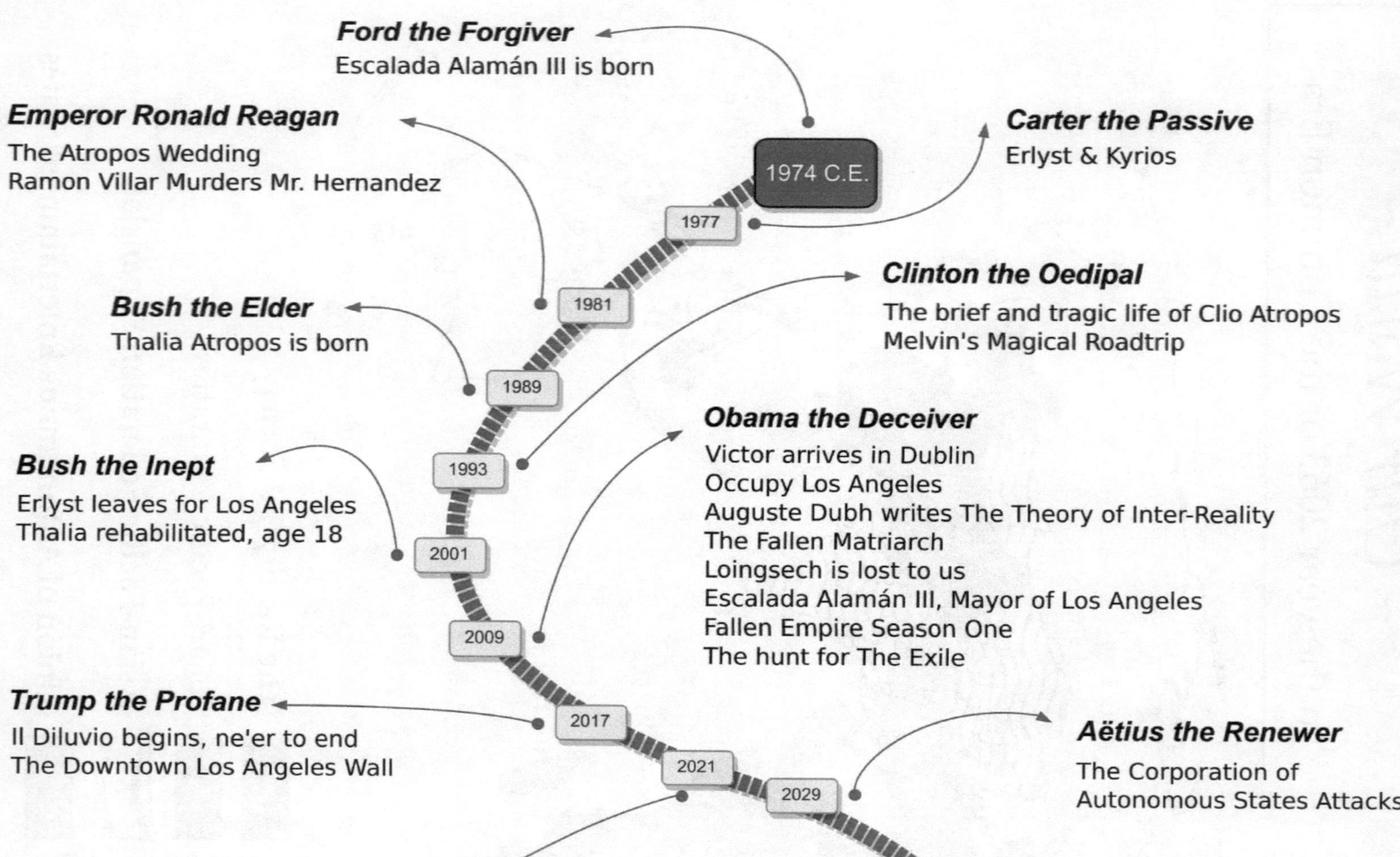

Ford the Forgiver
Escalada Alamán III is born
Emperor Ronald Reagan
The Atropos Wedding
Ramon Villar Murders Mr. Hernandez
Carter the Passive
Erlyst & Kyrios
1974 C.E.
1977
1981
Bush the Elder
Thalia Atropos is born
Clinton the Oedipal
The brief and tragic life of Clio Atropos
Melvin's Magical Roadtrip
1989
1993
Bush the Inept
Erlyst leaves for Los Angeles
Thalia rehabilitated, age 18
Obama the Deceiver
Victor arrives in Dublin
Occupy Los Angeles
Auguste Dubh writes The Theory of Inter-Reality
The Fallen Matriarch
Loingsech is lost to us
Escalada Alamán III, Mayor of Los Angeles
Fallen Empire Season One
The hunt for The Exile
2001
2009
Trump the Profane
Il Diluvio begins, ne'er to end
The Downtown Los Angeles Wall
2017
2021
2029
Aëtius the Renewer
The Corporation of
Autonomous States Attacks

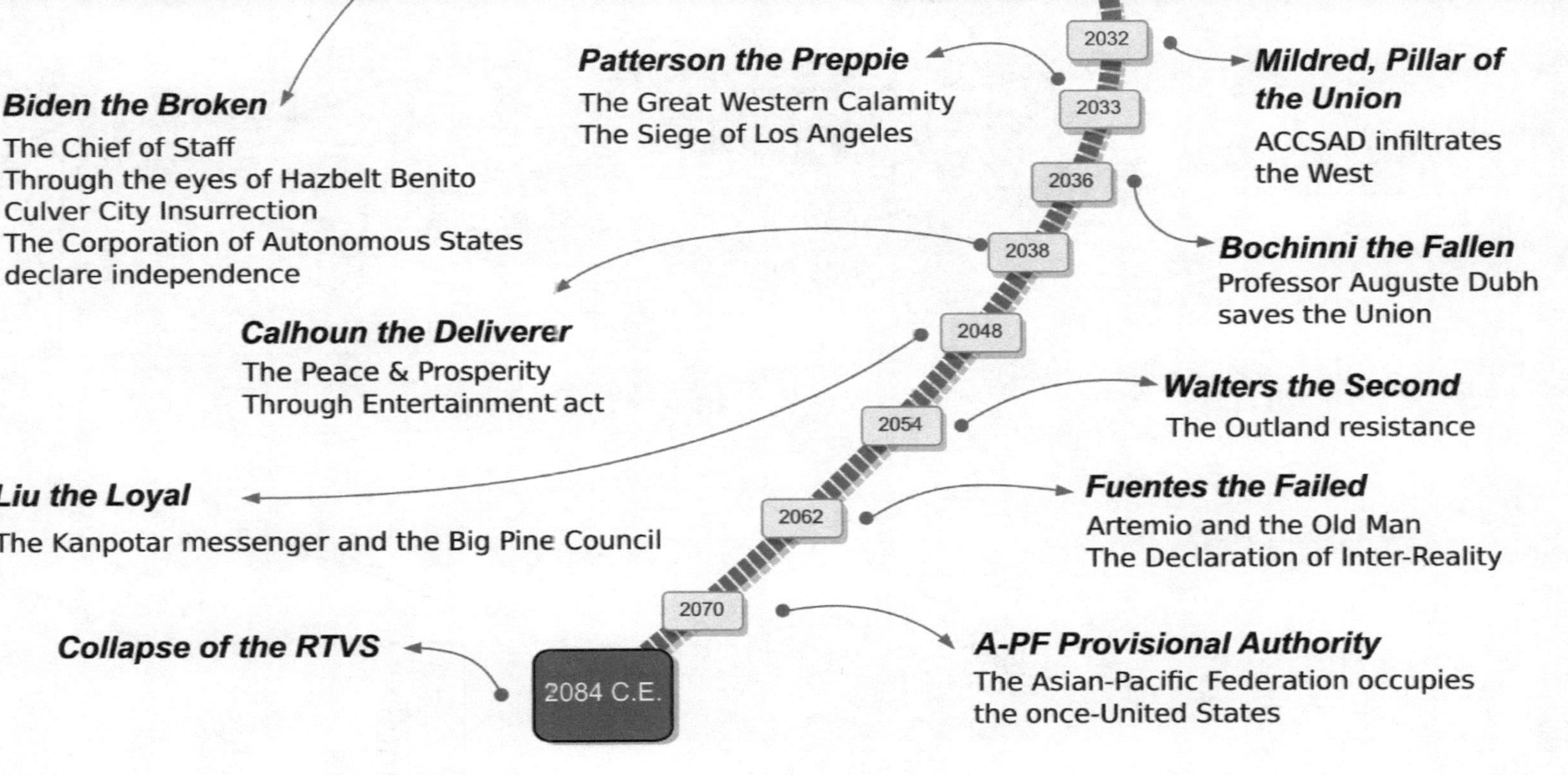

The Pageant of Power

Presidents and Chief Executives of the ever changingUnion

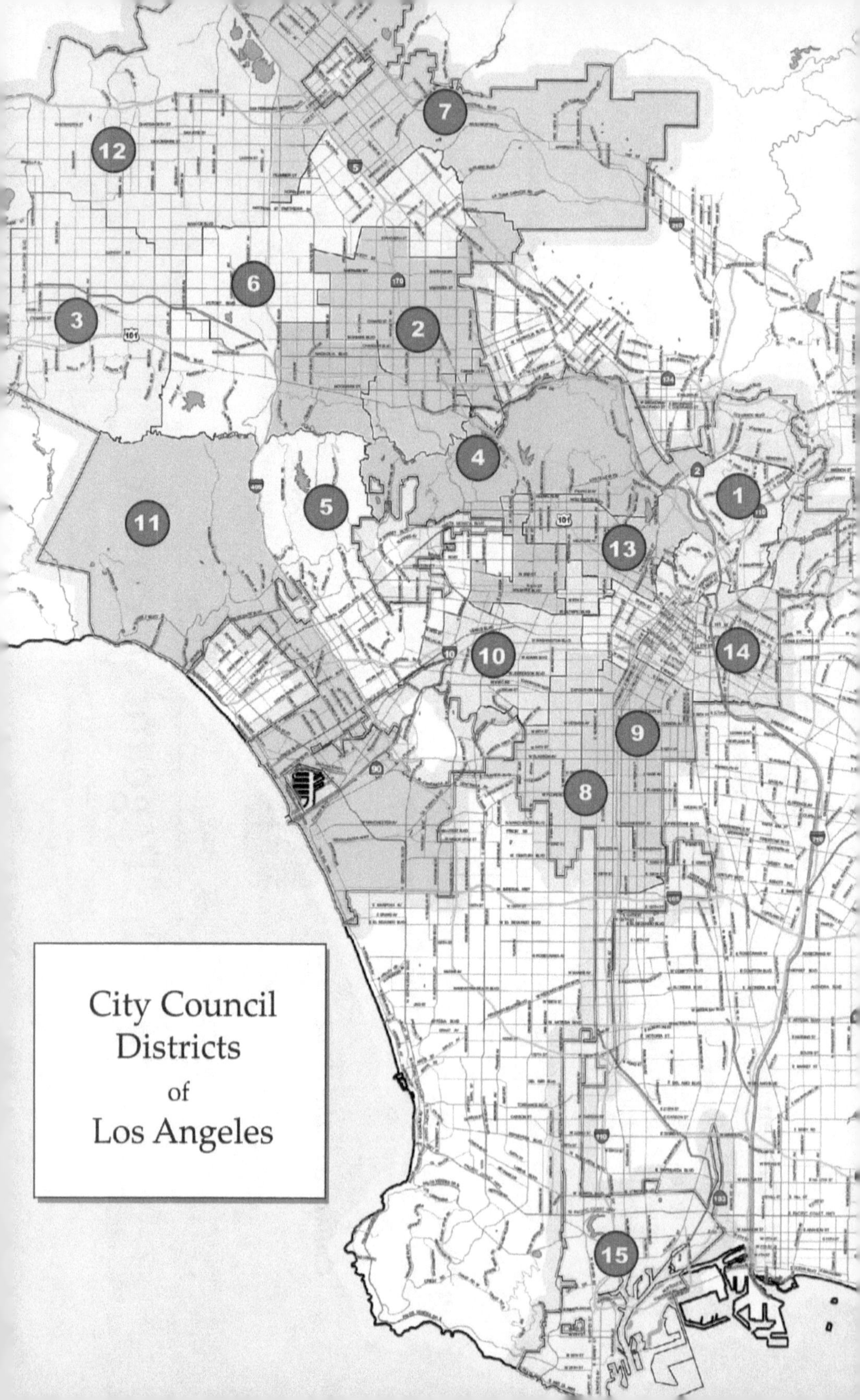

City Council
Districts
of
Los Angeles
1
2
3
4
5
6
7
8
9
10
11
12
13
14
15

Canon

Provenance

‡

I

Victor Loingsech fell from a polluted love nest,
Down to the grey Hollywood pavement.

3/15/2010

We were drunk, hunkered down in an old Hollywood dive bar. She was in Los Angeles searching for a reprieve from the Midwest, and I had not mustered the strength to leave. We smiled at one another and by the end of the song she crossed the bar and asked my name.

She flew home the next day but remained all around me. We exchanged long, desperate letters. When she decided to "Come out to Los Angeles, maybe start over again," with me, I said I would be waiting for her. I secured a small attic apartment, more than I could afford, and trimmed the nest with expectation.

Before she came, our conversations were wild confessions of devotion and certainty. As we settled into life in the attic apartment, our conversations became morose and pointless. Something had changed. Certainty seemed to be replaced by doubt, and we were strangers again. I had woven a grand romantic tapestry in my mind and forgotten the consent of my lover.

I felt betrayed, though I did not deserve to. I slept in the backseat of my car until Ian told me about a warehouse downtown that was renting offices as rooms. It was cheap and I could move in right away. I went to meet the 'landlord,' a punk kid called Jem from Conroy, Texas. Jem used the 50k sq. ft. facility for massive raves and renting rooms to a handful of rudderless humans.

The warehouse was sandwiched between truck stops and a strip club, beset overhead by 10 FWY. Though the night hums with activity, the warehouse feels cut off from the City. Unseen, and until the cops get called, unnoticed.

There were few words when I left. I said goodbye and she asked me not to blame her for what happened. She decided to stay in the attic apartment, and in Los Angeles.

The Mad Mayor

≈

LVIII

Winter ~ 1975

Escalada Alamán III began his life as Ramón Villar, heir to the South Bay Storage King's empire. His father abandoned his mother before young Ramón entered grade school, cutting her out of every aspect of his life. Ramón and his mother squatted in the family's large ranch home until L.A. County deputy Sheriffs removed them.

Ramón's mother never spoke of his father again. She had been a kept woman and did her best to find another keeper. Instead, she found a slick criminal with big shoulders and a dark hovel in Boyle Heights. The criminal, Mr. Hernández, sent young people with packages all over the neighborhood. When they returned to Chicago Street, they had money, lots of money. He always sent them away with another package, at times, after a merciless beating.

He had one of those for Ramón's mother anytime she angered him, but he stopped short of raising his hand to Ramón. The boy's shoulders were becoming as wide as his.

≈

As Ramón and his friends walked home from Prospect Park, he spotted Mr. Hernández outside a small bar on East Cesar Chavez.

"Wait. Guys. It's Hernández." Ramón stopped his friends.

The three boys waited and watched Mr. Hernández stumbling around the doorway of the bar. He tried three times to light a cigarette and threw his lighter into oncoming traffic. A pedestrian looked at him sideways and Mr. Hernández rushed him. The man took up running down the block and Mr. Hernández laughed until spittle flew from his mouth.

"Jaime," Ramón hit his friend in the shoulder, "that's your mom isn't it? She's asking Hernandez for a light."

Mr. Hernández tried to flirt. He got very close to Jaime's mother, reached out, and placed his hand on her backside.

Ramón leapt into the street and began running toward them. As he jumped the curb, Ramón swung and connected with Mr. Hernández's face. The older man's nose exploded, and he sank to the ground like a penitent pilgrim. Ramón breathed in Mr. Hernández's sobbing pain before he beat him into the sidewalk. People from the neighborhood stood around to hide the meting out of justice from any passing LAPD cruisers.

Ramón stopped punching. "Come here. Help me pick him up. We'll take my mom's car."

Ramón, Diego, and Jaime tossed Hernandez in the trunk and drove east on 10 until they were lost.

They killed the headlights and pulled the stunned man from the trunk.

Mr. Hernández cursed weakly as they carried him. "Don't kill me. All I ever did was take care of your slut mother."

Ramón chose a secluded colony of cacti and told the boys to throw Mr. Hernández into the dirt.

"This is it scumbag." Ramón approached Mr. Hernández and pulled a pistol from his waistband—Mr. Hernández's pistol.

"Please," Hernández crawled to his knees and clasped his hands in prayer. "You don't have to kill me."

"But I think I should, Escalada."

"No, please. I can pay you."

"I'm not interested in your money." Ramón put the safety back on. "You're going to disappear. If anyone sees you in the neighborhood again, you're a dead man."

Ramón turned and began walking toward the car. Jaime and Diego stood for a moment, stunned.

Mr. Hernandez leaned on his palms, spitting blood into the sand. He looked at the boys for a moment. Escalada Hernández raised his hands, "Boo!" and the boys jumped. His laugh rained down on the desolate sands.

Ramón knew that until he and his mother were buried in the ground, Hernandez would be right around the corner, knife in hand, posse in-tow. He removed the pistol's safety, brushed past his frightened friends, and put a hole in the criminal's skull.

The body dropped. It never kicked, or bucked, but Ramón stood over the corpse, ready to deliver a kill shot should the monster spring back to life. The growing pool of moonlit blood reached his kicks. "Let's go."

People listened to Ramón after that night. He was a very large man by the time high school came around, and although he had been an excellent athlete, he was at his best when arguing a point. His confidence and immensity swirled together into something resembling charisma. By the end of his senior year's football season, Ramón was cruel heart breaker.

His impressive SAT scores and geographical location were good enough to get him into a family-owned law school buried in depressing and perverse Glendale, California. His bored instructors either avoided him—star pupils make more work—or fawned over him. Ramón failed the bar exam four times, but eventually earned his degree.

Several of Ramón's friends from school encouraged him to run for a chair on the Boyle Heights Neighborhood Council. When he did, a contractor who was deeply involved in gentrifying Downtown LA destroyed him—twice. It was a surprise only to team Villar.

"We need a new strategy." Ramón paced.

"Maybe we should drop the promise of reduced fares for the subway, boss?"

"People like that," Ramón countered.

"Dumb people, boss. The Boyle Heights Neighborhood Council isn't going to get Metro to reduce fares exclusively in Boyle Heights."

"Dumb people swing elections, Carrie. It's like you fell out of a tree into this meeting."

Carrie sulked.

A slight, balding man spoke up. "Maybe we're not shooting high enough. Council positions are about results, not popularity. You haven't been in the game long enough to win on merit."

"And you are?"

"Anthony Bochinni, sir." Anthony looked permanently tensed, his shoulders swept forward, and his hands hung before him as if they were not attached; he affected a posture of contrived submission.

"That was a fucked-up thing to say Anthony, but you have a point."

"We know that transportation reform resonates with this demographic, *your* demographic. You need to position yourself for a mayoral bid."

"I can't even get on the Council..."

"Change your name."

"What?"

"Change your name, sir. We are in the pre-television stages; we can wipe the slate clean."

"Am I paying you?"

"No sir."

"Anthony, will you kindly fire everyone else on the staff and then join me in my office to see where this goes?"

"With pleasure, sir." For the first time, Anthony Bochinni's thin, tight lips stretched into a smile.

Bochinni brought in developer money; Ramón was alarmed at the excess. Over the next four weeks, Bochinni walked him through the parlors and corporate offices of the money behind a grand vision of a new Los Angeles. A city for the elite, unafraid to walk into the future by cleaning up its past. Bochinni needed to assuage the fears of the poor while assuring his sponsors that their grip on the city would continue. Ramón's skin was dark enough to pass him off as a liberal, but the developers liked their politicians white, so Anthony had to make sure Ramón toed the line and remained under his control.

≈

Bochinni received the vaunted nod from his masters and sent for Ramón.

"We need to make you into someone else. The name that tested highest with our groups was *Alamán*. Some sort of Mexican reactionary."

Ramón's eyes narrowed. "Yes. *Escalada* Alamán III."

"Then it's settled." Anthony smiled and clasped his limp hands.

Alamán's alma mater was an embarrassment, so he was scheduled to attend USC's prestigious Gould School of Law by powers he never encountered. During this do-over, at Bochinni's direction, Alamán began organizing marches and petitions for cheaper public transportation and greater access. His passionate vision of a fully functioning transportation system on par with New York City made him very popular with commuters who barely made enough money to ride the bus and could never afford a car.

He became a cult hero and posters of his website photo popped up along Cesar Chavez Blvd. In the mythology of East Los Angeles, Anthony Bochinni had created a false messiah. The huge bump in eligible voters with Alamán on their mind pushed him into dangerous contention with the city's highest polling politicians.

The Hollywood, West Hollywood, and Beverly Hills City Councils took interest. Bochinni had woven a very effective tale, a yarn that could be useful to the rest of the Councils. Alamán had only a blushing relationship with the truth and was capable of carrying a lie as gently as a newborn baby. During the 2013 Mayoral race Alamán entered as a dark horse backed by a tsunami of campaign donations. His competition saw the writing on the wall and saved their potential careers by slowly leaving the race or playing a calm and *clean* game against Alamán.

≈

Winter ~ 2013

Escalada Alamán III's mercurial rise from obscure community organizer to Mayor of Los Angeles was a testament to the strength and power of the city's corruption.

"Congratulations, Alamán." Mayor Hahnsen shook the Mayor-elect's hand.

"Thank you, sir, I appreciate your support and endorsement through all of this."

"You will be of great service to my *interests*, young man."

Alamán smiled, "I pledge to be, your honor."

"There's someone I'd like you to meet." Mayor Hahnsen led Alamán to the back of the celebration suite. They approached two men, opposites in every way, who were speaking softly over their respective drinks. Salvadore Garcetti VI, the movie star-handsome Chair of the Hollywood City Council, was tall, fit, and his gleaming incisors closed billion-dollar deals. Terry Bruce, the City's long-serving Treasurer, was neither tall nor fit, and his smile was more a warning than comfort.

Alamán whispered, "Your honor, I have already met Terry and Sal."

"Not as the Mayor of Los Angeles."

Alamán smiled. "Excellent point, sir."

"Sal," Hahnsen hugged Garcetti professionally. "Terry." No hug. "Gentlemen, I present to you Escalada Alamán III, the next Mayor of Los Angeles."

Terry and Sal golf-clapped and shook Alamán's hand.

Hahnsen continued. "Sal has a very big idea that I'm sure he'd like to hear your thoughts on, Alamán."

"Well, I don't think we went far enough with the Hollywood and Vine restoration project. We still have a pocket of bustling commerce surrounded by vast swathes of unlivable slums."

"Gentlemen, pardon me for a moment." Hahnsen made his exit.

"Selling a million-dollar condo to a popstar is tough when people are getting mugged up and down her street. And that subway station...I could strangle Hahnsen for that hobo tractor-beam. It should have been moved down the street, far from the Hotel entrance."

"You'd like to expand the gentrification zone?"

"Yes. I think we have an excellent chance of upsetting the balance if we have a surge of development and police presence concentrated in the area."

"I'd like to see the game plan, but I am in agreement that it is worth a try."

"Oh, well, Alamán, I assure you that..."

"This is my show now, Sal. I have some plans myself and when the time comes, I'll need Hollywood's backing, good name, and donor list."

"They'll be yours, your honor." Garcetti raised his glass.

After a short silence, Terry Bruce awkwardly spat, "What kind of plans Escalada? If you don't mind my asking."

"I mind, Terry." Alamán turned and bade Sal goodbye before walking back to the party.

"Asshole." Terry was not amused.

"Relax Terrence, no one fires the Treasurer. Besides, you are *very* good at your job."

"Don't call me Terrence."

≈

The Mayor's reign was one of silent terror; public transportation prices skyrocketed, and although money was set aside and spent, none of Alamán's rail line projects saw the light of day. The City's coffers were a wide-open, pungent trough to engorge private development.

As Garcetti's vision of Hollywood began to grind to a start, Alamán called him into his office.

"Hey, I really like what you did with the office, Alamán. Did you knock that wall out?"

"I did. The office was too narrow to inspire the kind of fear I aim to. I called you here to discuss my plans for Downtown. Don't sit," Alamán stopped Garcetti, "we're going for a little walk."

Alamán led Garcetti south on Spring Street.

"How often do you walk around down here, Sal?"

"Not as often as I'd like. I'm a city boy after all."

"It's beautiful down here these days isn't it?"

"It is. Filled with toned, tanned, hipsters and USC students. Quite a turn around."

"A very impressive turn around, but do you smell that?" Alamán inhaled dramatically. "Urine. Feces. Human filth and rot. I'd like to finish the proverbial tackle." Alamán led Garcetti to Broadway via 5th St. "That's the Millennium Biltmore Hotel. Beyond that, the Bonaventure. Luxury hotels, playgrounds for the rich, famous, and private. That's hard to pull off when only three blocks away you have this."

Alamán pointed south on Broadway. Crumbling structures from a long past age of beauty lined a filthy, indigent-littered gauntlet. Discarded humans crawled in and out of spaces between buildings and got what precious rest they could while the day's passers-by were too busy to molest them. Gaudy plastic trinkets and colorful quinceañera dresses clogged the innermost portions of the sidewalks.

"Beyond this human devastation is a god-inspired aesthetic. This was once a place of wonder, beauty, and pride." Alamán led Garcetti into Clifton's cafeteria. The dining room was silent save a few bored employees.

"You've been here before I'm sure. Never mind the ridiculous décor, I want you to look around at the people in these old pictures. I want you to fall back into that time: when you were dressed to the nines and walked down to Clifton's on a Friday night. Sometimes, you'd get lucky and see the Hollywood Elite."

"I'm with you, Alamán. Off to China Town for dessert or a Dodgers game, San Pedro for the view..."

"Exactly, Sal. *This* is Los Angeles, not Santa fucking Monica, not Venice. Fuck Hollywood. No offense."

"None taken. It's already happening, slowly. I mean, look at Spring Street. Residential rent is already at four-thirty per square foot and climbing."

"It needs to happen faster. Fifty percent of these buildings are either completely vacant or in bad enough shape to sell for a song. From China Town to USC, and all the way to the river, there are gaps in progress that need to be put to better use. These insulating blocks will help ensure the project doesn't suffer the same fate as the original Hollywood and Vine revision."

"How do we get our hands on those buildings?"

"We start in the worst neighborhoods and quietly, legally, condemn and reclaim the drug dens, the dance halls, and flop houses. At the same time, we coordinate with the deepest pockets on your developer list and pull together all the property that is owned by middlemen, or persons with whom we do not want to work. Somewhere between threat of imminent domain and cash payments, we should be able to weed the undesirables out." Alamán walked with his hands behind his back, surveying distant pawns on a battlefield.

"Ok, Downtown is owned. Now what?"

"I take all of the restrictions off your developers. They will not face punitive HUD quotas and permits will be rubber stamped; the mission is to create the most perfect living experience possible for the well-to-do. Failure to do so will bring a much higher cost than financial ruin."

"What kind of contractors do you want to bring in?"

"All of them. Gut the skyscrapers, tear the sidewalks and streets up, illuminate every square inch of alleyway, re-draw subway platform designs to prevent infiltration by scum, and most importantly, make the area independent from the rest of the city. I want the old underground tunnels[2] re-purposed for sewage, electrical, and water. We are building our Vatican City, and we are only inviting the most socially qualified."

"Morgan Freeman..."

"Think bigger, Sal."

"The bank president who manages Morgan Freeman's hedge fund assets."

"Now you're with me." Alamán smiled. "Everything is already here; we need only take it. You have two more years to work on Hollywood. Then, I'll need you focused on bringing the buyers Downtown. Are we on the same page, Sal?"

Avarice forced his smile. "Entirely."

---

2 During Prohibition, eleven miles of service tunnels became the byways to speakeasies deep beneath Downtown Los Angeles. Privileged patrons entered the underground tunnels via innocuous storefronts and got drunk on illegal liquor stockpiled by the mayor.

≈

Garcetti had been fighting for his life on the Hollywood City Council when Hahnsen approached him about their golden boy, Alamán. Garcetti's family had proven a stumbling block during his own re-election bid, so Salvadore was eager to be offered an inside track. [3] Mayor Alamán and councilman Garcetti VI formed an unholy union and the die was cast.

With the Hollywood and Beverly Hills City Councils in his pocket, Alamán leveraged most profit-producing cities within the Los Angeles Corporation to bob and weave within his grasp. Alamán's office kept its word and the city coffers bled into the private sector. Development ran amok and Alamán's dream of a fortified and cleansed Downtown slowly became a bleak reality.

Alamán coasted through the 2017 election, and by pedantic stroke of legislative pen settled in for an extended reign. [4] Several candidates made it very difficult for Alamán to return for his second term, but most were thwarted by the pull of rock-star politician, Garcetti VI, and Alamán's casual comfort with eliminating opponents—violently if necessary.

---

3 At the conclusion of a publicly quiet paternity lawsuit waged by Mabel Himmel, a judge ruled that former Los Angeles District Attorney, Gilbert "Gil" Garcetti, was not responsible for the welfare of her child. Mabel, erupted into violence and cursed the judge. She was immediately incarcerated, and upon release vowed to forever mar the former District Attorney's name by any means necessary. Hans "Stanley" Betrüger, Mabel's husband-to-be, legally changed his name to Stanley Garcetti, and together they birthed the 909-branch of the Garcetti political dynasty. Stanley and Mabel's progeny became ground level court clerks and paralegals. By the turn of the century, the 909-Garcettis had begun to dominate politics in Riverside County. The Garcetti offspring never won elections by virtue. Confusion regarding the—amply refuted—patronage of the bloodline sufficed as a positive memory of trust when voters visited the polls. Salvadore Garcetti VI was born to Genevieve and Jared Garcetti Jr. of East Hemet, California. Salvadore VI represented the family's proudest, most powerful, and most ruthless success. His great-grandmother Mabel wept with pride as she saw the families' names conflated by nightly news teams and the nation's paparazzi.

4 Mayoral elections in Los Angeles were held in odd-numbered years from 1909 until 2013. In hopes of increasing voter turnout, the Los Angeles City Council recommended consolidating city elections with gubernatorial and presidential elections in even-numbered years. In 2015, voters passed a charter amendment extending the term of the mayor elected in 2017 to five-and-one-half years.

Erlyst & Kyrios

§
XXIX

End of Summer ~ 1980

The summer was as breathtaking as it was brutal. For three months the skies had opened and turned tiny Athens, Georgia into an equatorial rain forest. As the rain receded it was overwhelmed by another passing front—each day without a glimmer of sunlight, or hint of hope. The University gave the tiny hilltop town a reason to exist, and as the summer waned, the returning students spoiled the silence of the quaint deserted streets.

Shaking water from her long coat and folding her umbrella, Erlyst walked into Rocky's Pizzeria for her mid-Sunday shift. The restaurant was lively with returning students, new students, and their parental escorts.

"Hey Erlyst." Shannon waved from the cash register.

"Hey Shan, looks busy tonight. Christ, did you pierce your nose again?"

"Sure did, looks magnificent, yes?" Shannon preened. "I don't recall rush week being this crazy last year. I thought they'd all be gone by now."

"One last drink before melting back into the nether regions. There are more and more people every year, it's the nature of things," Erlyst replied.

Shannon grabbed a tub of ranch dressing from a below counter fridge. "Are you heading out to the Fullilove farm? Pylon's playing, and Twisted Kites. Wait, they call it something else now."

"Little Mikey's band?" Erlyst helped Shannon scoop ranch into tiny cups.

"Right. What is their name?"

"Erlyst," Eric called from the back, "Are you here to work or not?"

"Sorry, coming," Erlyst called out. Eric was easy to dismiss; he was the boss, but that only mattered to him. "Shan, listen, I'm not really into this sort of shit, but this morning when I came out of my house three hummingbirds were standing on the porch rail."

"Crazy." Shannon responded vacantly.

"In a row Shan, facing my front door. They were standing at-attention like they were waiting for me to walk out."

"You're mental."

"Maybe. Nonetheless, it's a special day as I see it, so if anything *interesting* happens, let me know." Erlyst gripped Shannon's arm.

"Okay nutso," Shannon laughed.

"Erlyst!" Eric shouted from the kitchen.

"Coming!" Erlyst walked swiftly toward the swinging kitchen doors. The afternoon's rain pattered on the roof of the restaurant.

Erlyst checked her hair in a mirror next to the kitchen door. She was a mess. It was a summer afternoon in the South; everyone was a mess. Tiny freckles on her sun-warmed skin made her look 12, but her pale emerald eyes were weary beyond her eighteen years. She was pleased she wore her hair up; she had always admired her sleek neck.

The dull hardwood aisles between tables and booths were awash in feet, children, and sundry items of luggage and/or shopping bags. The lead up to—and subsequent weeks of—the school year were a cash boon for sleepy Athens. Without it, the town would quite literally melt into the redneck landscape and disappear. Erlyst watched the students come and go year after year—should a fissure appear in the walls of her tiny southern prison, Erlyst would claw her way through.

The rush began to slow down and Erlyst retreated to the kitchen. Three orders hung from the cookline while Cortez, Darryl, and Slim leaned against the counter. Erlyst counted her cigarettes, one, two, three—she'd have to stop on the way home. Before she could escape for a smoke, Shannon slammed through the kitchen doors.

§

"Whoa sister, you on fire?" Erlyst caught her excited friend.

"Sort of," Shannon's Irish eyes twinkled. "Y'need to take over on table three. That *something interesting* you were waiting for just walked in."

Erlyst remembered her hummingbirds. "Table *three*. Of course."

The rain subsided and tendrils of sunlight bore through the storm clouds. A dark-haired man sat by himself in booth three near the front window. His tousled hair looked purposely disturbed, and his pristine light wool suit set a soothing grey shadow amid the newly lit dining room.

Erlyst began walking toward him, hoping he had not seen her staring like a dumbstruck fawn. His cool amber eyes never left hers.

"Who put you in this big old booth all by yourself?"

He smiled. "Your hostess was kind enough to..."

"Kind enough? A family should be seated here, we're kind of busy if you hadn't noticed..."

"I slipped her a tip. I mean no harm. I'm having a very difficult time finding a quiet place to have dinner before retiring."

"Downtown is far from private during Rush week Mister."

"Mr. Atropos. Kyrios, Atropos." He reached his hand to hold hers.

"Pleased to meet you." His grip was intense.

There was a long silence, during which Erlyst remained focused on Kyrios' smile, and seemed not to notice...

"Any chance I can get a glass of Burgundy, Miss?"

"Yes, sorry about that, I'll be right back. Erlyst. Call me Erlyst."

Shannon ran over to the bar, "Dude, what gives?"

"Nothing. He's a filthy narcissist. Look at him."

"Yeah, I've been looking at him. He's fucking perfect. How is he not dying wearing a suit in this heat?"

"Shan, get a hold of yourself."

"Whatever. If you're not interested, I'll..."

"Thanks love, I have this under control."

Erlyst walked back to table three with Kyrios' wine.

"Anything else, sir?" Erlyst held her breath.

"No. I think that I'm quite alright for now, Erlyst."

Erlyst exhaled silently and turned. He remembered.

Kyrios ate his meal quietly while reading a local newspaper from front to back.

Eric mocked Erlyst to the joy of the cooks and dishwashers. "You better get out there, he's leaving. Go give him a big juicy kiss!"

"Fuck you," Erlyst hissed under her breath. Why are the men in this town such children?

Kyrios paid his check, saw her face through the kitchen door, and waved before walking out into the night. Erlyst felt like a coward, and if Eric walked in and said another word she'd reach for the pizza peal and hack him in half.

Shannon rushed through the kitchen door again and grabbed Erlyst's arm. "Come 'ere a sec..."

Shannon pulled Erlyst behind the cookline, up the rickety back steps, and into the alley behind the restaurant. She looked around conspiratorially. "Okay, I'm your best fucking friend after this missy."

Shannon held out the check for table three with a perfectly, hand-written business card:

110 Clayton, Rooftop Lounge.

The other side of the card read, in fine embossed script, *Kyrios Atropos - Admit One*

"What's on the roof?"

"Who cares?" Shannon shouted. "Don't be an idiot, go meet him."

"You're right. Can you..."

"Yes, I'll cover you, go."

Erlyst flew from the restaurant. Her mother was mercifully asleep. Erlyst pulled her favorite cotton dress from the closet. The dark blue fabric was dotted with tiny white flowers and three grey buttons at the neck. She pulled her hair up into a respectable bun and took care to sparingly touch up her makeup. It would not do for this stranger to think of her as too eager. Erlyst headed back to 110 Clayton.

§

The downtown sidewalks were dense with drunken revelry. Though she had no idea what to expect, she was relieved that they were not meeting in one of the bars at street level. Erlyst pulled her shawl tight as she entered the tall brick building. The tuxedoed elevator attendant took the card from her and handed it back. He smiled, as if to wish her well. And then shook his head, as if she had no hope.

Commencement

‡

II

8/15/10

I booked passage to Dublin before my severance ran out. It'll be tight but I'll make it. I'll have to go back to work as soon as I return to Los Angeles, but that's how it is in our country. Work or die.

Airports have evolved into highly militarized processing centers where customers are herded through a series of gates and asked to periodically remove clothing to stand inspection. The entire enterprise is fraught with opportunities for delay.

I kept my head down while the glitterocracy flitted to and fro in Dolce & Gabbana sunglasses, and pink velour track suits.

Leaving Dallas—

The Dallas International smoking room was dense with bright morning sunshine that pierced the windows facing the airfield. The room was littered with young soldiers in desert camouflage that bore ISAF patches. None seemed giddy or anxious; they were all silent. They have seen the sands of Babylon day after day, month after month, and year after year on one deployment after another. The soldiers were a collection of tired eyes, exhausted conscience, and maddening threadbare excuses for hope.

Late, maybe three AM, far above the Atlantic Ocean— I have the sunrise to look forward to, but until then the world is bathed in darkness. Only the stars reveal that the universe still exists outside this metal craft.

Later still—

A small sliver of sunlight spreads against the eastern horizon on the far side of the dark, dark night. Sunrise over the Atlantic, trapped tens of thousands of miles in the air—it gives the experience a sad sense of voyeurism. If I could raise my face and feel the warmth of the coming sun, it would feel real. Instead I watch a TV-sized facsimile of the phenomenon. Everyone around me fell asleep long ago; I envy their slumber.

Four more hours, and I land in Dublin. I can make it.

The remaining sleepless hours finally concluded. I watched excitedly through the tiny airplane windows, breathing in the onslaught of unfettered green. Below the cloud line, Ireland was enshrined in grey mist, the beginning, or the end of a day's rain. The airport sign shone through the mist in tall, proud, green letters— Baile Átha Cliath.

My taxi wound into Dublin and crossed the dark and choppy Liffey. We curled past Trinity College, south on Saint George's Place and soon stopped at a large red brick building: Avalon House. I stood on the corner of Aungier and Whitefriar Place looking up at the former medical institution, several floors taller than its neighbors. The ancient stone walkway beneath my feet was slick with rain.

Avalon House was awash in sound. A bank of computers lay beyond a seating area and a hotel-style counter greeted all weary travelers. After a short transaction, I secured my belongings in the hostel's cage, changed my shirt, and walked out into the cool morning in search of a pint.

I continued wandering, smoking the last of my American cigarettes.

Dublin was eerily silent, the small shaded streets east of Aungier were warmed by pinpricks of bright sunlight, and the tiny windows above the shops remained shuttered. Soon, business started moving people 'round and it began to resemble a city. Little ones in school uniforms or in soccer jerseys, raced away from their parents, or remained silent and respectful at their sides. They kicked rocks, slapped each other's shoulders, and hid around corners for their friends; they were no different than the children on Alvarado Street.

At eleven's first chime, I entered a silent pub. The early morning sun poured through stained and unstained glass alike and the old walls of The Hairy Lemon were plastered with a century of memories foreign and domestic. I took a seat at the bar and the bartender came up from washing glasses to greet me.

The patio was quiet. The open space was positioned between the four wings of the building and lined with an old iron staircase to the second floor. Small pricks of rain dotted the cement floor of the patio. Thank you, Dublin.

After several pints, I turned my sights toward dinner. The streets were calm but populated by early evening walkers. I wondered how much of an American vibe I put off. Fashion-wise I'm neutral: t-shirts, workpants, boots, and flat cap. My beard is dark and getting full. In a crowded bar no one notices me.

I left and walked along taking note of patio cafés and long alluring bars for a later imbibing. I finished my cigarette on Chatham Row in front of Sheehan's, then snubbed it out in a metal tray affixed to the neatly painted wall, red as an old-time engine and half as bright in the waning sun.

Sheehan's was warm. The wood planks in the floor creaked under my boots as I approached the bar. A man in his forties was blind drunk and rambling off at the mouth about being a workingman and getting the short stick. The bartender rolled his eyes and put him straight, "Tommy, you're over the line, you need to get on home."

"Well, sorry, I'm just saying that I have a... have a..." Tommy shifted on the stool perilously.

"That's it then, you won't break your neck here Tommy," The barrel-chested bartender picked Tommy up and showed him the door. He returned from the doorway after watching that Tommy carried on down the road.

—3am

I've been wandering the hostel's common areas, periodically sitting down to attempt an internet connection; spotty though it often is.

§

XXX

August ~ 1981

Erlyst was whisked by sleek black jet to JFK in a little over two hours. An entourage met her at the gate. She followed them through back hallways, and they emerged from a staircase in the center of the parking structure.

One of the security guards finally spoke as he ushered her into a black SUV. "Here we are Ms. Spell. Mr. Atropos rode ahead." Three total vehicles left in a flock and Erlyst was crossing the Queensboro Bridge by sunset.

Athens was far away. Erlyst's life was far away. The immensity of the buildings bewildered Erlyst as they got closer and closer to the city. They seemed to cradle the sky the deeper they plunged; the streets and sidewalks were filthy.

She rested her chin on her hand as the trucks slammed in and out of traffic, marching toward Central Park East. The walled park was an emerald sight for sore eyes. Erlyst was relieved that Kyrios lived next to his very own forest. A Georgia girl bereft of trees is a wilting petal.

They stopped in front of 2 East 61st Street. In an amusing symphony of wrist microphone muttering and changing of guards, Erlyst was helped from the vehicle and commandeered into the building's cavernous lobby. The elevators were flanked in mirrors and imposing gold statues. Part of the entourage stayed in the lobby as Erlyst and her three handlers sped forty-one stories into the New York twilight.

The elevator doors parted on a grandiose foyer framed by a black lacquered staircase. The staircase split, providing two ways to the second floor. Erlyst caught her breath as she ascended the staircase. The second floor was an endless open space separated into individual sitting rooms, and a dining room. Erlyst's skin tingled as she ran her fingers over the fine polished woods and the regally upholstered furniture.

Kyrios emerged from behind Erlyst and walked toward the long ceiling to floor windows looking out on Central Park.

"I apologize for the rush. The circumstances being what they are, there were very few options. I wish we could go back and..."

"Don't worry, I understand."

"I hope that someday you will be happy here."

"I will be. Some day."

Kyrios smiled. "Welcome home, Erlyst Rae Spell."

Everything, everyone, was far, far away.

§

Shortly after Erlyst arrived in Manhattan, Kyrios was called away to a distant land and returned only once in the following nine months. Kyrios never proposed, he never had a chance, but as the next autumn began to fitfully cede to winter, Erlyst was besieged by a brood of wedding coordinators, chefs, executive assistants, assistants to assistants, and well-wishing female peers. She was ripped from the sweaty carelessness of poverty and shown her place in the Atropos Empire—an immense bloodthirsty organization no one would speak about.

From morning to night, she managed thirty-four wedding contractors. No small feat for a grown woman, but Erlyst was not quite that. She cried herself to sleep some nights, but she began to understand what it meant to hold someone's livelihood in her hands. After dispatching the first few consultants who let their bad day make them forget their place, Erlyst began to feel the length and breadth of her tentacles.

Time with Kyrios was fitful and sporadic. One week she'd barely see him in the night before he retired, and another he'd call off his entire schedule to remain in bed with his young bride-to-be.

"Kyrios, say that thing to me." Erlyst purred into a portable phone while tasting wedding cakes.

"Erlyst, I'm busy..." Kyrios sighed and relented, "Η αγάπη είναι μια ψυχή που καταλαμβάνει δύο σώματα."[5]

"Kyrios come home. Please." Erlyst was frustrated and trying to seduce.

"I will be home in two hours."

"Promise?"

"I do."

"I don't want to have to beg."

"It's a very busy time my pet, but a window approaches and through it I see you and I on a silent island, with a long white yacht anchored just offshore."

"All you have to do is make me feel like I'm not the last thing on the day's list. That's all."

"Duly noted and taken to heart."

§

Erlyst stood on a platform in a gown she had already decided to dismiss.

5 Love is composed of a single soul inhabiting two bodies.

"I understand completely Ms. Spell, but that is unfortunately not an option."

"Everything is an option. Please see yourself out."

"But ma'am."

"We're done, leave before I lose my sense of decorum and replace your entire staff."

"Yes ma'am, thank you ma'am."

Erlyst stared at the back of the dismissed assistant's head as she slowly exited the suite. "Cyan, please come here."

Another assistant approached hesitantly. "Yes ma'am?"

"Stop fucking calling me that. I'm nineteen years old."

"Yes ma...miss."

"That dreadful woman tells me that it is not possible to make the cake I asked for. Do you understand thus far?"

"I do, miss."

"Very good. Make this cake happen for me. There are two more weeks; I don't understand why there is a problem. It will be expensive, but we're not concerned with that are we?" Erlyst looked the new assistant dead in the eye.

"No miss."

"On your way." Erlyst dismissed her assistant with a petulant flip of the wrist.

A rotund and repugnant man walked into the penthouse.

"Erlyst, Erlyst, Erlyst, it's so good to meet you!"

"Who is this clown?" Erlyst asked a dozen consultants within earshot.

"Lawrence E. Robertson. At your service." The round man bowed with effort. "I'm Kyrios' personal attorney. I've been looking forward to meeting you." Lawrence leered.

"Pleased to meet you." Erlyst ignored his outstretched hand.

"Ah yes. Well, the big day is fast approaching is it not?"

"Why are you still here?"

Lawrence's suits were very expensive and perfectly tailored; yet he perpetually looked like he'd just gotten off a twelve-hour bender at the racetrack.

"Miss Spell, you have a call." A male assistant whose name Erlyst had not yet learned called out.

"Excuse me." Erlyst brushed past Lawrence and took the house phone from the young man. "Hello?"

"Erlyst, it's Shannon."

"Shannon. How did you find me?"

"She's dead Erlyst. Your mum's dead."

Erlyst collapsed to the ground and wept with her knees pulled to her chin in the third wedding dress she'd tried on that day. The entourage kept a wide berth and let Erlyst console herself silently in a crowded room.

§

A meager service was held for Erlyst's mother beneath churning storm clouds at the Old Athens Cemetery. As the attendants passed to offer Erlyst their condolences a light rain began to fall.

Shannon turned to Erlyst as the last mourner disappeared into their car.

"You want to get a drink 'er somethin', Erlyst?"

"Badly. We need to ditch these clowns though," Erlyst pointed over her shoulder to three immense men in black suits and sunglasses.

"No problem, I have a plan. Get us to the Georgia Theater." Shannon grabbed Erlyst's arm and they walked toward the waiting SUVs.

"Take us to the Georgia Theater," Erlyst barked at the driver. She turned to Shannon, "We can have some lunch and a drink. What do you say?"

"Perfect," Shannon winked.

It thrilled Erlyst to watch the slumbering brick buildings slip past. Downtown was a postcard from a distant relative, a reminder of simplicity. The aging water oaks threatening on cue to crumble at 75 years still provided a warm canopy along Clayton Street. The girls took a seat near the railing on the rooftop bar and looked out over south Athens.

"What the fuck happened to you?"

Erlyst whispered, "Remember table number three? His name is Kyrios Atropos and we fell in love. He swept me off my feet to Manhattan."

"So where is Kyrios?"

"Iceland."

"Oh. He knows your mum died right?"

"He does. He sent his condolences. It's complicated."

"Nothing complicated 'bout death."

Erlyst turned to Shannon with tears forming in her eyes. "Shan, I miss you and this backward town so much."

Shannon wiped Erlyst's cheek. "Save it. Here's the plan: I'll slip out the back and get the car. You hit the bathroom, climb out the window, and I'll pick you up on Clayton. We'll be on my front porch before they know we're gone."

Shannon left first, and after a few minutes, Erlyst tapped her closest guardian on the shoulder.

"Hey, He-man, I need to tinkle."

The guard spoke into his wrist microphone. "Hummingbird is in flight."

"Are you serious? Give me a fucking break, I never should have told Kyrios about that... "

Erlyst walked petulantly as her entourage fell into place on the staircases and landings. She'd have to time her escape perfectly. "Buh bye He-man, ladies only." Erlyst pushed open the bathroom door as two guards fell in on either side. Erlyst waited to hear the guard report in his microphone and tried to wedge open the window. Decades of desiccated paint formed an impenetrable barrier in the channels along the side of the window. Erlyst slammed her palm against the sill but to no avail.

*Shit shit shit...*Erlyst looked down at her precious Louboutins, "sorry girls, it's for the cause."

The finely crafted heels dug through layers of laziness and the window began to move. Erlyst struck it again and it moved a few inches. "C'mon fucker... "

"Everything ok ma'am?" A guard knocked on the bathroom door.

"Go... "a few more inches, "fuck... "almost there, "yourself," the window heaved open.

Erlyst heard the door give as the guard pushed his way in. She scurried down the fire escape and hit Clayton Street as

§

Shannon squealed around the corner in her mom's '75 Buick LeSaber.

Erlyst jumped into the passenger side and Shannon skidded the wrong way down one-way Clayton Street. Erlyst's confused entourage poured out of the theater—mouthing profanity into their wrists and mounting their black SUVs to give chase like some inept posse in an old western.

"Whoo!" Erlyst shouted out her window as they sped down Pulaski Street.

Shannon parked under some trees beside her house on the end of Tibbetts Street and the girls waited in the car for a few minutes to make sure no one had followed them. As promised, they were soon on Shannon's porch, each with a bourbon rocks in hand.

"That was amazing Shan. I owe you one."

"No biggie, love. Can't possibly match the excitement of New York." Shannon reached into a small wooden box she had placed on her lap and busied her hands with its contents.

"New York is intense, there's no doubt about that. It's hard to find a quiet moment." Erlyst looked down at her own hands resting in her lap. Her manacles were not visible. "Rich girl problems, eh?" Erlyst forced a laugh. "What's going on with the Rocky's crew?"

"Same bunch of arseholes. Eric is still in love with Sapphire, she is steadfast in leading him on. Slim is back on the drugs, doubt he stopped, right?"

"Highly unlikely," Erlyst agreed.

"Everything else meanders on."

"There's something very comforting about that."

"Ha, says the girl that ran off to the bigtime city."

"Guilty." Erlyst blushed. "It's very lonely Shan. It's hard to explain, but everyone around me is a stranger. I know nothing about my husband-to-be's empire, but I am daily reminded to keep its best interests at the forefront of my mind."

"Empire, oooo," Shannon waved her fingers. "Here, this should help quiet things down a little." Shannon proudly presented Erlyst with a thin joint and a lighter.

"Thank you, Shan. This is going to help a lot." Erlyst lit the joint and hit it several times before handing it back to Shannon and staring unrepentantly at the dense foliage all around. "You have no idea Shan, the extreme wealth. *I have no idea*. All I know is when Kyrios speaks, mountains lift and scuttle where he demands."

"So, milk baths and massages?"

"Potentially. So far, it's been a lot of meetings and wedding planning—all, very unpleasant."

"Why'd you run off, Erlyst? I mean, I get it, Kyrios is beautiful, and it turns out super rich as well, but you never even told Bea, your own mother."

"I know it doesn't make a lot of sense, but mom would not have understood. It happened really fast and I had to leave." Erlyst passed the joint back to Shannon. "Sorry, think I was holding that."

"Were you?" Shannon asked, sincerely befuddled.

"Maybe?" Both women giggled and Shannon coughed.

Erlyst looked at her phone. Fifty-one messages. "I should get back to the Brute Squad. Maybe they kept their mouths shut."

Shannon stood slowly, stretching the moment.

"No, no, don't get up. It's been a little while since I've walked Pulaski."

"Are you going to invite me to the wedding or what?"

Erlyst dropped her eyes. "I can't Shan. I'm not permitted to invite anyone."

"Permitted? Says who?"

"Erlyst," a gruff voice came from beyond the tree line. "We have to depart for the airport."

"How long have you assholes been standing there?"

No one answered.

"Un-fucking-believable." Erlyst stomped off the porch.

§

Winter ~ 1982

Holy Trinity Cathedral was trimmed in white: petals, silk, linen, and ribbon. Erlyst's big day had arrived. She held her breath and walked out to the foyer where the mayor of New York City waited to walk her down the aisle.

"Are you ready young lady?"

"Yes, your honor, I'm ready."

"Please, call me Ed." The Mayor held out his bent arm.

The large doors parted, and organ music flooded the cavernous sanctuary. A three-story chandelier gleamed down from the ceiling over the altar where Kyrios and the wedding party waited silently.

Every person in attendance was a stranger. Heads of state, foreign dignitaries, and a movie star here and there, filled the room with expectant silence. The crowd turned and stood in honor of Erlyst's entrance as the music began. Every man, woman, and child devoured the sight of the young bride slowly moving between the masses of onlookers. Though Kyrios' goon squad had mirrored her every move, she now passed into the unblinking gaze of the public. For those without power she was a fearsome mistress to be obeyed and worshipped, for those in power, she was a fresh young girl to be inspected and judged. Hers was a watched life now.

Kyrios beamed from the altar, his hands were perfectly clasped against his Dunhill suit. The gleam of his teeth, the casual escaping curl against his forehead, and his commanding, yet humbled stance were framed for the rolling cameras. Ed made petty small talk with Erlyst as they walked down the immense aisle. *They're old friends musing on a special day* the viewers sighed romantically.

The Mayor stopped at the base of the altar and Kyrios descended to take Erlyst's hand, as he had a dozen times during the rehearsal. Erlyst smiled. though it all felt as contrived as a Barbie doll thigh, Kyrios' unabated attention always made her swoon. She ascended the steps to be in his embrace forever. For better, or for...

A man leapt to his feet and shouted "Free West Beirut! Drown the Zionists in the Sea!" before unfurling a homemade poster of Yasser Arafat. A score of security personnel and Secret Service engulfed the man and whisked him out of the church in seconds. His cries of protest finally subsided behind slammed SUV doors and squealing tires.

"Well that was interesting," Archbishop Iakovos addressed the congregation. "May God bestow peace on that man's heart very soon." The audience applauded. "Shall we continue?"

Kyrios' face was twisted with rage. The Archbishop paused until Kyrios waved his hand, in blessing, for the ceremony to continue.

"Be thou magnified O Bridegroom, as Abraham, and blessed as Isaac, and multiply as Jacob. Walk in peace and work in righteousness, as the commandments of God.

"And thou O Bride, be thou magnified as Sarah, glad as Rebecca, and multiply like unto Rachel, rejoicing in thine own husband, fulfilling the conditions of the law, for so it is well pleasing unto God.

"Na zisete!"

It was finished, the framed portrait complete. Kyrios' lips fell warm and tenderly on hers, as practiced, as hoped for. The newlywed couple turned to the audience and waved. The sanctuary erupted in applause and music once again flooded the cavernous hall as the Bride and Groom slowly walked the gauntlet to the church doors, shaking hands and receiving hugs along the way.

When the limousine pulled away Erlyst hiked up her dress and straddled Kyrios' lap. "We have plenty of time before we get to the airport."

Kyrios smiled and began to unbutton his trousers. "I believe we do *Mrs.* Atropos."

‡

III

Victor struck out into the city. He walked down Grafton, getting lost in the crowds of shoppers.

> *8/17/10*
>
> *The children and their parents alike stopped to watch and tip street performers. Musicians playing familiar songs, puppeteers, and human statues lined the walk-*

way like riot cops at a May Day march. The University's ancient stone barrier curves slowly along the busy intersection while buses, cars, and bicycles whisk between pedestrians crossing in three directions. Dublin provides chaos when I need it.

O'Connell Bridge ends beneath an immense statue of Daniel O'Connell, sodden from centuries of avian defecation. The road ahead stretches endlessly out of sight.

There are myriad American chain restaurants lining the thoroughfare, shamefully sandwiched between legitimate pubs and restaurants as well as vast rows of consumer caves waiting patiently to part tourist with euro. On North Earl Street I found a humble and animated statue of James Joyce. Two old men in varying states of inebriation were collected on the base of the statue. One tried through bleary eyes to light a short broken-off cigar.

His counterpart, on holiday with the grandkids, sat regretting his last pint as the aforementioned children and his wife wandered in and out of the endless shops and curiosity-purveyors. An exhausted woman sat on the third corner of the base. She busied herself with her purse while her children ran laps around the statue, periodically waving at the old men and screaming gleefully when they waved back.

6pm

The sky continued its grey silence and finally, as I stepped onto Parnell, tiny sprinkles of rain began to frame my footfalls. By the time I turned onto North Great George's Street the ancient stone walkways were sullen with dampness and the skies had darkened considerably. I took refuge in the Joyce Center. I was completely alone in the three-story structure, save the woman at the admissions desk. I took my time, wandering around the mock-ups of Joyce's room and workspaces, watching each video presentation, taking note of important locations such as the Irish National Library where Joyce had composed much of what would become Ulysses.

The journey ended on a small patio next to an enormous bull bearing quotes from the Artist's varied works. Unfortunately, smoking was not permitted on the patio, so I made my way back to the entrance.

What am I doing? At the not-so tender age of thirty I have already fallen in and out of love with the concept of long-term solitude. Walking around a dusty epitaph for a scribe compounded it: you must disengage to put it all on paper. Writing is work. It is a commitment; writing isn't a spiritual spasm and a rush into the abyss.

There are two kinds of people: people who live life and people who reflect on lives lived. It is rare for people to have a foot planted firmly on both sides, like the shaded eye of a Venn diagram, living as well as reflecting. I have placed my weight advantageously on the live side and my writing block isn't a block at all, but a lack of will to disconnect and reflect. When I crushed out my cigarette, the sky was charcoal in whitewater rapids, and translucent oceans of rain were forming between the pebbles lining the museum's courtyard.

I walked into a mild downpour, my flat cap kept me dry, and my wool overcoat beat off the cold.

945pm

I have been productive, and on holiday no less. I traveled to the other side of the wide, sprawling Liffey, explored the roads I first saw entering Dublin, and devoured a large serving of history. Not a bad day's work.

I returned to the south side of the river in search of calm. Even the men in tweed at J.J. Smythe's slapping the bar when Ecuador scored a goal, were not interested in dancing on the table or shouting someone down over their religion. On occasion, one or more patrons may find themselves embroiled in a rowdy game of dominoes with a couple of flirty pensioners whose cheeks have reddened in coy seduction. Still others, anchored by life and pride to the very stool beneath their arse, make their territorial declarations of exception:

"Look, I won't have it. I will not be t'rown out of this bar." The slight, quiet man who came in every night as far as I can tell leaned heavily on the bar.

"You can say one more word about it and I'll t'row 'ya out m'self." Eamonn, the bartender, half threatened, half-announced to the amused five-person audience sprinkled about J.J. Smythe's.

"Ya can'a dooooo it," the drunk slurred.

Eamonn assured him, "I can, right over the shoulder with 'ya like a baby, I'll have 'ya on the curb before you can say..."

Everyone began to laugh as the drunk rose from the bar and tried desperately to hold his head and pointed finger up. "Feck you, no no no, feck you. You can kick me out, toss me, you can pull me by me feckin' hair. Well, what's left of it," rowdy laughter from his audience, "but I, on Mary's feckin' name, refuse to be t'rown out!"

≈

LIX

Spring ~ 2020

An overcast winter slowly died, and spring skies broke apart in great shattering mirrors. The citizens of Los Angeles, at first sign of darkened clouds scattered like insects, terrified and confused. The sun never seemed to come out for long.

The summer rolled in on wet grass, with occasional bursts of sunlight between the clouds. Persons living without air conditioning longed to be anywhere but home. The city, still adamantly opposed to competent public transportation, was forever choked with cars. Every summer month reeked of exhaust.

Il Diluvio wafted slowly onto the shores of Catalina Island. Pockmarked beaches dimpled under the first strands of soft, warm rain. The golf-shirted, Jimmy Buffet-brainwashed pedestrians trolling the island's Luddite byways felt run afoul by the interruption of rain. For the heavens to piss on their hard-earned facsimile of bliss was just...rude.

Los Angeles welcomed Il Diluvio as the storm endlessly gathered onshore. The oppressive summers of the early century had not abated as promised and winter became cultishly anticipated for the cooling and soothing effects it had on the battered coastline. Soft, inert warmth condensed Il Diluvio and allowed her to spread and incubate high above Los Angeles. Temperamental clouds erased the buildings looming over Pershing Square. The stark colors of the Square's framing skyscrapers were dulled as the mighty clouds slowly descended.

Then...the rain began. Ne'er to end.

The low-lying coastal regions felt the wrath first and with the most fury. As weeks dragged into months, the streets of Santa Monica, Venice, and Marina del Rey began to succumb to the waters building deep in the entrails of the city. The Westside was awash in dark, sodden rivulets and began to resemble a Caribbean dictatorship. Decayed, crumbling infrastructure forced stranded workers and professionals alike to commission boats and rafts to continue commuting. Water vessels soon became currency to those left behind when the affluent elements of the Westside evacuated to higher ground.

The harder the rain fell, the faster the western neighborhoods succumbed.

The Coastal diehards resorted to violence and pillage. A lot of people drew on experience in crisis times, whether through training on some flavor-of-the week humanitarian effort or through simple common sense in a period of trial—as observed on myriad *Survival Shows*.

A pioneering sliver of the well-to-do decided to stay behind: Burning Man aficionados composed miniature societies that remained isolated and seemed content to wait out the storm and keep to the highlands. *The beach will come back some day*, they murmured endlessly. *The skies will part once again*. Though their orgies were legendary, they were petty dictatorships that dissolved rapidly.

In the flood lands and the ruins of the old Westside, no amount of money could save you if you were left alone. Those who stayed behind recomposed and began to live the life that was unfolding around them.

The Elite's abandoned five-bedroom homes became theaters of combat as upper-middle class Angelinos vied for occupation rights. Robbed of their chance to truly *make it*, the embittered ladder-climbers squatted in the sewage-ravaged homes and muttered *I did it, I win*.

The canyons were safe for a time, but mudslides brought on by years of cyclical droughts demolished the rickety cliff-hanging homes at the highest heights. By way of trickle-down, the city below shared in the mountaintop community's excess: massive gushing waves of rock, mud, and debris carried SUVs and disturbed foundations down into Hollywood like an errant meteor shower.

Mayor Escalada Alamán III recognized the gravity of a domestic refugee crisis while the Union was facing a long economic depression and escalating wars abroad—*help* would forever be "on its way." The Mayor's office rapidly put contractors to work building a retaining wall that stemmed the tide and temporarily ended the seawater's eastern push at I-405. The haphazard, rushed installation mowed down homes for several blocks on either side of the freeway. A blessing to some, to others an unwelcome additional horror.

In time, Culver City, Hancock Park, Wilshire Corridor, and all the central low-lying plains and valleys began to relent under the sustained pressure of the storm above. Block by block these bustling border cities were abandoned as citizens with the capital to do so hired private security and took to the hills and high rises.

Il Diluvio turned the Los Angeles valley into a series of deep, tepid Lochs.[6]

Life became the storm, and the storm became life.

≈

The success of the 405-retaining-wall inspired Mayor Alamán. While visiting the newly formed Del Rey Bay, Alamán incorporated hints about a protective barrier surrounding the successfully gentrified DTLA[7]. Work had already begun on fortifying the newly renovated police headquarters—expanded and redesigned to encircle City Hall. The floodwater-driven flight downtown and the ignition of brutal gentrification efforts pushed the mayor's ideas for the barrier before the councils and the L.A. County Board of Supervisors.

No one could deny that the 405-retaining-wall had been a brilliant success, yet it was also commonly held that the Mayor's insistence on encircling Downtown, like a fortress, was madness. Alamán and Garcetti's pet plan was scoffed at in Committee and buried behind an impossible schedule of pre-review investigations. The Board of Supervisors felt quite clever, but Alamán was not amused.

"The meeting is being moved. I just got word." The councilperson from District 8 whispered into the receiver.

"Where?" District 10 asked nervously.

"Sub-floor meeting room."

"Sounds like a trap."

"Of course it's a trap, but what kind of trap?" District 8 was no longer whispering.

---

6 Iconography p. 22, Los Angeles in the wake of Il Diluvio

7 Downtown Los Angeles: coined in the early 2000's during the first push to gentrify the downtown area.

“You need to calm down James. Look, I know there have been rumors...”

“False, I might add Sandra. False, and demonstrably so.”

District 10 sighed. “Here’s the thing. The paper trail leads to your district. [8] You and Krekorian over in District 9 stand to gain quite a bit by threatening Downtown's access to the Harbor.”

“But you know we didn’t...”

“Doesn’t matter what I know, James. Someone in your District left her stink on this; Alamán is your primary concern now. I just want you to know that I will support the Mayor's Office if it comes down to it.”

“Are you threatening me?”

“I won’t waste my time threatening you. See you at the meeting, Jimbo.” Sandra couldn't help but get James stirred up. Most of Alamán's gentrification projects had financiers in her District, financiers that had stayed mostly above water, and counted on Sandra to keep them there.

The air in the sub-basement room was dense and still. A small, local Press gallery clogged the meager space, and large men in sunglasses lined the aisles. Garcetti sat at the center of the platform surrounded by Districts 4, and 5, and the Chairs of the Beverly Hills and West Hollywood city councils. Alamán sat far to stage left, leaning back in a fine leather chair, and slowly smoking a large cigar. The rest of the Districts made their way to the front rows. Representatives from a select few of the Eighty-Eight Cities[9] filled the rest of the formal meeting chairs.

As District 11 sat uncomfortably next to 1 and 9, Districts 12, 7, 2, 6, and 3 grouped together in mammalian fear—no one paid much mind to the twelve-seven-two-six-three. District 15 sat alone, the new guy, and the favored son. They all smiled carefully at one another. None wanted to seem too happy to see the other, and none could afford to hesitate and deny any potential allies their vanity.

Garcetti brought the meeting to order. Alamán remained in the shadows behind a stiff drink and a grey cloud of smoke.

---

8 Iconography p. 32, The Los Angeles City Councils 2021

9 Los Angeles County is a haphazard mosaic composed of 88 municipalities, countless unincorporated areas, and millions of residents entirely unaware of where they are at any given moment.

"Welcome and thank you for accommodating us on such short notice. We have all faced ordeals. Shared ordeals, and personal ordeals in our own backyards. The rain brought great pain and misery, but it also brought us strength. Our once splintered government now functions as an anointed entity for good." Garcetti waited, a seasoned dramatist, "Yet, that's not enough for some of our esteemed leaders."

Murmurs rose in the room. Alamán rapped his hand loudly against the table and the room fell silent. Like a vicious patriarch he held the room against revolt.

Garcetti continued, "This fetish for blaming our failures on City Hall ends today. Bring her out."

The crowd turned as second-term councilperson Muri Sahli from district 14 walked solemnly toward the stage. Her eyes were vacant, and her movements were imitations of a rehearsed arrival. They had dressed her smartly in a high-necked blouse and business jacket, careful to spare the audience evidence of her long and brutal "interrogation." Her face was eerily calm, yet her hands shook as she placed them on the edges of a podium. She removed a folded piece of paper from her jacket and smoothed it out as she inhaled purposefully.

She looked straight ahead, beyond the audience.

"I am here to confess. I have conspired to commit the vile and treasonous act of subverting the Mayor of Los Angeles."

The room erupted. Alamán stood and raised his hand. The room came to heel before he had to slam it on the table again.

"Our goal was to combine our efforts with the cities of the South Bay, Vernon, Bell, South Gate, and Lynwood, to eventually block the City of Los Angeles' access to the ports." The accused looked around, panicked. Most of them were innocent, but Alamán wasn't meting out justice, he was making a point. They were guilty of *something* and there would be no defense against their detractors.

Sahli continued in monotone, "I will now read a list of my co-conspirators.

Deanne Jensen.

Sandra Jillibrunch.

James Eirelipsön... "

District 10 and 8 looked at one another sheepishly. The large men in sunglasses began to wave in their direction. Both stood obediently and walked out of the room with no resistance. One by one, the accused were escorted from the meeting.

District 12 stood and desperately shouted, "Long live Alamán!"

Cautious cheers rose all over the room.

Grown adults began flailing like fish as the large men pulled them from their seats. Protests for mercy and decency were ignored. Alamán sat silently and smoked his cigar, occasionally tipping his drink beneath his broad, dark mustache.

"Marqueece Krekorian.

Antonio Villa."

Sahli folded the list and looked to Alamán for her orders. He nodded and she walked into the custody of the remaining guards.

The room had thinned by half. Downey and the Vernon-through-Compton corridor took the hardest hits, but no district or city had been spared. All five members of the Los Angeles County Board of Supervisors were pulled gruffly from their seats, shocked and shouting curses. Alamán's message was loud and clear...

Garcetti crossed his hands in front of his microphone. "Allegiance to the City and its divine purpose is paramount. Are there any objections from the remaining representatives?"

—silence.

"Councilpersons and representatives, please follow me. The Press will remain inside."

No one was willing to give an eyewitness account of what happened next until Alamán had been dead for years. According to an anonymous deathbed confession, each remaining member of an active government post was given a pistol and paired with one of the dismissed *conspirators.*

Garcetti was reported to have given the command to execute.

For Unity, for Strength, for the City.

Among the remaining, no man, nor woman, staid their hand.

≈

When the bill for the DTLA wall was re-introduced as the Los Angeles Youthfulness and Core Revitalization and Redemption Act (LYCRRA), it was passed unanimously. The councils shrewdly agreed to a program with a sunset clause of thirty years.

Plans were drawn to construct the DTLA barrier using the Harbor, Hollywood, Santa Monica, and Golden State Freeways as superstructure. Neighboring communities rose up and tried, finally through violent means, to stop the construction. In spite of their righteous indignation, they were small flickering candles amidst a firestorm.

Immanent Domain took on an entirely new blush under Alamán and the decayed and neglected parts of downtown Los Angeles were sucked up by the machines. The City erected a winding chain link fence to create checkpoints. As the final posts were set, drones dropped leaflets over the communities inside the fence.

NOTICE FROM THE OFFICE OF THE MAYOR OF LOS ANGELES

This region and its surrounding neighborhoods are now under the jurisdiction of the City of Los Angeles pursuant to Cal Code Civ Proc § 1230.030. This will serve as thirty (30) days' notice to vacate all premises, domestic, commercial, or industrial, within the demarcation barrier. All persons, places, and possessions will be subject to impound, imprisonment, and execution after 30 days.

We are all thankful for the opportunity to serve the City and Its Greater Good.

- James Blankenfeld
DIRECTOR, OFFICE OF SPECIAL OPERATIONS

The City began leveling large swathes of land surrounding DTLA—repossessed, without hesitation, without due process. As the demarcated region was slowly evacuated by force, workers replaced the infamous chain link fence with layers of haphazardly spaced blast walls. The barriers insured that no clear path of egress to the Wall ever materialized. Temporary sentry houses could be erected in less than an hour, and fiat choke points were ordered routinely in response to threats. It was impossible, even for the guard battalion, to know from day to day what byways would be impossibly blocked, or free and clear. The demarcated region became randomly dissected, cutting apartment complexes in half and turning bustling thoroughfares into dead ends.

Construction of Alamán's magnum opus commenced. Helicopters began dropping multi-ton containers at Dodger Stadium and an endless march of trucks rolled down through Chinatown. Immense, sloppy, curtains of iron rods encased in football fields of concrete grew slowly from the earth until they tenderly scraped the underbellies of overhead freeways. The Theater, Gallery, and Jewelry districts of south DTLA were gutted as appropriate and dynamited with extreme prejudice whenever permissible. Buffer communities of mildly expensive and starkly depressing apartment buildings were constructed along the demarcation barrier to provide further insulation from outside.

The hills and high-rises began to empty as the craven, moneyed citizens flocked to their walled, sterilized Eden. The strictly controlled streets were free of all signs of poverty, consternation, or suffering. Massive walkways awash in fresh flowers and chamber music joined the highest floors of towering high-rise apartment buildings, saving their residents from mingling with those closest to Earth. Elaborate webs of vertical and horizontal elevators connected the stratosphere of the Downtown skyline, further removing one's feet from solid ground.

To come in under twenty floors meant a building was fit only for store-housing low-caste workers. Ambitious Owners simply built up, expanding on decrepit, abandoned husks, and turning them into the teetering foundations for glittering towers that stretched deep into the low clouds.

The mayor's office used donations from the newly settled DTLA elite, and re-appropriated Homeland Security funding, to re-grid the area within and immediately outside of the Wall. The city within the City had its own electrical power grid and cut services to those outside of the wall. In spite of damning them to a pre-technological wilderness, the Feudal lords still commanded lust in the hearts of their subjects.

And all the while, it rained.

≈

Spring – 2025

For Hazbelt Benito's fifteenth birthday, his grandfather gave him a rough, wooden box.

"What is it?"

"Open it, come on."

Within, lay a mechanical alarm clock from the mid-Twentieth Century.

The elder Benito struggled to rise out of his chair and look his grandson in the eye. "This belonged to me for many years. It tells time, and it can do so without electricity, and without a receiver connection."

The clicking of the gears, and the chime of the bells fascinated Hazbelt. Time had been told via satellite for so long that Hazbelt's little machine was a mystery; its need for human attention was so foreign that Hazbelt treated it like an elderly family pet.

After Il Diluvio, electricity and receiver signals became a luxury in neighborhoods like Highland Park, and Hazbelt had forgotten to wind the gears before climbing into bed. For the first time, his trusty mechanical alarm clock had failed; he woke with only five minutes to spare before the first bell at

Franklin High School. He rushed through his morning routine and ran all the way to school in the rain.

It was also the first day Hazbelt had heard of the Sunset Camp.

Mr. Sown stopped lecturing the class when Hazbelt took his seat.

"Thank you for joining us Mr. Benito. You've been to the Office already, I trust?"

"Yes, Mr. Sown. I'm sorry, my alarm..."

"No worries Mr. Benito, it happens to the best of us. So, let's bring Mr. Benito up to speed. Ms. Merkovich, can you tell me what year the Downtown Wall was built?"

"..."

"Ok, Mr. Jacobs?"

"The year after Il Diluvio started."

"That's correct. What year was that Mr. Jacobs?"

Ryan Jacobs fidgeted in his seat.

"That's ok, make sure you write down that the DTLA Wall was constructed in 2021. As Mr. Jacobs pointed out, in response to Il Diluvio. Mayor Alamán divided the downtown area into four sections. [10] You should all be writing this down.

"The City Zone is comprised of the City offices, including the Mayoral compound. It remains one of the most heavily guarded places in the nation. Olde Los Angeles is the largest section. Ninety percent of residential, commercial, and retail operations are within the Olde Los Angeles section. It's the city within the city." Mr. Sown forced a laugh, but no one got the joke.

"In the center of Olde Los Angeles are the Great Gardens. Alleged to be a second Eden by those privileged to see it."

Lillian Contreras raised her hand. "Have you seen it Mr. Sown?"

"No, no, I don't qualify for that."

"But you're a teacher." Lillian pleaded.

"And old." Ryan Jacobs added.

Mr. Sown blushed. "I am old, and I am indeed a teacher. Unfortunately, the only way I could get beyond the wall is by

---

10 Iconography p. 24, The Downtown Los Angeles Wall and Sections

getting picked at the employment rally. As you can see, I am already employed, so let's move on.

"The last section is Sunset Camp. This area, which is along the eastern border and across the LA River from the rest of Downtown, serves as temporary housing and confinement for thousands of workers. Sunset Camp is also the only civilian entry point to Downtown. The remainder of Downtown is an industrial belt surrounding Olde Los Angeles. The utilities, fabrication, and manufacturing necessary to keep Downtown autonomous cramps this outer region."

The bell rang.

"Shit. Ok kids read chapter eleven tonight. If you have any questions about Downtown so far write them down and we'll go over them tomorrow." The room had already emptied. "Or not."

"Mr. Sown?"

"Oh Hazbelt, what's on your mind?"

"You were talking about the sections, and you said that some of the people from outside, people like us, were able to get in."

"Yes, but only for a short time. The purpose is to trap desperate people into working for very low wages. In return, one can gloat about having been inside, and proudly send the pittance home."

"You think that's bad?

"I do. People who put themselves under the City's control no longer make their own decisions—they must only obey. People stripped of control over their own decisions are prisoners. It's sick young Mr. Benito, don't you think?"

"Sure. Sick. How do we, *they*, get in?"

"Well, Olde Los Angeles, the Great Gardens, and the City Compound need menial workers. Cooks, cleaners of all stripes, chauffeurs, gardeners, wait staff, et cetera. Annually, there is a perverse version of an employment rally in Hollenbeck Park, more like a cattle call, really. Hand-picked deplorables are permitted to do hard labor inside the wall for one year."

"What happens after a year?"

"If they make it that long, they're kicked out. Booted, like spoiled food. No one from the outside community is permitted to set down roots. The City fears so-called anchor babies that would tarnish the elite luster of being a downtowner."

"Still. A whole year, that's something..."

"The price is your soul, young Mr. Benito. Your very soul."

Hazbelt was an atheist. "Thanks Mr. Sown. See you tomorrow."

"On time we hope, yes?"

"I'll wind my clock as soon as I get home."

Hazbelt dropped his backpack and sat next to his grandfather.

"Why are we so poor?"

"Hm, that is a complicated question Hazbelt. We have never been a wealthy family."

"Did one of our ancestors make a mistake? Do we suffer for his sins?"

"We do not suffer. We have a home, we are well-fed, and well-loved. In these ways, we are a very wealthy family."

"But we cannot see the Great Gardens."

"Ah, the Great Gardens. They were not made for us. There are people who have a special kind of wealth. It comes from their ancestors and their ancestors' ancestors. There is a second kind, that kind of wealth is only possible with permission from the first group. Both groups are wealthy because they are powerful and are powerful because of their wealth."

"But we can be whatever we choose to be, Mr. Sown reminds us often."

"That is true, but you cannot choose your parents. You will live your life on this side of the wall."

"That doesn't seem true. If I work hard enough, I should have just as much chance as anyone. Besides, the Mayor's name is Alamán! He's one of us."

"Mayor Alamán is nothing like us. He may have grown up on the East side, but he left all of us to die when the rain began falling."

Hazbelt was silent and his grandfather feared that his lesson had gone too far...

"I say these things to you because you are a man and not a child. There is no justice in this world, so we must be just to one another. Do you understand Hazbelt?"

The boy hugged is grandfather. "Yes, I understand now."

"I love you, now go do your homework."

But Hazbelt didn't understand.

Hazbelt thought that his grandfather had given up. Mr. Sown always said opportunity is only for those that seize it. The only thing Hazbelt's grandfather seized was an extra nap in the afternoon.

≈

"Hey! Yeah you, fuck head."

Hazbelt kept walking, avoiding puddles where he could.

"Haaaaaz-beeeeelt, come 'ere sweety. You mad, bro?"

"Leave me alone."

Leonard circled Hazbelt. "You got a dead body in that backpack?"

"No. I have a project."

"Oh, okay a project. For school?"

"Yes."

Leonard stopped. "Then why are you walking away from the school?"

He was right, Hazbelt panicked. "Am I? I have so much on my mind, thank you..."

"Nice try. I'm not a narc, man. Unless you're planning to shoot up an elementary school, I wanna know what's up."

"Quiet down. Come on, walk with me." Leonard walked next to Hazbelt. "I'm going Downtown."

"For what? Sick of being alive or something?"

"I'm getting in."

"How?"

"The employment rally. The one Mr. Sown was talking about. I found out it starts in a couple of days. I'm getting in man, I'm going to see the Great Gardens."

"You're whacked. Don't let Senile Sown send you on a suicide mission. Even if you get in, you'll be cleaning toilets."

"It's my destiny."

"Fucking whacked. I'll walk you to the Gold Line. Did you bring a gun?"

"Don't be insane." Hazbelt proudly produced a pilfered billyclub.

The boys slowly entered the platform. After the floods, most people stayed indoors. Riding the automated trains made one a target. They checked for thieves behind the ticket dispensers and pillars. A creeping Gold Line train pulled into the Highland Park station. The doors parted and several men moved back from the doorway.

"Thank you." Hazbelt nodded and entered the train.

The doors closed as Leonard mouthed, *you're whacked.*

Everyone watched Hazbelt carefully. Two of the men looked familiar, neighborhood familiar, and the third was a white guy. It was the first time he had been in the presence of a Caucasian, so he tried not to stare. The man's suit was remarkable. Hazbelt kept his hands in front of him and backed toward a seat.

"You don't want to sit down young man." The white guy warned without taking his eyes off the other two men. "Good chance we'll have to fight or run before it's all said and done."

Hazbelt addressed the other two men, en Español: "Are you guys okay? You seem pretty spooked by this guy."

The man in the futbal jersey kept an eye on the White Guy. "What's he doing outside the wall?"

"Bad family, same as us. Who cares? We're all outside, doesn't that count?" Hazbelt shrugged his shoulders.

"No." The man in coveralls answered abruptly.

Hazbelt turned, "Sir, I'm Hazbelt Benito, what may I call you?"

"Dennis."

"Dennis, it is a pleasure. How do we prepare?"

"If the platform is full, press your bodies against the door and hold them shut. If people get on, we want them as far away from us as possible until we know their intentions."

"And if it is empty?" The futbal fan asked.

"If it's empty keep your eyes open and your mouth shut. Empty stations are perfect for an ambush."

"How do you know?"

"I make my way up and down the line when the money is right."

"Smuggler." The man in coveralls huffed.

"He's a bodyguard," Hazbelt interrupted.

"Very observant. Look sharp, we're here."

The four men watched the Southwest Museum platform for movement, but nothing stirred. The train doors swished open as the men waited; only silence entered the train.

The doors began to close and a shock of black rushed toward the train and disappeared between the doors two cars away.

"Shit, shit, shit," The coveralls guy started chanting.

Futbal guy tried to calm him down. "Whatever that was, it's not in here with us."

"We're fucking dead..."

Hazbelt pulled the billyclub from his backpack and moved it to his pocket.

Dennis peered through the dirty windows between the train's rumbling cars. It was a waste of time. "No one is moving around back there, and no one is on their way toward us, so let's just keep it down and watch the doors."

Futbal jersey, "You're not in charge gringo."

"Just advice, take it or leave it."

"Are we all going Downtown?" Hazbelt tried to chip the tension.

En Español: "None of your business kid. Besides, you don't want this white guy to know where you're headed."

"Probably a cop. Looks like a cop."

"Talks like a cop."

Hazbelt shook his head, disappointed. *In English:* "I'm going to secure a job at the employment rally."

"That's a bad idea kid."

"It's a very good idea, thank you. I am a smart and competent candidate. There's no reason I'll have any trouble."

"Is this your first time?"

"It is." Hazbelt smiled proudly.

"Look kid, you don't know what it's like down there. The Annexes are no place for a rookie, and tens of thousands of desperate people have been lining up in Hollenbeck Park for months."

"I won't be stopped. I've come this far..."

"Looks like we have people on the platform, you boys mind helping me hold this door?"

The four passengers pressed their bodies against the doors and held the edges of the window. Several men trotted along with the occupied car until it stopped. Their eyes were hungry for violence.

"They've seen us, get ready..."

Hazbelt wailed and fell to the floor, a long blade pressed between the train doors, slick with the boy's blood.

"Mind the gap, the locks will engage soon, just hold on."

A fire raged through Hazbelt's side as warm blood began to soak his shirt. Through stinging tears, he saw a shape in the window between cars. The shape that had entered the train watched in silence from behind the filthy glass.

Hazbelt howled, "Dennis, Dennis, there's someone..."

"Hang in there, kid."

The angry men from the platform started to clear away as a man with a shotgun approached the train. Two blasts hit the car and everyone dropped to the ground.

Dennis crawled to Hazbelt. "Is the cut deep kid?"

"I don't think so. It's not bleeding as much now."

"Good." Dennis reached into his jacket and produced a small strip of clear paper. "Lift your shirt."

"What is that?"

"It will suture the wound for now. You need to get to a hospital."

"I'm fine. I'm not weak."

Dennis finished setting the suture. Hazbelt did not flinch.

"Guys help me pick him up. Guys?" Both men sat slack against the railing. Each had taken buckshot to the chest. "Probably better that way."

"Better? How can that be better?"

En Español: "It was only a matter of time before those guys ganged up on me."

Hazbelt did not like being tricked.

"I saw something. Or someone, in the window there, while we were being attacked."

"Are you sure?"

"Maybe?"

"Okay. Let's get you down near the other side of the car and we'll keep an eye on that door. We're not going to be able to repel attacks now that we're down to four hands, so stay away from the windows. There are snipers all through the canyon anyway."

"Why do they shoot at the trains?"

"For fun, kid."

Hazbelt felt sick to his stomach. He thought he understood cruelty, but he was wrong.

They pulled slowly into the Lincoln/Cypress station. The neighborhoods crammed against the rail line were deserted, it was too dangerous to be outside.

"Get down under the seat," Dennis offered.

Hazbelt complied, stifling a yelp as he disturbed his knife wound.

A masked man wearing body armor stepped slowly onto the train. His outstretched arms cradled a long automatic rifle. At his hip, a soiled string of human scalps.

Someone called from outside the train, "Come on, there's no targets on this one."

The man started backing out. Hazbelt's sneaker squeaked against the train floor. The armored man froze and raised his rifle, scanning the car. "Hold on, someone is hiding on this one."

Hazbelt heard boots running toward them. He was too far from the other door to leap, and he was a sitting duck if he stayed. Dennis sprang from beneath the handicap seats, grabbed the safety rails with both hands, and kicked the masked man backward onto the platform. The doors slid softly into place and the train began to accelerate. Machine gun fire collapsed the windows of the car.

Hazbelt raised his head. The men did not appear to be following them along the tracks.

"Are you okay?"

“Yep. Might’ve pulled something. I’m getting too old for that sort of thing.”

“Are you a cop?”

“No. I was a military man for a time.”

“Which military?”

“Does it really matter anymore?”

“It has always mattered.”

“I was more like a consultant. My loyalty was to the mission.”

Hazbelt walked slowly toward the window. “What is that?”

Spreading like a vast asphalt prairie in all directions, the long abandoned Golden State Freeway unfolded below the train bridge. Encampments of varying sizes littered the massive roadway and its borders.

“That used to be an interstate Freeway.”

Hazbelt muttered, “It’s massive.”

“Millions of cars used to pass through here. Look ahead of us, that’s the Chinatown Annex.”

An immense grey wall rose from the western shore of the distended LA River.

Hazbelt was overwhelmed.

“Station’s coming up. Let’s get on the door.”

“Shouldn’t we hide?”

“I’ve got a feeling we’re past the rough parts.”

Two large red beasts formed an arch above the Chinatown platform. Hazbelt’s eyes were wide, it was the first time he had seen Chinese dragons. When the train stopped and the doors parted, Dennis put his arm around Hazbelt.

“I’m lucky you’re handsome too.”

“Say what?”

“Handsome. People pay more for handsome boys down on Figueroa. You’re going to set me straight for a few months.” Dennis heaved off the train with Hazbelt in his arms. The boy struggled, and his billyclub fell from his pocket. The older man was too strong for Hazbelt, and the pain ringing through his head kept his hands low and eyes closed. He began to scream when it was clear he could not win.

"Come on handsome, it's not so bad. Maybe you'll get one of those daddy types that will spoil you..." Dennis' hands suddenly fell away, and he slumped to the platform.

A woman in a long black cape pushed Hazbelt back onto the train and held a taser, ready to fell Dennis should he rise again. When the doors closed, she placed the taser under her cloak and removed her hood.

"Hello. I am sorry that I could not help you sooner. Are you alright?"

"I think so. Thank you. Thank you so much, I don't know..."

Hazbelt started to cry. The stranger embraced him. "You are safe now. Why are you here?"

The boy wiped his eyes. "I plan to impress the job pickers so I can see the Great Gardens for myself."

The woman smiled. "Those are very big plans."

"I am no child."

"There are more people like that white man and the people from the platforms, thousands of them. Ride with me through to Boyle Heights and we'll watch over one another."

"Yes. Thank you."

The vast train yards beyond Union Station were now host to thousands of commissioned City vehicles. From helicopters to armored cars the sea of black and white stretched out of view. "That's a lot of equipment."

The woman replied, "The Mayor is preparing for war."

The track carried the train over an immense canyon, the once vital Hollywood Freeway. Bodies littered the strategic moat separating Chinatown Annex from Downtown. Beyond the Hollywood Freeway, immense steel girders rose three hundred feet into the air forming the Downtown Wall. The tops of gleaming glass skyscrapers rose higher still. A cramped opening emerged in the endless steel barrier.

The train remained in a tunnel cut through the wall for several seconds. When they emerged, Hazbelt's eyes were alight with wonder. The pristine spires surrounding the Mayor's compound reflected sunlight-creased storm clouds. The clean, brightly lit streets didn't seem real. The sky was obscured by a web of glass and steel. In the distance, the city ceased and gave way to a rippling sea of green.

"The Great Gardens," Hazbelt whispered.

"Yes, they are deadly, but very beautiful."

"You have seen them?"

"I have, but for a very short time."

"Tell me, please." Hazbelt became a child once again.

"Of course."

The woman kept her eye on the electrified barriers encasing the track. Below the First Street Bridge, the rain-dimpled LA River played slowly toward the Pacific. Within the City Zone section long esplanades of flowers-in-bloom, manicured lawns, and sprawling covered walkways consumed the shores of the swollen river. As the waters passed beneath the barrier and into Sunset Camp, the environment returned once again to the decayed, concrete ditch that it had been for three score and five years.

"You remind me of my father. He was also a man of great vision. When the downtown purges began, he was able, always, to find a place for us just beyond the police line. He laid the first concrete for the Civilian Crossing at Sunset Camp."

The train slipped underground before reaching the towering East Barrier of the DTLA Wall. "He was able to keep me a secret. No one cared about my father beyond his ability and willingness to work. I lived my life in a series of cramped apartments, most overlooking shops, long closed. But I was happy. I did not know fear, and I could not conceive of what my father endured. I craved the outside. I begged my father to let me play somewhere, anywhere. There were no children in Sunset Camp. He risked everything by permitting me to play on the rooftop. He fashioned a tarp to conceal me from overhead helicopters, but I was not satisfied. The rain was monstrous, and in the end, I retreated to our tiny cell. We began riding the Gold Line from beginning to end every day. Though we never dared to leave the train, it was enough. On my sixteenth birthday..."

"I'm fifteen. Almost sixteen." Hazbelt stated proudly.

"My father smuggled me in a large walking trunk to the center of the City. When he found a safe clearing, he let me out. I had never seen beauty like I witnessed in that small clearing. The Great Gardens filled my eyes, ears, and nose with exotic gifts. Above, looming in the sky like satellites, gloom-covered skyscrapers sat in silent judgment beyond the emerald rain forests."

"I knew it would be incredible..."

"As I twirled, an angry voice called to my father. He responded quickly and ordered me to stay put. They shouted at him while he removed his sleeve. Once they had scanned his ID, he rolled his sleeve down and began pleading. Soon he was begging and then one of the men struck him. As he fell to the ground he screamed, *run.* But I could not. I watched the security officer approach me cautiously, and strike with his baton. They dumped me on this train."

"Where is your father?"

"This is our train. When he is free, he will find me here. We have arrived."

Hazbelt sat up and scanned Mariachi Plaza station. Though it looked empty, the air was thick with anxiety.

"Come with me. We are both better off with a friend."

"I cannot leave."

"Something feels wrong. Please. Come with me to the park and then return."

"Move very quickly. See the stairs there, beyond the ticket machine? Move to the surface without hesitating. You will be fine once you are on the surface."

"Thank you."

Hazbelt stood before the doors. When they parted, he sprinted onto the platform, tripping over the first step. He reached the top of the stairs and looked back. A mass of bodies emerged from beneath the far escalator and rushed the train doors. Hazbelt heard the woman scream before the train carried her into the silent underground tunnel.

The boy collapsed to the ground. Tears gushed from his eyes and his body heaved. The sobbing enflamed his knife wound, but scuffling feet at the base of the stairs sent him sprinting for the long escalators to the surface.

As Hazbelt reached the top of the escalator he gathered the courage to turn and look back into the subway chasm. Bodies slammed at full speed into the base of the escalator. They looked up at Hazbelt and writhed around in an insect mass.

They wanted to rend Hazbelt from limb to limb, but they would not ascend to the surface.

The boy ran across First Street and south on Boyle Avenue. Several blocks of quiet, tree-shaded homes had passed before Hazbelt's legs would stop running.

A dome of light bloomed in the darkening sky just beyond the Golden State Freeway overpass. The air was vibrating, and he began to feel an immense sound curling around the bend. Massive loudspeakers crowned Hollenbeck Park and shouted orders to a sea of human bodies. Helicopters circled, sweeping the crowd with spotlights. There were no gaps, no fissures in the immense organism, only a writhing cancer 300,000 cells strong.

Just beyond the lake he saw the processing center. Hazbelt had to try; if the entire Eastside stood in his way, he must be smarter and find a way in.

Guards in body armor were frisking candidates before allowing them into the inspection stalls. Several got rough and slammed two women to the ground. As more guards gathered to join in the beating, Hazbelt leapt from the shadows and sprinted toward the processing center. His heart threatened to rupture, its deafening thump filled his ears. He did not hear the rifle report nor feel the bullet rattle around in his skull. Hazbelt Benito fell to the ground, far from his goal.

§

XXXII

Spring ~ 1986

As autumn and winter passed, as sure as the sun rose, Erlyst slept alone. Kyrios' weeklong trips to far-off towns—small Southern towns—entombed her in doubt, but she held her tongue.

The phone rang across hollow chambers. After three rings it ceased. Erlyst heard footsteps approaching.

A knock at the door, "Madame. You have a telephone call from El Matador."

"The restaurant? I don't have any business with them."

After a moment, "Madame. I apologize, but they insist it is urgent that they confirm your reservation, lest it be given to someone else. They will not be dissuaded."

Erlyst threw open the door and snagged the cordless phone from her butler. "Thank you. You are dismissed. Asshole."

Erlyst put the phone to her head, "This is Mrs. Atropos, what seems to be the problem?"

"No problem ma'am. We needed to confirm your reservation and we have not been able to contact Mr. Atropos for several hours. We know that losing a reservation here can be very...*frustrating*...so we wanted to make certain Mr. Atropos *intended* to relinquish it." It was true; flaking on a reservation at El Matadore was like committing social suicide.

"But I don't have a reservation idiot...wait. Yes, I recall now." Erlyst knew what to do. "What time was the reservation again?"

"8:30pm."

"Well, well, Mr. Atropos is looking to impress." Erlyst hissed politely.

"Yes ma'am, it is a very coveted table. I hope you'll forgive the intrusion."

"Your establishment is forgiven. Thank you for the call."

Erlyst showered and dressed, taking great care that every hair, line, and curve was perfectly in place. She called her car and strode to the curb. The click of her heels against the blank sidewalk and the soft swish of her gown carried her into the long black automobile.

El Matadore's lobby was lined with men, seated, and women, standing, because one cannot sit in those damned dresses. All eyes fell on Erlyst as she closed in on the Host.

"Has the Atropos party been seated?"

The Host checked the list smugly. "No, and you are?"

"*Mrs.* Atropos."

"Of course, I apologize." Not recognizing the face of your master is a grave sin. "The party is having a cocktail in the lounge; shall I escort you... "

"That won't be necessary." Erlyst repaired to the lounge and stood at the entryway scanning the room.

Kyrios was surrounded by three obese men and a young, professional woman in a smart suit and excellent shoes. One of the men said something amusing and everyone feigned paralysis. As they laughed, the young woman traced Kyrios' necktie with her finger and looked up into his eyes as she flicked his belt buckle provocatively. Kyrios looked down at the small-framed woman and smiled his crooked, *I mean you great harm* smile.

Erlyst strode calmly toward the young woman and struck her face with the 40-carat ringed back of her hand. The young woman collapsed to the ground, lip split, cheek cut, cowering in terror.

"Kyrios, walk away." Erlyst paused briefly. "Now."

He smiled, stifling a chuckle. "As you wish my love." Kyrios and his three partners nodded their heads to Erlyst and began to walk toward the dining room.

"Mr. Atropos?" The young woman cried.

Kyrios walked out of the room and did not turn to offer his young prey protection from the scorned matriarch.

Erlyst thrashed the horrified young woman while the crowded lounge looked on. A surrogate, but it did not matter, she had to destroy what beauty the young woman might enjoy before slipping into middle age.

≈

LXIII

Summer ~ 2025

Peals of thunder ripped through the skies above soaked and defeated Culver City. The portions clinging to the rising Angeles Hills had been spared complete devastation, and although it came at the eleventh hour, the 405-retaining wall had saved much of Culver from becoming part of del Rey Bay.

The sun had long since set and the positive-minded citizenry were outside in the mercifully light rain trying to piece together an old idea of *Friday night*. Lightning streaked the warm summer sky, and the continual grinding of filthy white thunderheads produced monstrous claps that echoed against the low buildings and asphalt byways.

People thought it was thunder when a massive explosion scattered the contents of a quiet café as shrapnel. Citizens were engulfed by the eviscerating plume: chair legs, tabletops, porcelain, and slices of shredded metal from espresso machines, danced within the deadly cloud. Thirty-five people died instantly, and several dozen outside the cafe suffered eventually fatal wounds.

Within hours, two more cafés, a high school, and an office building suffered similar fates. A faction calling itself The Local Militia released a video prior to the evening news cycle calling the Mayor an abomination to the *freedom* movement...

> **clip**
> "...and making some pretty...what would you say Mark? *Outrageous*, almost comical, demands. Here's Tom Uncle with a special report on the Local Militia."
>
> "Members, masked, explained that they: *demand the immediate resignation and imprisonment of Escalada Alamán III. His reign over our fair city must come to an end. We can no longer wait for a brighter day, Alamán and the criminal Council Coalition must be brought to justice.*
>
> *We are patriots. We are warriors. We will not relent until we are free once again.*
>
> "We don't know who they are, but we know who they are after, and we know they are willing to kill. An attack on our glorious Leader is, of course, an attack on us all, Tina. So, it seems we are dealing with some very insane, or very stupid terrorists. We'll have more on the story as it unfolds... "
>
> "Thanks Tom; now, in Celebrity news... "
> **clip**

≈

The city was appropriately alarmed.

≈

Culver looked to Mayor Alamán for help. Secretary of the Treasury, Terry Bruce, sent a spokesperson to hold an emergency press conference. He denounced *terrorism* but continued to express concern over “a troubling wave of resistance to Council Coalition mandates and sovereignty.”

He could not openly say Culver City deserved to be attacked, but he did not say it was unjustified. “It is our sincere hope that this problem won't upset the delicate rule of law in Culver City any further. The Mayor’s Office will begin deploying consultants to advise the Culver City Council on counter-insurgency methods.”

The Local Militia was smoke and mirrors, a distraction manufactured by the mayor’s office. This was an Occupation. The Culver City Council rightly feared for their lives and began to meet clandestinely. They quietly stockpiled weapons and stopped using accounts with the city.

Culver knew it was no match for the Mayor's Office or its proxies, but if necessary, they could attack West Hollywood and drag Hollywood into the fight. City Hall would be forced to spring to the defense of its lapdog.

Culver City authorities refused the Consultants at the city line and threatened a civil war. They had learned from America's Imperial folly that one must only hunker down into an insurrectionist posture and wait until the oppressor runs out of fuel or loses interest. If Culver City could keep the mayor engaged long enough, and to an annoying enough degree, he'd relent after a few years and leave them be.

The newly formed rebel government in Culver City prosecuted Alamán and his major players in absentia and vowed to imprison anyone who entered their territory that was under warrant. Alamán taunted Culver City's leadership and they responded by decimating three expensive restaurants along Sunset Blvd. with an off-duty SWAT-deployment. Alamán was called to act by the Beverly Hills elite and the mayor moved gleefully to wipe Culver City from the Corporate Charter.

≈

Terry Bruce convinced Alamán to send a diplomatic party to make nice with the rebel leadership. They made a large production of it: newscasts, online engagements, even an under the table login code to spectate in real-time. The pageant began with a large parade of Alamán's men leaving the main city gates and heading to a garland-laden helipad erected outside the DTLA walls for the occasion.

The party landed at the designated Culver City site and exited the aircraft under heavy vanguard.

A man in a worn uniform pilfered from an ARMY surplus store approached the Mayor's ambassador. Many had already died and suffered so that the elites could live in isolated excess, but the rebel leader remained focused; he had promised not to show his people's ire and to return home safely. He shook the ambassador's spray-tanned and many-ringed hand roughly.

"In spite of being degenerate scum, you have been granted an audience with his High Honor Escalada Alamán III. What have you come to offer his Honor?"

As the rebel leader began to speak, one of his Lieutenants broke rank and raised his pistol, aiming it at the ambassador. "How can you shake that monster's hand?"

The ambassador cowered shamefully on the ground begging for his life.

"Stand down soldier!" The rebel leader shouted at his Lieutenant.

The rebel line began to dissent and demands for the execution of the ambassador eclipsed pleas for sanity. The cacophony started to cause panic in both heavily armed camps.

"If you do this, soldier, you will sign our death warrant, every man, woman, and child in Culver."

With great effort, the Lieutenant lowered his pistol.

"Good thing you listened to your boss," the ambassador snarled just before his neck split open. A tiny crimson hole formed an arcing rush of blood that gushed down the ambassador's white, pressed shirt.

≈

The bullet came from a hidden position somewhere among the rooftops, but all in attendance assumed that it came from the rebel Lieutenant's weapon. Viewers nationwide were convinced they had just been subjected to a public execution.

"Perfect." Terry sneered.

Alamán angrily turned on Terry, "What? He just killed him in cold blood...in front of cameras!"

On the screen behind Alamán, both rebels and representatives of the Mayor's Office scattered, looking for cover. The viewing screen became a blinding white flash, and the men were gone, vaporized. All that remained was half of the burning rebel command vehicle.

"What the fuck just happened?"

Terry straightened his tie. "I ordered an air strike to be ready in case those savages started shooting. I had a feeling things may go south."

"I should throw you off the Point Fermin cliffs."

"Escalada," Terry begged, "let me explain."

Alamán perched on the edge of his desk waiting for any sudden movement or hint at flight.

"I saw an opportunity, and I overreached, your Honor. I take full responsibility."

"Do you, Terry?"

"Yes sir, full responsibility. It will never happen again."

"Tell me Terry, what precisely were you trying to accomplish?"

"Chaos."

"Obviously. To what end, Terrence?"

"Destabilization. We've barely explored the possibilities of federal disaster funding, not to mention the foreign aid channels I've opened. At present we stand to increase our federal funding by eleven percent in the new fiscal budget. I firmly believe that an unstable, yet contained, state of upheaval will push us further still into the twenties or thirties."

"You'd light the Westside aflame for twenty-percent?"

"For five percent." Terry replied, unashamed.

Alamán chuckled. "Let's have a drink."

"Thank you, sir, but I am quite alright."

"That's an order Terrence." Alamán dropped a perfect globe of ice into both glasses.

"As you wish."

"How long have you had this project in the works?" The Mayor watched like a tired old lion as Terry sipped his drink.

"Not long. We created the Local Militia and made sure they integrated into the rebel leadership. After that, it came together rather simply."

"You started a war."

"Well, that was the idea wasn't it? It gives the governor and D.C. a way to throw money at the problem but stay politically distant. It also serves as a nice warning to anyone refusing to play nice."

"False Flag operations are so passé Terrence, so Twentieth Century."

"Your honor, with all due respect, I prefer to be called Terry..." Terry clutched his throat and his eyes widened.

Alamán laughed a little as he eyed the half-empty crystal tumbler in Terry's hand. "You were right, you should have skipped that drink. If Los Angeles can't control its own backyard, we'll never have an argument for secession. This isn't about some hippies that think shopping at Trader Joe's makes them Che Guevara. This is about leaving the Union behind and running the show. You okay, Terry? You look...ill..."

The Secretary of Treasury stumbled; the poison restricted his breathing. The side-table lamp leapt into the air, papers were made into a snowstorm, and Terry crumpled to the ground looking up at Alamán with pleading eyes, "Please...please *choke* I was just following orders..."

Alamán placed his boot on Terry's forehead, "Come now Terrence, you may have been following orders, but they were not *my* orders. I won't waste my time asking who you are working for, I give no quarter to traitors."

Alamán dialed a number on his receiver. "We have a slight setback; we need to plan our way forward in light of today's events in Culver City." Alamán looked down from his phone call and made the sign of the cross in front of the gurgling Secretary of the Treasury. He lifted his foot and buried it deep into Terry's chest, crushing his rib cage and delivering a muffled deathblow.

Alamán continued his conversation, "Forgive me, I had an internal issue to deal with. Contact our partners[11] and arrange for a conference call tomorrow. I want a plan in place to move forward within forty-eight hours, and I want the names of every fucker behind this Culver City bullshit."

---

11 The Alliance of Caribbean, Central, and South America Democracies (ACCSAD) was established following the inglorious departure of the 45th US President. ICE implemented 45's executive order calling for law enforcement to engage in operation Great Renewal. With unspoken blessing from the White House, ICE rampaged through legal and illegal immigrant communities alike.

Refugee crises sprung to life all over the state of Chihuahua, exposing ICE's tactic of driving massive 18-wheelers crammed with deportees to the El Paso-Juárez border and kicking them out, at gunpoint. Cuba suffered a similar fate as ICE operatives and anti-Castro elements in south Florida set scores of immigrants afloat in the Caribbean on massive, precarious flotillas. Miami-Dade elementary school students signed the side of the rafts with heartfelt taunts like, "Here's a Commie for your Mommy!"

Mexico, Cuba, Haiti, and Venezuela formed ACCSAD to contain the crisis. The new regional power soon tempted Nicaragua, the Dominican Republic, Panama, Jamaica, Guatemala, El Salvador, Costa Rica, Ecuador, Peru, Bolivia, Paraguay, and Brazil to join the Alliance. Chile, Uruguay, Argentina, and Colombia notably abstained.

Muses

‡

IV

Victor took a seat on a long booth in J.J. Smythe's next to a small octagonal table. The booth ran the length of the pub on the north side and the tall bar occupied half its length, centered against the south wall. Pint coasters were arranged in a pentagon, or gram, on the wood surface. The building had been the birthplace of Thomas Moore, whom Victor admitted he knew nothing about.

8/20/10

I woke up with a thick head, my first taste of hangover in Dublin. J.J. Smythe's and Sheehan's are my homes away from home. I spend most of my time in one or the other. By week's end both pubs began pouring a pint as soon as they saw me coming up the street.

As I strolled south on Aungier large wet drops began falling from the sky and striking the ancient street with tiny shattering hammers. I wandered dense south Dublin for several hours before returning to the neighborhood. McDaid's was just around the corner from Sheehan's. Their floors creaked loudly, and the bar room was dark, save for elongated rectangles of light pouring in through stained glass windows high above the front door. The high ceiling made the room feel immense and reverent. The almost black wood of the bar and wall behind absorbed light and the bartender seemed to float as he pulled levers and dispensed potions.

While the sun began to dip below the buildings I turned onto Chatham as the still spattering rain shined brightly in the sunset's fiery wake.

Freedom poses a curious paradox. On the one hand, I require and violently defend my ability to act autonomously. However, on the other, I long for the sense of purpose that comes with companionship.

Although I command all authority over my actions, it would be nice to be joining someone for pints tonight, instead of awkwardly mixing with the drunken hordes and sitting in silence.

—Never pleased: me.

Victor booked his flight for London: a few days in another town, another country for that matter, seemed just the thing to help Victor reset.

‡

Victor took Fredrick Street north from Parnell Square. Rain began falling. A light rain, but the clouds appeared to be foretelling a raucous afternoon storm. The buildings started to look more closely packed together. Indeed, the intersection at Lower Dorset reminded him of Brooklyn neighborhoods he had been shuttled through. Victor neglected to turn left onto Bolton and began a long trek away from Dublin.

8/21/10
1pm

I am in safe harbor for now. Still lost, make no mistake, but I found a cigarette machine and I have a pint of stout. I made a wrong turn and as far as I can tell I am on the northeast outskirts of town. I kept walking...and walking...and walking, until the cramped store fronts melted into an ancient, stone wall. Behind the wall stretched an emerald blanket as far as the eye could see in all directions. Across the street, tightly neighbored town homes with narrow front lawns rested behind gates. The mossy wall was periodically sprinkled with sunrays, as the clouds broke overhead.

The wall came to an end near another waterway in a provincial looking square. I had gone too far. I headed back down what was now Lower Drumcondra. Before returning to the nicely tended yards lining the street ahead, my attention was drawn to a long sign: Kennedy's.

An old man sat at the bar having a one-sided conversation with the bartender. They both looked up when I entered and then went back to what they were doing. The bartender walked down the bar and asked me what I drink.

The thrill of discovery seems to be morphing into a love of familiarity. I am seeking acceptance and inclusion from the city; haunting visited places and reveling in recognition. Dublin's vast, sprawling maze of streets curve in on me at times, and I can no longer bear the silence.

I am certainly off the path I have beaten since landing in Dublin. There is a definitive feel of permanence, of home, beyond Parnell Square. Near Trinity, young transient faces dominate the landscape, but in the slow, sleepy side of Dublin, school children play in grey dilapidated playgrounds crowned with names like Sacrament and testifying to someone named Mary's virginity. This Mary character doth protest too much.

I met one of my roommates this morning, Andrew from Boston. It was interesting to speak of the US with an American. The ingrained feelings of recognition and solidarity surface immediately, Stockholm syndrome, I surmise. Yet, after the initial thrill of commonality, the honest truth is that even though they wave the same flag, Boston and Los Angeles may as well be on different continents.

And what to say?

I'm not a patriot, and I am not proud of anything the United States has accomplished. If you believe in a god, I'd rather not discuss it. Without those anchors, I remain invisible to most Americans.

845pm

My return to town was guided by the Dublin Spire, looming 121.2 meters above the city center. The stainless-steel implement of divine penetration shone gold and tangerine in the setting sun. I knew I could follow its siren song to the center of gaudy commerce and O'Connell Street.

I cut across Smithfield via Mary's Lane, through back road wholesale stores, industrial textile buildings, swap meet style collective markets and sporting stores—in the midst of cut-rate food, medicine, and housing, one still had an opportunity to buy a 35€ Robbie Keane jersey.

The sunset shined on the brick walkways and reflected from the glittering store and mall fronts approaching O'Connell. People shuffled in all directions. A puppet clown beat on a tiny baby grand piano, costar to a marionette. Human statues came to life, delighting children with their silver-painted vacancy. Local music, pub cries, and the ravings of religious zealots mingled on the Atlantic breeze.

930pm

I was devastated to find that my room had been given to someone else. There was a mix up at the front desk, and I had paid in cash so there was no record with my name on it. I suddenly felt the full weight of being 5,157 miles from any sofas I could crash on.

I ended up at the Jacob's Inn Hostel, watching the night shift count their drawers. The Avalon House manager was kind enough to call over on my behalf to see if they had a room.

Outside, a group of Irish taxi-drivers huddled, waiting for tourists to pour out of the Jacob's Inn Hostel for a night on the town. I've become very comfortable at Avalon House, very comfortable in my little neighborhood.[12] My anxiety isn't based on the situation, but on resistance to change. Feelings of distance, the seven-mile Diaspora earlier in the day, and temporary homelessness, got the best of me.

I hope they have a room.

1030pm

Though I longed to end this chaotic day at J.J. Smythe's, walking over to the other side of the Liffey would take close to a half-hour out of my drinking time. The seven or eight men sitting in the corner bar were watching a futbal match, so I took a chance.

1130pm

My demeanor has changed, my spirits have been raised, and I am looking up at one of the most beautiful moons I have ever seen. The air is wet on the Irish port's edge.

8/22/10

The disruption of last night threw my haphazard universe-away-from-home into a woodchipper.

The morning air was cool and crisp; I lit a cigarette and looked out over a new part of Dublin. The stark backyards below teetered between junkyard-storage and personal effects of one or more families sharing a

12 Iconography p. 20, Victor's Dublin

common area. The elevated tracks poured north and south and even on the top floor of Jacob's Inn the Liffey was out of view. That fuck awful spire though...it stared imperiously into the rising sun as an immense outstretched middle finger from the people of earth. I snapped a photo of myself. My eyes were tired but determined, a smoke-clouded visage framed by a yawning Sunday morning above east Dublin.

I had to secure a room at Avalon, the sooner the better.

Talbot Street was bathed in soft blue shadow. The sun was not yet high enough to crest the taller buildings and the lane of walking path to O'Connell Street was bathed in the same catatonic haze—whose borders mussed the focus just so to obscure Dublin with expressionism.

Deserted O'Connell was immense, though the bridge was a quarter mile south it seemed to loom in a mythic distance, departed and separate from the lazy, abandoned commerce center. I shared the street with morning birds and my thoughts.

The Liffey was silent. The endless pedestrian bridges were lit slowly in turn by the coming daylight. Grafton Street was devoid of life; a rarity I had come to find. I walked south on the famed brick road and began to hear a low, sweet violin. The vibration of the sad minors and a deepening reprise stopped me in my tracks. The man looked up, smiling, and dipped his baldhead to continue. He was a simple man; A man who had discovered that his passion could contribute to his welfare.

I've been searching for that for far too long. I'm tired of the quest, though I know the quest will never tire of me. Am I, or am I not consumed by my convictions? I emptied my pockets into the violinist's case—cash, change, and cigarettes—and kept walking to Chatham. As I passed my cherished pubs, all with locks and steady shutters drawn, I walked away from fear and in turn walked away from the past.

§

XXXIII

Summer ~ 1990

On through Reagan and Bush the Elder, Erlyst pursued Kyrios. She thwarted his efforts at every turn, showing up at parties she had not been invited to, making certain that Kyrios' *date* looked her in the eye before disappearing into the night with her husband.

For a time, when she acted out Kyrios was amused. When she became a nuisance, he froze her accounts, and disengaged utilities to the home for the week; torments rained down, ranging from petty to sadistic. Kyrios often changed the locks to the doors and dismissed the staff without warning.

Erlyst became ill, disoriented, and began to gain weight. She couldn't banish the thought that her dear husband had infected her with some malady from one of his whores. She had her assistant make an appointment with Dr. Catchem for the following afternoon.

"Mrs. Atropos," Dr. Catchem smiled broadly.

"What is it doctor? I feel like I'm going to die."

"Well, it's good news..."

"It's not cancer right, I hope it's not..."

"Cancer? No, no, I wouldn't refer to that as *good news*. No, rather, I would say you should *expect*, or be *expecting...*"

"You don't know what's wrong? Fuck, fuck, fuck, you're supposed to be the fucking best..."

"Relax, Mrs. Atropos," the Doctor addressed her abruptly. "You have a little one growing inside you."

"A little one *what*? Tumor? Stroke?"

"A baby, Erlyst. You're going to be a mother." The doctor forced a smile.

It was something about the way he said it—*growing inside you*—the way he had described an alien form writhing in her womb, pressing against her body from the inside. She wanted to claw it out with a spoon.

"Thank you, doctor."

"Mrs. Atropos, don't you want to..."

"No." She rushed to the door. "I know what happens next."

Lawrence E. Robertson answered the telephone wearing a pink dog collar and a pair of yellow rubber shorts. "This had beeeter be gooed..."

"Lawrence, it's Erlyst. Why do you sound Swedish?"

Lawrence cupped his hand around the phone receiver. "Erlyst, yes, I'm so glad to hear from..."

"Enough Lawrence, I need to speak to Kyrios. Now."

Lawrence swiveled his head. Kyrios was beneath two Haitian teenagers, one of whom had already removed his board shorts for a little spare change.

"Erlyst, there's absolutely no way, he's behind closed doors with clients."

"Look, put him on the phone, I promise to pretend I don't hear moaning in the background. Otherwise, I'll be making a very serious and life-altering decision for both of us."

Lawrence muted the phone.

"It's Erlyst. She's insisting..."

"Speaker phone." Kyrios flung his wrist at Lawrence and let it fall on taut, impressionable flesh.

Lawrence shouted, "Erlyst? Can you hear me?"

"Yes, idiot. Kyrios. I need to tell you something."

"I'm here Erlyst."

"Are you alone?"

"Don't waste my time."

"It finally happened you corrupt bastard. You polluted my body with your demon-seed."

Kyrios moaned and growled, *Fuck* as the second teenager removed her bikini.

"That's what I said, *fuck*. Look, I don't feel like either of us have time for a baby..."

"Is it a boy?"

"It's too early to tell."

"You have all the time in the world, Erlyst."

"What?"

"My son will be treated as a burgeoning god. That is what you will dedicate your precious time to, Erlyst. Are we clear?"

"No, you piece of trash, I'm not having your kid, and I'm definitely not raising the little bastard...Kyrios? Lawrence?"

The call was dropped. Erlyst placed the silent phone into her lap. She smoothed her dress down over her stomach. "Between you and me, I hope you're a girl..."

§

At eighteen weeks...

"Back again doc, this is the boy or girl visit, right?"

"Yes, it certainly is. I assume that means you would like to know?"

"Yes," Erlyst's face grew dark, "it is very important to my husband."

"Then let's see, I'll get the wand."

Erlyst waited, round-bellied, youthful in pregnancy, dreading the doctor's declaration.

"Hm, okay? Yes. Hm. Okay." The doctor manipulated the wand and clicked on the computer screen. Erlyst couldn't make heads or tails of the blurry mess on the screen. She laid back and tried to practice her speech to Kyrios about his new pride and heir, but the doctor's muttering interrupted her thoughts.

Dr. Catchem played with a few images before turning to Erlyst.

"Mrs. Atropos," the doctor pulled up the first image and expanded it dramatically, "it looks like you will be having a lovely baby girl."

"No. Are you sure doctor?"

Erlyst's terror surprised him. "Here are a few more views, but yes, I feel confident that this is a darling baby girl, congratulations." The doctor tried to salvage the sentiment.

"What am I going to do?"

"Mrs. Atropos, is there anything you'd like to talk about..."

§

"No. I'm very pleased, I'm going to name her Thalia and wish her joy."

Erlyst wasted no time running from the office and onto the street. She bent at the waist, dry heaving into oncoming traffic.

Weeks after her appointment, Erlyst finally dialed.

"Lawrence?"

"Erlyst. Hello...do you want me to get..."

"No. It's a girl. Turns out he should have let me handle it."

"Oh, Erlyst."

"Fuck you, Larry. Give him the message."

"As you wish. Erlyst, if you ever want to talk..."

"You have to be joking Larry." Erlyst disconnected the call.

Lawrence E. Robertson kicked his stubby feet against the ground. He was incapable of empathy, but somewhere in his blank conscience, he had room to be obsessed. The young bride was never far from his mind. His intentions were never wholesome, and had Erlyst known, there would be no reprieve from the heads that rolled.

That weekend, Erlyst lay by a large pool hidden on the rooftop of a Park Avenue hotel. With a rousing treatise on sexism open on her chest, she breathed in the mid-summer air and tried to feel intoxicated by its warmth. Nothing took the sensitivity of sobriety away. With this child inside of her, it would be reckless to chance it—a child forever marred by an alcoholic mother would not do; would be both bane and curse. After all, she could not count on help from...

Kyrios caught her eye. As Erlyst gathered her things Kyrios walked onto the pool deck and loomed above her. "The child no longer interests me Erlyst, but I cannot allow you to destroy it."

"You're going to bring a child into this world to avoid a scandal?"

"Don't get up, I'm not staying."

"That's not surprising. Where to now, sir?"

"It would bore you to death my sweet. Look," Kyrios softened his tone, "I can't wait to meet Thalia." Kyrios smiled at Erlyst and stroked her cheek. "You'll make a wonderful life for our child."

With that, Kyrios evaporated back into the building and was gone. Erlyst was confused, but grateful for a gesture of kindness. If only she could keep her cheeks from reddening and her heart from fluttering when Kyrios was kind to her.

Thalia was born on December fifth. Kyrios called into the delivery room from the deck of a newly christened oil freighter now under his purview and command. "Well done, Erlyst. All the fingers and toes are present?"

"Yes, oh Kyrios, she's beautiful, I wish you could..."

"Indeed, same here, look, I have to..."

Erlyst hung up.

Thalia, new to the world, but wise to the turmoil ahead, began to cry softly.

"Oh yes, my little love, it's you and mommy. Until the end. Bitter though it will surely be."

Kyrios claimed to admire Erlyst and Thalia's relationship, *jealous* he would say, as if his wife had somehow abandoned him for the love of the child. His manipulation was maddening, but each time he held Thalia in his arms and swung her proudly around, Erlyst forgave him for pieces of the past. Had he been capable of staying consistent, she'd have forgiven him for all things.

§

Winter ~ 1997

Kyrios burst through the door screaming at no one.

"Kyrios? What...is that blood?"

"Stay away from me Erlyst. I'm giving you fair warning."

"Do you need a doctor?"

Kyrios walked briskly down the hall and slammed the bedroom door. Erlyst remained in the library and made a neat bed of the love seat across from Kyrios' perpetually empty desk.

Erlyst felt shaken, unable to call sleep. When she heard the shower sputter to life, Erlyst walked down the long hall to the master suite. The bloody clothing was nowhere in sight. She entered the steamy bathroom and between curtains of warm, condensed rain, Erlyst saw her husband scrubbing his hands. His back was a collection of deep and superficial cuts, some desperate and long from shoulder to waist. Erlyst removed her clothing and opened the glass shower door.

"Erlyst?"

"Of course. Who else?"

Kyrios turned rapidly and grabbed Erlyst by the waist. "What are you doing here Erlyst? I told you to leave me alone."

"I was just worried..." His chest was cut far worse than his back, stripes, like claw marks, lined his stomach.

Kyrios pressed several fingers between her thighs while she gasped. "I know why you're here."

Erlyst's legs clenched as he tried to bury those same fingers in her womb.

"Kyrios, I..." she moaned before she could finish. Her head fell to his shoulder. She pulled him closer and deeper. "Your back, what happened?

"Really Erlyst? Now?"

"Just tell me," Erlyst panted.

"I broke someone's neck tonight." Kyrios pressed her back against the shower wall and gripped her neck. "He looked at me strangely on the way into a bodega on Blah Blah Street. I wasn't angry really, more, indignant." Kyrios weighed his words. "I did wonder what it would feel like to teach him a long, painful lesson."

Erlyst's eyes were pinned open. Her breaths were short with fear.

"I followed him for hours. Most of the day. I threw a rock at his head at one point and quickly hid. Like a child, Erlyst. I'm sure he suffered a concussion then; it was quite a large rock. As he staggered, I emerged from the trees. He cried out and I smashed my fist into his mouth. I caved his teeth in. It was..." Kyrios could not finish.

Erlyst struggled and Kyrios tightened his grip. "He fought back, Erlyst. Quite a bit more than I expected, as you observed. I snapped his neck because it became boring, beating him unconscious and then waking him over and over. By the end, the fight had simply left him, and I was no longer amused."

Kyrios smiled while Erlyst struggled to remove his fingers from her body and his hand from her neck.

"Kyrios let me go please, I can't breathe..."

"It was strangely compelling, but I felt none of the excitement I expected to."

"Kyrios, please..."

Kyrios growled through the steam. "I know what you're thinking. My good little southern belle. There are no positive outcomes when a woman accuses me of a crime. They will strike you down as mad. Do you understand?"

"I do."

"Every human on this planet owes, or will owe me, their lives. You will not be missed Erlyst, and you will never be mourned."

He released her and left the shower.

Erlyst wept.

When Kyrios began to snore, Erlyst rushed into Thalia's room. "Darling, wake up," she whispered until the young girl opened her eyes.

"Mommy?"

"Come on sweety, put your shoes on, and this jacket. We have to leave right away."

"But why mommy?"

"Thalia," Erlyst grabbed her arm. "Do as I say, now."

Thalia recoiled and finished putting her shoes on.

"I'm sorry, precious. Daddy's security guards will be back soon. Please hurry."

The two raced into the night and hailed a passing cab. Kyrios had a car stored in Paulus Hook. If Erlyst could get to it, they could head south and figure everything out with Virginia in their rearview mirror. The parking garage was silent; Erlyst walked rapidly and quietly with young Thalia in tow.

The car started. Erlyst began to relax.

"I don't remember this car mommy."

"You father uses it."

Erlyst sped south on the Turnpike, in hindsight, a bit too fast.

≈

A New Jersey Highway Patrol car flashed its red and blues as 78 gave way to Interstate 95.

"You have to be fucking kidding me."

"Mommy! That word, you said... "

"I know baby, not now."

The officer knocked on the car window. "Good evening Mrs. Atropos."

"Is there something amiss, officer?"

"You were exceeding the speed limit ma'am."

"I apologize officer, it won't happen again."

"I'm glad to hear that. Here's the thing. I also have an order to take you back into the City."

"I beg your pardon."

"Yes ma'am. You're to be returned home immediately. My backup will be here shortly."

"No, no. We can't go back, we're not safe there, officer. Please, you can't send us back. We'll spend the night in a cell if we have to."

"Now ma'am, I know life can be hard sometimes but at the end of the day, you have it pretty good, don't you?"

"Fuck you, you don't know anything about my life. He hurt someone tonight. He came home covered in blood and cuts."

"He said he hurt someone?"

"He said he *killed* someone. For fun."

"Well, that seems a little far-fetched Mrs. Atropos. What would a guy like your husband be doing killing people? He's got too much to lose. Take it from someone who knows, your husband is *not* a killer." The smug flatfoot smiled.

Kyrios was not waiting at the door as she had expected him to be. He slept soundly as Thalia and Erlyst walked slowly back to their respective beds, bound to one another in their prison.

≈

LXIV

Autumn ~ 2025

Mayor Alamán, in conspiracy with his Chief of Police and Garcetti VI reached out to the leadership of New York, Houston, and Atlanta:

CLASSIFIED/PRIVATE: EYES ONLY
Our once great cities have decayed. No longer are we leaders of industry and beacons of social and financial success. We are all victims of our Federal Government's corruption and incompetence.

We received an early taste of Federal neglect long ago during Hurricane Katrina. The Federal government allowed one of the Nation's proudest and oldest cities to drown. Most recently, their criminal neglect destroyed of our fair city, Los Angeles. Disasters and pandemics have victimized large swaths of American society and our government has responded with false promises wrapped in rhetoric from the Executive, Judicial, and Legislative branches.

In our proud history there have been two Americas: One an honorable companionship of like-minded states, and one a tyrannical Federal entity that mimics the Kingdom our brave forefathers overthrew.

The Federal government has left the American people to suffer while it advances its fruitless foreign wars and occupations. It has abandoned the will of the People to the will of foreign and domestic corporations, and in doing so has invalidated its jurisdiction over the People. It is time to sever the head of the Imperial Snake and revitalize our People's unique and exceptional destiny.

I ask you, esteemed leaders, to join with me in denouncing this fractured system. If the American people are to be free, truly free, we must stand in unison and renounce the abomination that American Federal government has become.

≈

Yours in peace and prosperity,

Escalada Alamán III
Mayor
City of Los Angeles

Salvadore Garcetti VI
Council Chair
Hollywood City Council

Lance Milthau
Acting-Chair
Culver City Council

Sheldon Masters
County Supervisor
Los Angeles Third District

Nancy Khahn
County Supervisor
Los Angeles Fourth District

Jaime Pinkerton
Chief of Police
City of Los Angeles

Anthony Bochinni
Chief of Intelligence
City of Los Angeles

"Look Escalada, you may or may not know this, but Texas has the right to legally, and peacefully, cede from the Union at will. Hell, we can even break into five states if we like." Honorable Mayor of Houston, Leopold Riordan, countered.

"You're giving me a fucking Social Studies lesson?"

"No, no, no, compadre. I am simply pointing out that the citizens of Houston are not specifically enriched by that part of the plan...hello...hello?"

Riordan hung up his antique desk phone. His Chief of Staff lingered in shadow near a permanently closed window.

"That was the last time he'll call." The young Chief of Staff was concerned.

"I know. We need to extend a proposal for a ceasefire with New York and Atlanta, if this thing is going to work, they are going to need our ports, resources, and manpower."

Afternoon light glinted off the Chief of Staff's round, thin-framed glasses, "Besides, Alamán doesn't want Texas working with its southern neighbor against his interests."

"Over my dead body." Riordan sneered.

The Chief of Staff pleaded. "Sir, I think..."

"There will be no cooperation with Mexico. We own Mexico and we always will. They're no better than apes down there."

"Sir," the Chief of Staff protested wearily.

"This is the part where you leave." Riordan motioned to the door. His Chief of Staff nodded and exited the office.

Riordan's ignorance prevented him from contingency thinking across racial divides. The Chief of Staff knew that no alliances were certain. Alamán needed Houston's ports in case New York and Atlanta did not play ball. With Houston's and Los Angeles' port infrastructure Alamán could surround Central America. If he did, he would stand a good chance of pulling the diseased US gov't to its knees.

The Chief of Staff walked out of the mayor's office, down a long corridor of waist-high cubicle walls. His expensive size $10^{1/2}$ shoes tapped a disconnected march and his employees stood, looking concerned. He waved, hoping to reassure them.

The Chief of Staff returned to his modest apartment. The sensor on his front door read the card in his pocket and released its locks. The Chief of Staff dismantled his laptop and destroyed his papers. When he was comfortable that all potential contraband had been eliminated, he placed his clothing into a small suitcase. The Chief of Staff disappeared into Scholes International Airport, flew away from the early morning sun, and never looked back.

"There's someone here to see you." Justine poked her head into Alamán's office.

Alamán made slow, stabbing motions on his desk.

Justine tapped her foot impatiently. "I am *certain* you want to speak to this man; shall I show him in?"

Alamán looked at Anthony Bochinni, his Chief of Intelligence, and Bochinni nodded subtly. "Send him in Justine." Alamán dismissed her.

A slight gentleman in a simple grey suit and round, thin-framed glasses walked into the room. His grey eyes siphoned the mid-evening light from the western windows. He held his shoulders slightly forward, as if playing the victim, but the young man's presence filled the vacuous and palatial office.

"Good afternoon gentlemen, I am Mayor Riordan's *former* Chief of Staff. Though Mayor Riordan is of no use to you, I know how to cut Texas out by bringing Louisiana in...for now."

§
XXXV

Spring ~ 1998

The second course at Crème du Monde was impeccable, and though she had heavy thoughts, Erlyst could not help but smile.

Kyrios was distracted, elsewhere. That was nothing new.

“Kyrios?”

“Yes?” He scanned the room, seeming to sample each person in turn.

“I’ve been sick as hell lately.”

“I’m sorry to hear that,” Kyrios huffed.

“I’m sure,” Erlyst muttered quietly. “It seems every morning something has me over the toilet for about a half hour. Weird, right?”

“Bizarre, Erlyst. Truly.”

He was consumed by every passing thing.

“Since you are on some distant planet, I’ll just slide you a note. Like grade school.”

“Erlyst, really. Don’t mock me...”

“Some things are better read than said.”

“That rhymed. Have you practiced this Erlyst?”

“Fuck you.”

Erlyst flipped a thick piece of ivory card onto the table in front of Kyrios and made her way across the immense dining room of Crème du Monde. When she reached the back hallway, she turned to see Kyrios’ reaction. His attention was focused on a young waitress. Not their waitress; their waitress was not quite as lovely, not quite as young, and fresh. Erlyst’s mouth twisted bitterly. The young woman walked off with her tray and he watched her young backside sway all the way into the kitchen.

He turned and picked up the card Erlyst had left. It was blank. *She's an idiot* he thought before flipping it over.

I’m pregnant again, asshole.

Kyrios looked across the crowded dining room and stopped on Erlyst as she turned to enter the powder room.

While Erlyst fussed with her hair and straightened her gown in the long, sensuous mirrors along the lounge's wall, Kyrios rushed her. Before she could react to the menacing blur, her feet had left the tile floor and her back had slammed against the mirrored wall. Erlyst struggled; Kyrios stood above her, pulling her face closer, straining the neckline of her expensive gown. He raised his fist in the air and paused; he wanted to enjoy her terror.

A shrill scream emitted from the doorway of the ladies' lounge. An unwelcome witness.

Kyrios lowered his fist and whispered to Erlyst, "There will be no more children. You should not have told me Erlyst. Take care of it, or I will."

He left his wife sobbing on the floor of the bathroom and walked out of the restaurant.

When Erlyst repeatedly called her husband from the emergency room he unplugged the phone. The hospital staff pitied Erlyst. She accepted their offer and spent the night in an empty room in the trauma ward. In the early morning, Erlyst returned to their mirror-lined suite and silently showered, awash in reflections of her tired, tear-stained eyes. She crawled into bed. Kyrios never moved.

Erlyst refused to terminate the pregnancy, and though he was often somewhere else, Kyrios began to appear suddenly. His visits were slow burning conversations over food, grown cold from neglect. Thalia, still enchanted by ignorance, would excitedly beg her father to tell her of his adventures. Erlyst would wait silently until Kyrios addressed her—even then, she considered her words carefully.

As reward for her exemplary etiquette, Kyrios would announce his intention to spend the night with his *darling wife*. His affections were an obvious disguise. At times, he insisted on being intimate, athletically, as if he were providing a great husbandly favor to his engorged wife.

She woke one night to Kyrios' shadow, risen from bed, and calling her name softly. As her eyes creased and focused, he brought his closed fists down on her chest, stealing her breath.

§

Erlyst tried to scream and kicked as Kyrios mounted her and pinned one of her arms beneath his knee. Her free hand swung wildly and connected with her snarling husband's nose. He leapt backward, bleeding, and Erlyst bolted for the door. His blind swipe just missed her braided hair as it swung behind her. Erlyst tripped and fell, wiping crimson streaks across the mirrored halls, staining them in blood.

Thalia, still a mere child, walked out of her room and into the hallway.

"What's wrong mommy, why are you crying?" Thalia rushed to help her mother.

"Nothing's wrong baby, nothing." Erlyst tried to soothe her daughter's fears through her own tears. "Go back to your room honey."

Kyrios entered the hallway, "I'm not done with you..." he paused, "Thalia. Darling, go back to bed."

"No daddy." Thalia threw her arms around Erlyst and buried her face in her shoulder.

Erlyst wrapped her arms around Thalia and kissed her neck. Kyrios retreated.

It was late the next morning when Erlyst woke, curled around her daughter. She rose and stretched. The house was still; she entered the hallway cautiously and looked into the foyer. Kyrios was sitting cross-legged at a table smoking a cigarette. She approached him in a trance. When she took a seat next to Kyrios her body tensed.

"Erlyst, our time has passed. What I once felt for you is no more. You are the mother of my only child; nothing can change that. Keep this *other* child if you must but know that I will not recognize it as my blood."

"It?"

"I tire of trying to change your mind, and I tire of the façade. It is over between us, but I will continue care for you and the child."

The blood still clung to Erlyst's face and neck. "You are pathetic."

"And you are incapable of carrying on a rational conversation, it has always been so." Kyrios sighed heavily and returned his attention to the cigarette burning in his left hand.

Erlyst knew that divorce would ultimately end in disaster. Kyrios needed a matriarch to please his family. He would be excused liberal use of painted women, but he could never be excused for demolishing the sacred matrimonial contract. To do so was to open oneself up to questions of core-integrity. Kyrios could be trusted to remain bound to his contracts and that was precisely why he was in the position of power he enjoyed.

Kyrios did not leave. He remained, day and night.

In her eighteenth week he rushed her in their kitchen. If she would not sleep, he protested; he would put her to sleep. Dr. Catchem threatened to alert the authorities and Erlyst reminded him that him that no one gained a thing from threatening Mr. Atropos.

In her twenty-third week Erlyst succumbed to a sudden, crippling pain—as if every injury she endured had suddenly ruptured.

"Help me!" Erlyst shrieked.

Erlyst's assistant flung open the doors.

"Call a fucking ambulance," Erlyst clutched her belly, "now!"

Erlyst's assistant summoned EMTs and tried to soothe Erlyst as she rocked violently and struck the bed. Erlyst began to lose consciousness and her assistant slapped her face.

"Erlyst, stay with me."

"What the fuck is wrong with you?"

"Mr. Atropos ordered that you be awake at all times, to experience every part of childbirth. He was very specific... "

"If you touch me again..." Erlyst curled into a ball to weather a tsunami of pain.

A pair of twenty-year old boys in a painful rush to field their next travesty burst through the door, sidled up to Erlyst, and palpated her abdomen. Little Boy A smirked at Little Boy B and slipped between Erlyst's legs. Little Boy B caught Erlyst's fist before she broke A's nose.

Erlyst struggled mightily.

"I'm sorry Mrs. Atropos, you are having this baby right now." Smiling, plastic empathy, practiced concern, and authority.

"It's too soon, I can't, not yet... "

"I know, nonetheless, the baby is coming. Please help us out by giving a push. Everything you learned in class is perfect for right now."

Little Boy B remained on the sidelines cheering Little Boy A on and condescending to Erlyst as she bucked and screamed in agony.

Clio Atropos was stillborn to this pair of smiling impersonations, and before the umbilical cord was severed, Little Boy B had packed their gear and was tugging on Little Boy A to remove himself from between Erlyst's thighs. Clio's tiny heart sat empty in her chest. Her eyebrows pursed in question, frozen in confusion. Erlyst begged them to let her hold Clio but the house staff refused, on Mr. Atropos' orders.

Several days later Kyrios entered Erlyst's room. "How are you feeling?"

Erlyst was silent.

"One less bastard child in this city," Kyrios smiled. "You did the world a favor."

Erlyst could not respond. Tears slowly dropped from her eyes as Kyrios left the room. He could hear her crying and turned to watch her pain before leaving. They never spoke again.

≈

LXVII

With New Orleans in-tow, Alamán no longer needed Atlanta and he had no desire to impress the Floridians. In the past half-century, the northern parts of the state had become extremely dangerous to all outsiders—rumored to be an insidious ploy to put an armed human barrier between the rich Southerners and the rest of the Union. The southern climes became a fortified refuge to the out-of-touch billionaire political sect. As Utah had been through much of its history, Florida became an autonomous entity under a pseudo-religious banner that superseded the Stars and Stripes.

"Your hon-oooor?" Justine's voice sang over the tiny speaker embedded in Alamán's pen.

"Yes Justine?"

"Rein Sarbays is here to see you."

"Send him in."

Alamán straightened his papers and occupied his enormous desk like a many-eyed predator waiting in his web.

Rein popped his head into the office, "Hey! Olly-MUUU-AHN!" He walked in swiftly and extended his hand to shake Alamán's. Rein's *hair* was an obvious toupee. The dark, luxurious waves barely concealed the remnants of his once proud mane. Sarbays' internal organs were rotten with drink and held together by sheer refusal to expire.

Los Angeles was rife with people who were professionally fraudulent and whose paycheck depended on their façade. Sarbays was part of a sub-caste of entertainment: the promoter. Ancient and decrepit bottom-feeder though he was, Rein had deep connections all over the country.

"Are you drunk?" Alamán asked.

"Yes, I am. Speaking of which," Rein pointed over his shoulder to Alamán's crystal canter.

"Oh yes, please do."

Rein rose and poured a drink.

"How's the young girl you keep locked up in that studio?"

"Oh, you know, she's a pain in my ass but I love her."

"Wasn't she supposed to be deported after the rehab thing?"

"No." Rein slurped the ice at the bottom of his glass.

There was an awkward silence. Alamán knew that to be false.

"I need an *escort* in New York two weeks from now."

"Male or female?"

"Female. However, this is more than coital, I need a complete escort with access."

"Understood, I'll send you the details this afternoon." Rein pointed to the canter, "May I?"

"Of course." Alamán sighed.

Rein rose, poured a belt, slugged it back, poured another, and waved as he walked out of Alamán's office dripping alcohol in his wake. He stopped a moment to whisper something scandalous in French to Justine and began to unbutton his trousers. She slapped him across the face. Rein smiled, finished his drink, and set the glass of ice upside down on Justine's desk. “Maybe next time sweet-tits, maybe next time.” He continued smiling adolescently and strolled casually to the elevator.

“Justine, have Jaime come see me.” Alamán howled into the lobby.

“I'll try him...”

“Now, Justine.”

Chief of Police Jaime Pinkerton poked his head into Alamán’s office, “Your honor.”

“Come in Jaime. Have a seat old friend.” Alamán pointed to the plush pair of leather chairs near the windows. The *Kill Zone* Pinkerton used to call it. He had made certain that the windows were fitted with bulletproof glass, and always insisted that the thick, lead lined curtains, be drawn.

Watching Alamán murder Mr. Hernández in cold blood all those years ago had *affected* young Jaime. In the moments just after the fatal shot was fired, Jaime shrunk in terror, waiting for Ramón to turn the pistol on him. When it didn't happen, Jaime was overcome with a new sensation; he wanted to know what it felt like to pull the trigger. Jaime was too much of a coward to be a killer, but he made it a point to hurt people, pouncing on the weak. His parents had eleven other children to look after and sent Jaime away to a cruel uncle's house in Lawndale. Jaime weathered his uncle's abuse formidably and ran off at age thirteen with five hundred dollars from his Uncle's sock drawer. He was arrested in less than twenty-four hours for shoplifting some potato chips.

Once in custody, Jaime refused to speak.

Late the following day, he had not uttered a word. The police were not able to identify him and no matter what they tried their intensity only steeled him against their techniques. A social worker intervened and placed Jaime with a retired Pittsburgh PD captain. The boy tested Captain Pinkerton's resolve immediately and learned that the Captain never threatened anything he couldn't back up. Each time he had warned the thin boy to not *test him*, Jaime felt the swift fury of an authoritarian—composed always of a need to punish and a need to find absolution through punishment. Jaime was deeply inspired; he wanted to be a police officer.

The Captain was proud when the boy asked to take the Pinkerton name and cast away his heritage. He felt that he had *done some good in this world* when Jaime chose law and order over the violence that seemed to be welling up inside him. The Captain did not see that his son was evolving, and that his cruelty would only escalate under the guise of *duty*.

The Kill Zone curtains had been pulled back, so the Chief of Police unconsciously drew them shut before removing his jacket, smoothing his Stalinist mustache, and relaxing into the only chair with its back to a wall. Alamán smiled, *same old Jaime*. The Mayor had taken care of the other witnesses from the night he shot Hernandez, but Jaime had slipped out of his hands and into the LAPD.

Alamán promoted Pinkerton out of the Sergeant ranks when he needed to send a message to his officer corps, grown fat and happy on pillage and politics. Pinkerton evolved into a mindless sycophant and an opportunist. Amid Culver City's brief secession bid he provided oversight for anti-insurgent policies including detention facilities, interrogation techniques, and executions. He could be trusted to obey orders, but Alamán had lately been informed that *his* orders may be falling into a tertiary category with his Chief of Police.

Alamán handed Pinkerton a drink, "Here you go; how are you these days?"

"I'm well." Jaime retrieved the tumbler of clear liquid. His visage remained marble, disciplined to a fault.

"You're off to the inauguration in Manhattan next week, aren't you?"

"I am. Looking forward to it." Jaime clinked his glass against Alamán's.

"So, you think Leary is the right guy for Police Chief in Manhattan? Didn't he call Dongan a *liberal pussy* during the last election cycle?"

Pinkerton coughed, "Um, yes, it appears they've worked through that. New York needs a stronger hand in the streets; the economy has unleashed a great deal of ill-tempered ruffians. Leary is on-board with our suggestion that the tunnels and bridges to the island be heavily fortified. When Dongan gets re-elected they will be ready to implement those suggestions within the year."

"Excellent, we can't have Manhattan integrating with the rest of the boroughs. Getting the scum off the island for good was no small feat. I want to ask you something, Jaime."

"Of course." Pinkerton sat at attention.

"What is Thomas Dongan meeting with Harriman in Tallahassee about?"

"Last I heard he and Harriman had a plan to privatize the rest of I-95. Only the tobacco states are resisting but they're just holding out for leverage."

If Pinkerton was lying, he didn't show it. He may not know anything, Alamán concluded.

Pinkerton flinched when Anthony Bochinni entered the room. "Don't you knock Bochinni?"

"No."

"Have a seat Anthony. Jaime and I were just discussing Harriman's plans for I-95."

"It's not going to work." Bochinni stoically took a seat opposite Pinkerton. "Dongan won't win."

"I beg to differ," Pinkerton countered.

Bochinni opened a slim leather case and extracted a tablet. The tablet's screen came to life with dozens of photographs for Pinkerton to survey and Bochinni set it on the table. "According to our sources, this man," Bochinni expanded several print sheets of digital photographs, "has other plans."

Pinkerton looked over the photographs; they focused on a man of purposely plain description waiting, sometimes pointing a camera, sometimes a high-powered riflescope. "You're trailing a P.I.?" Pinkerton huffed indignantly.

"Not quite," Bochinni switched screens and opened a satellite image of Jupiter Island, Florida. Bochinni typed a command into the tablet and illuminated the area in pinpoints of deep red. "You'll recognize these locations."

Pinkerton sat back and took another belt from his glass. “You think he's after Dongan?”

“I know he is.” Bochinni sneered.

“Who is he?”

“Retired USMC Lt. Col. Praetorian. He spent fifteen years in special operations as an assassin, running between Iraq, Afghanistan, and Syria after the fall of Egypt. It is rumored that he has over five hundred kills, on and off the books.”

“What does he want with Dongan?”

“Jaime, this man has never missed. He doesn’t just hang around for kicks. He's being paid, handsomely, to collect intelligence. This guy is the closest thing humanity has to the Grim Reaper. I suggest you quietly let Leary know that Dongan is a marked man. At this point, he either needs to dedicate every moment to protecting Dongan, or he needs to start vetting his replacement.”

“Of course, I just can't wrap my head around it. Why Dongan?”

Alamán stood and returned to the canter. “Look Jaime,” Alamán kept his back to his old protégé, “we all need Dongan and Harriman to succeed in every way. Without friendly parties on the coast, the revolt is doomed to fail. I am personally impressing on you that I consider it of the utmost importance. If *any*thing happens to this partnership it will bring about contingency plans neither of us are interested in entertaining.”

The Chief of Police loosened his tie, “I understand your honor. I am confident we can take care of this quietly.”

“While you are in Manhattan,” Bochinni stated flatly.

“Well, it would have to wait until I could get to Florida...”

Alamán cut Pinkerton off, “You're not going to Florida. If Dongan can't handle this problem with the intelligence we are offering, I would seriously reconsider calling him your guy. Take care of it in Manhattan.”

“Of course, your honor, forgive me.”

“You are dismissed Jaime.”

The Chief of Police stood, shook hands with the gentlemen, and closed the large oak door behind him.

≈

On the eve before his departure, an encrypted packet marked *Eyes Only: CoP - J. Pinkerton* flashed across the Chief of Police's tablet. It contained scanned papers devoid of official markings. To Jaime it looked like Alamán was taking his hands off the evidence. Alamán made it clear that Leary was not to be trusted. Pinkerton was to speak directly to Dongan, "...we cannot chance tipping Leary off if he is orchestrating this."

Pinkerton was puzzled by the Praetorian situation. The Lt. Col. could be purchased, but in all of his publicized missions, he was always sent to kill. If he had intended to kill Dongan, Dongan would already be dead. Someone within the movement had to be targeting Dongan; the situation didn't feel *Federal.* Alamán was acting strangely and Pinkerton had never trusted Bochinni, but both men needed Dongan elected.

Pinkerton put the device in its case and tucked it into his neat, organized briefcase. He pulled a cigarette from a miniature humidor case in his breast pocket, an illegal vintage 1990 from Winston-Salem, perfectly preserved and in mint condition. He ran the antique carcinogen beneath his Stalinist mustache.

≈

Rain battered JFK International airport. Leary's men emerged, phantom-like, to escort Pinkerton to a waiting car. Once in Leary's office, he relaxed and unbuttoned his jacket. Leary entered soon thereafter and shook the hand of his *blue-line* partner in crime.

"How the hell are you?" Leary bellowed.

"I'm well," Pinkerton smiled. "The mayor sends his best."

"I'm sure he does, *old snake,*" Leary half-muttered. "How is Escalada these days?"

"Paranoid as usual."

"Do tell..."

"He's reintroducing curfews in some of the satellite districts instead of dedicating manpower to the problem. You know, politician bullshit."

Both men laughed with caution. "Thank you for making the trip out, Jaime. I greatly appreciate it."

"Of course."

"Look," Leary dipped his head, searching the floor for his next words, "...this Dongan-Harriman thing has everybody on edge around here. You're not in New York to warn us of something are you?"

"No. If I were, this meeting would be taking place in Los Angeles."

"Right, of course." Leary forced a smile. "Sorry friend, have to ask, you understand."

"I do. I also know you are a busy man...Chief." Pinkerton smiled, shook Leary's hand and saluted before dismissing himself. "If I don't see you prior, I'll be directly to your left on that stage Saturday night."

Pinkerton retired to his luxury suite and washed the day's filth from his body. He sat in a warm towel looking out the window wall at New York City fifty floors below. A soft knock at the suite door pulled Pinkerton from his thoughts. When he opened the door a young woman with soft, dark eyes in a thin red evening dress intoned shyly, "Is High-May here?"

"I'm Jaime, come in." The young woman walked past the Chief of Police. Her perfume wafted; her hygiene was impeccable. She was perfect: pretty enough to be easily insulted, but lacking the confidence to react, large enough to put up a fight, but too frail to win it. Pinkerton shut the door softly on the dark and abandoned hallway.

Jaime Pinkerton's alarm woke him at precisely 430AM, as it had for the last thirty years. His room was silent in the moments before impending sunlight. His sepia, mostly hairless skull peered out from twisting landscapes of cotton encased down while he moved to stretch out the last kicking effects of the Sandman. When Pinkerton's eyes focused, the sun was creating fuzzy blue shadows against the expensive furniture. Jaime's belongings sat in perfect linear conformity on the hotel's lacquered side table: wallet, keys, receiver, weapon, and money clip—empty: his money was laid out in individual stacks by paper and coin denomination. Everything in its place.

The rising sun revealed splashes of red and black against the calm eggshell-colored wallpaper. In Pointillist arcs, the young woman's blood painted the room in soft crimson.

Smeared stains of tears, sweat, and mascara muddled the pristine sheets and pillows. Pinkerton's smile returned; someone had suffered needlessly, long into the night. Everything in its place.

Thomas Dongan was scheduled to have a drink at The Campbell Apartment perched quietly above Grand Central Station. Pinkerton showered and shaved, taking great care to trim his mustache and to scrub any remaining blood from his cuticles with a heavy brush and a heavier hand. The bustle of Grand Central Station quieted as Pinkerton walked up the luxuriously carpeted steps leading to the long lounge. A calm din of conversation blanketed the large, dimly lit room. Dongan was standing at the end of the long antique bar surrounded by security and sycophant alike.

"Mr. Dongan." Pinkerton tapped the Mayor of New York on his shoulder while he flirted with the Police Commissioner's niece.

"Who are you?" Dongan whirled around searching the bar for his security detail.

"Jaime Pinkerton, Police Chief of Los Angeles." Jaime reached out his hand.

"Right, right, we met at Escalada's last inauguration," Dongan pretended to recall. "We were scheduled to speak tomorrow afternoon if I remember properly."

"We'll keep that meeting so that there is a paper trail, but it was important that I meet you privately. How have you been?" Pinkerton changed the subject as a young woman passed within earshot and winked at Thomas.

"I've been well, and busy of course, lots going on behind the scenes." Dongan hit Pinkerton on the shoulder fraternally. "What brings you out tonight?"

"Our office has stumbled onto something we think you should know about."

"Did Alamán send you?" Dongan began avoiding eye contact, scanning the room.

"He did."

"Alright, let's go somewhere else."

Dongan signaled and his entourage emerged from the crowd and swept them into a car. Pinkerton started his warning and Dongan stopped him, asking that he remain patient, “We are almost there.”

The car stopped in front of a silent doorway hidden in an alley off Dey Street. They entered and followed a dank hall deep into the entrails of the building. The hall ended at a padlocked door, behind which awaited a luxurious VIP room. Immense curtains parted on a large glass wall overlooking a nightclub far below. The glittering, writhing dance floor dropped six floors beneath the street. The ancient structure's core was now a yawning chasm of electronic aural debauchery.

“Can't beat the view,” Dongan looked down on the crowd and waved Pinkerton over.

“I'd rather not be seen here but thank you,” Pinkerton said with subtle disrespect.

“One-way glass my friend, I'm *never* here. I’m assuming Leary got you past my keepers.”

“He did,” Pinkerton answered.

“I see. Thank you for your candor. Now, what have you been asked to tell me?”

“Someone has been watching you, specifically while you are on Jupiter Island. The individual is a retired sniper who has been on the take as a mercenary for private corporations and governments alike. He hasn't made any offensive postures, but he does appear to be researching your interaction with Harriman.”

“Could it be Harriman's man?”

“It seems unlikely, Harriman would be better suited and protected from accusation by having you followed in Manhattan. Alamán thinks he means to prevent you from being elected. By force.”

“Who is he working for?”

“Right now, my best guess is that he's tied to Washington. For all their ignorance of the big picture they know that we aren’t working together out of friendship. It could be that this man has been sent as a subtle reminder that the Federal government is still in charge. If he is working for the Feds his mission is intelligence gathering, they have no reason to eliminate you...”

“And if he's not?”

"He is not being as careful as he has been in the past, and we will neutralize him. Thomas, we need to talk about Bochinni."

"Anthony? The guy is a sociopath, but that's part of the job description."

"He has retreated further into the shadows lately. When I met with him monthly to report on the SMO-MAX[13] he still allowed his scent to mark his deeds. He has become a phantom, but his hands are on every policy decision Escalada considers.

"He has a new Deputy Chief, one that has avoided being introduced to anyone of importance, except Alamán. This man materialized, whispered in their ears, and has disappeared to work in absolute secret. It makes me uncomfortable; I can't pinpoint why the Deputy Chief concerns me, but the timing is a little too convenient."

"Have you spoken to Escalada?"

"No, I don't feel I can have a candid conversation with him regarding the issue."

"Just keep an eye on him. Escalada is too smart to subvert his military control by chasing the fantasies of secret-intelligence. Bochinni is all smoke and mirrors."

"I certainly hope so. Look, I'm not trying to be alarmist, but I think you and Harriman should put this deal to bed ASAP. Without it, Alamán's interest in New York will wane."

"Well, not everyone is sure they want the two coasts united."

"I'm not suggesting..." Pinkerton retreated.

"It's alright Jaime. Alliances are not always what they seem. Praetorian was our idea."

"I don't understand..."

"The fastest way to check someone's reach is to feed them false information. Compelling, false information I might add." Dongan smiled. "We needed to know if Bochinni had eyes on us

---

13 Santa Monica Airport Super Maximum-Security Detention Facility: The grounds of the former Santa Monica Municipal Airport (SMO) were used during the multiple west Los Angeles insurrections to detain current and potential insurrectionists. Its population expanded with the eventual inclusion of persons accused of providing insurrectionists with safe harbor, facilitating their agenda, or in any way outwardly (or inwardly...they always find out) sympathizing with anybody in direct or indirect opposition to the Mayor's Office. Historians and human rights groups point to the creation of the SMO-MAX as one of the catalyzing events that sparked widespread armed revolt against the Mayor's Office.

and we needed to know if you were the man to tell us. Alamán was necessary in the past to seduce Harriman, but now that Harriman is on board with I-95, Alamán is incidental, and we can cut him out at will. I will need something from you, Jaime."

"That depends..." Pinkerton answered slowly.

"This is not a request. I can assure you that if you have doubts, Alamán knows about them. It's only a matter of time before he takes that as a threat. Hell, that may be why he sent you to tell me about this sniper blarney."

Pinkerton shifted uncomfortably in his seat, "What do you propose, Thomas?"

"I'll need someone to lower the drawbridge when we come for Escalada's head. After we strike, you'll disappear, and I'll see to it personally that you are taken care of."

Pinkerton's forehead wrinkled; his discipline was evaporating.

"Alamán is dangerous. You know it, I know it, Harriman knows it. His desire for power blinds him to the obvious: if we are not united, we will fail. He has become an albatross and we must cut him from our neck."

Pinkerton remained silent.

"Do you understand, Jaime?"

—silence—

"I need to know that we are on the same page," Dongan leaned in closer.

"We are."

"Excellent. Look, let's lighten the mood a little and have another drink. Shall we have some girls come by?"

Pinkerton was swimming in anxiety, but nothing motivated him like the female form. Nothing spoke to him like *the war*, the endlessly varied seduction and then annihilation that addicted him. Pinkerton requested a link-up and had a brief conversation before turning back to Dongan. "I'm inviting a friend. She is very, very obedient."

"Very well Jaime, it's your party."

≈

≈

"Yes, I understand." The young woman placed her phone on the seat as *Leary* disappeared from the screen. She straightened the straps on her dress and flipped her cropped ebony hair as the driver entered an alleyway off Dey Street.

"Gentlemen..." A large man in dark glasses entered the room after a half-hour and nearly half a bottle of twenty-year-old Scotch. "She's here."

"Good, please shut the door behind you." Dongan ordered.

The young woman entered the room and smiled shyly, "Hello High-May." Her discreetly tattooed arms and chest bore fresh wounds, lashes no more than a day old. Her thin black evening dress clung desperately to her lithe body and her soft brown eyes were a mixture of fear and awe.

"Dance for us." Pinkerton demanded.

The men remained seated, with their eyes trained on her.

The woman set her purse down and began to sway to silent music. With subtle hand gestures Pinkerton conducted her movements, occasionally commanding her to remove a strap from her dress, tease, and then replace it. Dongan was mesmerized by the sick little game.

Pinkerton compelled her to stand still, facing them. Obeying a wave of his hand, the young woman let the soft material of her dress fall to the ground. She stood bare, stockinged and gartered, with her hands obediently clasped behind her back. Burned in a tattooed arc above her mons veneris, lay Dante's infernal warning, *Lasciate ogne speranza, voi ch'intrate.*[14] She raised her delicate porcelain arms, there was a quick flash, and she began dancing again.

Pinkerton was visibly perturbed, "Charlotte, I did not ask you to start dancing."

The young lady turned to face Pinkerton and held a pistol silencer to his forehead.

"What is this...?" Pinkerton felt Dongan's blood pooling on the leather sofa beside him, "Oh fuck, Thomas?"

"He's dead Jaime. Alamán sends his regards." The young woman smiled and blew a fine crimson hole in Pinkerton's skull before disappearing into the frigid night.

---

14 "Abandon All Hope, Ye Who Enter Here." From Dante Alighieri's *The Divine Comedy*, Canto III: The Gate of Hell.

≈

POLITICAL ASSASSINATION—
screamed the New York Times
ENEMY OF THE STATE MURDERED—
shrieked the Washington Post
DONGAN DYNASTY DIES—
lamented the Los Angeles Times

Alamán stirred his drink, smiling. "Those fucking idiots fell for it."

"They certainly did." Bochinni clinked glasses with Alamán. "Leary played it perfectly, and we made certain that all evidence leads directly to Jupiter Island."

"The Feds will be so far up New York and Tallahassee's asses they'll have to pull out of the movement."

"What if Florida goes to the Feds?" Bochinni asked.

"And hang for treason? No chance." Alamán finished his drink. "We consolidate now and wait."

"Wait for what precisely?" This was the first Bochinni was hearing about *waiting* for anything.

Alamán locked eyes with Bochinni's Deputy Chief.

"The Fed is still too strong to challenge directly." The Deputy Chief continued. "We need time to stockpile and move forces into the States."

"Then," Alamán paused dramatically, "we decapitate the viper from within."

"Precisely." The Chief of Staff added.

"If we strike now, the Fed will snuff out the resistance in less than a year. We need to be inside the borders. Then, there is no turning back."

"Salut." Bochinni intoned calmly. He did not appreciate being kept on the sidelines, but he could tell, for now at least, that his Deputy Chief had Alamán's ear. Any resistance would be read as a threat.

Descent

‡

VI

The day was bright and cool; Victor leapt from his post-breakfast perch and had a final cigarette on Aungier before heading back upstairs. Cleaned and dressed, he stepped out into the August morning. Victor walked beneath the Fusilier's Arch and east down a path saturated in greens. The shaded pathway wound around a large lake rife with birds and early morning pedestrians. Victor sat on a quiet, empty bench and stared out over the body of water.

8/25/10
830AM

This is a true municipal common. It exists to enhance a citizen's life, a concept long lost on Americans. Beauty, community, and a sense of commonality are all victims of our lack of empathy. I paid nothing to be here and bowed to no authority for entrance into this breathtaking landscape. I am autonomous.

1045AM

As I approached the Irish National Library, I tried to imagine James Joyce walking toward the large domed structure during a torrential downpour, manuscript in hand, determined to utilize the reverent silence and warmth of the library to create.

I was berated by a scowling librarian. He angrily pointed to a "NO PHOTOS" sign as I aimed my cell phone at the vast reading room. The Librarian never softened his scowl.

I walked around the book-laden walls and eventually took a seat at an empty desk, far enough from the main desk and prying eyes. The antique green-glass reading lamps sit like silent rows of corn in the vast Midwest, and the sea of brown desktops provide the topsoil from which they sprang.

1055AM

I've got nothing to work on. It's dreary somehow to be here and not on the streets. My mind is blank.

Noonish

A rather large person was standing at the front desk of Avalon House. The person seemed agitated by the kid behind the counter's unhidden awe. Apparently, the employee had never seen a six-foot tall man wearing a lady's blouse, skirt, and heels. Honestly, she looked like she had just gotten off a long flight and needed a little understanding.

9PM

California, for all its propaganda, is not the open-minded and compassionate savior of the Union. The Los Angeles Basin teeters back and forth between enlightened cohabitation and declared class-warfare. Developers are permitted to wrangle billions into a pen for City Hall to feed on at will. The targets of their wrecking crews are always the poor. Scores of people who barely retain their humanity trying to make it onto a complex spreadsheet as Tennant: LAHD-886557.

1115PM

I was invited upstairs at J.J. Smythe's. There will be music, I was told. The dark room has booths on both walls with similar octagonal tables. The band was sitting on stage conversing when I sat down. Shortly thereafter they picked up their instruments and the guitarist started things off. The ensemble built into a crescendo before breaking off into improvisational interludes by each player and a finale.

In hindsight, an entire month alone is a bit of a stretch for a first-time trip overseas. I need to regain my stamina. Soon I will be in London among writers.

‡

8/26/10 730PM

Caught up in the King's life here. It will be so difficult to go back to the life of work and deprivation. It suits me so to haunt the pubs, to blow with the winds and land where I may. I cannot reconcile real life w/ the life I want, w/ the life that inspires. Grey-clouded existence, the occasional sun-bathed cigarette—beauty oppressive beauty—

Victor drifted in and out of the futbal match splashed against J.J.'s large mounted television set. The stout had crawled on top of Victor and was harassing him for his reverence.

10PM

Fucking drunk.

8/28/10 9AM

A sort of swooping and irrational scribble followed that last, not so poignant, notebook entry; after admitting I was done for the night, I pulled myself straight and stumbled out of the door; up Aungier to the hostel. As I ascended the staircase clumsily, I wished upon a star, or whatever else was available, that my room would be empty so I could slip into bed silently to wait for the painful morning to come.

I heard shouting through the door, peer pressure mixed with painful violations of the Queen's English. The din poured under the door and into the hallway, filling me with dread. I turned the doorknob and faced my destiny.

Six South Londoners turned and looked as if their mother had walked in while they were circle-jerking to Guns & Ammo.

I waved.

Alcohol flew around the room and each hooligan hugged me into the crew and shouted profanity.

You going to sleep? —One of the guys asked.

No, no, I figure I'll at least have a drink with you before you go out. You're going out, correct?

Oh yeah! —The boys had popped over to Dublin for a few days of dance clubs, alcohol poisoning, and unprotected sex with strangers.

They were playing a game called 'King's Cup,' during which 'winners' dump part of their drink into a single cup. There was a splash of everything they had on hand in the King's Cup. One of the hooligans was supposed to drink it as punishment for losing the game, but he was being a bit prissy about it, so I stood up and took it from him. I hoisted it up in the air to primate cheers and swallowed it in one gulp. The bottom of the cup was littered with disintegrating Skittles candies that I struggled to choke down.

I was in very big trouble. There was nothing short of profuse vomiting that could help me.

I blacked out on the walk to Temple Bar but when I returned to empirical reality we were standing in a loud nightclub—squinting in the flashing lights.

I was fired as tour guide. The bar I had taken the boys to was full of old men and tennis was on the television.

‡

Two-thirds of the boys had paired off with girls in the next club and the final two were looking around nervously.

I never said goodbye, simply turned and walked out into the night.

The path to the hostel was a series of flashes, first of herding six rowdy kids a mile down the road, then leading a charge into a bar. Climbing Aungier, I took solace: as long as the boys were partying, the room would be empty.

Morning brought blinding pain. A large blank spot in my vision and an excruciating stabbing pain behind the eyes welcomed me back to the living. Waves of nausea rolled from toes to forehead and back again. I pleaded with my body to please stop.

The room was empty, either the boys had slept elsewhere in the city or had not made it anywhere at all. Jail came to mind. Who am I to talk, thirty years old and drinking myself unconscious with six twenty-year-old hooligans?

The warm shower felt good, but it came nowhere close to cutting through the violent pain. A walk to the store for some headache medicine and some water was necessary, so I collected myself and walked down to the café. The smell of the food turned my stomach. I ordered a small coffee but couldn't bear to order food.

The air outside was mercifully cool and the wind made me feel a bit human. I lit a cigarette. After three inhalations I regretted it. Breathing in and out made me sob and hold my temples. I wasted a perfectly good cigarette and headed back inside.

I wandered the hostel, trying to sleep in chairs, and trying to stretch out on the sofa, but could not get comfortable.

I popped chalky Paracetamol pills from the corner drugstore and trudged south on Aungier to a pizza place I'd seen advertised. The friendly Pakistani men running the parlor were excited to be at work and excited to see customers. The shouting hurt my head a bit, but their good cheer rubbed off. I took a seat at the back of the parlor and watched SkyNews: an MI-6 agent had been found murdered and stuffed in his own luggage, Pakistan was embroiled in an immense Cricket insider betting scandal, and two British pop stars from a boy-band of days-past were burying the hatchet and recording an album together. Same old shit, different country.

I could not finish the pizza, but for the first time all day I felt like sipping a pint of stout. John Lynch's place sat across the intersection from the hostel. The pub was almost silent. The two pints I was able to tackle before closing time sent me to bed peacefully.

The boys were gone again
In Temple Bar no doubt
And I,
Welcomed the calm.

I'll close my eyes
On the starry night
And rise
To drink Éire's stout.

Stumble her streets
And coddle her pride
Before sleeping,
A poor, pickled lout.

I saw the boys off this morning, one shouted his email address as they filtered out and I pretended to write it down. They left a shock of rubbish and potential stains behind, so I did my best to tidy up before housekeeping came around.

‡

Victor toured the neighborhood as all the shops began to open and collected thirty postcards. Having accomplished this with relative grace, he took his stack of cards and seated himself on the patio of the Hairy Lemon to put a bit of his mind on the permanent record. The city of Dublin had reminded him of beauty and of a lyric rhythm between people in awe of beauty. It made him miss Los Angeles, his family, even the dank warehouse he called home.

The postcards bent beneath his pen, murdered by a possessed hand. In some he planted hints regarding his state of health and mind, to ease worry, and in others he wove the fringe, outlandish, and painful, to bring them into the tale. Finally, to some, admission of deep longing to see their faces again, tomorrow would do, but another two weeks seemed far too long.

Long after he'd dropped his paper missives in a post box, Victor wrote on the final page from a worn notebook:

Tomorrow will mark two weeks in Dublin. Friday, I fly to England. Three days with Stasia and Dahvit, back to Dublin for one final week—then home.

It will be an odd transition, being back in Los Angeles. Lovely and odd. So strange to not walk Aungier, to not stroll down Stephen's or Chatham, so strange to not see John at the Hairy Lemon, Eamonn at J.J.'s, or Brian and Stephano at Sheehan's. I have carved out an alternate existence here and I will consider it a loss when I leave it behind. I know that, should I stay in Éire, Los Angeles would lure me back some day, enraged by my insubordination.

—DUBLIN AUGUST 30, 2010—

Resurrection

§
XXXVI

Autumn ~ 2001

A young NYPD detective with a mortgage and a taste for the ponies sold the news of Kyrios' death to the Times before the authorities notified Erlyst. She read about it as the announcement scrolled beneath a CNN anchor's bosom. She smiled and finished her tea. Her large hat and dark glasses let her relish in the news privately; no one knew that the Widow Atropos was cooing quietly into a steaming cup, imagining far off lands and meager attempts at communication.

Lawrence E. Robertson flashed across Erlyst's phone. She denied the call.

He texted. "Erlyst. Kyrios is dead. Please call me."

"For christ's sake." Erlyst dialed the lawyer. "Yes Larry, I already know. Thanks. No, and go fuck yourself."

By the time The Chief of Police and the acting director of the FBI rang Erlyst's bell she had paid multiple designers to set the rooms to a mourning tone and she had donned an eclipsing veil.

"Come in, gentlemen."

"Mrs. Atropos, we'll just stay if it's alright with you."

The Chief's cool tone surprised Erlyst. "Of course."

"On behalf of the city of New York and its servicemen, we extend our condolences to you."

"I thank you gentlemen very kindly." Erlyst smiled humbly.

"We will find out what happened ma'am, and you can be assured of our absolute discretion."

"Thalia and I thank you." Erlyst slowly closed the door. It was clear that the Chief had been ordered to conduct a clean investigation. He was not pleased.

§

Erlyst, with Lawrence's loyal assistance, laid the Atropos Empire to waste—drawn and quartered, the carrion was flung north, south, east, and west. Corporate pirates far and wide were all too willing to preside over the dismantling of the modern Leviathan. By the next year's Q3, the planarian beast woke from its slumber stronger, regenerating and become whole again beneath hundreds of covertly coordinated and consolidated banners. Though nothing material was created, the appearance of increased competition rewarded all stockholders with a windfall profit.

A regiment of lawyers dispatched by Lawrence connived with a federal judge to freeze sales of the Empire's assets. The lawyers argued that the haphazard way these assets were flying around endangered the investments of core financiers. The judge ordered a two-week moratorium and billions of non-existent dollars flooded the accounts of thirty-two men and one patient widow.

It worked; the Atropos empire was no more. Erlyst was free.

§

In the wake of Mr. Atropos' death, a tsunami of paternal suits crushed Lawrence E. Robertson's office. Women from as far away as Indonesia and all continents between clamored into courts to testify to their child's rights.

Desperate to be *elsewhere*, Erlyst pulled Thalia from school and they flew by private charter to Buenos Aires. While Erlyst languished in a sub-par seaside villa with Thalia, a small entourage arrived, purchased a refined hilltop residence in Barrio Parque. In South America they were untouchable by the greedy hands awaiting them in the United States, and in moments of weakness Erlyst vowed to stay an expatriate, no matter the cost. Her mind changed when she discovered her young daughter running around the slums of Buenos Aires with a local peasant and con artist.

Erlyst spotted them while on an errand.

"Who is that young man?" Erlyst asked a bored clerk enjoying a light nap next to snow globes encasing beach scenes.

"¿Que? Oh, you mean Santiago?"

"Santiago. How do you know him?"

The clerk, mistaking her attention for affection leaned closer, "He trolls Palermo for rich women. He's nothing, a street thief who sells drugs to kids. Lo que necesitas es un hombre. ¡Un hombre grande!"

Erlyst backed slowly away from the store clerk. His leer had turned unnerving. She was pleased to have the busy market to her back.

She had to admit Santiago was a very beautiful creature, far more stunning than Mr. Atropos had been in his youth, but he was a man and Thalia was still a very young girl. Before long he would teach her the ways of the world by force or by coercion, and Erlyst could not be asked to endure a peasant branch to the bloodline.

"Where are you off to my love?" Erlyst asked absently, trying to hide how important her daughter's answer was.

"Nowhere, just to Palermo to shop. Maybe some dancing."

"With friends?"

"Of course. I'm not pathetic." Thalia sniffed.

Thalia had learned to lie. She had even learned to believe her lies.

"Well, have fun. Are you sure everything is ok?"

"Okay? Quit being weird mother, I have to go."

Erlyst grabbed her arm. "I want you to stop seeing him. It ends now."

"What are you talking about, *mother*?"

"The street thug. Santiago."

Thalia froze. "You're insane mom, there are no street thugs in Palermo." She laughed, a practiced, casual laugh.

"I'm *mom,* now am I? If you are lying to me, it will be the last time."

"I'm not lying!"

"Then leave. I've said what I intended to say."

"You are such a lunatic *mother*, I swear... "

§

Erlyst followed her daughter down the hill and into the tourist havens. The car stopped at a small storefront next to a busy bar. Thalia exited the passenger side wearing remarkably less clothing than she had been when she left the house. Her face was painted for seduction and her shoulders were thrown back in defiance. "I knew she was lying."

Erlyst barked at her driver to park.

Thalia sent a text. A broad smile spread across her young face before she disappeared into the noisy bar. Erlyst could not decide whether she should wait or try to catch her in the act. As she vacillated, Santiago walked past the car and toward the bar.

"Stay here," She ordered the driver and exited the car.

Erlyst made her way into the bar after Santiago had disappeared to the back. Music and conversation throbbed against the black-painted walls. The back of the small front room opened into a large courtyard filled with shaking bodies. Erlyst scanned the crowd and found her daughter. Thalia looked coyly up into Santiago's eyes as he reached out his hand. She followed him onto the dance floor.

He guided her, closing the space between their bodies with each passing measure of deafening bass and laser light. He crouched to place his lips on hers. She wasn't sure what he was doing at first and she flinched. Santiago would not be deterred. He grabbed her chin and pressed his face against hers until she melted into the embrace.

Erlyst had seen enough.

"*Mother.*"

"I hate when you call me that."

"You're my mother, aren't you?" Thalia kept her eyes fixed on her cell phone.

"It's not *what* you are saying, it's *how*, you say it my darling."

"Well, I haven't had much luck teaching my asshole to talk, but as soon as I climb that hill... "

"You're staying in tonight."

"What? Why? Come on, that's so not fair. You started it!"

"You lied to me, Thalia."

"About what?"

"Last night, in Palermo. I watched you give your body to that trash. I saw how you danced. If you have not spread your legs for him, it cannot be far off."

"You are sick, Erlyst."

"I'm you *mother.*" Erlyst mocked her daughter's petulant tone of voice. "We will put this ugliness behind us."

Erlyst forced Thalia onto a coach flight to New York City and Thalia cried silently. She had no name for the tiny pain in her chest that had erupted into a paralyzing ennui. She did not know enough to blame it on love, but she now held vengeance and loss closer to her heart than wonder and comfort.

Erlyst remained, and at nightfall stole away to Palermo and got herself lost in the large open-air party. Before long, her short red dress caught the attention of a young man with long inky hair and a workingman's filth. Erlyst winked and the man stood.

By the time he reached the dance floor, Erlyst had pushed the hem of her loose dress beyond her thighs, an unsubtle invitation that the powerfully built young man knew far too well.

"You should be more careful. Dancing alone, even in Palermo, can be dangerous."

"How dangerous?" Erlyst asked, wrapping her arms around his neck.

"You are in no danger from me, senorita."

The young man had not developed the stamina necessary to challenge an Irish belle to a drinking competition, and though he tried mightily, he succumbed to agave before she bent to rye.

He regained his senses periodically: once, while Erlyst helped him walk home; again, as Erlyst removed his shirt and then her own; and a final time as Erlyst looked down on him, numbly saddled. She smiled sadly as his eyes lidded for the last time.

Santiago woke to an empty bed. His hips were covered in dried blood. A wide gash toured the length of his flaccid penis. Resting in the blood was a soft, slowly saturating piece of paper with pristine blue letters on one side.

§

Santiago Benitez,

By now you've noticed that I spared your manhood. I did not have to. You would do well to stay away from impressionable young girls.

- Mother

Erlyst slept with a revolver beneath her pillow. Santiago seemed hot-blooded enough to be shamed beyond fear. The staff was in-house, so Erlyst left the windows open. The soft linens drifted in the Atlantic breeze and an unsettling darkness fell over the house. Shadows danced listlessly, and below her room something shifted.

Erlyst gripped the weapon. She let go only when she heard the hushed voices of security staff clearing the floor. Erlyst relaxed her grip and closed her eyes. She was being paranoid.

Erlyst.

Erlyst sat straight up in her bed.

She was alone. She shared the room only with the sound of the tides crashing.

Erlyst. An oily voice fell from the ceiling.

Erlyst recoiled. *You're dead.*

Am I?

Yes. I saw the body.

The shadows in the room shifted, mimicking a bright day's sun climbing through the sky.

You did something...delightful last night.

No.

The voice hung in the damp air, dense as smoke. *Oh, but you did Erlyst. You were impeccably cruel. Thalia will never forgive you.*

Stop.

No. Not yet.

Please.

I saw your eyes. In spite of your tears, I watched you use that young man's body.

Erlyst smiled. *Did you enjoy it, Kyrios?*

She stared into an empty room. Her burden persisted; the torture had just begun.

§

When Erlyst joined Thalia in New York, she banished her molded memories and sold Mr. Atropos' prized Manhattan apartment for a song. She felt like seeing the sun every day, so she dispatched her assistant to Los Angeles to inquire about the crowning floor of the Millennium Biltmore Hotel. The infamous downtown landmark at the corner of West Fifth Street and Olive was profiting from the gentrification wave near the Pershing Square subway station. The hotel's management was eager to learn how much the Widow was willing to allocate to their cause.

Erlyst insisted that her employees take special, high-priced care to preserve as much original wood, marble, iron, and decorative work as possible, but to otherwise gut the architectural masterpiece and tailor it to her needs. [15] They installed a private elevator from the hotel below that opened into a circular foyer. A finely carved array of curved Queen Anne sideboards lined the pristine silk adorned walls between openings to a concentric hallway. A single delicate table held a vase of pure white hydrangeas; no other flower was permitted on the floor.

To the west the brightly lit hall led to the staff quarters and offices before opening into the grand dining room. The cavernous space occupied a quarter of the floor looking out over the City's distant coast. The canopy and walls surrounding the long formal dining table were composed of a photosensitive synthetic glass and dimmed according to Erlyst's comfort.[16]

To the south lay the kitchen, abreast the dining room, and behind, chambers meant for her daughter. To the north lay Erlyst's quarters, ever guarded from the outside world and impassable to all but a few. Erlyst's master suite opened into her private study, creating a self-contained domicile looking out over City Hall.

---

15 Iconography pg. 18 Crowning floor of The Millennium Biltmore Hotel

16 The thirty-thousand square foot experimental form put a face, and a dollar amount, on the research by a group of structural physicists at MIT. The for-profit project served as vindication and funding for further research—what's another ten-thousand feet between scientists?

§

Stretching across the eastern face of the apartment, Erlyst had the designers divide the space evenly into a visiting library, a sitting room, and Erlyst's private study. The titanic halls were lined with biliothéque libraries clinging to every inch of wall from floor to forty-foot-high ceiling. Between the archives of ancient knowledge, immense windows laced in iron drew light from the rising sun. Erlyst commissioned a massive recreation of Bosch's triptych *The Garden of Earthly Delights* spanning the ceilings of all three halls. In Erlyst's private study: serene and surreal Eden, the lost symbiosis between human and beast. In the Library: humanity in all its beauty, terror, and ignorance. The sitting room: a demonically funny depiction of Hell as seen through the eyes of an orthodox adherent to christ-worship in its infancy.

Mad Men and Their Myths

≈

LXIX

Winter ~ 2028

The twenty-first century's ravenous addiction to wars of aggression destroyed the USA's long toiled-over web of control. Hubris, and an inflated sense of freedom from accountability, warped the vision of America's leadership—they became convinced of their own moral superiority, and invincibility.

The ruling party continued to pander to its addled constituents by offering increasingly ridiculous and outlandish figures for the highest offices of the land. If a politician was incapable of at least one divisive public comment per week, said politician was vulnerable to being labeled an "insider," a "conformist."

Entranced by the theater of politics, our Imperial Senators began more and more to resemble the reviled and deluded Senators of the Roman Empire. The immense Fasces hoisted on the walls of the Senate chamber serve as an unseen, though unhidden, reminder of our State model. As Iraq and Afghanistan erupted, dictatorships across Asia unraveled. Some conflicts were short-lived, and others crushed deeply instilled puppet regimes permanently. The Iraq War[17] had given birth to a second generation knowing nothing but foreign conflict and domestic silence.

US citizens had no clue. Those that cheered for war—prepared for it and executed it—had learned to whisper about the dangers that *peace* would bring to the United States. These armchair patriots shrieked that, *if the United States stopped policing the world, the chaos outside would soon engulf our shores.* As

17 ...still technically an Authorized Use of Force. War was never declared.

the eternal police force, the United States faced eternal enemies, old, new, and manufactured.

Alamán sat back in his chair staring at the news anchor reporting the invasion of yet another small country by the United States. The Mayor's hair had hints of silver at the temples and his eyes were lidded and deeper set than they had been when he first seized office. Alamán pulled Anthony Bochinni up on his receiver.

"Alamán. Did you see?" Bochinni asked.

"Yes. Why do you think I'm calling you?"

"Of course."

"It's time to cement the relationship and move forward. Call the men together. Send your Deputy Chief to my office and get over to the Mexican Consulate."

"But your honor, shouldn't I be..."

"If you can't handle the straightforward tasks I give you Anthony, how can I trust you with the complicated matters?"

The Corporation of Autonomous States, or CAS, conducted their first aboveground meeting in the ballroom of the Alexandria Hotel deep within Los Angeles' Great Gardens. California, Texas, Hawaii, Alaska, and Louisiana seceded from the Union by virtue of inalienable States' Rights to decide its citizen's fates independently from the Federal Government.

The burgeoning Southwest Territory (formally Arizona and New Mexico) signed in solidarity (to protect their newly formed government), as did Oklahoma and Mississippi. Alabama had voiced a desire to join in secession, but Alamán intended to make Alabama and Georgia into a demilitarized zone. He considered the hostile environment perfect for housing prisoners and fomenting border chaos with Florida.

Within forty-eight hours, Mexico, Guatemala, Honduras, Nicaragua, Costa Rica, Panama, and Cuba recognized the CAS declaration. The US media treated it as the misguided intentions of "Anti-government thugs and anti-White racists who want only to destroy *freedom*." [*sic*]

As it had been decade after decade, the *frightening-leftist* meme and a few well-planted pamphlets during house raids were enough to lull the American people into complacent sleep. While the Fed soothed themselves with petty raids and mass arrests, coalition troops from the CAS and the Alliance of Caribbean, Central, and South America Democracies (ACCSAD) began moving into position.

"We're nearly ready." Bochinni intoned.

"We must be patient." His Deputy Chief muttered. "We are tilling the soil."

"Tell me what you mean by that. What are you up to?" Bochinni sat back. The slight, spectacled Deputy Chief looked like too much of a pushover to strike.

"We are ensuring success."

"*We?* This isn't the first time you've left me out of the loop, but it *will* be the last..."

"We had to be certain that everything was in place before we disseminated the mission."

"What mission? Who belongs to this *We* you keep referring to?"

"We can't make the same mistakes as our predecessors, Anthony. The twentieth century gave revolution a bad name. Over and over, the message and purpose of revolution became propaganda used to coerce subjugation. The ideals were co-opted as marketing and the *sponsor* called the shots.

"We are slowly creeping in under the Fed's nose—we are creating infrastructure. As long as they consider us a pesky militia movement, we can continue to occupy and fortify turned cities while they wage war overseas. By never "attacking" anyone, by never calling thousands into the streets, we make it hard for the Fed to consider us a real *enemy*. Without firing a shot, we now occupy most of the old territory of Mexico. We will soon have a direct line to the Oval Office."

"If the Feds ignore CAS where will this *revolution* come from?"

"That, sir, is privileged information."

"You're insane." Bochinni stood to leave. "I'll put an end to this tonight."

"Good luck sir."

"Good luck? Who the fuck do you think you are?"

"This is already taking place, Anthony. It is beyond the point of no return."

"Is that a threat?"

"A threat? No, please have seat. You needn't be in the dark any longer."

The Chief of Intelligence relented.

"To be completely honest Anthony, de-centralization of power has never truly been our aim..."

Alamán used the amassed CAS and ACCSAD battalions to leverage regular meetings with President Pelagia Aëtius, just as the Deputy Chief had predicted. While completely focused on the outside world the President didn't have the resources to move against CAS. Her Cabinet assured her that placating the extremists in the domestic regions made more sense than compromising any of our fledgling wars in the Fertile Crescent. As long as CAS behaved themselves, they'd be allowed their angry protest. The Fed would put the dog down if it became rabid.

State after state considered a CAS-style declaration, but they did so behind closed doors. This did not stop the state governments from providing distribution, transportation, and military securities for CAS. The Fed looked the other way while Alamán filled State coffers with tax money and remained peaceful.

≈

President Aëtius was persuaded to send her Vice President and a young, bright-eyed representative to Caracas as a last-ditch effort to undermine the CAS. "Young lady, I want you to always hold your head high. What you and your mission represent is a desire for peace. It is... "

"Madame President," her Vice President interrupted politely, "we should be moving along."

The President looked deeply into her young protégé's warm, earthen eyes, "Make us proud."

The representative whispered something in the President's ear, and they embraced.

The Vice President escorted the representative to a waiting car. As the entourage entered Baltimore the Vice President broke his long silence.

"What did you whisper to the President, honey?"

"Did you just call me honey? Sir?" She asked on the edge of offense.

"I did. I also asked you a question. Answer it." The Vice President's tone intensified.

"This is a highly inappropriate conversation. Let me off at the next exit, I'd like to disembark." The representative reached for her cell phone and the Vice President batted it weakly from her hand.

"Look kid, just tell me what you said to the President. It's very simple."

"Fuck you, psycho."

"This is who Aëtius picks to wrangle with the Alliance?" The Vice President and the driver began laughing; the representative was paralyzed by sudden and vivid terror.

"Mr. LeVander...Mr. Vice President...I asked her to pray for me, I am nervous." The representative searched the Vice President's eyes for a sign of compassion; she was disappointed.

"She's lying." The driver yawned.

" Okay, little girl, the hard way it is." The Vice President fired a taser into her side.

The driver pulled under a bridge as a second black car pulled up behind them. "I'll go get Graham, get rid of her." The driver smacked the representative's head against the window frame to knock her out and pulled her to the side of the road.

Graham, a clean-cut recent graduate of Yale made his way to the running car and the entourage moved toward Ronald Reagan Airport. The Vice President, a minor army of security, and Graham boarded a private flight to Caracas.

Upon arrival they were ushered past writhing crowds of angry people. The airstrip's barrier threatened to cave in as peasants vowed to throw themselves on the runway, if only to kill the monsters they expected to ooze from the private jet.

The Venezuelan government allowed the riotous protest, a cordial slap in the Empire's face—a long overdue slap. The windows of the airport were dense with fists and faces trying to break into the concourse; the Vice President asked, "How are we going to get out of here?"

"We're not." Vargas Lleras, the rogue ACCSAD representative spoke for the first time. "We're going upstairs, change of venue. As you can see, we have a little crowd control problem outside." They entered a small, warm meeting room.

Lleras waved to empty and half-destroyed desk chairs for the American diplomatic entourage, "This was the best we could do last minute. Please, gentleman, have a seat." Lleras and his security team seated themselves in high-backed leather executive chairs on the opposite side of the cheap, coffee stained, conference table. "What can we do for you esteemed gentlemen today?"

"Wipe that sneer off your face for starters." The Vice President sat forward, causing his chair to creak.

"Your threats mean nothing here, LeVander. Calm yourself or wait in the airplane. Better yet, have a stroll outside, *connect* with the people."

"Your Excellency, we are here to pronounce a new vision of South and North American cooperation." Graham interrupted diplomatically.

Lleras sat back, satisfied with the dodge. "So I've heard. However, I was told a young lady would be your representative. A protégé of your President, no?"

"She was unable to fulfill her duties in that capacity. My name is Graham Jenkins, sir."

"Graham, it is a sincere pleasure," Lleras cordially insisted. "Mr. Vice President, on further contemplation, I do feel that it would be best if you waited elsewhere while I speak to Graham."

The Vice President reluctantly rose and made his way toward the broken doors.

"Mr. Lleras, I want to cut to the chase." The young salesman rolled into his pitch. "The United States cannot allow our citizens to engage in a brutal civil war. We are prepared to make a concession to the ACCSAD in return for their unilateral declaration of war against the CAS scourge threatening our country's security."

"Declare war?"

"Yes. We need your help covering our western shores."

"That is true, Graham. Tell me about your concession."

Graham pulled a thin computer tablet from his suit jacket and set it in front of Lleras. The screen flickered to life dramatically (an old business school trick) and an unseen hand sketched a map of the United States. "The ACCSAD Annexation: beginning on the coast of California, and running along the 37th parallel, this annexation will terminate along the Oklahoma and Louisiana borders. The Annexation would return most of the land ceded by the Treaty of Guadalupe Hidalgo."

"That's it?" Lleras rapped his fingers against the cheap table.

"Sir, the possibilities are limitless. The United States is also prepared to offer structural support."

"In what way?"

"Our proposal is to create a free port structure for the Annexation. Businesses and institutions could remain as-is. However, these entities would answer to an ACCSAD administered occupation until hostilities with the CAS are quelled. Think of it, Vegas, Tijuana, San Diego, Hollywood, *and Coahuila y Tejás.*" The slick graduate leaned back in his creaky chair confidently.

Lleras sat back as well, smiling. They were clever to cut California in two, but Graham had to be a moron if he thought Lleras, a native Venezuelan, gave a fuck about Texas. Were he not compelled by his superiors to take the American offer, he'd have openly mocked the young bigot. "You strike a hard bargain, Graham. What about the resources and existing communities?"

"Taxes, infrastructure and above all, *profit*, will be the purview of the ACCSAD to do as it pleases. The gulf and Angeles ports alone should net... "

"Enough," Lleras raised his hand. "When must this declaration of war take place?"

"Within the month. Our garrisons in the west will stand down and push back behind the Annexation line. We expect your troops to stand their ground in the west as we push Alamán from the east."

"I understand. Now, explain something to me. Why aren't you a young law student with beautiful brown eyes and a master's degree in international business contracts?"

"I don't understand... "

"The President and I were very specific about the conditions of this meeting. I don't understand why she would send you instead."

"The Vice President... "

"That's enough," The Vice President burst into the room.

"Ah, LeVander, I'm glad you're here. We're going to solve this once and for all. Have a seat."

"This young man is a bright new addition to my staff. It is no concern of yours. Are we finished?" The Vice President grunted defiantly.

"No LeVander; we're not. I was promised an American head to hold up to my people, a blood sacrifice for the horror and agony they have suffered. Personally, I requested an attractive sacrifice. Who knows? I might have decided to keep her...for a while. I intend to hold the President of the United States to her word."

"You can't be serious," Graham rose from his chair, rightly terrified.

"Very serious," Lleras stared coldly into the Vice President's eyes.

If LeVander flew home empty-handed the President would find out about his switch and have him buried deep within a secret Romanian prison. "Graham. Sit down. Close your eyes and recite *The Star-spangled Banner*." The Vice President shook Lleras' outstretched hand. "We have a deal."

Federal troops pulled back beyond the Annexation Line and ACCSAD flooded each state's major cities and capitals with battalions of occupying troops. The US Government was lulled back to sleep. President Aëtius addressed the core of American power in the White House Rose Garden on the morning of ACCSAD's proposed declaration of war. She gave a rousing and unintelligible speech calling on Americans to have *the vision to defend their future from enemies current and emerging*. The press conference concluded with subtle applause. The President looked to the sky and squinted when an object briefly eclipsed the sun. A mushroom cloud formed over the Pentagon, and the shockwave evaporated all in attendance.

In an underground bunker, the Secretary of Labor was sworn in as the President of the United States. Secretary Mildred Walters was the only ranking government official who had skipped the President's speech; her brutal battle against Vicodin addiction had turned her bowels to cement. By 11AM she was the Commander in Chief of the United States Military. ACCSAD remained in position and severed diplomatic ties with the Federal Government. Congress panicked, and immediately placed blame on the CAS. High-level members were gathered up en masse and subjected to torture and imprisonment. The shock of being attacked so intimately rippled outward and the government's raids were extended to CAS sympathizers and alleged co-conspirators

The CAS machine ground into action. Noble, newsworthy people crowded the streets begging their government to stop. The international media embraced the CAS fawningly and soon the United States government was accused of instigating a *Great Western Calamity* by international legal bodies. Foreign aid sent from abroad began to clutter American ports under CAS control. As they received international support and tacit approval, CAS ensured that a rapidly escalating, brutal, and immediately *full-scale* civil war consumed the United States. The conflict involved the most advanced munitions techniques and weapons systems known to humanity and its out-rippling sadism threatened to gush beyond America's fragile borders.

The world paid little mind to the American skirmish. They went about their business and waited to see if the fluffy little subsidized revolution would beat the big bad guys, or if the bad guys would keep their jobs. Most people tended to side with the CAS call for something *different*, and US citizens began to identify CAS as the *little guy*.

Alamán lead the charge, flipping counties and states one by one simply by marching through and recruiting the locals. In the distant wake of a 2010 Second Amendment ruling, [18] Americans armed themselves heavily with little resistance. Those who chose to join Alamán's forces did so equipped for war.

The Federal Government had to admit a stalemate and started bringing troops home from dozens of warzones abroad. By the time the first platoons of US Armed Forces began returning to polluted, blood-drenched American soil, the CAS was a prevailing physical and philosophical presence in three of the four time zones.

American soldiers went AWOL in droves, and the deeply entrenched CAS troops welcomed their decades-earned and combat-hardened expertise. The soldiers that remained within the Federal ranks were a match for the CAS forces, but no more.

A man claiming to be from Alamán's inner circle asked for a brief audience with President Brock Patterson.

"Mr. President? Anthony Bochinni is here."

"Please send him in," Patterson responded solemnly.

The President moved to the center of the Oval Office. His Secretary of the Interior stood and buttoned his suit jacket.

Anthony Bochinni seated himself without shaking the President's hand.

"Thank you for meeting with us Anthony." President Patterson sat on the Resolute desk. "I'm told you have a proposition for us."

"I want immunity first. When it's all said and done, I want to be made comfortable and powerful."

The Secretary of the Interior pushed back, "We can't really make any offers until we know what you...."

"Then call me when you can." Bochinni rose from his seat.

"Wait, Anthony..." the President stopped him from leaving, "you are granted immunity from prosecution. Now what are you offering?"

---

18 McDonald v. Chicago, 561 U.S. 742 (2010): US Supreme Court decision that found the right of an individual to "keep and bear arms" as protected under the Second Amendment is incorporated by the Due Process Clause of the Fourteenth Amendment against the states. The decision cleared up any uncertainty regarding the inalienable right of every man, woman, and post child, to become weaponized—all local wisdom on the subject is null and void.

"Alamán's head." Bochinni smiled. "I will leave a hole in our security big enough to squeeze your team through. Once you have established an offensive position, hit Downtown with everything you can. I'll take it from there. When Alamán is eliminated, I will unilaterally declare hostilities over and CAS will fall into line. I need three weeks."

Both heads-of-State smiled. "We have a deal." President Patterson replied.

"There's one more thing. My Deputy Chief needs to disappear."

"We can take care of him."

Bochinni stood and buttoned his suit jacket, "Be certain that you do. He is dangerous."

The Secretary of the Interior waited until Anthony had left the room. "We can't trust him."

"I know, but he wants Alamán dead. It's personal. We can trust revenge."

≈

The Siege of Los Angeles

By the light of a half moon, carefully placed and remotely detonated explosives pulled down the power grid and blanketed the Los Angeles basin in darkness. Crews dispatched to assess the damage reported complete decimation. "The substations are just gone. It'll take weeks to get power back to this district."

Bochinni walked into Alamán's office and paused at the doorway. His Deputy Chief and Alamán were speaking softly next to the windows. He could see the Deputy Chief's lips and was able to decipher *inside job.*

Bochinni coughed loudly and entered the office.

Alamán smiled, "Ah, Anthony, good of you to join us."

"The most optimistic reports have us down in most of the city for several weeks. Eight substations were wired with C4 and detonated from elsewhere. We are scouring the power companies' employees for potential saboteurs. This was definitely not pulled off by the Fed."

“Agreed Anthony. But you think it was employees? Seems like a stretch.”

“Maybe they were Fed sympathizers. We’ll find out, mark my words.”

“It’s not like the Mayor is popular around town.” The Deputy Chief smirked.

Bochinni looked relieved. “That is also true.”

Alamán turned to face the window. “I want every person involved punished publicly.”

“Yes sir.” Bochinni bowed his head and left the office.

The Deputy Chief warned in a hushed tone, “Watch him carefully. He knows who did this.”

Early that Saturday morning, twelve masked men fell from the sky. Each expertly landed in turn on the former City Walk atop Universal Studios in North Hollywood. They packed one another’s parachutes and checked the perimeter with rifles raised.

One of the masked men spotted a couple of drunks when his flashlight scanned a tight alleyway. He called out to the team that he had targets and approached the men.

The drunks threw their hands up, laughing.

“Ay, we give up man. We’re peaceful.”

“Get on the ground, now!” One of the masked men screamed while the other motioned toward the ground with his rifle.

“Oh shit, okay, okay,” the drunk tried with effort to get on his stomach.

The other drunk teetered a bit. “I fought in the Egyptian Conflict; these clowns are fakes. A real soldier would be wearing the Federal Flag, not...whatever that symbol is.” The drunk attempted to focus on the insignia adorning the masked man’s breast pocket. “In fact, I should beat their dis’pectful asses.”

The drunk lunged and the masked man dropped him with a bullet to the forehead.

“We have to kill you too. No offense.”

“No, no, I won’t say anything.”

“I have to be certain.” Another clean shot to the second drunk’s forehead.

The masked men made their way down the eastern slope of Universal Studios, and followed Lake Hollywood Drive to the dusty, winding trails leading to Griffith Observatory. When they reached the summit, the masked men established a perimeter and watched the observatory for movement. The city below was blackened, and Downtown Los Angeles shined like a fallen star in the vast night.

Headlights rounded a corner below the summit and the masked men took cover.

A black SUV entered the observatory parking lot and killed its lights. The vehicle came to a slow stop in the center of the lot. The doors opened and private security surrounded the car.

Anthony Bochinni stepped from the black SUV. “I thought these morons were supposed to be here already. I can’t just stand around waiting. I shouldn’t even be here. I can’t believe Patterson...”

A gloved hand covered Anthony Bochinni’s mouth and he drifted to sleep.

When he woke, he was in a vacant aircraft hangar and his security team was laid out on their backs. “What the fuck happened?”

Bochinni’s head of security groaned, “I think they drugged us.”

“Of course they drugged us, idiot.”

“They must have arrived before we did. They got the drop on us, boss. It won’t happen next time.

Bochinni pulled a small tracking device from his jacket pocket, left by the masked men.

He smiled, “There won’t be a next time. It has begun.”

The masked men secured an equipment drop zone at Griffith Observatory. With no air force to repel the deliveries, Alamán watched as massive canons began to line the hills, pointed toward Hollywood and Downtown.

Artillery shells rained down on the Great Gardens, and the Chinatown Annex day and night, for three weeks. The low rain clouds provided the illusion of protection, but at any moment death could drop through the billowing white to maim and terrorize.

Anthony Bochinni repeated himself, "Alamán, please listen to me."

"It doesn't make sense."

"It's only a matter of time. They took Dodger Stadium late last night. They have the high ground, we have nowhere to hide."

"Why aren't they hitting us directly? Why are they pummeling the Great Gardens?"

"That's my point your honor, we need to get you out of here before they decide to start."

"It's like they are warning shots, or a diversion. Something's not right..." The grey downpour outside turned the Mayor's windows into mirrors. Alamán watched Anthony Bochinni between the raindrops. "Where's your Deputy Chief?"

"I'm not his keeper."

"You're supposed to be."

An immense explosion just beyond the DTLA wall shook the office windows. A plume of orange fire lit up the morning clouds. Alamán turned to Anthony and his elite guard. "Let's go."

The six-member guard detail ushered Alamán and Bochinni through the immense tunnel system beneath Los Angeles. The concrete hallways grew more narrow as they continued. The forward guards unlocked a heavy metal door and rushed the two politicians into an empty room.

"Wait a second," Alamán pulled a small revolver from his jacket and shot the guard locking the door.

The rest of the detail pulled the mayor to the ground and disarmed him while Bochinni paced back and forth.

Alamán sneered. "You're a dead man, Anthony."

"You smug fuck. You're in no position to level threats."

"I am your lord and master."

"Oh, so deluded." Anthony shook his head. "You never deserved to run the show. It was always me, Escalada."

"Did your Deputy Chief put you up to this?"

"No, the Deputy Chief will be dealt with shortly. He has a little tracker in his hat band that will lead the Feds to his doorstep. I won't get to witness his death because I insisted on being present for your execution."

Alamán struggled mightily as a guard pulled his head back, exposing his neck.

"You got too greedy and forgot how you got here, and who got you here. You never should have crossed me." Anthony blew his boss a kiss.

The guard carved a canyon in Alamán's throat with a large hunting knife. The security detail released him as he convulsed. Escalada Alamán III died gasping and slipping around in his own blood.

During Bochinni's betrayal, a black Apache helicopter fired a missile into the building where the Deputy Chief was headquartered. No bodies were found among the rubble and the President moved rapidly to keep the strike quiet. The Deputy Chief would be allowed to fall into obscurity. "Good riddance, someone did us a favor," he was rumored to say in later unauthorized biographies.

The smoke began to clear on The Great Western Calamity[19] and once again, centralization had won the day.

‡

IX

9/2/2010

Met a man from Italy last night named Pablo. Ireland has thus far refused to honor his Italian credentials as a Physical Therapist. He has been living in the hostel and searching for administrative work. I cannot help but feel for him, he must return to Italia in the morning.

Ireland and the rest of Europe are facing the repercussions of our economic collapse. Dublin is flush with

19 Iconography p. 26, The Great Western Calamity

both Irish and foreigner in search of a job...any job. Feels a lot like home...

Dublin has rain forecast the entire time I'll be in London. It's been three days since the heavens lowered and bathed the soiled streets. My demeanor is degrading; the smallest provocations threaten to set me off into a negative spiral. I am restless, yet I bristle at breaking my routines.

Ian sent an address to help ease the solitude: 79 Queen St Dublin 7 - Dice Bar. Harper swears by it, when she was in Dublin, Dice Bar was her spot. Ian wrote. Younger crowd, but not Temple Bar douche-baggery. Used to be rockabilly-ish, writers and musicians.

Tantalizing, but I have reservations.

Midnight, last call on the South side of the Liffey -

I felt a dark and indescribable need tonight. I wound through offices of state and ancient Viking cathedrals with reinforced castle walls. The carefully placed lights on the edges of the immense monuments shone up in arranged illumination; history behind a glass case, preserved but still misunderstood; still lacking the essential confession of violence and control; these accouterments of power are treated as symbolic of our civilization when they are proof of our barbarity.

I crossed the Liffey with one eye on the inky night sky. I penetrated farther west and the stroll along Inns-to-Arran Quay was pleasant in the cool air. The Supreme Court of Ireland loomed bureaucratically in the dim municipal light.

The Dice Bar looked a little crowded and I hesitated as I finished my smoke. I heard dance music coming from inside. According to the flyer taped to the door, the DJ would be there all evening. The bar itself was grand, a proper grungy bar in the storefront of a two-story

> *brick building. The bartenders both reminded me of the bored intellectuals slinging drinks in downtown LA from time to time.*
>
> *I finished my pint, gathered my belongings, and walked back into the night.*
>
> *I pressed back east dangling perilously between desperation for a way to fill the time and a desperation to cherish and preserve each moment I had left. The trek had been a mistake, my 4km jaunt would cost me precious hours at J.J.'s, but the fact that I felt that way drove me mad. What was there to be angry or disappointed about? Life unfolds as we live it, we do not live it as it unfolds.*
>
> *I felt divergent, this new life I had fleshed out in a few weeks' time was coming to an end, but in moments like these I'd have gladly boarded a plane for the United States. I took the Quay all the way back to Eustace and crossed the Liffey on a mission to wile the night away in quiet comfort. I had failed myself; it had been my own rigidity and desperation that had forced me to quell my nightly insomnia in silence.*
>
> *The night became peaceful, cathartic. My mind was racing with ideas and disgruntled diatribes, I want the universe to suddenly open once I step foot on English soil. Though I feel confident that Stasia and Dahvit will be impeccable hosts, I crave isolation.*

It was a frigid night—the night that the dreams began.

‡

Victor sat up in the early morning. A long, detailed dream ran like a pieced together film in his mind.

9/3/10

Sitting in the common area of three buildings, a cross between a Westside court and a sleepy Georgia compound. A rainstorm is coming, dark sky, dusk, the air chills rapidly. Lightning strikes cause a small fire in a tree, but it is rapidly put out. Then it begins to happen over and over. Small, manageable fires are started in two of the homes, one being mine. A man I do not know, the tenant of the third building rushes into my place. He begs me to come with him. The fire in his home is near the microwave and he is scared. I try to put the melting wires out as his family stands looking on from the dining room. The home is warm and cramped with furniture and rugs. The walls are covered in their entirety by icons of Catholic dogma, predominantly Thaddeus. The fire proves more difficult to put out than the original fires and I am afraid I will not succeed. I run to my home (which I never see) and return with a fire extinguisher. I have difficulty pulling the pin and my mind is awash in adrenaline. It finally gives and I empty the extinguisher onto the flames. I am taken aback; the extinguisher is powder, not foam. The fire goes out and the family encircles me.

The skies suddenly gush, and floodwaters climb my legs in the courtyard. Immense walls rise from the earth into the sky, encircling the apartment complex. The walls seem to slow the flooding but amid the peace there is an immense explosion and a blinding flash of light. Once the hum in my ears and the brightness recede, I am standing in a vast wasteland. A child pushes her little hand through the ashes of her charred family and walks slowly toward me pleading. I realize I am holding bread; I break it and hold out a piece for her.

§

XXVIII

When Kyrios Atropos died Erlyst no longer had the comfort of her revenge to cling to. His heart failed, no big surprise, though she had hoped it would be a slower, more painful death. The authorities never suspected Erlyst, for that she was thankful. Lawrence E. Robertson, however—owing to his intimate, if limited, knowledge of Mr. Atropos' activities—found the circumstances of Mr. Atropos' death very suspicious.

"Erlyst, I have to speak to you." Lawrence's voice was muffled.

"Are you on a payphone? Christ Lawrence..."

"Yes, it's the only way to reach you privately."

"Well then, carry on..."

"Not on the phone. I'm landing in three hours."

"Okay...is everything alright?"

Lawrence had already hung up. Erlyst's wall console faded back into a looping view of a spring meadow. It reminded her of home.

When Lawrence was shown into her room, Erlyst was asleep.

"That will be all." Lawrence dismissed the butler who bowed slightly and retreated from the room—careful to leave the door open.

Lawrence stood for a moment admiring Erlyst's smooth skin. Though she'd soon be midway through her forty-second year, Erlyst was as youthful, stunning, and poised as she had been when she first arrived in New York. A long streak of grey now adorned her temple, waving amongst her auburn tresses.

Lawrence harbored closeted desires: dark and humiliating fantasies, of Erlyst succumbing to mad lust and becoming his hobbled, ignorant foot servant...

"Erlyst. Sweet Erlyst, please wake up." Lawrence placed his hand on hers.

Erlyst's soft emerald eyes parted, she could scarcely make out the face of the child whose small, soft hand had driven away her nightmare. When the mid morning's bright background receded, she saw Lawrence. His tiny brown eyes were pinned shut in ecstasy as he held her flesh against his.

Erlyst convulsed.

§

"If you touch me again Lawrence, I'll have you disposed of. The butler is obviously fucking fired."

Erlyst rose from bed and put on a robe.

"Your husband's body was discovered by FBI agents who had been tailing him for three months."

Erlyst paused. "That's a very heavy intro Lawrence. Can we walk back a bit?"

"Yes. Kyrios' death always seemed odd to me."

"You've mentioned that. Really Lawrence, what's so mysterious?"

"He was supposed to be somewhere else."

"He routinely lied about where he would be. I can't say I've heard anything *mysterious* yet." Erlyst opened the wide doors to her armoire and pulled a dress from within. "You have five more minutes to get to the point Lawrence, then I'm banishing you."

"Kyrios was expected at a meeting of great import. Not just to the Atropos Family, but to the continued relations of the United States and several Southeast Asian nations. The effects of his absence were soon felt worldwide.

"Kyrios became more and more unpredictable with age. You, of all people know that."

"Yes, he had always been *mad*, but that's the point. Something else was happening. That's why I did some digging on my own. I found someone who was willing to talk, and now I know why it was so expensive."

"Two minutes."

"Do you recognize this woman?" Lawrence produced a photograph from a manila folder. Erlyst was repulsed by Lawrence's barely subdued fascination.

"Can't say that I do. Why?"

"She was in the room with Kyrios when he died."

Erlyst's eyes lowered.

"Do you know these women?"

Erlyst took the photographs from his hand, "No."

"Kyrios was responsible for their disappearances."

"Responsible?"

"The woman they found with Kyrios had been held captive for some time. Kyrios was hurting her all along. They think she died last month, but he kept her as a trophy, or perhaps because he had not intended to kill her. He made mistakes with these other women, mistakes that led the FBI to that hotel room. They say he devolved, that whatever was keeping him together fell apart. He was a monster."

"You know what he was, you know why he brought me here."

"We don't speak of that Erlyst."

"He killed that boy the night we met..."

"And you watched him do it. Neither of us can play the victim."

Erlyst remained silent, stoic.

The FBI had conducted and concluded the investigation without press leaks or public question at the request of the Departments of Justice, Commerce, and Treasury. The horrors perpetrated by Kyrios Atropos were buried in the civil and criminal paperwork of New York City forever.

How many times had Erlyst hesitated? How many times, had she failed to pick up the phone? Would she have said anything if she knew how far he had gone? She watched the City coming to life from her window and long after Lawrence had left, she still could not decide.

§

Winter ~ 2006

Thalia Atropos lost her way along Hollywood Boulevard. Her young high school eyes were wide with admiration, and every wavy-haired actor or producer she met pulled her strings while she danced merrily into depravity. Erlyst retreated into her own silent sorrow. Her book-laden perch overlooking Pershing Square kept her in solitary confinement. The world outside was pain and being bound in space was its own agony.

A pair of LAPD lieutenants were escorted into Erlyst's sitting room.

"Mrs. Atropos, we're sorry to interrupt you so late in the evening. We have your daughter in custody, and we need to verify her age."

§

"Wait, what's going on, what has she done?"

"Ma'am, please, how old is your daughter?"

"Seventeen."

The cops both sighed and looked at the ground. "Mrs. Atropos," The higher-ranking lieutenant broke the silence, "your daughter is in trouble. She's known up and down the Sunset Strip as the welcoming committee for touring musicians."

"How welcoming is she?" Erlyst asked, though she dreaded the answer.

"Very. We came here with the intention of leaving her in your care. But I must insist that she be watched over," the officer pleaded.

"You have my word," Erlyst answered, distracted. She was imagining a cell in a high tower for her only daughter.

"Okay, go get her out of the car." The lieutenant waved his colleague off. "Mrs. Atropos, your daughter is in trouble."

"You said that," Erlyst responded as a matter of fact.

"If we hadn't been called, she would probably be dead ma'am."

"Where was she?"

"Backstage at the Hollywood Bowl. She was entertaining a new Swedish rock group. The band's lawyers insist that the members were unaware that she had lost consciousness during intercourse." The officer paused, "So they continued for an estimated half-hour after she'd succumbed to an overdose. She's very lucky she didn't..."

The partner arrived with Thalia; she was wearing hospital scrubs and her olive skin was pale.

Erlyst embraced her exhausted child and walked her into the foyer.

The police shut the door behind them and returned to the street below.

"We're gonna pick that one up dead next time" the officer said to his partner as they drove off.

Erlyst sent Thalia to a rehabilitation facility in the newly branded NoHo Arts District. Thalia did her time quietly and remained coherent, but she replaced her thirst for booze and heroin with the soothing seas of legal narcotic relaxants. The treatment center was awash in prescription pills and most wandering its halls did so in a doctor ordained, voluntary haze.

Rein Sarbays slipped into the conjugal room as the inmates were being shuffled in one by one. Rein saw Thalia sitting alone.

"I'm Rein."

"I couldn't possibly care less."

"Come on, that's no way to be. I brought you something."

"What?" Thalia's drug alarms went off. "Tell me."

"Easy there, cowgirl. What's your name?"

"Thalia." She tapped her fingers impatiently.

"Here, tenacious Thalia."

Thalia could tell his smile got more charming as the oxycodone kicked in.

"Come on over and give me a hug Thalia. I feel like we're going to be close."

Rein was in and out of the facility and kept Thalia on a short enough leash to inspire puppy love. Thalia's neuro-receptors were deeply infatuated, and though Rein never inspired lust, she trembled while he was away, and that was good enough.

When Thalia's ninety days had expired, Erlyst returned to the dismal, prison-like structure to collect her daughter. They had barely spoken to one another while she was in residence. In Erlyst's care, Thalia made no attempt to keep up appearances and Erlyst capitulated through egotistical denial. Within a few weeks Thalia was sneaking up to the rooftop garden to take calls from Rein.

He loves me.

She had said.

He is the only person who understands me.

She had also said.

I will spend my life with him.

She had finally concluded.

§

Autumn ~ 2012

Erlyst stood before a wide mirror set in the center door of her armoire. Fifty years had made their various cruel marks on her body, yet she suffered less than she had anticipated. She'd been spared breastfeeding; Thalia refused, and Clio was never permitted a choice. Her hips had widened optimistically in motherhood and she'd never looked as fetching in a tight gown. She could still see faint reminders of her youth in the tiny freckles dancing along her nose, but her eyes had hardened. She was a wealthy east coast blueblood now—more Kennebunkport than Myrtle Beach. The small grey vein of hair that began near her temple had metastasized; her long Lake curls now cascaded entirely in lustrous silver.

Though Erlyst had proudly earned several striae, her skin had not distended. Her aversion to *too much* sun had spared her maladies of the flesh, but as her dermis thinned to rice paper, Erlyst became ghostly.

She slowly fastened her garter to her stockings and ran her finger down the pre-War silk. She could still play the seductress; that was not the problem. What becomes of an old seductress whose audience dies? Erlyst had become her own master, yet, she remained everyone's plaything.

Erlyst opened the wide armoire door and retrieved a pristine Gilbert Adrian wool suit with severe lapels. The suit was a muted teal, almost slate, a unique and dignified color. Every stitch was perfect, hand tailored to her body.

It would be easy to blame Thalia: for drowning herself in misery, for breaking Erlyst's heart and forcing Erlyst to break hers. It would be far easier to blame Kyrios for his cruelty and violence, but Erlyst had never been a victim.

And now, beyond the security of pity, she intended to finally wrest control over her life. As the world ebbed and flowed, Erlyst would rise and fall no more. She mindlessly ran her fingers over the corners of her Tiffany writing desk. If it were possible to be nostalgic in death, she knew she would miss this sanctuary.

But think of everything else you'll miss.
Nothing, Kyrios. There is nothing to mourn.
You'll miss me.
Erlyst did not answer.
You cannot live without me, Erlyst.
That's what I'm afraid of.

Erlyst walked along Sixth Street to catch a final glimpse of the Central Library. She swam into the romantic chaos Downtown was becoming and resigned to take her last breath among the young and alive. She stepped below ground at the 7th St. Metro subway entrance, leaving the black daytime clouds and city above.

Erlyst did not believe in an afterlife, and somehow that had always made this life all the more remarkable.

Peace & Prosperity Through Entertainment

≈

LXX

Summer ~ 2036

The former American Empire was an isolated shell. Indigenous peoples and foreign governments seized abandoned US fortresses all over the world. High-tech equipment and technology became the purview of street-rat and Lord alike—a carnal Christmas with an American Reaper driving its sleigh over the horizon. America licked its wounds as it had watched its television heroes lick theirs. While the frail Eagle limped and fell prey to disease, the rest of the world's economic giants picked at her carcass, feeding on the starving, yet addicted consumers within. Like the vernal equinox in a calm meadow, life was beginning to slowly open—fragile petals closed for so long to the chaos, spreading and reaching toward a sun no longer possessed by Western gluttony.

The American Judicial and Legislative Branches were mired in apathy and their own brand of unflinching corruption. The Unitary Executive [20] continued the business of government while all else sat in paralysis, happy to be relieved of duty, free to give endless press conferences and fundraising speeches.

Consolidation of wealth became viewed as a saving grace as politicians clasped hands with corporate admirals and injected

20 The Vesting Clause of Article II in the US Constitution provides, "The executive Power [of the United States] shall be vested in a President of the United States of America." Proponents of the unitary executive theory argue that this creates a hierarchical, unified executive branch under the direct control of Chief Executive. The general principle that the President controls the entire executive branch was originally innocuous, but extreme interpretations claim that neither Congress nor the federal courts can tell the President what to do or how to do it, particularly regarding national security matters.

manufactured capital into the economy to maintain a consumer edge.

Nothing matters more, the Chief Executive Administrations insisted. Like *weapons of mass destruction* or banks *too big to fail* the lie was big enough to cow the skeptics and isolate dissent. The American Dream was laid bare for all to see—it was never about ambition or ingenuity; it was about lust. The American Aristocracy created demand by living beyond most persons' means and always insisting that in *America, ANYone can achieve what I have if they work hard enough*.

The true Aristocracy was born into wealth, had been raised to maintain it, defend it, and to pass it to the next generation unsoiled by peasant hands. It was a holy crusade to billionaire and millionaire alike. They shrieked like wounded hyenas when asked to consider true charity or mercy. The middle class were properly and thoroughly convinced that they had more in common with their masters than the masses below them who wallowed in filth and crime.

All anti-social activities were deigned anti-*consumer* rights or anti-*consumer* freedoms. The nation *was* the consumer and its people were the trapped, sick, cells of a yearning, addicted organism. With no eyes to see, no hands, feet, nor tentacles to pull its feast to its gaping maw, the organism began to slowly wither. The top-down mythology that *to consume is to transcend* began to unravel again.

Executive Patterson stepped down at the conclusion of the Great Western Calamity and retired from public life as a concession to the defeated CAS. The Federal government allowed the CAS leadership to place a candidate in running for Chief Unitary Executive—sealing the deal. Substance and moral character (or a sincere health evaluation) should have kept Anthony Bochinni out of office, but invisible hands in the Federal government put him in position. It was rumored, but never confirmed, that Bochinni had clamored to deliver Judas' kiss to Alamán's inner circle.

“Anthony. You have to read this.” Vice Executive James Calhoun entered the office.

"What is it, James?" Executive Bochinni sat back in his chair while a photographer for a glossy, corporate-sponsored Beltway website snapped official documentary footage.

"Can we ditch the cameraman for a moment?" the Vice Executive asked earnestly.

"No." Bochinni took the file from his Vice Executive and turned to the windows of the no-longer-Oval Office. He positioned himself in the waning afternoon sun and parted the curtains looking philosophically out at the White House grounds, now safely encased behind thirty-foot-high blast walls and a dense phalanx of perimeter guards. The official photographs would later carry the State Department-authored caption: *With the truth about evil in one hand and the fate of the nation resting on his shoulders, Executive Bochinni faced the coming darkness with valor and unerring strength.*

"Good stuff Mr. Executive," the cameraman fawned.

"Thank you. Now leave us, I'll call for you later."

The cameraman collected his gear and bade the gentlemen farewell.

"This had better be important, James," Executive Bochinni spat impatiently.

The Vice Executive knew the significance of his next few sentences. He took the long route around the couch before sitting down and relighting his cigar with a box of wooden matches—striking outward as a gentleman should. "An economics professor from Yale has proposed an interesting solution to our predicament." The Vice Executive answered.

"Do tell."

"In layman's terms, Professor Dubh argues that we can preserve a consumer-based model without resorting to industrialism and isolation."

"We have to start making things again, James. You know it, I know it, and Congress knows it. We can't afford to import, and we have nothing to offer for export."

"He argues that the only problem we have to solve is de-capitalizing products shipped to the US."

"I thought you were giving this to me in layman's terms." Bochinni sniffed.

"We need to have our products *donated*."

"Well, christ on a crutch James, I'll call Santa Claus and have him get to work on it, after all he owes us one..."

"I'm being serious, sir. I'd like to talk to him and see how he would implement such an undertaking. I am prepared to go to Yale with a Senate commission to speak with Professor Dubh."

"Take your nerd-commission to see this professor, but if any hint of this hits the internet you're a dead man."

Vice Executive James Calhoun set up camp in New Haven and extended an audience with the United States government to Professor Auguste Dubh. For eleven months the team met behind closed doors. Dubh had organized the ideas behind his philosophical and fictional texts into a prototype society model. This grouping of social imperatives and structures were the only strong, innovative chance the Vice Executive could see for the barely United States.

≈

Vice Executive Calhoun poured a drink and called Professor Dubh.

"Professor? Yes, it's James. Look, we need to talk."

"Go for it, I'm expecting a call in twenty minutes."

"Offer your sincere apologies and re-schedule."

"It's with Beijing, Mr. Vice Executive..."

"Auguste, I need you on a plane to Irvine immediately. I'll meet you there as soon as possible."

Calhoun entered the lobby of a Hilton near John Wayne Airport and shook hands with the Professor.

"Mr. Vice Executive, it's always a pleasure." The Professor was a very unassuming man, his neat grey suit sat comfortably on his body, and his round-framed glasses glistened in the cast mid-day light.

"Professor, thank you for not hesitating. Come with me." The men moved to a large black car waiting outside the service entrance to the hotel.

The car parked in front of a non-descript home deep in the tedium of suburban Irvine and the men entered without speaking. Once seated in the staged living room, The Vice Executive leaned in urgently.

“We have a situation Professor. Bochinni is pulling the plug on the project.”

“We expected this; it's time to move into an alternative phase of the plan.”

“Alternative? I didn't expect this, who expected this... “

“Yes, alternative. We must eliminate Bochinni and you must implement our plan.”

“I can't believe you are suggesting we kill the Chief Executive.” Calhoun retreated.

“Come now, elimination can mean many things. It'd be much easier to put him in a room with a young girl and have her press charges. By the time he is exonerated we will be testing social groups nationwide.”

“That sounds like a coup.”

“You act for the good of the American people. Anthony Bochinni wants to doom our country to pre-corporate industrial servitude. Just like Stalin, just like King George, just like his old boss Alamán.”

“This conversation makes me extremely nervous.” Calhoun began wringing his hands and pacing the floor. “We're talking about overthrowing the government.” At his core, James played in gentleman’s politics, *sedition* was still a naughty word.

“Let's say...” the Professor began, “we do what you say and close up shop. You know the position we are in now that the world's power centers are in the far-East. We have already sold this idea to the A-PF.[21] If we are not able to begin test-groups within the calendar year we will be in serious breach of faith. It will be an enormous embarrassment for our few remaining allies and the United States will be permanently crippled. Bochinni cannot repel an economic lifeboat from the Federation. We have no other... “

“What about talking to Bochinni, reasoning with him? He's not an idiot.” The Vice Executive pleaded.

“Talk to Bochinni? About how he gains? About how his angle is represented? You are this country's savior in the new

21 The Asian-Pacific Federation, (A-PF) comprised of three initial countries—China, Japan, and Indonesia—had expanded to include India, Pakistan, and large swathes of former USSR satellite states: the 'Stans, southern Ukraine, and the infamous Balkans. The A-PF developed deep ties with South American trade organizations and the Corporation of Central Caribbean United National Trade.

century. Bochinni cannot comprehend our work; he cannot see that we are creating a real future for our people. He is content to strip-mine the present, future generations be damned. Do not make this mistake James. With our help the once-United States can again hold her head high on the world stage."

"The world stage? You sound like you're selling something." James muttered.

"We can bring our people into the light James, by force, if necessary. I have a plan..."

On a warm January day in Hiroshima, elite police forces from all eight Japanese Chihō surrounded and locked down the Forest Hills Garden Hotel. As Executive Anthony Bochinni stirred an antacid powder into his green tea, several loud pops interrupted a meeting of private security firms from the US, Japan, and India.

Bochinni motioned for his Secret Service agents to investigate. The luxury suite's door exploded, and armored police smashed the large windows looking out over the sea. Before Bochinni's teacup hit the floor, his personal guard had all taken a single bullet in the neck.

Bochinni stood slowly and buttoned his suit jacket. "I'm not sure if you know how bad you just fucked up. I'm the Chief Executive of the United..."

An armored police officer struck Bochinni with the butt of his rifle and Anthony collapsed to the ground.

Okinawa Prefectural Police Chief Kishimoto approached the crumbled American. "Anthony. I am here to arrest you for disgracing one of our citizens. A child. Do you understand?"

"Fuck you."

"I believe you have that backward Anthony."

The armored police pulled Bochinni to his feet and into custody.

Executive Anthony Bochinni's arrest was unprecedented in United States history and the American media immediately revived post-War nuclear rhetoric: Japan should be *turned to glass*; Japan had *forgotten WWII.*

It was nauseating in extremis and the world looked on as the tiny American Dachshund pathetically barked orders at the Mastodon before it. Traditional Western allies of the United States spoke softly of their *regret*, and their *concern*, but none dared challenge Tokyo or the Asian-Pacific Federation.

The Japanese Prime Minister spoke from Tokyo on live international Receiver channels: "On Thursday morning US Chief Executive Anthony Bochinni was placed under State custody. He was questioned regarding the rape and murder of a female minor in Okinawa. At present we are in communication with the State Department of the United States.

"There will be no extradition; Mr. Bochinni has viciously violated one of our citizens. I will not be another official, in a long history of officials, who pardons such behavior based on fealty to a depraved foreign power. Mr. Bochinni will be arraigned in seventy-two hours and will stand trial by week's end, in accordance with his rights on Japanese soil."

According to court documents, the Executive and some friends decided to purchase an adolescent: drugged, caged, and delivered to an enormous luxury suite in Nagasaki. Anthony had a thing for role-playing—girl in a cage, twenty-one men in uniform, and a yearning for the days when war was a *good thing*—he could barely contain himself.

The Department of Justice swore up and down that even though sex with Bochinni may resemble rape, he couldn't get it up unless it was consensual.[22] The Japanese government giggled and refused to negotiate. The Justice Department wrote voluminous and finally humble requests to review the documented evidence. Japanese officials would at times appear

22 This Dadaist technique of argumentation was immortalized by the Memorandum RE: Standards of Conduct for Interrogation under 18 U.S.C. sections 2340-2340A, authored in 2002 by then-Deputy Assistant Attorney General of the United States John Yoo and signed by then-Assistant Attorney General Jay Bybee. "...We further conclude that certain acts may be cruel, inhuman, or degrading, but still not produce pain and suffering of the requisite intensity to fall within Section 2340A's proscription against torture. We conclude that the treaty's text prohibits only the most extreme acts by reserving criminal penalties solely for torture and declining to require such penalties for "cruel, inhuman, or degrading treatment or punishment." This confirms our view that the criminal statute penalizes only the most egregious conduct. Executive branch interpretations and representations to the Senate at the time of ratification further confirm that the treaty was intended to reach only the most extreme conduct."

on international programming and openly mock them, but primarily the requests were read, distributed, torn apart, and ignored. The Department of Justice wailed to every International court that would listen, but none felt compelled to help the vast nest of vultures.

The United States government held its breath, and the US media was ordered to erase the scandal from American minds. There was no functioning nuclear arsenal to speak of, no longer a standing army on every continent, and no far-reaching forward bases from which to launch attacks. The hulking State was a ghastly beast gushing life's blood from fetid wounds, but it was the creature's rank voice, it's seething, writhing hatred for the truth that made the world look away—first in detached embarrassment, and finally in disgust.

Anthony Bochinni was executed unceremoniously on March 24th.

≈

Upon officially assuming the office of the Chief Executive, James Calhoun offered his condolences to Anthony's "friends, family, and the American people. Let me also take this opportunity to offer my condolences to a fallen idea...

"The United States of America has slowly been forced into the fissures of the global stage by greed. From this day forward, we will not reward cowardice and vice. We will no longer honor the dishonorable or allow them to shape the lives of this great nation's citizens. For too long, we have been kept mute in the face of overwhelming power. We will throw open the shutters and let the light shine on America once again."

Though he had said nothing of substance, Executive Calhoun had charged a lethargic nation. James was thirty-six years of age when he assumed the office of the Chief Executive; his handsome looks were uninterrupted by corruption.

He appointed an unknown human rights activist as Vice Executive and summarily dismissed the existing Executive Cabinet. Within ninety days, speaking from Jakarta, Calhoun announced a trade pact with the Asian-Pacific Federation.

American congresspersons and talk show hosts issued calls for Calhoun's head. He was called a traitor; he was alleged to be plotting to turn the US into China's sweatshop.

For two and one-half years Calhoun's administration rebuilt America's façade, even insisting that the media refer to him as the *President*. As Calhoun's first term in office came to a close, the A-PF began launching large shipments of goods to US docks. Hundreds of thousands of harbor, transport, and logistics employees were put immediately to work. As the first video game consoles arrived from Japan, Executive Calhoun returned to American receiver screens.

“My fellow Americans, we have seen dark days. As Americans have been reminded recently, a hard days' work for hard earned pay is what makes this nation great. Soon, we will be putting *everyone back to work*!” Calhoun paused to let the applause die down.

“In the next few months, I will be introducing the Peace and Prosperity Through Entertainment act to Congress. With this historic legislation, we will reclaim one of America's most proud industries and bring American Entertainment back to the world. I ask you to join with me and usher in a truly *American* century.”

Reports of enormous test groups from every state in the Union splashed across American receiver screens. Entire neighborhoods were being filmed day and night and then edited for content. These neighborhood programs were then packaged and marketed internationally to test groups around the world. Products from the member-nations of the A-PF were featured in the daily lives of on-screen *families* as the premier products that every American held near and dear. Within the first year of community-testing, nations spanning the globe began clamoring for access to these *US-Entertainments*.

The corporate heads of Communication—what was left of it—began disseminating the message. The United States was offering its people the opportunity to live the American Dream. Certainly not the Dream as mythologized in the twentieth century, but the true and heartfelt Dream of all Americans: to do nothing and have everything.

≈

Americans signed up in droves, pouring from every corner of the social and economic landscape to be a part of the True American Dream. Massive census-level casting calls took place at gutted, abandoned sports arenas and concert halls.[23]

Once cast, a citizen's life became the script: the Sponsor paid for the chemicals bleaching their clothing, their hair, and their conscience. The toilet-paper in their cupboard, the cupboard's hinges and screws, the carcinogens in their veins, the alcohol numbing their beleaguered sense of dignity, even the sheets they swaddled in before falling into fitful, drugged slumber, were bought and paid for by the patron producer of State. The asphalt on the road, the petrol in the family auto, and the very blue skies above one's balding cranium, belonged to the Sponsor.

In most cases, entire communities were asked to perform as usual, to *struggle* to *earn* on-camera and relax in a perfect cocoon otherwise. By the third season, a slight majority of American citizens were either on a program or were a part of the mechanism bringing these RealCommunities™ to life.

At the close of Calhoun's second Administration, Chenguang Liu, his loyal Vice Executive, earned an unprecedented eighty-five percent of the popular vote for her campaign, effectively giving voters an extended Calhoun administration. No one living high on the PPTEa[24] dared change America’s course in the slightest. Behind the perceived prosperity, the PPTEa created a purposeful and damning

---

23 Register. Perform. Thrive. During registration, a candidate was assigned a video casting call. Personal data and a brief audition were uploaded to a massive database in Utah* to be “placed” on a show. Citizens were analyzed and “cast” into neighborhoods, given a domicile and an identity. In most cases, people were more successfully “dramatic” when kept among loved ones, but at times families were split to facilitate a market or upon request, and in rare occasions because of a promotion.

* The NSA surveillance facility created for the collection and retention of the world's internet and cell-service data fell into disuse as the US dropped from the perch of Superpower. The facility had been mostly abandoned but the new Calhoun Administration repurposed 10% of the functioning storage and effectively replaced fingerprints and Federal files for participants in the American experiment.

24 The Peace and Prosperity through Entertainment act, introduced in 2038 by President James Calhoun following Anthony Bochinni's distasteful exit from public life.

schism. Those who were deemed unworthy for casting, and those who refused to participate in the social program, were instantly disenfranchised.

The Apple Thief

‡

XII

When Victor booked his flight to London, he did so in geographical ignorance. He was to land at Luton, far away from his destination, Golder's Green. Any number of places would have been more ideal.

The airport's bus counter employees were slow with advice but quick to shut Victor down when he was misinformed. He ended up with a bus ticket to somewhere "near Golder's Green." The woman pretended to ignore Victor when he asked, *how close to Golder's Green? What should I do then?*

The large bus was stuffy, and he looked out the windows searching for serenity. The bus lurched into action and soon they were hurtling down M1 toward London. The vast and rolling countryside was beautiful and reminded him a bit of the eastern farmlands along 580 near San Francisco.

Victor had wanted to feel the same exhilaration he felt coming into Dublin, but London had already been stressful. He decided to get off the bus when they came to a crowded city street, assuming that shops and people meant payphones, cell signals, bathrooms, and food. When the bus dropped him off, Victor took a good look around and pulled out a cigarette. The street, Finchley, was choked with small automobiles and its sidewalks were invisible under pedestrian commuters and wanderers alike.

A large man in a blonde wig and a purple dress asked Victor for a cigarette. He politely handed one over and lit it for her. The violent shock of blue eye shadow against her smooth onyx skin turned her eyes into warning-beacons. She smiled and thanked him in a slow English accent. Victor watched her walk a half block to a charity bin with her battered rolling-suitcase. She propped it against the box and busied herself with something Victor could not see behind a pillar. An old woman in a headscarf, crouched low by a rugged life, walked immanently toward the suitcase.

"That's mine! Stay away from it you fucking bitch!" She hissed.

Victor was taken aback by the previously docile person screaming a warning at a hunched old woman.

The hunched woman flipped her off and waddled down the street still shouting, "Fuck you stupid bitch! Fuck you!" It felt like home to Victor. The employees in the London airport were no ruder or disinterested than the employees at LAX

"You got a fag?"

"Pardon me?" Victor asked, confused.

"Fag, fag, you got a fag?"

"Yes, hang on." Victor reached into his pocket and retrieved a cigarette for the man twitching to his right. His salt and pepper beard stubble, sullen-bouquet, and unkempt clothing gave him a vagabond aura.

"You wanna buy a book?" The man held up a copy of Tony Blair's newly minted autobiography.

"No thanks, that guy's a piece of shit." Victor sneered.

"Yes! Yes?" The man started shouting. "Fuck him, and Bush too! Fuck them all! You see, I'm an artist. They don't like that. I perform against their agenda, I am a performance artist, I've nailed myself to crosses before." Victor noticed the intense scarring on his earlobes and lips. "They can't take it, can't take someone pointing out their LIES. You see?" Victor remained cautiously silent. "You live around here?"

"No," Victor answered.

"Where you headed?"

"Golder's Green."

"Oh yeah, okay, I used to live around there."

"Oh great, how should I go about getting there? Does the tube go there?"

The man's eyes widened in horror. "No, you don't want to go down there. Confined space, if they attack, they'll attack in the tube. Gas, poison gas, nowhere to go, no way to escape." The man became agitated, and Victor regretted bringing the subject up. "You know, those bastards they took my car. Yeah, just drove right up and towed it away. Said I had parking tickets. I lived in that car, parking tickets, I don't even know what that's supposed to mean." The man started flailing his arms. "Hey, I'm staying nearby, you want to stop in? Use the toilet or something?"

"Thank you very much, I appreciate it, but not today, I need to get moving."

"Okay, come on I'll show you."

Victor decided to follow him, at least he knew where Golder's Green was...allegedly. The man suddenly darted across the busy street and leapt over a metal rail on the center island between north and southbound lanes. Victor chased him into the street as a light rain began to fall. His courage faded as he approached the rail and envisioned catching his boot and tumbling into traffic. Victor walked the island back to the light and crossed legally. The man, regretfully, was waiting for him.

"Why'd you do that?"

"If I don't make it to my friends' house alive, I lose."

"Lose what?" The man looked genuinely confused.

"Nothing. Just a figure of speech. How do I get to Golder's Green?"

"Oh, right, come on. There's the tube, don't... "

"Right, don't get on that, I got it."

"It's a shame, you need so much money just to live. People don't realize that the things we need are just waiting there for us. Waiting to help us..." The man reached into a crate of apples stacked on the sidewalk, selected one, and kept walking. "See, now I'm eating, didn't cost a thing. Paying for what you need is a sign of idiocy. See?"

While Victor appreciated his anti-consumer stance, he was not interested in spending his first night in a London jail cell with the Apple Thief.

"Okay, here." The man pointed to a large and convoluted bus map on the side of the bus stop shelter. "You want this one here. See? See? 52. See?"

"Excellent, thank you so much," Victor reached out his hand to shake the Apple Thief's, and stepped onto the bus that had just arrived. Once on the bus he started placing coins in the slot and asked the driver if he was headed to Golder's Green.

‡

"Oh no, that's 52, this bus is 56."

"Shit." Victor stepped off at the next stop. The Apple Thief was digging in a trashcan near the bus stop, so Victor slipped into the entrance of a shopping mall to wait for the man to move on. London had been treacherous compared to Dublin and Victor had only been there for six hours. After having a coffee Victor boarded the proper bus and was soon watching cramped identical homes rush past as the bus bounced north.

Golder's Green had several stops, so Victor chose one with *station* in the name hoping it was a hub and easily accessible for his hosts. He exited the bus; glad to be free and roaming again. After purchasing some cigarettes with his newly exchanged Pounds he placed coins in a payphone and called his host, Dahvit.

"Ah, brilliant," Dahvit was pleased to hear from Victor, "Stay put and we'll be there in ten minutes."

"Lovely," Victor hung up the phone and returned to Golder's Green Station to wait for Stasia and Dahvit. He enjoyed the moment of isolation to observe the neighbors and watch them walk on and off large red buses, some of fabled double-deck status. As two buses parted ways on the circular drive, Dahvit and Stasia emerged from a sea of pedestrians.

Dahvit was wearing a brilliant white 1920s equatorial fedora and carried his linen suit jacket over his shoulder. Stasia's coat tore through the grey London dusk, an inferno of red wool.

Victor waved but the couple had already seen him; precisely as he had written he would be, clad in black under a grey flat cap, holding a lit cigarette and in need of a shave.

Stasia ran up and hugged Victor warmly and welcomed him to London. Dahvit stepped forward with his hand outstretched and Victor gave him a hug as well. Adoration was immediate, the couple were luxurious brushstrokes on a canvas filled with desiccated asphalt.

The trio began discussing dinner and soon they were walking arm in arm toward an eastbound bus. While in London, Stasia and Dahvit had fallen in love and inspired one another to pursue their shared passion: writing. They had lately left a far louder life on the east side of London and begun a nicer, quieter life.

They exited the bus near a precarious curve. Once around the bend, Stasia explained in her warm, smoky voice—to Victor's ears, newly perfumed with a London lilt, "This is the Spaniard's Inn. It was once the last Inn before the gates of London. If one was caught inside the gates when they were closed, one had to stay at the inn and leave in the morning." Stasia pointed through the darkness at a large ancient wall. "It is also haunted." She smiled and wrapped her arm around Dahvit's as they crossed the Inn's threshold.

Soon, the drinks were flowing.

"What are you up to these days?" Stasia asked, adjusting her glasses.

"I am gainfully unemployed. I've been trying to stretch my severance and avoid taking the next step."

"Do you have a next step?"

Victor slowly peeled the label from his beer. "That is part of the problem. The longer I mull it over, the more creative I become with poverty."

"Does Sarah still send you projects?"

"She does, Saintly Sarah has kept my belly full on many occasions." Victor lifted his glass. "You are doing amazing things, I hear. Public relations in the literary realm, right?"

"Yes, for *Rhee* magazine." Stasia became shy.

"Very impressive."

Dahvit asked, "How do you and Stasia know one another?"

"We don't, not really." Victor answered. The beer label was free of the bottle, so he began to fold it.

"Victor rented a room from Sarah, we met once on her front porch."

"You were leaving the next day for London."

"That's true. I, of course, continued to hear stories about Sarah's writer roommate, so when I heard Victor would be visiting our fine city, I insisted he drop us a line."

Dahvit gathered up a steak knife. "So, Victor here could be an American serial killer and we wouldn't know."

"It's true," Victor smiled.

"Not if he lived with Sarah," Stasia assured him.

“Welcome then, writer ex-roommate of American Sarah.”

“Where did you end up after Sarah’s? A little birdie told me you fell in love.”

“I stayed in Hollywood until my job ended. When I got laid off, I ended up downtown.”

“Of course you did; where are you staying?”

“I’m renting a room in a warehouse off Alameda. Most weekends it’s a full-fledged punk rock venue, and lately a massive rave.”

David grimaced. “That can’t be cozy.”

“My landlord told me to buy a padlock for my door as soon as possible. I didn’t get the lock, so I figured that I’d kick back in my office to see how rowdy things got. By 10PM, four hundred people had crammed into the warehouse and hallways outside my door. I smoked cigarettes while the walls tremored for six hours.”

“Cops?” Dahvit wanted to know.

“Oh yeah. I listened as they raided a rave once. I shut my lights off and watched the shadows of feet pass under my door. The cops beat on my door several times, found it locked, and moved on. The next day there were people sleeping all over the warehouse in muddled paralysis.” It felt odd to say those words rather than write them down.

“How is LA?” Stasia had waited patiently to ask.

“Stifling. Sullen. Heartbreakingly gorgeous.”

“I miss her so.”

Victor could no longer fold the beer label. “Hey, I'll be back,” he said abruptly and stood.

“Are you going to smoke?” Stasia asked mischievously.

“I am.”

“We'll come too,” she replied.

The back area of the restaurant was a sea of platforms on varying planes, filled with chairs, benches, and tables lit by small candles. The trees were sparkling with white string lights. The distant bar and the restaurant behind bathed the darkness in a subtle and warm glow. As one cigarette became several, Victor and Dahvit began discussing typewriters—a passion of Dahvit's as well. The darkness of the space around them and the flickering light from the small table they huddled around cocooned the trio and spun them off in fractal conversation long past the death of the long day's sun.

When they arrived back at the flat Stasia curled up on a sofa, while Dahvit started a warm fire. Their fireplace was flanked by a summer's worth of chopped and carefully stacked firewood. The walls were otherwise consumed by art and bookcases. Victor always felt best when surrounded by books. The trio kept the conversation going into the tenth hour and never, upon pain of missing something epiphany-inspiring, allowed the distraction of fatigue to douse the flames.

Before ascending the stairs to bed, Saskia turned to Victor. “You never mentioned her. The girl you fell for.”

“It was a mistake. I fell, but not in love.”

The Fallen Matriarch

§
XLI

Erlyst woke in a room gilded by pristine sunrise. The darkness of the wood soothed and absorbed the bright oranges and purples spilling carelessly across her floor. An enormous down comforter devoured Erlyst's entire body. Her head (if it were attached; she had no proof) bobbed above a tumultuous ivory sea. She could feel neither her fingers nor her toes. Adrenaline leaked into her bloodstream and slowly she began, in vain, to thrash her body.

She had intended to fall before that train.

She was so close to ending the pain, ending everything, but the man stopped her. Instead, she fell head-first to the concrete. The last thing she recalled before consciousness fled, was a stranger holding her ankle. His terrified eyes apologized but his fingers were wrapped so tightly that his knuckles were white. The man forced her hand and damned her to a new day.

Erlyst wept.

A woman approached from her bedside, clad in white.

"Erlyst? Can you hear me?"

Erlyst turned her head slowly. "How long have I been here?"

"This is your home Mrs. Apropos, do you recognize it?"

"Answer the question, imbecile."

"You were brought here a few weeks ago," the nurse answered carefully. "Wait, maybe it's been a month..."

Erlyst could only muster the feeling of a few days' absence, as if the air around her sat stagnant while the rest of the world meandered about its inane business.

"Is my condition permanent?"

"The doctors think so, yes ma'am, but they can't tell what is causing your paralysis.

"They can't tell?" Erlyst paused. "Bring Lawrence to me at once and begin scheduling visitation and therapy through my personal assistant."

"Yes ma'am, anything else?" The nurse squeaked.

"Pain killers."

Erlyst had done her best to take matters into her own hands. She wandered onto that subway platform intent on passing responsibility for the empire on with no kicking or fighting. She had been robbed of that escape. Damned to her chambers high above Pershing Square, damned to its death shroud, the best terminal care a buried emperor can buy.

Lawrence E. Robertson, unfathomably high-priced Attorney at Law, walked in unannounced.

"Erlyst, it's so good to..."

"Enough Larry. What do I need to know about my absence?"

Lawrence took a seat on a low antique tête-à-tête close to Erlyst's bed. His balding head reflected the morning light and Erlyst asked that he put his hat back on.

"I'm happy to report that everything is still intact. Your order to resuscitate was fulfilled each time as indicated in your living will and all assets remain under the control of the Atropos Trust and will be turned over to you *upon your adequate recovery*. Which is today." Lawrence smiled kindly. Erlyst knew her attorney had no glimmer of kindness in his cellular composition, he had simply learned to feign empathy, as every good sociopath must.

"Thank you for keeping me alive, Lawrence."

"The police said they thought it was an attempted suicide. Is that true?"

Erlyst looked down at her broken body and sighed. "That's preposterous Lawrence. Please continue."

"Thalia is no longer in residence. She has...moved on."

"How long has it been since she visited?"

"Erlyst," Lawrence looked up from his small, clasped hands. He could see that she would not be refused. "It's been five weeks."

"She couldn't show her face around here after she fought to pull the plug?"

"You've been through a great ordeal, Erlyst." Lawrence oozed condescension.

She turned her head and stared at the ceiling. "What do you propose, moving forward?"

"I suggest that we convert your role into board-director and majority stockholder for the trust and dissolve your corporate directorship. You will retain ultimate say over Trust matters and spend your time worrying about more interesting things. Everyone adapted quickly in your absence, so it shouldn't be any trouble..." Lawrence looked up again, "Sorry, Erlyst."

"Start drawing up the paperwork and let's put this to bed."

"What are you going to do?" Lawrence looked into her eyes with a longing he had barely kept concealed while Mr. Atropos was still alive.

"I'm not sure yet." Erlyst smiled for the first time. "But that's part of the fun."

§

Erlyst tried in vain to reach Thalia; each snub was a stinging slap in the face. At the conclusion of her third week awake Erlyst's assistant entered to announce the Prodigal Daughter.

"Mother?" Thalia looked shyly around the corner.

"Come in," Erlyst intoned mechanically.

"It's been a long time. I'm sorry." The young girl approached her mother pensively.

"No need for apologies, Thalia. Come sit with me."

Thalia entered the room. She was uncomfortable in her dress, as if she had chosen something brand new for the occasion. Thalia was humiliated and she wore her shame as a thin, viscous mask. The young woman's smart, conservative attire was clearly a ruse to deter Erlyst's judgment. Yet, she failed to conceal the bruises on her arms and the tired, stimulant-carved lines marring her sweet young eyes.

"It is good to see you. Your father's businesses will provide an allowance for you. Do you understand?"

"Yes mother. I understand. What about school?"

"School? Let's be honest child, school is a very low priority in your life."

Thalia started to defend herself, and Erlyst cut her short.

"It does not matter now. You may do as you please." Erlyst's eyes grew icy.

"I understand."

Erlyst recalled Thalia's long dark locks spilling down the back of her soft white birthday dress. As a child her emerald eyes were wide with the wonder. Those days were long past.

Erlyst needed to pour a little daylight into the lives of those around her—scatter the vermin scurrying about in the dark. And the man from the subway platform? Yes, he must also be made to survive under watchful eye. The man had walked away, anonymously. Erlyst could never do that; she could never just *disappear*. Someone was always watching, looking out, even on the edge of her own death she was halted by *that man*.

As dictated on this sixteenth day of
February Two Thousand Twelve—

It is in my darkest hours that I am granted the power I lacked for these eternal days and nights. Lacked since I let that wretched shell of a man put a platinum band on my finger. I was never in love, and Kyrios was incapable.

He was the collapsed star I introduced into my galaxy to clean up and dispose of my pain. Self-destruction by the firelight of entire nations ruined, all in the name of aristocracy. No act sounds quite as poetic after it is committed; it is the anticipation that sucks beauty from the world and infuses desire with mythological power. Once these desires are satiated, they crumble, shattering as grey leaves in winter-beaten hands.

Kyrios fucked me like a whore for three years before I became his brooch. A symbol, until death do us part, of his virility. He had hoped for immortality through fatherhood, but his maniacal behavior and sour genes have guaranteed him nothing of the sort. My late husband's name bears a legacy of failure and I intend to strike the final blow.

- Erlyst Rae Atropos

Subversion

≈

LXXI

Autumn ~ 2047

Nearly six-score years after being forced to integrate their schools with Indigenous families, Big Pine, California had become the purview of the remaining Panamint band of Paiute Shoshone. Rarely did a Caucasian face pass through the tiny mountain town crushed between the Sierra Nevada and the White Mountains. Flight to the PPTEa communities had allowed numerous *out-of-the-way* locales to revert to a more or less *natural* condition.

The owner of the only bar in town sent word to the city's council that a strange woman wearing a headscarf had arrived from an outsider community in the south, close to the Los Angeles Basin.

The council deliberated:

"We should have her in a cell before she utters a word." —vengeful

"Come now, that's a little extreme, don't you think?" —naïve

"Extreme? It's like you were born yesterday." —afraid

"Gentlemen, you are both correct. We can't trust this person but locking her up will only worsen whatever problems she may bring. Let's hear her out and send her away. Agreed?" —optimistic

"Agreed." — reluctant

"Agreed." — relieved

The strange woman was called into the conference room of a storefront office. As eight men escorted her down a hall, she could see the three Council members waiting patiently at an aging table.

"Thank you for meeting with me. I am in debt to you; you have my deep respect." The woman bowed as she removed her headscarf.

"What is your name?" —suspicious

"Dr. Elizabeth Monk. I come from the Kanpotar community in Lucerne Valley."

"Why are you *here*?" —curious

"We need your help but allow me to explain. *We*[25] began by rebuilding the industrial and mechanical infrastructure in our valley. Light manufacturing was more successful than expected, and we are now able to share our training and services with similar communities as far as Pennsylvania, Illinois, and Oregon. The PPTEa has begun to turn the non-televised regions into a vast sea of disconnected islands. As a result, our ability to move back and forth between Syndicate hubs has become greatly hindered."

"Syndicate?" —wary

"We are the governing bodies for the manufacturing process, composed entirely of employees. We oversee operational decision-making along a non-hierarchal chain of responsibilities; ownership is a shared commodity. It has allowed us to address local issues first, and then plan and prepare to help address local concerns elsewhere in the non-televised regions.

"The Federal government ignored us; we certainly weren't bothering anyone under PPTEa jurisdiction, but once we achieved interstate networks, they shut down I-15 and 40. Both are now walled and heavily patrolled, and we can no longer risk approaching Bakersfield. They signed over their sovereignty last spring before the roads cleared. That's why we need your help. We need safe passage over the border into Death Valley. We mean you no harm, we are, ourselves, an outsider community trying to survive."

"We have not heard of the Kanpotar; why should we believe what you are saying?" —skeptical

---

25 The Kanpotar community formed from the large swathes of undesirables Alamán dumped in the Lucerne Valley region near Victorville, California during Il Diluvio: the homeless, addicted, and mentally unstable, lived alongside Alamán's political enemies: lawyers, physicists, actors, doctors, accountants, mechanics, and normal, critically-thinking Los Angelinos unwilling to fawn over the Emperor's invisible robes.

"You may not believe, but *we*, are willing to take that chance. We have fought valiantly against the Owners of these factories and have suffered to bring this community to life. We have the chance to help isolated groups in the non-televised regions escape starvation. We can build an alternative life for those of us on the outside."

"We've heard enough Dr. Monk. We'll adjourn and reconvene in the morning. I hope you'll be present for our response." - patriarchal

The stranger left Big Pine under the cover of night.

"Absolutely not. We don't need any trouble from outsiders that skulk off before dawn. We are secure in our isolation. We know Bishop looks over us as a buffer." —incensed

"Right, a *buffer*, against people like us!"—offended

"For all we know these *Syndicates* don't exist. Let's find out what we can before jumping to any conclusions. It's been many years since anyone has travelled beyond our borders, we do not know if what this stranger says is true." —sober

"I've heard of this, from the young people. The government is filming whole cities and making tv shows." – hopeful

"You can't be serious. The rich white people left because the economy went to shit, not because of some tv show." — rational

"But what if she is telling the truth?" —radicalized

≈

Prior plans to recreate American industry were placed back on the table by the Kanpotar community. Local, small-scale syndicates began forming to take over state and municipal functions outside of the PPTEa communities. The decrepit shell of American labor unions coughed back to life with a new goal: creating a life for the disenfranchised. Industry from sea to sea had been abandoned in the latter half of the twentieth century. That capital flight never abated, and with the PPTEa's inception, all capital for manufacturing raced offshore permanently.

Though the people outside of the RealCommunities™ were crippled by the umbrella power of the Federal government, they were allowed to flourish unless deemed a threat to PPTEa affiliates. Reprisal was swift and brutal. The instant success of the RealCommunities™ was another excuse—in a long line of excuses—to devote public resources toward wooing lobbyists and foreign corporate sponsors rather than saving lives.

Capital retained ownership of the factories and machines (or so they told themselves) but refused to sign leases with outsider syndicates. Their vain personal interests were better served keeping the factories locked up and hoping that a production company would need their facilities for the great American Show. Power was offering no concession, so the syndicates made their demand.

At times in the dead of night and at times in the brazen mid-day sun, men and women began to pry the locks from the factory doors. They put their hands to the machines, fixing what they could, and improvising where they could not. Low-level assembly-line manufacturing was possible with the manpower and limited fuel resources available. As more people came forward with expertise, the syndicates began re-engineering the existing infrastructure. The latchkey treatment of the factories by their Owners would soon come to a violent end.

In October the first battalion of war-hardened police-for-hire invaded and occupied a chain of textile mills along the Taunton River. The mercenaries took no prisoners; the unarmed workers and their families were slaughtered en masse.

The Owners of the facilities sent their emissaries to conduct press conferences on the steps of the various seized warehouses and factories.

"Today, the theft of legal private property by anarchist thugs and their brainwashed families comes to an end. Let this day stand as *day one* in the War Against..."

The news feed was cut.

"What the fuck just happened?" The cameraman peered around his lens. "We've got nothing, no live feed, no signal, no..."

The cameraman froze.

The reporter berated him, "Finish the sentence moron. What are you looking at? ...oh shit."

Hundreds of syndicalist workers emerged from the dense forest and formed an ominous wall just beyond the press conference.

"We're just here for a quick take and then we're gone." The reporter panicked.

The government emissary cowered behind the far sturdier, far earthier, cameraman and remained silent.

A slight man stepped from the trees and approached the reporter. He placed his thin, round-framed glasses back on his long Roman nose and brushed his parted hair to the side. "We are here to hold you accountable for Taunton River. We do not choose a violent struggle with you; we want only to feed our families.

"By stealing." The reporter replied.

"We will not allow you to murder and abuse innocent people with impunity. We have the means to work these factories and to make them whole again, and we have the means to take them by force if you so choose."

"Hey, start recording," the reported nudged the cameraman, "and to whom are we speaking?"

"You tend to refer to us as Outlanders."

"Yes, that is clear," the reporter sneered. "What do you call your little, *gang*?"

The thin man smiled, "We are no one. We are invisible, and we are prepared for war."

"There you have it, folks. A filthy band of trash diggers are coming for your children. The wonders never cease with *these* people."

The man walked away, and the syndicalist barrier evaporated into the tree line.

"Those hippies just got themselves into a lot of trouble..." The reporter stared into the forest hoping to catch Syndicalist eyes peering out at him.

The Corporations reared their reptilian heads and searched for victims. Disenfranchisement of the non-televised regions had created a glut of out of work foot soldiers. Superfluous security, military, and police details were absconded by private parties and positioned eternally as watchdogs in vast empty lots. The primary kills by these roving bands of bored, rudderless, mercenaries were innocent bystanders wounded by stray bullets or by unreported fire on civilians.

As the barbarity increased, the Syndicalists began to emerge from the background. Private mercenaries were lulled into comfort and began dining in small Massachusetts towns. In a single night, seventeen Private Security International personnel met their slippery end at the tip of a Syndicalist Bowie knife while *fraternizing* in Fall River. The commanders took the hint and brought all personnel within the walls of the facilities, forbidding contact with the townspeople. The soft, overpaid, guns-for-hire began to defect; it seems sleeping on a cot in a bivouac isn't a hardcore, high-maintenance mercenary's idea of a good time. The commanders were able to squeeze funding for barracks from the corporations, pleading that the final front against private property seizure by peasants was a well-oiled and well-coddled extermination machine.

From within the high walls, droves of private security teams waited for an attack. At night they lay awake, poised to hear an onslaught, to witness violence under cover of night, to have a *purpose*, but it never came. The psychological burden was debilitating: fighting a cold war that could erupt into chaos at any time, against an enemy that hides comfortably outside of the walls you constructed to keep them there.

Syndicalists launched a triad of small destabilization campaigns: one rendering a primary supply line impassable, the second, an assassination of a high-ranking officer on the wrong side of the wall, and the final, a Trojan horse of sorts involving the introduction of a particularly nasty and enduring breed of bedbug within the factory walls. The rotations of sick or mentally handicapped security personnel began to bleed the coffers.

The *war that wasn't there* was costing the Owners billions to wage. They demanded an assault meant to completely eviscerate the Syndicalist communities in a final and brutal push. Armaments, armor, and cannons arrived via airlift.

Personnel carriers and short-range missile delivery systems began to dot the horizons and hills. Syndicalist leaders and sympathizers were rounded up without warning and publicly executed while the Federal government pretended not to notice.

The Syndicalists moved swiftly to garner the sympathy of the Union-backbone of the PPTEa: the persons milling about off-camera making the Great American TV Show happen, feeding the faux neighbors and crews, watching their children, servicing their cars, building the roads that carried them to plastic surgeons, grocery stores, and private golf courses.

≈

"Henry."

"Who's asking?" Henry did not look up from his lunch.

"It's me."

Henry slowly set his sandwich down and kept looking forward. "You're not supposed to be here. Your kind are shot on sight these days."

"Used to hang us from trees. What's the difference?"

"The difference is you chose to give up. Some of us are still in this fight."

"I love you, Henry."

"Don't start that shit. Why are you here?"

"We need your help."

"I knew it. Please, just go. I don't need any trouble, and you're a dead man walking these streets."

"There are cameras everywhere, I know. We need you. I need you. They are slaughtering us."

"That's none of my business. Plenty of good, legal jobs on the Show."

"There are camps now. They send more of us every day. No one comes back, Henry. Pretty soon, there will be nothing outside of the Show."

"The Show is why we still have a country. I know it's vicious, I know it takes no prisoners, but what can I do about it? Nothing."

“You can organize. They can’t operate without the millions of people working behind the scenes. Without you, there is no Show. We are only asking to live.”

“That’s not my life anymore, Marcus. Besides, they’ll never negotiate.”

“We have to try.”

Masses of workers gathered in PPTEa cities. A call beginning in the machine shops of western Indiana and reaching to the ports of San Diego rang out *to unify and take back our power*. From small screens in back rooms, a pirate broadcast sputtered to life during a situational comedy. Henry wiped his nose on his hand and straightened his back, “Hello everyone, Henry Ocasek here.”

Cheers rose from sea to sea.

“Hopefully some of y’all remember me, it’s been a while. Here’s the thing, good people are getting killed and we need to do something about it. Lot of us got family and friends that became outsiders instead of being on the Show. Most of them didn’t have a choice. Some real bad things are happening. People on the outside are being rounded up and sent off to camps. These camps are set up to do only one thing.” The broadcast flashed to drone video of long lines of people being marched between tents. An armed man strikes down a woman moving slowly in the line. She raises her hands to shield her face and the man puts several bullets in her head. “Once the outsiders are gone, they’ll need someone else to fill the camps with. It’s time for us to come together again. We have to stop this madness now; it will only get worse.

“On May 1st, everyone, and I mean *everyone*, is walking out. Go to work, do your job, and at high noon Eastern time, we walk out. It’s been a long time since we’ve had a voice. We’ve gotten comfortable, pretending that comfort is justice. Together we can make sure that the PPTEa is working for the people.”

The Unions demanded that the Owners sit down to negotiations. The Owners snubbed their attempts. The Union masses began demonstrating their solidarity through small walkouts, but the Owners remained granite.

May the 1st spread, Rapture like, through the RealCommunities™ as the clock struck 12:00PM. Cameras dipped, microphones failed, and RTVS hubs rushed to replace the unscripted chaos with recycled footage. Princes and princesses, greatly put out by the slightest dip in subservience, raged in empty dressing rooms to no one. The interstate Place and Part transit system ran a final lap to remove all riders, and then shut down in the dark corners of the tunnel system. Actors, crew, administration, and management of The Show were stranded, paralyzed. The macrocosm of the PPTEa could not endure the loss of foundation; every millisecond spent off-screen murdered the bottom line.

The Corporations and politicians soon sang the sweet song of undercover-*Socialism*. Facile pride kept some corporations addicted to the power of denying the Syndicalists a helping hand, but by and large Syndicalists were able to sign temporary leases and occupy thirty percent of their target facilities within the year.

The Masters turned these scraps over to the hounds, and after centuries of carnage, Power was forced to allow Peace a safe place to incubate.

≈

Outside the PPTEa, localization became a necessity, and albeit grudgingly, Americans soon learned how to work with one another toward a common goal. Strange and foreign as it felt, Americans began to participate in the lives of their fellow citizens without the over-arching impetus of *earning* representative capital.

A family needing water needed exactly the resources and humanpower necessary to complete the task. Earning the money to *pay someone else to do it* is an entrancing farce until people begin dying from lack of thin strips of colored paper. Americans had been indoctrinated by an inescapable paradox: help others but help them within the context of their benefit to you. The cult of *individuality* and the cult of *the common good* were placed uncomfortably side-by-side in American educational curriculum, in its media, and in its foreign policy.[26]

Just inside the PPTEa borders, the social strata of the United States, as personified by the rapacious consumer, was the order of the day—preserved pristinely in the viscous amber of apathy. Every filthy, trod-upon, open space reeked of vapidity: staged, engineered, manufactured, and dreamed. For a brief, stroke-inducing moment the international viewers started to lose interest in the American experiment.

§

XLII

Autumn ~ 2000

Melvin R. Wurtzel arrived in Los Angeles at the turn of the century by way of a pilgrimage around the country with his estranged father. To rekindle their relationship, Melvin followed *the worst father in the world* through the deep-south peddling pressure cookers to rednecks afeared of the coming Y2k apocalypse. It was a depraved and exploitative endeavor; Melvin had not fallen far from the proverbial tree.

---

26 The American version of Western Capitalism required two distinct faces. It lauded the nobility of the poor and downtrodden, the leper, and the sex worker, but could never stoop to provide them with justice. Those that fell to the side, by deign of deed or birthright, were held up as an archetype, a vision of what will come if you cannot conform. It is by this sleight of hand that a society criminalizes its lower castes and places the impetus on the individual to rise above the community, rather than on the community to rise as one.

It was the forced contrivance of individual-participation that consummated the façade and focused attention inward rather than outward—a cult of subjectivity at war, always, with reality. It was espoused that the individual must perfect oneself before being useful to the community, when in reality, being useful to the community is what perfects, and ultimately defines, the individual.

With the impetus of wealth no longer available as a means to one's ends, Americans sought alternative inspiration to participate in each day. Success abroad inspired American philosophers to experiment with evolved economic models borrowed from the Mondragon Corporation of the former Santimamiñe Peninsula.

Life slowed, stimulation ebbed, and Americans in the non-televised regions walked, narcoleptic, into a real empirical world shading their eyes from the Hydrogen-lit truth bombarding them. The rotted carcass placed around American minds at birth became an archaic paradigm, fit only to be mocked and warned of in Huxley-esque pop fiction.

When he returned to the coast, Melvin was lured to Los Angeles by friends from high school and wandered the midnight Hollywood bondage clubs. He was in his element: dominant, unhindered, and loved for the extremity of his arrogance. As the girls and boys clamored to catch his eye, he made it simple, "just tell me I'm pretty and buy me cigarettes."

Melvin's wild tangle of sun-sodden curls was soon sheared down to a smart platinum cut befitting a business suit, leather harness, casting call, or wake. As his pairs of pants made from PVC began to overpower his trusted jeans, and as MDMA graced his lips more often than bottom-shelf whiskey, Hollywood Melvin was born.

By way of fucking someone's girlfriend properly at an orgy, he landed at the helm of a B-movie and soft-porn casting company. Melvin's new casting couch had the power to compel actors to disrobe and Melvin never tired of their awkward tendency toward insecurity. The *willing*, as he called them, were far less interesting. Without the *awkward*, Wurtzel was not amused.

When the casting company folded, Melvin changed gears and accepted a low-level administrative position for D6, a fledgling cable channel devoted to video game culture. One of the company's founders realized Melvin's potential early on.

Jacob Tarshish admired Melvin's stubborn resistance to the new century's pervasive anti-smoking stance. Though Tarshish only smoked chronic, he understood Melvin's low-level misanthropy. As they shared the patio, and more than one joint, Tarshish realized that saying *no* to Melvin was the purview of the strong-stomached, and that mere civilians would fold immediately under his abusive charm.

Tarshish put Melvin on the phone twenty-four hours a day selling the new channel to cable conglomerates coast to coast. Melvin carried the channel into production with over fifty percent of their *'dream clients'* in their back pocket. A few unpopular mergers and cancellations nullified the channel's only competitor, and its dedicated viewers were brought into the D6 fold by force. Dominion belonged to the last channel standing.

§

When the masters of Entertainment came knocking, Melvin commanded the internet-presence of the half-billion-dollar corporation. The channel was purchased by a significantly larger cable conglomerate—for an obnoxious sum of money—and Mr. Wurtzel became a Vice President. The same Melvin Wurtzel who had attended precisely one college class and simply walked out, was now an engorged aorta in a communications beast that spanned the globe.

Tarshish, a more seasoned professional, was awarded the president's salary for his part in the channel's genesis and success. They both settled into comfortable lives, wallowing in high seven-digit salaries. Automobile-sized flat screen televisions, sports cars, and international holidays became frame to Melvin's self-portrait.

Melvin took Jacob Tarshish into his world; he invited him to attend after-hours parties hosted by his dearest friends that were rife with naked flesh and hallucinogens. Shaving ten years off Jacob's life by parading him through the seedy (and expensive) shadows of Los Angeles was Melvin's way of showing he cared.

As time passed, Tarshish, a deluded narcissist, took Melvin's hospitality for granted. The routinely fragile and inconsolable executive was a noxious presence, and a paralyzing tension replaced their friendship.

The industry morphed to accommodate the economic downturn of the first decade, and Tarshish fell prey to the chopping block. His salary had been the primary motivation for the attack, but it was no secret that Jacob was a pill. The company planned to let Tarshish go, pay Melvin slightly more, and force him to absorb complete responsibility.

"This is a very posh place for a man date, Wurtzel." Jacob flashed faux flattery.

"You're my special bitch." Melvin smiled as the waiter approached. "We'll take a bottle of whiskey, what do you have that's old and makes Irish dudes happy?"

The waiter pitched, "Midleton 26-Year-Old, absolutely exquisite."

Jacob gestured to Melvin, "I shouldn't do whiskey, I've got three Vicodin in me."

"Perfect, only one glass, now off." Melvin sent the waiter on her way.

Tarshish unbuttoned his suit jacket. "You're being odd, Melvin. If I were a suspicious man, I'd say you're about to break up with me."

"You're right on the money. They're letting you go."

"Wait, what? They who?"

"*They* asshole. The only people high enough up the food chain to plot your demise."

Jacob smiled and calmly folded his napkin in half. "How did you find out?"

Melvin felt uncomfortable. It was so rare, he tried to enjoy it. "They made me an offer. You're out, they'll give me half your salary and all of your bullshit."

"Ah," Jacob sighed, "so it's about money."

"It's always about money."

"What are we going to do? Who's behind it and how hard can we hit them? How much did they tell you?"

"I took the offer. I didn't even hesitate."

Jacob paused. "Well. I'm disappointed, but I guess I'm not shocked."

"Neither of us can afford to be out of a job right now, but you'll land on your feet a lot faster than I would. And I'm cheaper, this isn't personal."

"Of course it's personal. It's always personal. Maybe that's why they chose you. People that don't take things personally are easier to control."

"See, there you go, everyone is making a huge mistake. You're smarter, it's settled." Melvin looked over his shoulder. "Where's that whiskey?"

"I mean, holy shit, what are they thinking? I *made* you Wurtzel."

"Without me, there is no you."

"I can see how it would be comforting to tell yourself that. But, as you said, I'll land on my feet because I'm the one who *makes it happen* and you are just a cog in a machine of my making."

"Well, that machine of your making is kicking you out, so goodbye, adios, go fuck yourself, et cetera."

§

The bottle of Midleton arrived.

"You'll regret this, Wurtzel."

"Probably, but since I'm the only one drinking, I'm taking this to the patio to chain smoke. Buh-bye Jacob it's been...fun?" Melvin grabbed the bottle of antique whiskey and left Jacob at the table.

Over the next three fiscal years, Melvin became his channel's Atlas and as the foundation finally settled, he strode colossus-like through the halls of entertainment. The wear on his person was no match for his drive but when he sat silently, for long enough, he remembered a different time. A time when having enough gas and a roach to smoke meant a great day. Melvin's *give a fuck* was set to *broken* by default. He'd never been very good at giving a fuck in his youth, and now, he had given too much of a fuck for too long.

No one had ever seen Melvin with facial hair. He had entered the office hundreds of times after three days sans-sleep or after fifteen hours in an airplane, but never contrived. It began as a simple mustache that morphed into a mid-nineteen-seventies handlebar that framed his mouth and dropped beneath his jawline. Melvin's Finnish Tom sideburns grew to ridiculous proportions, and as they did, his hair became longer, kinkier, and wilder. By being alive he was actively saying, "Fuck you." To whom, it did not matter.

As entertainment folded into itself and three corporate Titans manipulated the entirety of American media, Titan the Second decided that a full house cleaning was in order. When the board discussed extraneous expenses, Management began writing their blacklists.

Melvin was widely beloved, but a threat to everyone. Fucking with Melvin, unless he had royally screwed up, was an exercise in the formidable girth of unbreakable confidence. None of that mattered because Melvin wasn't playing the corporate game. He wasn't playing a game at all, he was just, *that* good.

Daniel Bishop, Regional Vice President of Corporate Standards for the parent company, had uglier motivations than fear. He was an underqualified executive, pushed along by nepotism and handshake contracts. Bishop was a permanent member of *the club*, and that made him a bigot. He knew in his heart of hearts that craven, privileged men were charged by god with saving humanity from itself. Men like Jacob Tarshish—with whom he shared the four-thirty PM appointment slot at Mid-City Discreet Massage. Bishop resented that an outsider, like Melvin, had dared take Jacob's place rather than fall on his sword—*really? A Senior Vice President with a high school diploma?* People like Melvin Wurtzel needed to be shown their place.

Bishop's cowardly assassination attempt began with a tacit threat in front of Melvin's division. During a routine meeting, Bishop proceeded to throw Melvin's team under the bus for a slight dip in viewership.

"When I say that I am very disappointed, I am only scratching the surface," Bishop looked around the room, avoiding Melvin's fury. "We will not have another disappointment, or I will have your resignations."

When Daniel left the conference room Melvin followed him.

"Hey...Hey, fuckhead," Melvin raised his voice.

Daniel turned. "The meeting is adjourned, Mr. Wurtzel."

"Don't threaten my team over bullshit, Bishop. You'll regret it."

Daniel smiled, amused that he had prodded the lion from his den. "Your channel is bullshit Melvin. Its programming is bullshit, its market is bullshit. This is a sanitarium for the hopelessly insane, and it is run by a clown." He looked Melvin up and down. "Try getting a haircut and taking this job seriously."

Melvin stood in the busy office watching Daniel leave. "Bishop! When you said *disappointed*, did you mean, like when you whip your cock out, *disappointed*?"

Bishop turned to face Melvin and the entire floor peeked over their cubicles to watch. "I'm finished with this conversation."

"I'm just getting started you sniveling chump. If you want to take me on, say so."

Bishop began to realize that Melvin did not intend to back down. He was speechless.

"That's what I thought. If you ever pull that passive aggressive shit again, you're getting the pink tutu and shock collar."

The entire floor burst into hysterical laughter. Bishop turned scarlet as tutu and shock collar memes bearing his agonized face shot around the world millions of times over.

"Check your messages," Melvin taunted, "looks like you just lost your authority at D6. Have fun begging for a job at the Home Shopping Network."

Bishop charged at Melvin, flailing his arms pathetically as he ran. Smart phones zoomed in on the full-grown toddler man slapping at the air hoping to strike Melvin. When Bishop got close enough, Melvin raised his fist and dropped him where he stood. Bishop hit the ground shrieking.

"One last thing, Daniel. Fuck. You." Melvin smiled; the psychotic spark had created a firestorm.

"You're finished, Wurtzel. Do you hear me?" Bishop's reptilian lips stretched against his porcelain-capped incisors as he wept.

"I'm pretty sure I just quit, limp dick, but nice try."

The entire office applauded as Melvin walked slowly to the elevator and disappeared behind the fake mahogany doors.

A judge found Melvin's calm demeanor and bicep tattoo of Neil Diamond reasonable enough doubt that he was dangerous and dismissed Bishop's Assault and Battery charges.

To celebrate, Melvin spent several months traveling through the Spanish backcountry with Number One. Before they left Los Angeles, Ian loaned Melvin a new novel by an underground British philosopher. *The Theory of Inter-Reality* told the story of a family that loses their child to a reality TV program for six years.[27]

Melvin loved it; the trauma and the flagrant greed; he was deeply inspired...

---

27 The book's author, Auguste Dubh, painted a stark portrait of a young girl returning to a family she barely knows, and who barely know her. She struggles to participate above and beyond scattered stock-reactions to familial situations. The girl twitches sometimes as she looks for a camera but never finds one. Dubh warned of an *inter-reality*, a trap between real- and scripted-life, where the boundaries evaporate. It was a dark missive asking humanity to come back to the chaos of reality and walk away from the faux-reality we were creating in our society.

By the time he swallowed his pride all he could find to produce was high-level pornography. There were legions of *Daniel Bishops* in the Entertainment world; every studio board had at least three. Striking that pathetic little tubeworm got Melvin blacklisted across the board.

Hollywood rallied their troops to keep the major studios alive, and inexpensive professionals began seeping through the runs in the red carpet. Melvin pushed his way onto an underproduced reality program. It involved a Private Investigator tipping a slick-haired reporter to the scene of an infidelity. Said reporter brings betrayed spouse/lover and full-scale camera crew to the scene of the infidelity for a confrontation. The rest writes itself.

As time wore on, Melvin had to script more and more of the show to keep it afloat. This calculation helped edge him into a new bracket of reality television. His first, fully scripted reality-challenge revolutionized the genre. The studios blocked Melvin on all sides from producing blockbuster films—Entertainment's private, player's only, penthouse. Melvin loathed film but hit back anyway by undermining the studio's television markets.

Melvin R. Wurtzel held Old-Hollywood at bay with his pinky finger and he was precisely the man to carry out Erlyst's revenge.

§

Spring ~ 2013

Lawrence was forced to post up in the lobby of Melvin's production studio after multiple failed attempts to reach him by phone. Hours later, Melvin walked past the reception desk explaining to a group of interns the finer points of a glass bottom boat.

Lawrence called out. Melvin ignored him. "Melvin, it's Lawrence E. Robertson. It is urgent that I speak to you." Lawrence sprinted to catch the group before the inner doors to the sound stage closed.

Melvin whispered over his shoulder. "Who are you, tiny man? This is a restricted area."

"I'm Lawrence," Melvin did not shake his hand. "I'm Erlyst Rae Atropos' attorney. She would like to speak to you about a television venture she intends to fully fund."

"Erly-Sue who? What kind of name is that anyway?" Crewpersons dropped heavy bags behind them. "You fucks. You stupid, stupid fucks, get out of here before..." Lawrence scurried silently behind Wurtzel as he imperiously barked orders with a condescending flip of his glorious sun-like mane.

Melvin's massive office consumed the corner of the building. He kept a large, razor-sharp broadsword mounted to the wall, framed by various phallic implements of sudden death. The macabre arrangement of five daggers, a pair of braided riding crops, and a single flail mace fanned out like a medieval throne behind his endless desk.

"Mr. Wurtzel, Mrs. Atropos would like to speak to you about a business venture that she intends to invest in handsomely."

"Details Larry, I need details."

"Mrs. Atropos wants to create a reality television program featuring her family, and by extension the blueblood societies of the world."

Melvin snorted, "You're wasting my time..."

"*Atropos*, Melvin." Lawrence smiled. Suggestively, he hoped.

"Atropos. Atropos. Atropos? You mean the little rich girl that falls face first onto every cock in Hollywood?"

Lawrence feigned a cough of indignation, "Yes Melvin, That's Mrs. Atropos' daughter."

"Bring Erly-Sue to my office tomorrow."

"She's paralyzed."

"Fuck yeah," Melvin smiled, "this is going to be good..."

§

The hours, days, and weeks of solitude weighed heavily on Erlyst, but the vast black storm clouds marring her every thought began to dissipate. Erlyst realized that some of the feeling in her fingers had returned. By month's end, Erlyst was able to move her left hand and write meager missives into her journal. Her newfound clarity of thought and phantoms of hope had inspired her to memorialize the coming chaos.

Erlyst had her assistant stage the room for Melvin's arrival, bringing in fresh flowers and rearranging the books in the libraries to reflect an appreciation for Melvin's industry and his lower station in life. The Nurse gently brushed Erlyst's long silver hair and gilded her decadently in her best suit. Her exquisite Egyptian silk bedding was replaced and the Nurse strapped Erlyst into a large chair behind her writing desk. An antique blanket with a creased seam just below Erlyst's waist framed her upper body perfectly and provided a solid, taut surface to conceal her legs. Erlyst's presentation was of the utmost importance to her, indeed she felt it was at the very least, *everything*.

In her mind's eye she had a collection of trophies—the heads of her opposition—nailed to every wall. She sat, in fox hunting attire, and drank lazily from a decanter of brandy. Luxurious, illegal cigar smoke filled the room and clouded the staring eyes of her framed and mounted prey.

Erlyst's assistant called from her chamber door. "Madame, Mr. Wurtzel is here."

"Show him in." Erlyst waved her assistant away.

Melvin poked his head into Erlyst's personal library.

"I apologize, Mr. Wurtzel, for making you come to me." Erlyst raised her left arm and Melvin kissed her hand softly.

"Don't worry your pretty little head, I'll slip it into my final number so both of us can have a clean conscience." Melvin smiled and took a seat near Erlyst's desk.

"So, what can I do for you Erly-Sue?"

"I need your expertise, Mr. Wurtzel. I want to sell you my family."

"Sell? I'm not sure I'm your guy, but I know an Argentinean chap that could..."

"Yes. Sell. You see, Mr. Wurtzel, I want to lay this family open to prying eyes. Our empire reaches from pole to pole, from Kingdoms to Congress, and down into state houses and municipal courts. My late husband, may he putrefy slowly, was the grand conduit of all things financial. As you can see, I am no longer able to walk; I will likely spend the rest of my days in this state. My daughter is...a handful, to say the least, and I am daily descended upon by far flung throngs of royal well-wishers and potential business partners. I don't imagine there is a better template for your style of entertainment in existence."

"I've heard better. And recently. What's the revenge angle? This is all pretty lame otherwise."

"I'm not a monster, Mr. Wurtzel. *Of course* I have ulterior motives. None of which will hinder your ability to make obscene amounts of money from this family's utter lack of decency or control."

Melvin sat back in his chair. A secret revenge plot added at least a season to the show, "You have use of your left arm?"

"Yes, just lately. My paralysis may be fading."

If she made a full recovery, they could hide it until the final season. Thalia Atropos would become some sort of anti-hero to young American women, and feminist institutions worldwide would write articles about Melvin Wurtzel's criminal effect on young women. Each of which he'd gleefully frame and display next to his swords.

"I'll do it. Let's talk money."

"It is no object. Now, let's move on to logistics, what do you need to and/or want to know?"

"I researched your late husband, he's pretty last-century news. He died of a heart-attack, right?"

"There was a woman in the room."

"He was a cheater. Okay, good, anything really bad?"

"I'd prefer we keep him a philanderer, after all a large part of your sponsors will be interested in keeping his image relatively clean for business purposes."

"I don't love that, but okay. So rich businessman is boinking prostitutes and possibly the baby-sitter, mom is home minding the social duties. Young Thalia, wasting away in the darkness, is brought out into the sunshine only to be bragged about and then hidden again from sight. Where are you from? Originally?"

"A small town in Georgia. Athens."

"Tell me about growing up in backwoods dump like Georgia."

"Nothing to tell, really. The University of Georgia provides Athens with a raison d'être. It's a sleepy town on a hill between football seasons and beside that, completely backward and purposely antiquated."

"It's where you met Mr. Atropos?"

"It is."

Melvin stared at Erlyst...

"Should I go on?"

Melvin rolled his eyes.

"Kyrios came into the restaurant where I waited tables. I took his table from a friend. I recall saying something humiliating like, *That's an awful fancy suit for Athens, Georgia.* He smiled, the filthy narcissist. We had drinks after my shift, and Kyrios spun an epic tale for me."

"Fiction?"

"I remember wondering about that for a moment and then losing myself in his gaze."

"Go on..." Melvin cringed.

"He had been to all corners of the Earth, had tasted spices and spirits from secret jungles and far away monasteries, had touched, worn, and slept in the finest fabrics known to modern society, yet he was missing something."

"Someone to share it with?" Melvin smiled; he'd heard this one before.

"Something like that. He was never that poetic. He told me he needed a wife. *A wife, a matriarch, and a companion, in that order*, he would say. Poor southern trash isn't offered the moon by a beautiful and powerful man very often. We were married, with all requisite pomp, and I was the Queen of New York City for several remarkable years," Erlyst paused. "Then I found out."

"Found out what?" Melvin suddenly became interested.

"That Kyrios was a bit of a sex-addict."

"Wait, how did you not know that?"

"He satiated himself with other women in order to treat me normally, as befitting a wife. He had women living in apartments all across the five Boroughs. At times, he had a route and he had a schedule. I was the only wrench in his machine. Once I became suspicious I would actively thwart his attempts at privacy and long periods away from home. He escalated rather than backing off and when I finally confronted him with evidence he laughed in my face.

"I never pushed too hard, but I never let him off the hook. It became a game until Thalia came along. I began to expose him publicly and he slowed his pace considerably. In retaliation he would often involve himself with household employees to rub my face in his infidelities. I found this humorous because I had control over the hiring, and frankly...I never picked anyone that I'd have sex with. He was excited about the child until it became clear that she was a little girl. I resigned that it was better than running out on us; at least I had that to hold onto.

"Thalia was a joy, even as Kyrios sank deeper and deeper into secrecy. Thalia and I were co-conspirators on secret drives into the country and flights to Paris for timbales de mousseline de volaille."

"Kyrios beat me badly and Thalia witnessed part of it. She respected me less and less as each day passed. Her father terrified her, and she blamed me for staying. She could not understand my reasons; no child could understand the situation..."

Melvin interrupted her, "Erly-Sue, I can get down with your agony and everything, but I think we have enough to suck ignorant minds into your drama, and frankly, I lost respect for you a long time ago."

"I can't tell you how happy that makes me. I don't want your respect Melvin; respect will get in the way of your job. Do we have a deal?"

"We do. Is this the part where we get drunk and talk about our feelings? Oh right, we already did the last part..."

‡

XIII

While Stasia and Dahvit prepared breakfast, Victor took a seat in their backyard. Small stone steps below the patio led deep into the lush yard and were terminated by a small man-made pond. Victor walked down the path with a chair and his notebook. He scribbled an account of the Apple Thief and his flight anxiety. The chirping birds, warm but cloudy day, and overwhelming feeling of being taken care of put Victor in a very reflective state. His eyes tracked from the tightly-lined pages to the mossy surface of the small pond. Tiny flowers grew on the islands of green and glowed white under the blanket of calm grey sky above.

Stasia, Dahvit, and Victor wove through Golder's Green, passing houses that all looked the same. Occasionally a floor was absent or added, a bit more brick, or a bit more white—be it wood or artificial siding—but always, unceasingly, and systemically the same for blocks upon blocks on the winding Autumnal London lanes. They crossed beneath an immense brick bridge, arched like an old aqueduct above the quiet street. In a few seconds the South train would rattle overhead destined for Central London.

They reached a small gate to a park. The crowded, and tree-lined neighborhood street gave way to a vast green expanse as far as the eye could see. It was as if the city ceased, temporarily, to exist. Besieged by the veil of grey above and the soft eternity of emerald beneath his boots Victor wandered the vast, winding paths. He felt homesick for Dublin. A sudden desire to flip open his notebook and sip on a pint overwhelmed him.

They continued to penetrate further and further into the large open park. They crossed into Hampstead Heath, and deep into the trees. From the waves of green sprung immense snaking walls. Hidden in the dense foliage, a structure that was part fortress and part Xanadu pressed stoically through the flora.

Winding stairs took the group from the Heath floor to the first platform of the structure. The long, wide walkway was reminiscent of a forgotten Roman via, with long stonewalls, forming a seemingly infinite line of arched walkways and domed interchanges between. Below them a garden with a rectangular pond looked out over a large clearing in the Heath floor. Square stones lined the edges of the pond and several benches etched a border with the lush lawn. The final stretch was encased in foliage, and the roof of the walkway was a tangled ceiling of plants growing into and upon one another in search of sunlight and nourishment.

As soon as it had sprung from the trees, the structure ended. They crossed a final threshold and emerged on busy London street.

Stasia pulled the group down Hampstead Square and directed them through medieval streets, hemmed in by walls from ancient fortresses that now coddled elementary schools and tall thin homes. The cramped street bled into a bustling and sun-drenched lane lined with shops and cafes. Stasia chose a sandwich shop with quaint tables outside to permit smoking. Victor had one with Dahvit, in solidarity for the stout headache Dahvit now suffered.

"So, you've been to two cities now?" Stasia asked. "And do you fancy Dublin?"

"Indeed, swore to take my last breaths there just this week." Victor smiled.

"Then it's settled, when do you move?"

"I have entertained the idea of being an illegal alien for a while, but I've met more than a few people in Dublin looking for work, any kind of work, so long as it pays steady."

"The UK's no better," Stasia said.

"Nor Berlin," Dahvit added.

The trio strolled through Belsize, discussing the similarities and differences between American, German, and English responses to the economic crisis. Dahvit had lived in London for over a decade; he was often mistaken for a local, but he was a German-born transplant and returned often. He bitterly recounted the degradation of his native Berlin and feared that sections of London had, and were going to continue to, succumb to the effects Germany had experienced.

"Wait, which one is it, stop or go?" Victor was puzzled, the sign giving municipal permission to cross an intersection seemed stuck between yes and no.

"We call that a sleeping light." Dahvit offered authoritatively.

"Duly noted." Victor answered as they walked.

After a few minutes Dahvit turned to Victor, "It occurs to me that you are a writer, and although it is funny to pull your leg about the sleeping light it would not do for you to write about it."

"No, it wouldn't," Victor smiled, "but no worries, I planned on attributing it to you directly."

Regents Park lounged atop Primrose Hill. From Victor's vantage, London lay cramped against the snaking Thames. They descended the hill and strolled along Regent's Park Road to Trojka, a Russian tea and vodka house. The calm room was warm. Cups and saucers clinked along with knives and forks set down carefully against china. Ice rattled in glasses, and the conversation was a low murmur. Dahvit pulled them around to a table nestled in a back corner and they relaxed to pour over the long and verbose vodka list.

Stasia excused herself from the table and walked out of the tearoom. Clear alcohol wasn't really Victor's first choice, so he deferred to his host's tasting talents. Soon small glasses were set on the table with flasks of frigid, scentless spirit. Stasia returned as Dahvit filled her tiny glass.

"Thank you. Read that..." Stasia placed a newspaper in front of Dahvit. She was glowing.

After a moment he smiled broadly and removed his glasses, "Yes, yes well done. They certainly took their time mentioning *Rhee.*"

Stasia concurred, "Really, I was wondering if they'd be honoring their promise to us. What's important is that a Pakistani writer had his work reviewed by The Guardian. They were kind enough to mention the literary magazine and the issue. I'd call it a success."

"Oh yes, a brilliant success, and they even mention the lovely lady sitting to my left," Dahvit announced, beaming with pride.

Stasia dipped her head in a dignified curtsey and Victor applauded.

The tearoom began to slowly swirl as the replenished trio splashed inside on a near-rainy day. Warm, spiced air wafted through the room, from the kitchen below, from the cup to the left, from the waitress pouring boiled water on carefully chosen and cultivated leaves. In spite of a pair of well-placed smoking breaks, Victor had succumbed to the violence of the clear alcohol. On his third smoke break he vowed composure and returned to the warm room, now a slow-boiling din of words.

Stasia made plans to meet up with someone from the old LA gang who opened an American bar that served Mexican food.

"Gordon moved to the Eastside a year ago, after getting married." Stasia explained.

Victor interrupted, "Wait, Gordon?"

"Yes, do you know him?"

"I think so, has a thing for mustaches and submissive boys?"

Stasia laughed, "Yes," she caught her breath, "he's cooking up carne asada tonight for a party and invited everyone to come drink and eat."

The idea of trekking to the Eastside was daunting to say the least but it was finally decided that adventure was superior to comfort, and the trio set off by tube and bus. Once there, they walked along the river.

The bar was a few blocks away on the corner of a small, angled street. The bike racks on the corners were plagued with fixed gear bikes in an orgy of orange, caution-yellow, and white bicycular posturing. Twenty-somethings roamed the street and poured onto the sidewalk from the crowded bar. Victor felt like he was walking into a small Silverlake venue while the current Echo Park sweethearts fellated a mass of sweaty bodies—writhing to the music in thrift store hand-me-downs and three-hundred-dollar sunglasses.

The group pressed their way through the throngs inside. Dahvit and Victor flashed one another *let's bolt ASAP* looks as they snaked down into the basement level of the establishment. The warm, dense cavern below the bar was more lightly populated, but everyone was oddly dressed, as if they were flashing back to a prom-past. Horrid music, check, taffeta, check, photographer, check...

"Is this a wedding?" Victor asked Stasia.

"Oh yes, it's a reception, there's the bride." Stasia pointed to a woman in all white carrying a bouquet in one hand and a dark whiskey in the other.

"That makes sense," Victor conceded.

"In fact," Stasia continued, "I think we may be intruding."

"Oh." Victor took his drink down in one belt.

The reception's guests were eyeing the group. They funneled toward the staircase and Victor stopped; he recognized Gordon.

"Hey man."

"Wow, I haven't seen you since..."

"2006? 7?" Victor extended his hand.

"Seven I think," Gordon shook his hand and hugged him. "You used to date, wait, don't tell me her name, the brunette bondage model with the big... "

"Yep, that's me." Victor forced a smile.

"Well, it's good to see you, what brings you to London?" Gordon continued taking orders, making drinks, and preparing his carne asada.

"On holiday. No reason. Got laid off and figured I'd waste the money here instead."

"Nice. Don't leave without saying goodbye."

"No problem and thank you for the drink."

Victor joined Stasia and Dahvit outside for a cigarette. The Eastside kids were smashing pint glasses in the street and wrestling one another to the ground while their doting and vapid girlfriends looked on.

‡

Victor walked through the tree-canopied neighborhood and emerged on Golder's Green Road. A proper Italian restaurant struck his fancy first and he took a seat at a table on the sidewalk. He perused the menu and chose a specialty pizza and an Italian beer.

> *9/8/10*
>
> *I miss Dublin. Eating alone, writing in this notebook, a quiet moment of solitude, and I feel out of place again. The sense of belonging I had hoped for was here, waiting for me. Knowing that somehow makes*

me fear that I have compromised, and I long to fall back into silence.

There exists such a strange and indescribable difference between the pleasures of solitude and the pleasures of communion. One never overtakes the other, they vacillate between prominence and invisibility based on circumstance or act of will. I will never be satisfied with the constant stimuli of the city, and I realize I would be just as dissatisfied with a hidden cabin in the wilderness.

But we can't know how a moment will unfold until we are there, swimming in either its decay or brilliance. Ian says I'm a young and shapeless void, bumping against barriers, incapable of preventing repeat disasters. Ian's better at saying things than most people.

Wish he were here right now. I think I've started to rely on his friendship.

The boredom of unemployment pushed Victor into the pubs, chasing something long into the night, be it a stolen conversation or an inspired few lines written on a napkin. Victor was in Europe, he had chased his weight in stout, inexpensive meals, and luxurious walks. Yet, in that moment he wanted to crawl out of his skin, to feel something different, painful though it may be.

Victor paid, tipped heavily, and walked back toward the flat. It was clear that Ian needed people; he would short circuit in the absence of love, that absence being either real or imagined. Victor needed people because without them he was left to his own maddening thoughts. Without distraction, he inevitably found himself boring. In the bowels of the warehouse, the listless, penniless existence, had continued to convince Victor that he was not quite ready for solitude.

Golder's Green gave way to Ravenscroft and the clouds thickened over the northern horizon. Great white billowing columns announced a tyrannical war above English heads, hats, and umbrellas.

‡

Victor took a long shower, skipped shaving, and smoked several cigarettes on the back patio while the skies roamed in white and grey ripples across the domed autumn sky. He felt uncomfortable walking to the tube station; he had dressed too warmly.

London's underground system charges train fare in zones, ovals that overlap and border one another. Victor was mystified. He bought a day pass to be safe and slipped into the underground. It was a maze of crossing tunnels with varying flocks of people scurrying like frightened pheasant hens. The afternoon blew in small gusts past the platform, rolling and tumbling against the concrete while humming playfully. The ride to Euston was a bit nerve-racking, several announcements regarding the tube worker's strike alarmed Victor precisely because he had no idea how it affected his journey. All went well, one of the stops on his mission was to be closed, but Euston had already been closed and would remain open that day. It was an interesting strike; stations were closed in a pattern. Although it was uncomfortable (especially for a foreigner) the subway system had by no means been brought to a halt. It would be an effective way to keep Londoners on the side of the strikers for longer.

The ride was a straight shot and Victor relaxed. Once he exited the train at Euston he was once again thrown into a chaotic series of identical intersections. As he waded, salmon-like through concurrent waves of disembarking commuters Victor at last found a flight of stairs leading to the surface and freedom. Dahvit was waiting at the top of the escalator for Victor and patted him on the back.

"How was it, old boy?"

"No sweat," Victor lied.

The two struck back out on Euston, taking a brief detour through Dahvit's school, UCL and past an Italian restaurant where he and Stasia loved to dine on anniversaries.

They left the quaint neighborhoods and row houses for Regent Street. The busy London artery reminded Victor of Times Square as he stared north. The sun was prying through the clouds with enormous fingers of brilliant sunlight. Sensuous gold-lined rays cascaded against the BBC as they spilled into the intersection. The dying sunlight illuminated the windshields of commuting cars and was finally muted by the throngs of humans pressing against one another on all sides of the choked roadway. The buildings along Regent were majestic, the detail and decorative elements were stunning and regal.

"Mind the bike lane Victor," Dahvit taunted.

"Dangerous crew around here?"

"No, true professionals all, but addicted to speed."

"Duly noted," Victor put some distance between his footfalls and the dividing line.

"Whoa," Dahvit called out.

Victor looked up in time to see two bicyclists narrowly miss one another at an interchange. "That was close."

"It was. We certainly didn't need that distraction. Bound as we are to help."

"Bound?"

"Oh yes, British law requires *anyone who can* to *help anyone in distress*. Even foreigners on holiday. For example, had those gentlemen struck one another, we'd be bound to assist."

"How does one enforce a law like that?

"It's closer to social-engineering than criminal law. By making Britons feel responsible for one another they cultivate cohesion. A necessary element of a warring society."

Dahvit's disenchanted artist's tour of Central London carried them until turning onto Cork. Stasia appeared and kissed Dahvit on the cheek.

"Well hello," Dahvit wrapped her in his arms. "How was your day love?"

"Oh," Stasia groaned.

"Victor and I were thinking a pint and some steak would be best before we commit to the gallery."

"They have sandwiches and free wine."

"Brilliant."

Stasia had to attend the show for work and brought the boys along for a little culture. Unfortunately, the show was very disappointing. Abstract post-modernism at its worst in most cases. Indescribable but utterly forgettable pieces made up the remainder of the exhibit. The trio proceeded downstairs to the main room. A long table with a pristine white tablecloth held choices of four kinds of hors d'oeuvre, red and white wine, or soda water. Stasia located her target to accomplish the work aspect of her evening, and Dahvit and Victor wandered the gallery snickering and slugging back free wine.

‡

Victor spent the next day at the house. He had lunch at the Italian restaurant again and while he read, a man was speaking on his cell phone with someone about looking for work. When Dahvit returned from the library he cooked a shepherd's pie of beef mash and aged cheddar. While they sat at the table discussing religion and specifically their parents' take on religion, Stasia arrived. She kissed Dahvit and said hello to Victor.

“You were supposed to meet me so that we could train in together.” Stasia spoke softly in Dahvit's ear. She was visibly disappointed.

“I am so sorry, I completely forgot.”

Victor felt responsible. He thought of the overflowing recycling bin, stout cans threatening at the slightest provocation to spill out onto the kitchen floor in tidal waves. He thought of himself sitting alone in a pub.

“Hey, I was thinking about slipping out for a drink tonight if you two don't mind.” Victor abruptly stood with his empty plate.

“No, of course not, are you sure?” Stasia asked.

“Indeed, there's a place next to the convenience store on Finchley.”

“Oh, yes, we went in there once, on Patty's Day,” Dahvit added.

“The crazy place?” Stasia asked.

“Crazy?” Victor further inquired.

“The Irish place,” Stasia finished.

“Ah, perfect,” Victor smiled and put his cap on before walking out the door.

‡

The Grove was a large room. The gorgeous black-lacquered wood bar made Victor miss J.J. Smythe's, and the decor and seating reminded him of Lynch's near Avalon House. The pleasant young lady behind the bar had a slight Irish lilt to her accent and poured Victor's pint perfectly. One other man sat at a tall round table near the wall across from the bar. The room was otherwise vacant. Victor took a seat at a large table near the back of the pub. He meant to stretch out his notebook and make up for lost time, but he soon realized that the enormous table did not move, and it was just out of comfortable reach from the bench seat. He elected to open *Dubliners* instead. It only increased his homesickness for the Irish port town.

When Victor returned to the house Dahvit was walking through the downstairs hall.

"Victor, welcome back. Have a smoke before retiring?"

"Indeed." Victor joined Dahvit for the first of several cigarettes.

"Library tomorrow?" Dahvit asked as he crushed his last out.

"Yes, please. Just kick me up in the morning."

Victor was awake for another hour and finally wrestled sleep down near three am. The turbulence in Victor's mind was becoming desperate—

Artemio and The Old Man

≈

LXXIV

Summer ~ 2063[28]

"Come in Ambassador." Executive Fuentes offered the Ambassador a chair.

"Ah, Mr. Executive, I can't tell you how much this means to..."

"Yes, it is a pleasure to meet you as well, sir." Executive Fuentes seated himself without taking the ambassador's hand. "Normally, I'd never reach out to you directly, but we are facing an intense situation. Europe is threatening to end their contracts, all of them. Without Europe, the RTVS[29] becomes a burden to the A-PF."

The ambassador took his seat. "We are presently speaking on behalf of the Euro-Balkan Republic and the Union of Autonomous Entertainment States. There is nothing we can discuss impartially at this juncture."

Fuentes back-pedaled rapidly, "I lost my composure, it won't happen again."

"Mr. Executive, it is that insubordinate, primitive behavior that delineates master and servant. When Americans are well behaved, ethical, or dispassionate, they become boring." The Ambassador sat back in his seat and slowly unbuttoned his jacket. "I am here, Artemio, to solve *our* problem. We need to return your programs to prominence lest we lose our relationship with Beijing."

---

28 Iconography p. 28, Our World in the Sixty-third year of the New Millennium

29 Reality Television Society, a colloquial term for communities participating in the PPTEa Real-Communities™.

"I am all ears. I want nothing more than to perpetuate this relationship and its mutual benefits," Fuentes groveled.

"Very good. I'd like to introduce you to a man who was integral to the mapping of the first-wave RTVS communities." The Ambassador looked over his shoulder, "Please come in."

An old man in a plain grey suit and a weathered grey fedora entered the room.

"Good afternoon gentlemen. Pardon me while I find my way to the nearest chair." His wry smile splashed humility around the room and the Executive stood out of respect. As the Old Man took his seat and crossed his legs, the Executive caught a glimpse of the subtle exoskeleton just below the hem of his trousers. The light, flexible frame ran along the outside of The Old Man's calf and terminated within his archaic early-century shoe. The exoskeleton moved The Old Man's petrified limbs by responding to mere thought commands. He thus had the strength of a young, fit man, though his body could not hide its fatigue.

The ambassador took his seat and as the Old Man relaxed into a chair, he looked directly at the Executive. "Mr. Fuentes, Americans need to feel *besieged* again."

"By what?"

"Not *what*, but *whom*. Americans have lost the sense of fear that made them so compelling. We need to twist their arms a little. The struggle against *the enemy* is paramount; patriotism suffers liberal dilution otherwise. Without the nobility drawn from protecting the masses, we are left with the vacancy of your spoiled neo-aristocracy. Do you understand Mr. Fuentes?" The Old Man adjusted his tie and held his dark cane against his leg. A cane, Fuentes assumed, he still carried to *appear* frail.

"Yes. We need to rattle the cage of the hyena to make it laugh. Fine idea. How do we do it? The point of the RTVS was to put all consumer desires within reach."

"We need strife. Epistemological strife. I agree that it is difficult to foment strife while staying loyal to the brand. The threat cannot come from the outside world; we depend on that lifeline to survive. Are your intelligence services embedded in any lingering separatist groups?"

"There is only one left operating outside of our influence. The Inter-Realists want to put The Show to bed forever. They are a fledgling organization, but their strong populist appeal is cause for alarm."

"What do you know about the Inter-Realists?" The Old Man pressed.

"I can pull something up for you..." the Executive typed like a child, "...okay, here we go, this is from one of their numerous manifestos published by the Times." The Executive's desk flashed to life and zoomed in on an excerpt from a page-six news column:

> *The time has come to burn down the plantation houses. It is time to flush the rats from their gilded basements, to purge this infestation with fire. The scaffolding must be lit at its base, allowing the flames to engulf the wobbly supports of their State. There are no longer walls of perception erected around their crimes.* Inter-Realist Manifesto #37

"Perfect. Thank you, Mr. Executive. I will be in touch." The Old Man and the Ambassador began to stand. Fuentes obediently mimicked their ascent.

"But what the hell are we going to do?" Fuentes demanded.

"Don't worry Mr. Fuentes, this is quite out of your hands now. We only briefed you to ensure that you were culpable." The ambassador smiled and escorted the Old Man out of the once-again-Oval Office.

Executive Fuentes stood for several minutes, stunned. He could not shake the sense that he'd seen that frail old monster somewhere before.

"The Sarin canisters had *made in China* written on the side. The remote control came from Minato-ku and the components set sail from Jakarta. Mr. Executive, I think we must face the reality that the A-PF, either purposely or unwittingly, unified to attack a major US city. The question is what do we plan to do about it?" The Secretary of War took his seat.

"Thank you, Sanjib. Anyone else?" The Executive scanned his Cabinet.

"Mr. Executive, Mr. Secretary, I think it is rash to jump to aggressive postures," The Secretary of the Treasury contested. "The notion that we should shake a fist at the three pillars of the US economy is the sort of simpleton posturing that got us into this mess so long ago."

"Look, I didn't..." The Secretary of War stammered.

"Mr. Executive, I think the primary question to answer right now is *why*? It seems clear that persons within these countries were responsible, but we received no warning and certainly no requests for compliance, coordination, or assistance. I feel comfortable speaking for all of us in saying that it is most disheartening that we seem to be out of the loop on this." The Secretary of Treasury re-crossed her legs and waited silently for the Executive to react.

Fuentes's forehead remained smooth, his expression unperturbed. Either the Executive was counting daisies in a distant imaginary meadow, or he was incapable of feeling strongly in one way or the other.

"Thank you, Madame Secretary. Anyone else?" Silence... "We are adjourned. Thank you for your insight." Fuentes closed his notebook.

The Cabinet exchanged glances and slowly exited the conference room. Fuentes waited, wearing his mask of calm, then pulled up a connection on his handheld receiver. "Get the Ambassador. Now."

The Executive's console showed a broken, pixelated transmission of the Old Man who had accompanied the Ambassador. Fuentes sat forward, "What the hell did you do?"

"Mr. Executive, a pleasure..." the Old Man ignored his question.

"Tell me. Now." The Executive growled.

"You are not on the list, Artemio. I apologize, but this conversation is several steps above your paygrade. I assure you that you are safe for now and that we are only interested in replacing market-share. Do try to enjoy the rest of your Administration; we will take care of everything."

"This sort of attack on your own people is the beginning of the end."

"The beginning of the end? Of the Republic? Good riddance. The RTVS? Not yet, but eventually, yes." The Old Man smiled. "You have a facile grip on the underpinnings of history Mr. Executive. There is no end if the campaign is never completed. The show must go on for as long as the show *can* go on.

"We must push this society into its next chapter. I am only a facilitator of change, an agent of discord. It will be necessary to bring everything under the umbrella of the collective and then strip it away. We leave devastation, and in its wake, a society that must begin again."

"I don't understand..."

"That is clear. What you see beginning and ending is a façade. Physics famously teaches us that energy is never destroyed, that it simply changes form and continues in toto, devoid of autonomy. Control alters form, is crushed, re-distributed, re-planted, and sown. The rise and fall of Humanity, the rise and fall of Empires, religions, and nations, are all a thin veil hiding Control. What you see, Mr. Fuentes, is the reformation of Control in the former United States, our new National History. You would be best suited to interfere as little as possible. As a wise sage once wrote: *what you do is of little importance, however, it is of the utmost importance that you do it*."

"You're insane. Where is the Ambassador?"

"He's busy."

Fuentes's face reddened. He began to open his mouth and the Old Man interrupted.

"If the Ambassador feels compelled to speak to you, he will do so." The Old Man smiled, and the transmission ended.

Fuentes pounded his desk...and he remembered.

≈

Fuentes called his Vice Executive into the Oval Office near sunset.

"Have a seat. I don't know how he did it, Immanuel. I don't know how he pulled it off, but it's him."

"Who, Mr. Executive?" The Vice Executive looked up from his freshly poured scotch.

“He had his name washed from the record. He was a young Chief of Staff in Texas that joined Alamán's government. He worked behind the scenes on the CAS and was presumed dead after the Siege of Los Angeles. He resurfaced as the architect of the RTVS during the Bochinni scandal. Now he is whispering in the Ambassador's ear like a possessive lover.”

“Are you certain?”

“We found out that the real Auguste Dubh died back in '32. Almost ten years before he became known as the architect of the PPTEa. The Old Man, whoever he is, has assumed Dubh's identity, and is responsible for his work's influence.”

“Are you thinking intelligence agency? War Department, foreign agent?”

The Executive produced a portable console and showed side-by-side images of the Chief of Staff, Professor Dubh, and a screen capture from the recent conversation with the Old Man.

“It looks like the same man, at least the same suit, hat, and glasses. Is he really this generic looking in person?”

“No, quite the opposite, he fills the room when he enters. His presence is only ominous in its absence. He prattled on about control and energy being destroyed and re-made.”

The Vice Executive smiled.

Fuentes knew that he could not trust his second in command. “I think I know what his game plan is.”

“What is it boss?”

“Another drink, Jonathan, please.” Fuentes held up his glass.

“I'll take one as well...” The Vice Executive turned in his chair.

“No, you won’t. You need to be sober for interrogation.” The Secret Service filed into the room and surrounded the Vice Executive.

The Vice Executive pleaded, struggled, and kicked. “Wait, what are you doing?”

“Taking out the garbage.” Fuentes growled as the Vice was dragged from the building.

The Vice Executive was broken immediately. They continued interrogating him on Fuentes's orders for several weeks after he had confessed in full. They proceeded by torturing him until he admitted that his confession was false. His new confession invalidated his prior confession, so his captors began the process again to contrast his conflicted confessions and ultimately arrive at the *truth*. They pressed until the long-since-mad Vice Executive perished, screaming for his lost life. The Old Man disappeared, hidden once again.

≈

Autumn ~ 2066

Fuentes spent the following years in a constant state of fear, looking for the Old Man in every intelligence communiqué, and every exploding bomb on RTVS streets. The Sarin attacks continued against public transportation in every RTVS region. Before his deteriorating heart caught up with him, Fuentes witnessed the first volley in the Old Man's new order. In time for season finales, shadowy figures emerged to claim responsibility for the campaign of terror.

Consoles around the world crackled to life to watch and re-watch the *Declaration of Inter-Reality*. Three non-descript men whose faces were partially concealed by the brims of three grey mid-twentieth century fedoras appeared in front of an anonymous backdrop. Their eyes were hidden by light that reflected from their thin-framed, round, antique spectacles. The men were clean-shaven and wore identical grey wool suits. They read in unison, distorting any individual voice:

> *The stench of broken empire rose in the West and soon bathed the new earth in its swaddling decay. The Empire's illegal excursions into the Fertile Crescent at the birth of the twenty-first century marked the opening note in a tired, and painfully repetitious symphony—Our Death by Self-Inflicted Wounds.*
>
> *The civilized world had been watching the Leviathan's shining light sputter and flicker for a century. The world suffered as Americans blindly refused to*

hold their leaders accountable, refused to end the violence and slaughter.

The world learned from the Empire that Justice and Truth are subordinate to Corporate Nationalism. As the Empire funded, and cheered on the annihilation of men, women, and children, the rest of our world remembered.

For its entire history, The Empire has worshiped façade, honing it, perfecting it, distributing it. From our government's insistence that we are free, to the kabuki theater performed in our halls of legislation and judgment. The Empire cares not for its future or the futures of those it contaminates.

Though our country has been torn apart by civil turmoil and death, the people of the United States recognized their moment; it was only natural (was it not?) for our people to consider a watched life. Our receivers told us who we were, and whom our neighbors expected us to be—a person willing to sow envy in those same neighbors.

The late-century Hollywood reality phenomenon proved too attractive for the manipulators of lives to resist. The opening throes of reality were littered with just that...reality. Soon it became obvious that the allure of reality was strong enough to pull the viewer in but failed miserably to hold their attention. Alas, watching boring humans turned out to be...boring. Drama had to be amplified; it seemed, from the audience's standpoint, the more real a portrayal, the less real it felt on-screen.

But something happened. Something that had not happened in half a century of vapid, force-fed television programming: people actually became more odious simply by watching these shows. There was a demonstrable increase in apathy in persons exposed to high doses of reality programs. The subliminal message that the train wrecks they were watching on screen were somehow real, and therefore normal, altered the American psyche and distorted our concept of ourselves, others, and how we should interact.

We are no longer concerned, as a society, with what is real. The optimum we must hope for is recognition of the shared reality between each human being.

A realization of our unique Inter-Reality.

The efforts of the non-PPTEa communities must inspire our efforts to replace the RTVS and return to our humanity.

We do not choose violence, yet violence is inflicted on us for yearning to be free. When words and gestures of compromise are met with death, the Overseer must be quickened by steel. We call for unity against modern tyranny.

Demand a return to our natural, and long-suppressed, compassion. Demand an end to the collective prison of RealCommunities™ and our bondage to the Audience.

We will not stop until we are all free.

The short film was clean, stylized propaganda. Images of suffering, war, plastic neighborhoods, and plastic people were woven into brief reprises to the stoic reading men. The Inter-Realists were bent on pulling the foundations away from American Society. It was clear that the men fashioned themselves in the Luddite style of rejecting modernism, ultra-Conservatives masquerading as leftists and populists in America's post-millennial reality. A reality where *Conservatives* sought to conserve the near, rather than the distant past, to bind together forever the profit-wrenching machine the United States of Entertainment had become.

The Inter-Realist movement was to RTVS-youth what anarchism was to the fashion-obsessed London punks of the 1970s. The kids didn't understand what the Inter-Realists were calling for, but they refused to believe that such stylish anger could be anything but righteous. Men in old spectacles and suits began popping up on high school children's clothing, in music lyrics, and digital image-innuendo. By choosing the craven image in place of what the image represents, the coward is permitted to role play rebellion, to scream fuck you on bended knee, bound hand and foot in gleeful servitude.

≈

Winter ~ 2075

As Fuentes approached his final breaths, he witnessed his own grandchildren listening to bands screaming for the change the Inter-Realists were proposing. As he lay dying, he did so under heavy guard, expecting any one of his staff members to attempt or facilitate his assassination. It had been years since Fuentes had spoken face to face with any acting member of the US Government.

"Mr. Executive, it is good to see you." The Old Man walked lithely across the room.

"No...no..." Fuentes recoiled in horror.

"Don't worry Mr. Executive, I'm only here to wish you well on your next journey."

"How did you get past my security?" Fuentes wheezed.

"Don't be naïve, Mr. Fuentes." The Old Man smiled.

"You're behind this...all this destruction and chaos, you've been behind it for a very long time."

"Yes. It has been my duty to *facilitate* the re-direction of power over the years."

"You mean the re-direction of Control."

"Well, yes, to be candid. You have an excellent memory, Mr. Fuentes. There is a great deal of work still to be done, but you'll be *elsewhere* soon and none of it will concern you." The Old Man rapped his cane against Fuentes' luxurious deathbed.

"Then tell me. You have nothing to lose," the former Executive goaded.

"It would gratify my ego to provide you with a master plan old friend, but as ever, you fail to see the underlying truth. My journey began as a decision, and that decision has led me to many correlated and unrelated decisions. I am not especially talented, nor do I possess political prowess. I am a vessel for change, I am change, and when I am gone, change will continue to manipulate the world's stage in any way it sees fit. I may die before the conclusion of this chapter, but that is of little concern."

"Then this has all been for nothing?"

"Nothing? Do you expect that the world would have remained stagnant? Do you think that without me history would somehow have come to a sunnier conclusion? Please, Mr. Fuentes."

"Then what are you?"

"I am useful. Alamán found me so, but he was not ready to evolve. I helped grant the CAS a graceful defeat and in turn Executive Patterson tried to have me eliminated."

"The Apache strike after the ceasefire... "

"Precisely. I was paralyzed, but by no means dead. Strangely, the intelligence branches of the Pentagon felt I was more useful alive.[30] They leveraged a guarantee that the strike would not be fatal. Paralysis had not been intended either, but once they brought me in, I was able to continue working toward the PPTEa. When Bochinni tried to destroy my work he was set aside, as you have been."

The Old Man held the tip of his cane to Fuentes's neck. "My latest regret is not killing you years ago, but no one is perfect."

Fuentes closed his eyes and tears began to stream down his face. As death knocked on his door, he was above all a coward. When Fuentes opened his eyes, the Old Man was gone. Late that evening the Executive's heart failed as he lay asleep. When they discovered him in the morning his face was twisted in agony. He had thrashed violently in his bed, unable to speak as his spark slowly extinguished.

---

30 Specifically, an intelligence group that is mentioned only once in US government documentation, in the following footnote: "(316) The long schism between the DIA-████/Huntsville and the Department██████████ unwittingly caused the formation of a splinter cell within████/DIA DoE. This mingling of both agencies resulted in covert campaigns conducted on behalf of████/DIA warfare technology projects and ███████████ within DoE. The splinter group's intelligence and logistics capabilities are alarming; it must not be allowed to continue saturating both agencies. Immediate termination of the unnamed entity is suggested with prejudice."

A Watched Life

§
XLV

Summer ~ 2014

Thalia's soft olive skin glowed warm in morning light. Her long dark hair gathered in puddles at her sides as she lazily watched her feet mingling with Rein's. Thalia Atropos was a careless beauty. She had been scandalized by the haphazard and lecherous eyes of adults, but when all eyes were cast aside, she felt trapped in a deep, inescapable pit. Her young mind had been formed by unflinching lust from the immediate world and utter neglect from the two people whose blood flowed through her veins.

"How much Vicodin have you had this morning?" Rein asked groggily.

"Enough. Fuck off."

Rein always ruined the moment.

"Any vodka left?"

"Nope." Thalia stared at the wall smiling.

"I'll be back. Got any cash?"

"Purse."

"Where'd you get this thing?"

"I borrowed it from a friend."

"You only have eight thousand fucking purses..." Rein muttered under his breath, or so he thought.

"Get the fuck out."

Rein kept looking through the purse.

"Get the FUCK OUT!" Thalia shrieked.

Rein laughed to himself.

A full glass flew past his head and smashed against the wall. He kept laughing, "Thalia, your aim is improving. I'll be right back."

Thalia balled up on her bed and looked out the window. Rein strolled out of the building and whistled as he walked down MacCadden Place. He felt like a millionaire when he had someone else's money in his pocket. Thalia's eyes fluttered as the latest of several Vicodin pills washed over her body. Rein wasn't so bad, she recanted, at least he's good in bed and walks to the liquor store for me. The pills made everything make a little more sense.

As far as Thalia was concerned anyone asking her to be sober was obviously not on Team Thalia, her mother included. Though Rein had his moments of severe indiscretion, he never asked her to stop. He drank beside her, come rain or shine, and at the end of the night held her in his arms while he snored.

When Melvin and Lawrence walked into her living room, Thalia was climbing toward the light at the top of a deep, velvety well. Her eyes were rolling back in her head as she called, “Oh, honey, you came back.”

“Yes darling, now please take your pants off,” Melvin whispered.

“Um, Ms. Atropos,” Lawrence interrupted, mortified, “we need to speak to you for a moment.”

“Lawrence?” Thalia sat up and stared, doe-eyed at the wall adjacent.

“Thalia. I'm over here, it's Lawrence. This is my friend, Melvin Wurtzel.”

Thalia's eyes seemed to finally focus, and she limply offered Melvin a handshake.

Melvin shook her hand enthusiastically, “Nice to meet 'ya kid, real dump you have here.”

“Lawrence, who is this fuck?”

“Thalia, would you like a glass of water? This is a very important conversation,” Lawrence implored.

“You're mocking me as well? Wonderful. Do me a favor; just leave Lawrence. And take *Mr. Pretzel* with you.”

Melvin belly laughed.

Thalia sat up, enraged, “Get out!”

“Thalia,” Lawrence protested.

Thalia's fingers curled around the edge of a heavy crystal ashtray. With a flash of unexpected agility, she flung the heavy

§

projectile toward the two men. Lawrence belly-flopped on the ground as the ashtray smashed against the wall behind them. Melvin remained still, smiling at the heavily medicated goldmine piled on the dingy sofa like a coal miner's laundry.

"Mr. Wurtzel, please, let's try this again later." Lawrence tugged at Melvin's elbow.

"No." Melvin brushed Lawrence's weak grasp away and walked sternly toward Thalia.

He stood above her with his face inches from hers, "Look little girl, your mom wants to make a TV show, and we're here to make sure you receive your piece of the pie...ugh." Melvin grunted quietly as Thalia buried her fist into the crotch of his pants. He recovered slowly as Rein entered the apartment.

"Babe. BABE. Damn it, babe, why aren't you answering me...hey." Rein saw Melvin and Lawrence, "what's going on here, who are you?"

Rein looked around, scared, then charged at Melvin, who side stepped easily. Rein fell onto the sofa and as he turned around to get back up Melvin slapped him hard across the face. "Sit down and shut up. Lawrence, please finish and let's get out of this nuthouse."

"Thalia, your mother is trying to create a legacy for the family, and she would like you to be a part of it. It will be in a carefully edited and tasteful reality format."

"You'll be a star, doll-face, especially if you punch someone in the 'nads once per season." Melvin smiled and rubbed his testicles.

"What's going on?" Rein unconsciously rubbed his stinging cheek.

"Erlyst wants to turn her life into a TV show with these losers." Thalia flipped a limp wrist at Lawrence and Melvin. "They're trying to suck me into it."

Rein was certainly on board, $$ in his dim, unfeeling eyes. "You have to do this babe. Think about the exposure, you could be a god damn star like those fucking Jersey idiots. But you're way hotter!"

"And smarter...you forgot that part." Thalia smiled, basking in Rein's attention.

"Yeah babe, you know what I mean." Rein smoothed her hair back.

"I'll think about it." Thalia spat at Lawrence.

"Ah babe, come on... "

"Shut up Rein."

"We need to know missy," Melvin interjected.

"I told you imbeciles to leave. I have one more ashtray and now I know who to aim for, Mr. Wurtzel."

"Child, you have no idea who you are fucking with," Melvin sneered.

A second heavy crystal ashtray flew through the air in a flash.

Rein jumped up and ushered the men down the hall toward the front door. "Look gentlemen, put something in it for me and I'll make sure she signs the papers."

"Done, you're line producer for the pilot." Melvin slapped Rein in the face once more, for good measure, and walked out the door.

"I need the signatures tomorrow morning. Mr. Sarbays, do not disappoint me." Lawrence handed the contracts to Rein and walked down the hall toward Melvin.

§

Through her journaling, Erlyst was finally able to release some of her vile hatred by speaking its name. She agonized over her life's decisions and she wondered aloud in her writing whether her search for absolution would be empty. Thalia returned to her mother's bedside; this time she paid no respect to appearances; this time she strode proudly along the wood floors of Erlyst's chamber on impossibly high heels in a barely existent dress.

"Thalia, you look scandalous."

"Thank you, Mother."

"Well, I'm not certain you should take that as a compliment..."

"Enough, Erlyst. I want in on the show. I'd rather not discuss my life right now. What do I need to sign and whom do I report to?"

Erlyst leaned toward her daughter.

"Mom," Thalia pointed, "You're moving."

"Thalia, I want you to understand that this is meant to be a very public showing of our day-to-day lives. I think it best that you begin to surround yourself with your peers. Rein Sarbays is not your peer."

Thalia's eyes narrowed. She knew that she'd be mortified if someone lifted the rock she lived under. "I agree, I'll get rid of him tonight."

"You should move back into the Biltmore, for now."

"Okay. I can do that." Thalia was not thrilled about living with her mother.

"I'll raise your allowance while you are here, to ease the transition."

Thalia's eyes lit up. "I'll move back in by week's end. Is there anything else Erlyst?"

Erlyst searched Thalia's eyes a final time, "No, you are dismissed."

§

Fallen Empire splashed across boardroom receiver consoles from coast to coast. Even those who had no love for the concept could not look away from the obvious glut of wealth backing the project. Word spread fast and the pirates once again rallied, pulling in their studio markers, and making themselves and their financiers available for anything that Mr. Wurtzel desired.

Thalia returned to her mother's vast flat overlooking Pershing Square and tried to conduct herself like a lady worthy of her stature. She failed miserably, but never quite badly enough to warrant exile. To titillate investors, Melvin allowed a few video clips to leak of Thalia dancing half-naked at a rooftop party. Melvin had her followed inside the party and collected some *insurance* footage of Thalia manually manipulating Councilman Garcetti's twin sons to climax. Thalia was an instant internet sensation. Entertainment set them up and Melvin knocked them down. By year's end the project began filming.

Fallen Empire - Season One

Melvin's creation began with a 2015 New Year gala at the Atropos stronghold in the Hamptons with Erlyst presiding imperiously in a gilded wheelchair. She insisted on not being bed-ridden for the event. Thalia stayed in Los Angeles and received a battalion of visitors to her top-floor chambers throughout the weekend. She ended Sunday evening with three men, one of whom interrupted Thalia, the first man, and the second man, mid-coitus. In the scene that later earned Melvin infamy, Thalia, in shadow, pressed her finger out and ordered the late arrival to the bed. After a short and compelling silence, the man began to touch Thalia's lithe body, backlit in sensuous silhouette, while her original partners continued unabated.

So it was for much of the first season. Erlyst and Thalia witnessed their lives months later on receiver consoles alongside millions of Americans—one week at a time. Thalia's outrage spilled over when an episode featuring Rein aired.

Rein had walked into Hemingway's with a slip of a girl while *Fallen Empire* was filming Thalia's entourage. Rein's parasite looked all of nineteen, tall as a giraffe. Rein interrupted the group's conversation. Thalia looked up in horror and then looked away.

"Sir, sir? Yes, come here. This man is bothering us, and I would like to have him removed." Thalia motioned to the manager. He was very eager to do her bidding, especially on camera.

"Ah yes, Thalia, still a cunt." Rein smiled, his same blank excuse for a smile. "Look, I don't want any trouble, I just saw you and thought I'd say hello. This is Pam, by the way. She's from Denmark."

Thalia's entourage stared in awe as Pam reached her hand across the table. It took her a moment, but once she realized that Thalia did not intend to shake her hand, she retracted it, "Oh my," awkward giggle, "well, nice to meet you finally."

Rein saw security approaching. "Good luck with the show kiddo, you know my number." Rein and his Dane walked straight to the door and left.

§

"Was it just me," Thalia seemed to ask the camera, "or was that broad wasted?"

"They both were," a nameless tag-along intoned.

The on-scene director assured Thalia that he'd personally insist that Rein be cut from the episode featuring the restaurant.

Thalia lost her mind months later when Rein's face flashed across the screen. Within seconds she was screaming to the first *Fallen Empire* employee that answered, "I'm done! Do you hear me you sorry fuck? DONE!"

Thalia was unfortunately deluded about her position. To be *done* she was required to bond her potential stake in the contract, a tidy sum that even her late father would have had difficulty producing in liquid assets.

Thalia tried to sue, further humiliating herself; the show's popularity demanded that she stop whining and grow up. PR and real life fused for Thalia; if she walked away, she was finished, and she would leave the game a pathetic loser.

Legal representation for Thalia did not protest when the defense counsel asked the court to dismiss the charges. Both sides of the case shook hands before leaving the courtroom.

She knew the show owned her, but it was the first time it had betrayed her. Thalia became convinced that the entire point of *Fallen Empire* was to betray her—and she was partly correct. Her initial outrage led her to self-destruct weekly on American viewing screens. She had far more stamina than Melvin had anticipated. When the tantrum finally evened out, they began meetings for the breathlessly awaited second season. Thalia's meltdown had pushed the show's numbers through the roof and the Producers were willing to do anything, up to and including providing medical grade Dilaudid, to push the numbers. Thalia banished her feelings of autonomy and prepared to give the world the show they were obviously begging for.

During the second season, Melvin revolutionized the genre once again. On a sunny Saturday afternoon Melvin sat with Number One. "It's fucking bright."

"I know," she replied equally frustrated.

In the blinding 3rd Street afternoon, their lips and oversized sunglasses met over twin bottles of English brown ale. "Vicodin baby?"

"Um. Maybe in a little while." She scrunched her pale cheeks up while a soft, warm wind blew a strand of her crimson hair across her forehead. Melvin pointed his receiver's camera toward Downtown and framed her in skyscrapers against a neon sky.

"How do I look?" she demanded playfully. "Let me see... "

Melvin twisted, denying her a glance.

"Let me see it culero, hijo de puta."

Melvin belly laughed as her face grew red. "Wait, baby...that's it."

The whole *I want to see the picture before you post it* terror was an unspoken desire to create a façade as bulletproof and consistent as a celebrity. Emulation nests in mimicry, and if every kid watching *Fallen Empire* had a cheap disposable camera-phone, they'd turn their lives into a splinter reality show and sink deeper into the Atropos nightmare. They could cut production costs by wasting time on the audience footage and make them feel like part of the team. "I'm a brilliant fucking genius baby."

"I know. Part of why I keep letting you stick it in me." She fluttered her strawberry blonde eyelashes and Melvin shifted luridly in his seat.

"So, that's it?" Melvin asked. "What about my big, beautiful..."

"Yep. That's it."

"I'm going to have Larry call his telecom people and we're going to ship disposable *Fallen Empire* phones to lucky winners so they can run amuck as amateur paparazzi. If we're lucky, they will ruin some of their friends' lives with internet-worthy homemade porn." Melvin smiled, pleased with himself.

"Mr. Wurtzel, if we weren't in public... "

"I know baby, I know."

§

§

Summer ~ 2017

On the coattails of flushing the cell-phone market with cheap disposable product at maximum profit, Melvin leveraged Chinese, Japanese, and South American syndication before the conclusion of the third season. Though they'd be a little late to the dinner table, foreigners had been hearing about *Fallen Empire* for over a year in American and Ameri-phile entertainments. Thalia's escapades soon warped young Japanese and Brazilian minds alike; soon her poor choices about sex, prescription pills, and clothing were dogma to a generation of children who were proud to say *no matter what kinda' fucked up cretin I become I will never be Thalia Atropos*—far less subtle than Barbie and American family sit-coms. *Fallen Empire* set commercial aims at siphoning empathy from adolescent minds and replacing it with viscous, polluted lust for the next *it*; an emotional fracking that could be felt long into the adult years.

Thalia saw the inside of jail cells in seven states and her untouchable status echoed throughout pop-culture. In the fourth season, Wurtzel signed on with 'Chilz—an online subscription website with two billion users—to make original receiver content for their customers. Melvin and Erlyst said goodbye to network entertainment and NC17 ratings. *Fallen Empire* descended into a pit of depravity viewers found impossible to look away from. Though it permeated their minds, they refused to un-plug from the family's bottomless vapidity and Erlyst's imperial cruelty.

Thalia was permitted a few nights per month of freedom; a feature of her latest contract. Freedom from being watched, she was promised, though Melvin unerringly sent at least a camcorder to tail the queen of train wrecks...just in case.

"Did we lose him?" Thalia tried to catch her breath while spinning perilously onto Santa Monica Blvd.

"I think so baby. Wow, where did you learn how to drive like that?" A hard, yet malleable piece of masculine perfection flirted from the passenger side.

"I've been ditching cameras all my life," Thalia stopped at the curb, "get out."

"Wait, I thought... "

"Yes, I'd prefer you didn't think. We've been over this. Get out."

"Okay, okay. Call me?"

Thalia drove off, skidding back into the flow of Saturday night traffic in West Hollywood.

In the violet early morning, Thalia slipped from Club Sin-A-Matic with a man she'd just met. Her shiny PVC miniskirt was sodden with fingerprints and her long dark hair was tussled suggestively. Her prey was beautiful, bred over centuries as concubine to wealth. His stamina and his crushing grip would be the glorious little death of her if she could only keep him from speaking and keep his hands beneath her skirt. Thalia struggled to keep his impeccable body at the forefront of her mind, and by the time he mustered the dexterity to remove her miniscule black panties, Thalia was stimulated enough to hesitantly let him have his way with her in the parking lot.

She received what she had compromised for, the neural stimuli she needed to cope, and the soft warm sea of denial to which she became hopelessly addicted. All pain evaporated in pounding and thrusting amnesia. When the man pushed her to the ground, in the craven act of stealing a rich girl's purse, not even the pain and humiliation could wipe the ecstasy from her reeling mind.

A rabid *Fallen Empire* fan, on vacation from Oklahoma City, recognized Thalia through tequila-muddled eyes. As he stumbled down the street, she burst from a dank club, in the flesh. The fan nearly spoke but instead fumbled in his pocket for his official *Fallen Empire* digital recorder. A plastic hulk of a man followed Thalia and carried her down the sidewalk. The fan followed Thalia and her companion into the next parking lot. From a barely concealed position on Santa Monica Boulevard, the fan recorded the entire incident.

His close-ups on Thalia's bleeding knee, laddered stockings, and tearless expression of calm made Melvin Wurtzel a very happy man, "If you weren't such an annoying wreck, I'd offer you a job."

"I can change," the fan pleaded.

"Look, you're going to get a free dinner out of this, and if you behave yourself, I'll send a friend over to keep you company."

"Okay." The fan looked disappointed.

"Okay? How about thank you sir? How about, yes sir, that is very generous of you, sir?" The fan was about to defend himself when Melvin moved nose to nose with him. "Just don't."

The fan retreated and was escorted to a waiting car.

Melvin turned to his personal assistant, "When Thalia sees the episode that man recorded, I want you to personally give her that fuckwad's home address."

§

Fallen Empire – Season Five

"Melvin?"

"Erly-Sue, to what do I owe this intrusion?"

"Do you know what today's date is?"

"Um, fifteenth-ish?"

"Thirteenth, Melvin. Do you recall why that's important?"

"No, but I have a feeling you're about to tell me..."

"No cameras Melvin. I asked that I not see a single camera today. Why are nine *Fallen Empire* crewmembers dulling the finish on my Chippendale desk with spotlights?"

Melvin groaned. "I'll pretend to remember something about that if it makes you feel any better. Here's the thing, we need some specific footage. You've got a meeting today right?"

"Correct."

"Anyone you hate?"

"That's a long list Melvin."

"Perfect. We need Queen Bitch Erlyst, can you humiliate whoever this corporate yahoo is?"

"With pleasure. I don't want us to stray here, I'm not done scolding you..."

"We're not, princess. Your angst is duly noted, but you *are* the show. So, let's lace up those big girl panties and..."

Erlyst disconnected the call.

"Listen up felons and imbeciles." She addressed the crew strewn about her office in various stages of construction. "I am performing under duress. If you find me disagreeable today, please direct all inquiries to Melvin Wurtzel. Is makeup ready for me yet? Good, let's get this over with."

A young woman with stark black hair approached Erlyst. "Mrs. Atropos, it's a pleasure to meet you." The makeup artist curtsied, revealing a shock of mucus green hair tied into her ponytail.

"If you dare do either my hair or makeup like your own, it will be the last time you lay hands on another human being."

"Yes ma'am. I won't ma'am."

Erlyst sat impatiently. Her fingers clicked against the wood frame of her chair, and the smock, carefully tied across her chest, began to chafe her neck. The lights, set now in their broadcast constellation, burned down on Erlyst like menacing stars.

"You. Did you tell me your name? Don't bother. I can't believe you still have a job if it takes you this long to work. It's like you've never had anyone in a chair before. You've basically done what I do every morning in about five minutes."

"I'm sorry Mrs. Atropos, I'm nervous."

"Nervous? I don't have time for nervous. Did you lie on you resume?"

"No ma'am, I didn'."

The Irish lilt that the makeup artist tried so hard to suppress, surfaced. Erlyst could not push down her own thoughts of Shannon, her partner in crime so many decades past. She would not know Erlyst now.

"Where are you from?"

"Silverlake."

"I mean, before America."

"County Cork, Ireland, ma'am."

"I thought as much. I cannot keep you, but I bear you no ill will. My behavior was deplorable, and I apologize."

"Thank you, ma'am. Should I..."

"Yes. Just go." Erlyst raised her arms. "Someone fetch me a small tumbler of neat whiskey. If it's not in my hand by the time I count to ten, I'll stare directly into the camera *all damn day*."

Worker ants scurried and Erlyst submitted to her Nurse as she strapped the Matriarch into her gilded chair.

A meek director's assistant whispered, "Ten more minutes, Mrs. Atropos."

Erlyst shouted, "Why are you whispering? This guy's fired too. Anyone else feeling stupid?"

§

"Mrs. Atropos," Erlyst's personal assistant spoke calmly from her chamber doors. "Mr. Blankenfeld has arrived."

"Send him in." Erlyst continued with her work, shifting papers and making notes of mysterious import behind her large writing desk.

"Mrs. Atropos, I'm... "

"James Blankenfeld." Erlyst smiled and looked up, removing her reading glasses, and instilling a sense of full attentiveness. James Blankenfeld was an impressive six-five, give or take, too pretty and perfect to be intimidating. Most people would gladly sell him their first born and thank him for the pleasure.

"James, please call me James."

"As you wish. Please, have a seat, is this your assistant?"

"Yes, this is..." Mr. Blankenfeld struggled to recall.

"I'm Anne, thank you for seeing us today." Blankenfeld's assistant made an instant impression.

The lithe young woman took her seat confidently and tucked her mousy brown hair behind her left ear. Her suit was impeccable, and though she was his inferior at the office, her charisma made James seem small and frail.

"I'll cut to the chase..." James punched back in, grinning.

"I'm sorry, James, right? Please refresh my memory. What are we supposed to discuss this afternoon?"

Mr. Blankenfeld was not amused. His clean-shaven upper lip quivered. "Of course. We are proposing a partnership to block a massive solar panel farm in southeast California... "

"What would this partnership require from Atropos LLC?"

"My institution is prepared to fund the campaign, but we require a sympathetic ear in the media and, if it comes to it, friends on the bench."

"I understand. Why are you destroying this project?"

It was an improper question. Erlyst knew it, Anne knew it, and Mr. Blankenfeld felt he had to remind Mrs. Atropos that, "We don't go into the intentions of our clients. We are a conduit by which they accomplish their varied and sometimes sensitive goals."

Erlyst mused: *because solar power is hippie, commie bullshit; because we already sank trillions into wrenching the last molecule of petroleum from the earth's crust; because we can't* <u>*stand*</u> *to be proven wrong; because when you're this powerful, you don't need a fuckin' reason.* "You know the answer, James. I'm not asking you to sell out your demon masters, I'm only asking a question."

"But it's the question you are asking. It's simply not done."

"Thank you for your time. There won't be anything else." Erlyst dismissed him casually.

"I demand... "

Erlyst's back straightened and she struck the surface of her desk. "You demand nothing."

"Mrs. Atropos," Anne leapt to her feet, "I assure you it is not our institution's intention to bully or otherwise coerce you. Thank you, very sincerely, for your time. I hope that we meet again on calmer terms." Anne began to usher the enraged Regional Vice President of Special Projects Funding toward the door.

"Anne. see Mr. Blankenfeld out, but please return. I'd like to continue this conversation with you over tea. Are you available?"

P. Anne Twardowski blushed violet, "I am, yes. Thank you, Mrs. Atropos. I shall return directly."

"The rest of you parasites," Erlyst addressed the *Fallen Empire* crew, "be gone. We're done for the day."

Erlyst intended to grant Mr. Blankenfeld's organization its request, but it would be Anne that garnered the accolades.

‡

XVI

‡

Victor was disturbed by another dream.

> *9/10/10*
>
> *A giant park, with a child's playground in the middle. I am standing with another man. I know we are close friends. We are also having trouble finding an exit. We consider hopping the fence at one point; a fence made of imposing vertical, wrought iron bars. The trees are bare, it is autumn. I feel like I have already been there before and find it frustrating that I cannot get out now, I've been in the park too long.*
>
> *I walk past the front door of an angular, glass-paneled building and have to wade through a crowd leaving a wedding. I'm moving with much trouble, traveling perpendicular to the crowd, bumping into people, seeing faces flash by. The current of eyes and mouths refuse to pool into identifiable persons.*
>
> *The way out appears: a turnstile gate, black, with the bars bent to make sure you can only turn it one direction. It is hard to get to, even though we can see it clearly. We finally escape and head to a convenience store.*
>
> *I stand numbly under fluorescent light staring at the magazine rack. Nothing is compelling. I look out the window and see the park bursting at the seams: as if the wedding had enfolded billions of guests into a tiny space, before rupturing. Arms, legs, heads, bare shoulders, trouser cuffs, and eggplant pumps press between the park's wrought iron barrier like clay through a press. Flailing human bodies pour over the brim of the formidable fence, spilling and scurrying into the surrounding streets like a virus.*
>
> *Two young bodies crash against the window, laughing, filthy, and covered in chains, spikes, and tattoos. They notice the people inside the convenience store and leer into the window, as if something they really need is inside. I tap the glass with the edge of my right*

boot, scaring both of them. I am proud of my little joke.

I feel guilty about doing it while I am in the checkout line. I am not that person; I live in a decrepit warehouse with gutterpunks and their animals. I am better than no one.

A feeling, like a loud shrill sound, comes over me and I turn. One of the derelict boys is directly behind me. His face is scarred, either from being exposed to the elements or some sort of necrotic disease. His eyes are vacant, reddish, against eerie yellow clouds of cataracts. He has short, shaved red hair and a small prison tattoo of three circles and a triangle beneath his left eye. I turn back to make my purchase, not wanting to make the man feel odd.

The boy licks a square piece of paper and sticks it to the back of my neck where my hairline meets the skin, and he says, "You've got it now. friend."

I am horrified that he has just given me some sort of curse.

The derelict boy goes outside and is joined by a group of ten more derelicts. The store patrons watch, trying to figure out who they are, and the derelicts begin harassing someone who is sitting on the tailgate of a truck (like hooligans in a film). They rob this person and begin to walk across the street.

A stampede of mad humans, like the rush beyond a burst dam, overcomes the boys, the truck, and the victim. The wide windows of the convenience store are suddenly encased in faces—smashed against the glass, eyes snarling red and writhing against the crush.

The store windows begin to crack and splinter.

I am no longer in the store; I am on a desperate hunt to find a place to escape the maddening human deluge, seeking, always, higher ground. I need to clean myself, wash my hands, scrub my body. I walk in and out of identical tract houses, none are inhabited.

I come to one house and there is a man on a sofa. I feel like I am intruding, so I move on. I find a place that is enormous—the house is completely covered in wood-paneled walls, no carpet, so I think: this is the one. I walk to the back of the house, there is still nothing. I return to the front of the house and the sofa man from the last house is there and has aged decades. The old man is belligerent, wants money, some food, pills. I give him what feels like a lot of money—Sterling Pounds.

What I am looking for is under the sofa the man is sitting on. I locate soap and an astringent. "I could have told you that," the man scolds me.

I make my way to the middle of the house and find a room that has an enormous sink at the center. I scrub my hands with soap and astringent, thoroughly and compulsively cleaning every inch of my hands, beneath the nails, et cetera.

I feel a presence, I notice butcher paper scattered all along the floors, crumpled and in sheets (off-white). I think the old man is angry again and coming back to fuck with me, but a procession of people in humble clothing begin walking into the room in single file. I feel as if they are "showing themselves" to me, or "revealing themselves." I get the impression that they have always been in this house, as if they live in this place.

They are all sober faced and their cheeks redden with recognition when our eyes meet.

When Victor woke, he felt comfort, a forgotten calm.

The wood floors groaned.

"You ready?"

"Sure, give me a sec."

Victor dressed, brushed his teeth, and they headed out into the warm morning. Euston was slightly less crowded; the commuters had thinned as the morning rushed on. Dahvit lead Victor through backstreets and into the delivery-dock bowels of his school, UCL. The white hallways gave way shortly to a pristine courtyard filled with graduates and their friends, families, and loved ones.

"Ah fucking graduation, I forgot" Dahvit moaned. "I'm afraid we will not be able to access the library."

"Don't sweat it man," Victor smiled.

Dahvit and Victor left UCL behind and dashed behind the campus to a corner pub. Space was limited due to a lunch rush and the two friends vacillated between patience and scurrying off.

"Let's have a pint and a look at the menu and we'll see if we're moved." Dahvit suggested.

"Excellent, I concur." Victor removed his cap and set it on the bar.

"Well that was annoying. UCL does love its little soirees. To our detriment of course." Dahvit was perturbed.

"We're not in the club."

"But I *am* in the club!" Dahvit laughed and raised his hands to the sky.

"So, when do you aim to come to America? I mean, you'd probably better hurry."

"Of course, the end is nigh, is it?"

"Nigh may be a little strong. It's hard to say what everyone else will put up with. I assumed that by 2006 or 2007 there would be some sort of Allies to our Axis. We have been thus far spared our Berlin moment, but it can't go on forever."

"Unless it's meant to. I mean, the best way to hurt someone bigger than you is to wear 'em down first."

"True. It's a callous strategy in the short-term. I mean, we've slaughtered untold millions in the last decade alone, and the new president shows no signs of slowing any of it down."

"You don't think the accountability will come from within?"

"No way. Sorry, but no fucking way."

"Come now, one of the reasons people hesitate to judge the US is its reputation for righting its wrongs eventually."

"It's just too profitable and too easy to control the masses with fear of the "other." Our government has enshrined perpetual war and leaders that try to stop the madness are ejected with extreme prejudice. We have a long way to go, as a people, before we could rise up in any meaningful fashion. We have a saying: *if you sleep in a parking lot waiting for the newest smartphone, you're a good consumer. If you do it for social justice, you're a dirty hippy and deserve to be tased.*"

"That puts it very succinctly. Hyperbole?"

"Not from where I stand, brother. Dissent is suppressed without batting an eyelash."

The silky pints of stout were well received, but the menu did not move them at all.

"Well, fuck it, let's drink these and then look for food elsewhere." Victor offered.

"Yes, but where? I'm having a hard time with this at present. Wait, how do you feel about Thai food?" Dahvit smiled as he looked out the window.

"I usually love it."

They crossed the small street to a tiny white storefront. A counter and register bisected the long narrow room. Small, delicate tables with white chairs filled the space. They were seated against a bookcase near the kitchen.

"So, what do you think is going to happen?" Dahvit took his first sip of Thai beer.

Victor followed suit. "Nothing."

"Really? Nothing at all? No counter-American revolution flooding the streets? No dark horse candidate that surprises everyone by stealthily dialing back the horror?"

"No. Nothing perceivable. Nothing that will alarm anyone per se, not yet. There needs to be a spark, a catalyzing event. The way protest has been relegated to "freedom" zones, and police have been given the wink to beat first and ask questions later, that event may not be far off. But again, it's going to be crushed. What happens after will be the responsibility of the survivors."

"Books rarely have one chapter. Your people have a way about them. When it comes down to it, on the edge of the abyss, you cannot collectively suffer cruelty forever. You at least play a pretty good game, enough to inspire other countries to err on the side of less-repressive."

"I'm pessimistic I know, but I am from America," Victor laughed. "Right now, man, I think we are so far up our own asses that if the right television program came along and told us to jump off a bridge, most of us would do it. Have you listened to what our politicians say these days? It's really astonishing, and not in a good way."

"You can turn that off though. Cut the umbilical cord."

"Of course, but I wouldn't be surprised if our need evolved and found sustenance elsewhere. For fuck's sake, look at cable and the internet, it's just TV on steroids."

"TV was just radio on steroids."

"Right," Victor drank to that.

"Supposing it is something that is flowing through these mediums, how would we quantify such a thing? It serves so many purposes for so many people, it seems unlikely that there is a malignant guiding force," Dahvit proposed.

"With this beast, diversity is the enemy. Monopoly serves the message and keeps alternative ideas at bay (no dildo commercials on Sunday or during the evening news). It keeps the money flowing in one direction. For this organism to continue existing, it is necessary that it have some hook that carries it through the ages."

"Some people might call something like that *god*," Dahvit interjected.

"Precisely. That's one of the best hooks mankind has conjured up. Entertainment is on its way to taking the crown."

"The Sun worshipers had a pretty substantial, awe-inspiring, and reliable godhead to refer to. Telling everyone that you were the only one who knew *for certain* whether the Sun would rise each day...that's power."

"And yet, the Sun always rises. So, you must adapt. If your minions call your bluff and you threaten a sunless day, you are fucked pal. You have to mythologize contradictions instead of explaining them, and in the end you must market it to the masses as the one and only connection to the power of the universe." Victor raised his arms like a late-night shopping channel MC, "No magic powers necessary, just a sturdy and unquestioning faith among the flock."

"And you think this serves as the ultimate distraction?"

"The ultimate entertainment," Victor countered. "It's the *Get To Paradise* show starring everyone, whether they like it or not. The political distraction is pervasive in the US. The media has been hijacked and people are more than willing to allow that crew to shape the reality they conform to. They aren't idiots, they choose this lie. Choosing to be ignorant becomes a matter of patriotism, and to denounce it is like running into an AA meeting and screaming: *Couldn't handle it? PUSSIES!* We haven't bounced back from our 43rd president, haven't even started, honestly. We're walking down the wrong path and not looking back. It's sanctioned now that both political parties want war, espionage, and slaughter. Torture and mass incarceration have a global base; we can pull you from any street in any country and put you under indefinite detention."

"A grim affair indeed." Dahvit sighed.

They paid their bill and walked back onto the street. "Another pint before we head home?" Dahvit smiled.

"Sure, let's go."

The pub they stopped into had a small rainbow flag above the doorway, and a relaxing rustic feel. The pub's beautiful dining room and the bar beyond were a pristine dark, lacquered wood. Victor ordered pints and they sat at the bar, waiting for someone to clear a table.

"So, what's next for the US?" Dahvit continued.

"I think the US may be in for some turmoil if it keeps sucking all resources to the Executive Branch, specifically the Pentagon. People are still too afraid of losing their meager jobs, too frightened of not having a car, or a laptop. Our possessions control us. It will take walking away from all of those things to spark change from below."

Dahvit and Victor took two empty seats. Victor continued, "I don't think the American people have what it takes to stand on Pennsylvania Ave. for months until the President comes out to face them. I don't think Americans are desperate enough yet to mobilize in the way they would need to..."

"Before it's too late," Dahvit assisted.

"That's what I'm afraid of. If we need a revolution, it's already too late. Might as well start picking sides for a civil war."

"America in a civil war, live online. The world would stand still." Dahvit added.

"Shame we can't put the whole damn country on TV, might pacify the herd long enough to actually change our society."

"Wouldn't put it past your kind Victor," Dahvit patted Victor on the back. "Let's get the fuck out of here."

‡

As they waited for the train north to Golder's Green Station, it occurred to Victor that he'd be gone in less than twenty-four hours, back to Dublin.

"Would you watch it?" Victor mumbled, more than a little drunk.

"What?" Dahvit asked.

"A reality show about the United States."

"You're inferring that the US isn't largely a reality TV show now." Dahvit removed his hat.

"A majority of the population could be involved, relatively easily."

"All kidding aside, what happens to jobs if that takes place?"

"You've never been to LA," Victor smiled. "We function, from sewer to high-rise apartment, while under a blissful mask of façade. Your barista, trash collector, and city council person are all either trying to get on the big show or would drop their pants at the chance to try. The fawning, preening hordes of Los Angeles and its surrounding Valleys insist religiously that they create reality."

"But the rancid vapidity, man. How could it ever last?"

"Hey, I don't personally get it, but there are whole cable channels dedicated to this style of programming. For years it was a race to see who could think of the most reality TV scenarios, pilot them, and get them on. The reality TV junkies didn't care, the more the merrier."

"Shock and awe." Dahvit smiled.

"You said it brother."

"Within the US, the reality TV thing has become extremely obnoxious, but what of Europe, Asia, the Middle East? Africa?"

"I don't find that far-fetched at all. The world's affinity for blue jeans and blues-based rock is no less ridiculous than the idea that they'd waste their lives watching Americans be complete morons."

"Pardon me." A man in a subtle navy suit and khaki trench coat clenched the overhead bar as he leaned in. "Do you mind if I interrupt? I think you are correct, the world is ready, thanks to the internet, to give into the western concept of plugging in. If you don't mind my asking, how would you pull that off? I mean, making the population into a show?"

"We are consumers, so you would have to keep us distracted by products. If they were provided for people by advertisers, class structure can be re-administered on more arbitrary lines of story worth."

"3D Product placement," Dahvit added.

"Lifestyle placement," the man clarified.

"Sure, isn't *keeping up with the Jones'* a kind of social product placement? It's certainly been used in advertising since day one," Victor challenged.

"Interesting, so if you want your dish soap used internationally, what better way than to feature it than on the Great American Show?"

"Man, that is fucked up," Victor steadied himself against the center bar. "My name is Victor Loingsech by the way." He shook the man's hand.

"Auguste Dubh."

"Dahvit Herr."

"Nice to meet you, Auguste, and thank you for jumping in on our conversation."

"My pleasure. I felt compelled. I am a project manager these days, but once upon a time I was a serious philosophy student."

"Ah, this is my stop, pleasure to meet you both, and good luck sussing this one out." Auguste Dubh slipped between the automatic doors and disappeared down the chaotic hallways corralling the ants as they pressed immanently to the surface.

Dahvit and Victor continued the dark fantasy, imagining a United States divided up into neighborhoods based on a plotline designed behind the scenes. Victor insisted that a separate society of plumbers and mechanics would still be necessary behind the façade. Dahvit suggested it might resemble a colonial dynamic with the watched society preying on the others in order to pump themselves up as the elite. Victor added, "A new nationalism, one based on an image projected to the world. It could be the new religion."

"Nonsense, no one else believes in Americans like Americans do," Dahvit pointed out.

"Precisely, it is the new *American* religion. It is the ultimate proselytizing beast, sending its image of perfection and imperfection into the world as a beacon. The faithful have proven adequately able to re-imagine our tiny country as the center of a universe in which we guide the morality and meaning of the entire species."

"Although I think that is probably a fair assessment from a fair man, you give your people a little less credit than they deserve. After all, you're from America."

"I have a tendency to do that, curse of the thinking class, eh?"

"Europeans, probably more than Americans, appreciate how hard it is to keep so many people peacefully cooperating, and so diverse a people at that. It'd be like the EU suddenly having to act like a single country, a nation, instead of just head gangster. "

"Perhaps, but we have lost both authority and legitimacy and are staring down the barrel of making it worse by sticking our heads in the sand and pretending that we deliver freedom and prosperity to people at gunpoint."

"Delusional..." Dahvit grimaced as the train doors parted on Golder's Green Station.

"Yes. Purposely so."

Victor broke off and went on a final run to the market for cans of stout. When he returned, a white candle burned in Stasia and Dahvit's bedroom window. The walls flickered and the room appeared to be filled with tiny scattered lights. The overfilled recycle bin on the sidewalk dropped a stout can loudly on the silent pathway. Dahvit had joked that he feared what the neighbors might think, so he waited until the final night to place the bin on the street. Victor opened the door silently and placed the stout in the refrigerator. He exited the house as silently as he had entered and walked the cool streets back to the Italian restaurant. It seemed apropos that Victor spent his last evening in London retracing familiar steps. He seated himself outside the restaurant and the waiter approached.

"Allo!" He called, recognizing Victor.

"Hello to you. Same thing please?"

"Of course, right away."

A man, very very drunk, lunged toward Victor from across the doorway. He made several unintelligible statements. Victor was able to suss out that he was speaking Italian. In spite of the man's aggressive lack of coherence Victor wished he could at least communicate with him.

Victor opened his notebook to comment on the dwindling hours of his London excursion.

9/10/10

The wet streets are quiet for a Friday evening. Golder's Green is the 'burbs, sleepy-town, compared to the eastside. The heavily religious community holds great sway here. No matter how pervasive it becomes it is drastically absurd to see religion tamper with real life, especially the lives of those who chose not to pledge allegiance to theological abstraction.

Perhaps there is another dimension to Nihilism. Perhaps "nothing matters" is to be taken as a cautionary warning rather than a mantra. In other words, nothing matters, so do not let "things" ruin or make your life, treat "things" as they are: trivialities within a

> *lifetime. To apply too much meaning to the meaningless is a sickness, and a powerful motivator. So strange that persons enchanted by the sacred would be willing to commute it to crude and archaic symbols. Who among the faithful is faithful enough to stand and say, enough nonsense?*
>
> *It is clear: the contradictions and the travesties of faith lay squarely at the feet of dogma. Even if there be bloodshed, dogma must be defended. Now we have the proselytizing factions of Sun-Worship Monotheism who are not content to whittle their subjects into fine featureless masses. No, they now wish to market the divine: advertise, above all advertise, "We know the capital-T Truth. You need to get some of this."*

It began to rain lightly as Victor paid his check and bade farewell to the still screaming Italian. Tiny, mist-like raindrops collected on Victor's black clothing and boots like infinitely distant stars against the enveloping pitch.

He felt he would miss London when he left, more specifically Stasia and Dahvit, but he had not fallen in love with London like he had Dublin. London was a lot like home, both the people and the ways in which people carried on with life. London was a complicated city; Los Angeles was complicated as a matter of identity. Without the discomfiting allure of complication and mystery, the con artist and the politician wield no leverage over the human mind. When he reached the flat, the diminished white candle was still burning in the window. Victor could not decide if he should go back to the pub and wait them out, or just cuddle up with his stout and sit on the patio smoking cigarettes.

He smoked a cigarette on the front lawn to spare himself a moment to consider both options and to sit beneath North London's stars a final time. London was not as blessed as Dublin, with its luxurious and tilting cascade of visible night stars. Victor walked toward the front door twisting the end of his cigarette until it was no longer a fire hazard and slipping it into the rubbish bin.

"All's well that ends well."

‡

Dahvit was walking through the corridor looking thoroughly thrashed. His cheeks reddened and he apologized for being sequestered.

"Nonsense," Victor laughed him off, "I'm going to drink an unnecessary amount of stout and pass out before I hit the airport in the AM."

"Stasia and I will be down in a moment."

"No need mate..."

"I know," Dahvit smiled and ascended the elbowed staircase.

The couple came downstairs, Stasia's alluringly sleepy eyes were half lidded tonight, her week's work had come to an end and finally she looked forward to a day she could wake up whenever she pleased. They spoke long into the night and put a lovely bow on their mutual gift of sharing London with Victor before retiring to their beds and beckoning the Sandman.

Morning came rapidly. The sun rising behind billowing grey clouds had interrupted his light nap. He dressed, compiled his belongings, checked, re-checked, and re-re-checked his flight information and tickets. As requested, he knocked on Stasia and Dahvit's door.

"Hello?" Dahvit called. "Come in."

The couple epitomized Saturday morning, hair crazy with passionate sleep and disoriented.

"Hey guys," Victor leaned in to hug them before they got up, "thank you bastards for everything it's been absolutely amazing."

They hugged him in turn, "No no no, we're walking you to the station." Dahvit protested strongly.

"You don't have to..."

"We know, we'll be right back and asleep within the hour, worry not." Stasia smiled reaching for her robe.

"Fair enough, I'll see you kids downstairs then."

It was a bittersweet departure. Victor realized that he had needed to be in the bosom of compatriots and in following his instincts realized that he had also yearned intermittently for his solitude on Aungier Street. Ian had an old friend named Sil who insisted perpetual movement was the key—drop in rather than host—but could Victor live a life in that state? It would be the only thing he had not tried, and it would be a fine way for him to determine once and for all how to approach a lasting peace.

The bus approached and Victor hugged the couple.

"It was a distinct pleasure. I will return as soon as possible." Victor promised sincerely.

"Do," Stasia plead, "I miss LA and somehow having you here made me not miss it as much."

The bus ride to the airport was less rural than the one Victor had taken seven days prior. The terrain and infrastructure were denser and degraded by use and misuse. Victor fancied a read, but the scenery was too compelling and deep inside, he feared he was looking at it for the last time. If it took him thirty years to get to the UK, how long would it take to return? Victor re-checked his belongings, tickets, and the time to comfort himself.

The stark morning rained on the airport and rendered it a grey, dark-windowed bunker, emerging anti-aesthetically from a mound of earth. Once in the terminal, Victor had to follow a confusing series of signs re-directing him to a crowded and impossible counter. On occasion a customer would be sent away, shouting threats and denouncing airline protocol.

As Victor inched forward in the security line, an officer informed the waiting throngs that a fire alarm had been tripped and that they were not permitted to let anyone enter until the entire terminal had been searched. Victor looked down at his ticket, it was September eleventh, he had completely forgotten. They may all be looking at missed flights. Victor waited patiently and after forty-five minutes the line began moving again.

A bald man in a blue jacket stopped Victor outside the metal detector.

"Sir, we have to test your laptop."

"Okay." Victor replied, putting his belt back into his trousers. The man opened the soft case and removed his laptop carefully. He dusted the machine and sprayed it before wiping and inspecting it thoroughly. He returned it to its case and handed it back to Victor smiling, "Thank you, have a nice flight."

It had been harmless, but Victor still resented the search. As he walked through the terminal he wondered if London still looked at September eleventh as an automatic heightened security day. Victor had ample time before he had to report for his flight. He spied a restaurant advertising pizza and burgers.

The cover of the new *Rhee Magazine* Stasia had stuffed into his backpack, poked out from beneath the menu. "PAKISTAN" spanned the width of the cover. The artwork prominently featured Islamic crescents. With that book tucked conspicuously under his arm, or open under his nose, the dirty-capped, black-clad, heavily bearded American traipsed through a trigger-happy London airport on America's sacred Be Afraid day.

9/11/10

I was sitting in Sheehan's by half-four. At the hostel I realized that I stole Dahvit's copy of Dennett's Breaking the Spell. *I brought it along for dinner and pints at Sheehan's. Brian and Stephano greeted me like a brother returning from war.*

I am now quite drunk.

There are plenty of people on the street, but the people on these streets, in various states of mad inebriation, are simply calmer and more composed in their drunkenness than their American counterparts. I appreciate that quality immensely and it keeps me in this neighborhood day after day.

I lit a cigarette and took a seat where winding Stephen and William became quiet Mercer, to watch patrons milling toward all cardinal points. Some were returning from home—some were off to dinner before drinks—some to the post office, though it's closed—some with a bottle for home, alone—and some with daisies offered in fealty to wild and honest eyes.

Eamonn began pouring a pint for me as I walked in. He was discussing religion with a customer.

9/13/10

My final days in Dublin have been filled with a slow crawling dread—the purgatory of transition. I have fallen into a processional reverence for all five of my senses from daylight to mid-night, and whether the experience has been agonizing or liberating, it still must end. The grim idea of returning to an empty room, emptied of possessions by thieves, creeps in from time to time between pints. The greater fear is returning to an empty City, devoid of the pulsing and incoherent forces that break my heart and inspire me. What if I return to nothing?

But what do I have to lose? Perhaps more important, what do I have to gain? Forget about Los Angeles, why am I returning to the United States? I already know that I'm returning to a social experiment I no longer want any part of. Will I just pour my money down my throat until it's gone, go back to work and to apathetic payment of debts. Why?

Living in the warehouse had been an imposed hurdle; I did not pass that challenge as gracefully as I had hoped. Though I am not ready for a Buddhist retreat in the foothills, I can't help feeling like this is a moment to take advantage of, a moment that will, like returning to Dublin, take a long time to come back around.

Where can I go? I am wary of getting trapped against my will in sleepy, tree-shaded college towns. I'm not yet prepared logistically to go overseas. Unless I can find a way to work in another country I'm stuck in the US.

≈

What then? The men scattered about the pub, slouched, or sitting high and proud, are men made by their circumstances. I want out of that loop.

I am a shadow. My haunts, they haunt back.

≈

LXXIX

Spring ~ 2076

Alex rushed through a Real Community™ backlot and heaved open a production trailer door. "Where can I set these? Come on, I'm in a hurry."

A bored intern pointed to an empty corner of her desk.

"Perfect." Alex slapped the folders down and bolted. He had less than forty seconds to catch Dana Rorhbacjer before she made it to the makeup trailer.

As Alex cornered Studio 11, he saw Ms. Rorhbacjer. "Dana, Ms. Rorhbacjer, it's Alex from the production team, may I speak to you for a moment?"

Dana's frazzled assistant shook her head no beneath their immense black umbrella.

"Yes, I always have time for my fans. Alex, right?" Dana asked, adjusting her spray-lacquered hair, and slipping into her role.

"Yes ma'am. I mean miss."

"Not for long," Dana flashed an obnoxious ring—worth more than a generation of Alex's salary.

"My goodness, that's very impressive. Is there any way we can speak privately?"

Dana's assistant vigorously shook her head no and pointed to her watchless wrist.

"You know what, um, Alex? I need a soda anyway. Let's go to my trailer." Dana swiped the umbrella from the assistant's hand. "Thanks, that's all for now."

Dana ushered Alex into the trailer. "Did she follow us?"

"Whom?"

"That ghastly assistant?"

"No, I think we're alone now."

Dana slipped a pill bottle from her jacket pocket and cracked open a warm soda. "It's nice to see you by the way," she flirted, "Thank god you showed up. I have a fucking scene and she wouldn't let me take my fucking meds." A rainbow of barbiturates disappeared into her mouth in a flash, and America's favorite 'Farmer's Daughter' belched.

"Dana, I overheard something shocking, but no one will listen to me. I need your help."

Dana sank into a plush recliner to let the pills kick in. "Alex, right? Just because we hooked up once doesn't mean we're friends."

"Once? Are you serious? Listen, I was at Club Mindfuck last night, bored as usual, so I hit the bathroom to do a little skiing."

"Do you have any?" Dana perked up.

"No. Please listen, I was doing a line off the toilet paper dispenser and I heard someone mention Stacey Jacobs. *Apartment 1426C*, Stacey."

"I love that show. Even though it kicks our butt every week, I still watch it. The fucking parties they throw in that building are outrageous."

"So loud that bombs could go off, right? And nobody'd even know, right?"

"Sure, I guess. This is getting boring."

"Someone really is going to set bombs off. That's what these guys were talking about. It's the season finale for *Pershing Place*."

"The spin-off?"

"Yes. Look Dana, they're going to stage a fake terror attack. Something they'll blame on Outlanders or Inter-Realists; their bosses hadn't decided. But the point is to have Stacey *accidentally* discover this plot after it's too late. They're going to kill her too, Dana."

"Who were these guys?" Dana began to pay attention.

"I don't know, I couldn't see them. All I know is what they said made sense now that Stacey's dating that guy from *Pershing Place*."

"Okay, so you're not sure." Dana smiled, relieved. "Hey, it was probably just a couple of Hollywood types talking shit over lines of coke. What's the big deal?"

"I'm serious Dana, something is about to happen. I think we should at least call a reporter or something."

Dana stood and walked toward the trailer door. "You don't *know* what you *think you know*."

"They're going to kill people, Dana."

"No one that matters. It's Alex, right? Alex. People die every day, not much anybody can do about that. The thing is, we're in a fight for our survival. If no one watches, we disappear. All of us. Don't you think the Real Communities™ are worth a little collateral damage? Aren't we worth saving? Alex?"

Dana turned before closing the trailer door. "I'd leave the studio lot if I were you. You're kind of a dead man now, but ultimately you did the right thing, Alex. That's what's important, right?"

≈

The season finale inspired a small bump in ratings, but just shy of the goal mandated. Bomb attacks and kidnappings dominated evening programming and daytime Real Communities™ built the tension for sundown and the great gamble: stay inside or spend that money. The studios paved the way for the streets of Real Communities™ to run red with blood. The chaos had the religious on their knees and politicians begging for help.

The Asian-Pacific Federation (A-PF) mobilized its fleet at the close of the first financial quarter. As dawn broke on televised-Los Angeles, the Audience watched a show of force occupy Hawaii without firing a shot. Behind the curtain, A-PF led forces from the Union of Autonomous Entertainment States began to move over the Canadian and Mexican borders. An impressive naval fleet dramatically entered Los Angeles Port in a hail of cruise missiles and cannon fire. They provided set and setting for the slow infiltration of an occupying force—live, day and night, on receiver screens worldwide.

"Hello?"

"Romeo, it's Alex. I've been trying to call you all day."

"Alex, where have you been cuz? I'm sorry, they just gave my phone back. You'll never believe what happened last night."

"Save it. Something really bad is about to happen and I need your help."

"You *save it.* I just spent the night in a detainee camp. I'm not going anywhere as far as I can tell."

"Detainee camp, what do you mean?"

"Camp: fences, locks, mean hombres with machine guns, detainee: me. SWAT teams showed up last night and evacuated everyone in the pouring rain, said there was an emergency of some sort. They took us here; I think we're in Garden Grove. Anyway, like I said, I just got my phone, but no one is telling us anything."

Alex was terrified. "This is much bigger than I thought."

A guard in body armor shouted, "Candida. Romeo Candida..."

"Bigger than what? Hey, Alex, I have to call you back, it looks like they may be letting me go. Alex? Did I lose you? Stupid puto." Romeo waved to the guard. "Hey, yeah, I'm Romeo Candida."

"Let's go, Candida."

Romeo was processed and released. The guards were silent, and Romeo got the feeling the fewer questions he asked, the better. He tried to call his cousin again from the parking lot of a large abandoned shopping center. "No signal, of course."

Romeo found a local bus and connected with his daily commute on the Blue Line train toward downtown LA. When he got to work, his department was deserted. "Hey. Where are you fuckers? You'll never believe what happened to me."

The entire staff was in the conference room gathered around a receiver console.

"I've got some crazy shit to tell you guys..."

"Romeo, please be quiet. We are under attack." Angelina pointed to the console.

≈

A morning show host was pressing dramatically against his earpiece and announcing *breaking news* in disjointed half-sentences.

"...yes, we are now hearing that San Francisco and San Diego are also under attack. Wait...are you sure? That doesn't sound right. Ladies and Gentlemen, I'm being told that the ports of San Francisco, Los Angeles, and San Diego are being attacked by A-PF ships, anchored off the coast. KTLA is now streaming video from helicopters near Catalina Island of Japanese Yoritomo-class Destroyers firing cruise missiles into San Pedro, Wilmington, and Long Beach. Yes, ok, the Ports of Los Angeles and Long Beach do not seem to be the focus of the attack."

The office speculation began:

—That doesn't make any sense, what's the point of attacking the port if you don't shoot at the port?

—It's weird right? Wilmington, really? Why Wilmington?

—Refineries, it's always about the oil.

—Those refineries are worthless without the ports, which goes back to his original question...

Angelica shouted, "People are dying, what is wrong with you?"

The room got quiet; the scolded employees still giggled through their embarrassment.

"They probably got evacuated like I did..."

"You were evacuated?"

"Yes, last night, SWAT teams filled my neighborhood and started escorting people out of their houses. Said there was an emergency. Buses pulled up from every direction and off we went."

"SWAT, like LAPD?"

"Yes, I mean, I assumed so, though now that I think about it there were no badges or..."

"Where did they take you?"

"It was like a giant grocery store. One of those big fuckers. I think we were still in the South Bay. They let me out this morning, still no clue what was going on."

"This is what was going on." Angelica pointed to the broadcast.

"I need to get in touch with my cousin. He called me scared to death this morning; he thought something bad was about to happen. I need to check on him."

"Of course, Romeo. Everybody, I think we should all go home, call our loved ones, and keep an eye on the news."

A voice boomed from the office foyer. "Attention, this building is now under the control of the Sonshine Militia." Masked men in desert camouflage poured into the office from all sides. Romeo could hear the receptionist screaming and then a single gunshot.

The employees froze.

The voice from the foyer drew closer singing *Battle Hymn of the Republic* and dragging the receptionist's corpse by the hair. When he reached the huddled employees held at gunpoint he smiled and dropped the receptionist. "I didn't expect to kill one of you traitors so soon. It's going to be a good day."

"What do you want?" Angelica, ever the leader, pleaded.

"Want? That's complicated." The man behind the booming voice removed his skull facemask. "There's no ransom, this here is political. Some of you, hell, most of you, are going to die. A handful of you will be kept alive to give testimony, maybe even you, beautiful," the man caressed Angelica's chin. "We are god-fearing patriots and we are here to purge the Inter-Realist infestation."

"Inter-Realist? You are mistaken sir, this is a PPTEa organization, supporting the Real Communities™ through Human Resource services..."

The militiaman fired into Angelica's chest. "Ok, so maybe she doesn't get to survive. The point here is that a cleansing death will be your only salvation. Your conspiracy with terrorists and atheists must be met with brutal and enduring justice." The militiaman kicked Angelica's body. "I'm going to leave this here; in case anyone starts feeling brave. Any questions?"

The militiaman smiled and walked out of the room.

"Steve," Romeo whispered. "Steve, come here."

Steve scuttled cautiously across the floor. "I don't want to die, Romeo."

"Did you see the patch on that guy's arm?"

≈

"Yeah, a flag, so what?"

"It's a forty-nine-star flag. These guys are Southwest Territory militiamen, leftovers from the Great Western Calamity."

"If you're trying to calm me down it's not working."

"These guys hate brown people; this has nothing to do with Inter-Realists or the attack on the ports. They label us Inter-Realists, and the Fed looks the other way when they lynch us. We have to get out of here as soon as possible." Romeo's phone vibrated in his pocket. He quickly pulled it out. The last thing Romeo saw before a bullet pierced his skull was the name *Alex*.

Steve raised his hands in the air and the soldier backed up.

≈

The Audience was captivated as known Inter-Realist-sympathizers were sent increasingly violent and detailed warnings by the Federal government. [31] The occupying forces carried out coordinated attacks and ambushes, none but the willfully blind denied that the Federal government assisted A-PF forces by conducting covert domestic operations. The A-PF's mission statement was Manifest Destiny—no concessions and no tolerance for non-participation—but if it could last for a few seasons, why not?

Those outside the guidelines of the Real Communities™ were pariah, to be imprisoned and fired upon, but above all, a lessened citizen, a lower caste. Rebellion was frequent, but as shaman, priest, and politician had learned over the centuries, once instilled, the prime philosophies will always surface. The Federal government fought its most important war in the minds of its children, for without their blind acceptance, without their washed minds, the tradition of their ancestors, and thus their identity, would extinguish.

The Federal government duly preserved Invisible Hand economics as the necessary adjunct to its theological ends. The façade of the free-market requires the deeper necessity of worshipping capital over people. In the millennia marking

31 Operation Nineveh: eleven RTVS Human Resources Division staff members were kidnapped and held prisoner for forty days by a Fed-sympathetic militia.

human addiction to hierarchy, Americans had so convinced themselves that *someone* needed to be in charge that they worshipped a magical creature they could never meet, or address personally. Ignoring, of course, that if they are blind to this creature until after death, how is it that the Master got the message to them? *Secret meetings, you see, no notes, as it has always been with god. Please just trust me or we'll have to burn you alive, capisce?* [32]

No one in Real Communities™ asked *why*, no one asked *to what end*, they simply acted, re-acted, and looked to their dogmatic fantasies for the strength to commit atrocities—for the ability to justify their continued existence as a pawn in an

---

32 After the last Good War, the multi-national corporations became lazy about concealing their pet-investments in American religiosity and the tentacles of business wrapped tightly around the American Crucifix; the flesh of corporation replaced the flesh of humanity as icon. A "religious test"—expressly verboten in the holiest of American laws—existed for the highest offices in seven states at the turn of the twenty-first century.

Xenuites, in tune from the beginning with corporate hierarchies, surprised the Vatican by being the first to legally commodify a theology. Monotheism, in all its vaporous forms, sued Xenuites in courtrooms around the world for intellectual property infringement. The Catholic Church in particular, testified that its extensive archiving, molding, and preservation of Theology granted the Church rights to the primary tenets they felt Xenuites had plagiarized. Xenuites rebutted that the Catholic Church, indeed, monotheism in general, was a continuing meme and that ideas such as meditation, discipline, and giving one's self over to a higher being and/or purpose were arguably human traits and that the Catholic Church was trying to seize rights over basic human social and biological tenets.

In the Xenuite view, Psychology had proven that the positive effects people experience from religion are in fact effects that we will instinctually seek out in one form or another. In essence, shoving the absurd wedge of religion into the hole keeps the hole from being filled with something less...accepted. The Vatican, still reeling from its formidable, horrific, and continued coddling of child-molesters-et-rapists, could not bear the weight of its flock asking: if that absence in our lives can be filled by something else, why are we choosing to fill it with your god? if god isn't the only solution, why should god be my solution?

Xenuites welcomed the confused masses into its flock. In keeping with Catholic methodology, the Xenuites usurped local and regional icons and ideas and folded them into Church doctrine. The age of psych/self-help religiosity blossomed. Buddhist, Hindu, and esoteric texts sold in record numbers nationwide and dharmic-auditing became confession in the American lexicon. The underlying Humanism of the new spirituality appealed to a god-weary and ever secularizing world. Incorporation was a defining strand of the new spirituality's DNA, and modern churches addressed necessities that had been ignored by the ancient tribal myths.

Long before the PPTEa was passed, traditional monotheism had become a fringe belief-system, a looked-down-upon reminder of a tragic and brutal chapter in human history. Imposing religion upon children became taboo and the bloodlust of the post-Zoroastrian philosophies—Judaism, Islam, and Christianity's myriad splinters—lived on only in polluted minds. Their ancient racism, sexism, and hatred were stringently kept from ever dominating social epistemology again. In spite of the People's awakening, and in keeping with the true relationship between religion and power, monotheistic opinions and elitism continued to exist as whispered solidarity in the halls of Federal power, and among the aged, a silent cue that one was in the club.

unseen creature's sacred game. A game in which dependence precedes slavery.

In all, A-PF remained strategically violent, preferring to attack major city centers that had succumbed to Inter-Realist or similarly minded *insurgent* groups, and maintaining a modicum of on-camera control. Inter-Realism's refusal to accept the pop-culture-paradox of separate *realities* enraged the Real Community™ leaders. The Fed became *violently* determined to prove that their version of reality was *correct*, and the A-PF was all too willing to provide Coalition troops to assist—a Coalition from seventy-two nations eager to occupy a sliver of American society.

The Fed's blind devotion and intolerance of dissent made a blushing pass at the lunacy of the Medieval Catholic Church. Fed-sympathetic militias revived beheadings as a potent visual reminder of our fleshy frailty, all with silent reverence, invoking the presence of the highest power in the universe.

Spies and assassins entered communities disguised as next-door neighbors, mailpersons, clergy, porn directors, and daycare employees. Both physical and character assassinations slowly and subtly displaced and infected the community's peace of mind. Some communities recognized and challenged government cells, but inevitably another would emerge nearby organically. If a point of no return was reached, terror and slow agony marred the final days of the diseased community.

Once the target was effectively subjugated, A-PF bulldozers conquered suburban sprawl and reduced it to rubble. No laws existed in these demolished places of commerce and rest, rampant violations of human rights were condoned to maintain vacancy and chase away potentially returning refugees. Once the machine had ground all living things out of existence the battle line would move forward to another location.

The Fed was methodical and slow moving. After the A-PF moved on, the Fed littered the rapacious front with remote controlled machine guns, ensuring that the only life in these former towns and cities was a Coalition military presence.

Silent Centurions[33] exterminated any life detected in the battle line's wake.

33 Sixth-generation MQ-1 Predator, unmanned aerial vehicle (UAV) used primarily by the United States Air Force (USAF) and United States Central Intelligence Agency (CIA). The Centurion was the first UAV to operate equally as well in land campaigns, and infiltration operations. The Centurion program utilized nano-bio-tech advancements to manufacture the unique hull. Millions of flesh-like surfaces that connected to an electronic nervous system reacted to stimuli and collected information that the nervous system then converted into communicable intelligence. Weapons systems for the Predator's progeny were discarded when production costs were streamlined, and the Pentagon embraced a planned obsolescence model.

Last Rites

§
LI

Fallen Empire - Season Six

Erlyst summoned Melvin.

"What do you want, are you not making enough money?" Melvin took a seat near Erlyst's wheelchair.

"I need your help Melvin. I have identified the man who prevented my death."

"Cool. Are we bringing him in?"

"No. He must come to me."

"Okay Erly-Sue, I'll bite, why?" Melvin yawned.

"It is none of your concern Mr. Wurtzel."

"What do we do with him when he comes in?"

"Reward him, I want him lionized as my savior. The entire world will be waiting for him to come forward. And he will."

"I like it, MANHUNT, it brings a new dimension to the show, and people can feel like they are playing along in the hunt. Decals, cups at gas stations, basketball jerseys, let's run with it. When?"

"Now."

Still images materialized from the 7th and Metro platform on the fateful day that took Erlyst's mobility. Melvin reviewed the images with his production team.

"That guy?" Melvin pointed to a skinny kid alone on the platform near a very stately and poised Erlyst.

"Yes sir, in the Irish hat thingy." Melvin's intern called over his shoulder without looking away from the monitor.

Melvin recognized Erlyst's Good Samaritan. "They said they already found this guy, right?"

"Well, more like they know the three of four most likely places to find him. He smashed his cell phone when he grabbed

Mrs. Atropos, but the police were able to retrieve the phone's SIM card data. If Erlyst's people have the man's name they're being extremely tight-lipped about it."

Melvin considered his next move...

...then barked to his team, "Alright my children, let's make him the most infamous man in America."

clip

A slow, sweeping shot of a dark, foreboding subway platform begins as soft cello music plays low minors. The subway platform is deserted, filthy, and painted in shadow. The frame shakes and splinters to black.

After five long years a wrong may be righted.

Erlyst sits at her desk, writing in the warm evening sunlight. Her body is harnessed to her chair and her mouth is troubled. Each buckle and strap holding Erlyst upright gleams as the camera circles her.

After five long years of questions, the world may find an answer.

The grainy image from the subway platform flickers as it zooms in and the silhouette of a man in an Irish flat cap fills the screen.

After five years of pain, a Matriarch may finally know peace.

Images of suburban streets, city alleyways, Arab deserts, and Pacific jungles, cross and recede behind an antique atlas zooming in on each continent in turn.

WHERE... IS... THE... EXILE?

end clip

— cut to faux newsroom—

Chase: Folks, it's been a hell of a journey so far, but our sources tell us that Fallen Empire's seventh season will make the rest seem timid.

§

Stacey: That's right Chase. And if the trailer we just watched is any indication, we are in for a real-life manhunt.

C: So, Stacey, what can you tell us about this mysterious man? What did they call him?

S: The Exile. Our sources close to Mr. Wurtzel's team tell us he was not only there on the fateful day, but that he caused Erlyst's paralysis.

C: Why would she want to find such a person?

S: He saved her life, Chase. If he hadn't stopped her, a train would have killed her.

C: Stacey, that's ghastly!

S: It sure is, Chase, but here's the best part: our favorite Mommy Dearest wants to thank him personally.

C: What does that mean?

S: We'll have to watch...

C: Who could resist? Thanks for clicking on Action Entertainment Voice, I'm Chase Covington.

S: And I'm Stacey Stacerson. Goodnight and remember, we're your Voice for Entertainment in Action!

The Man's face was flashed around the world, and soon a meta-cult grew up around "The Exile"—soil tilled furtively by TheGreatSamaritan.org and SamaritanInExile.org. T-shirts of the strange man, silhouetted in an old Irish flat cap, soon overcame sales of Che Guevara t-shirts, and finally became a must-have item in high schools and night clubs both foreign and domestic. Every week, someone tried to turn The Exile in. Elaborate conspiracies between neighbors sought to impersonate The Exile; the viewers simply could not stand the suspense and sought a conclusion, be it truthful or concocted.

§

Twenty-fourth Day of March Two Thousand Nineteen
A confession as dictated to an undisclosed third party

As each day passes and as each moment's storm clouds obscure the sun, some new part of my body fails me. In the beginning, scores of fake well-wishers made their way in and out of my chambers, pacing above me like a murder of crows bickering over carrion. Then the empathy gave way to pity and they smelled their opportunity to punish a helpless victim. Deserved? Yes. And I deserve far worse.

On the night we met, Kyrios and I left that rooftop and fucked in an alleyway like teenagers. We were discovered by an inebriated college student, blind drunk and slurring. The student insisted on "joining the party" and unzipped his khaki shorts. Kyrios grabbed the child by the neck and pummeled his head against a brick wall until his skull collapsed. I never screamed. I tried to run but Kyrios grabbed my arm and pulled me down the alleyway to his entourage. He explained on the drive to Atlanta that we would take separate private flights and he would see to everything being taken care of. I need only join him in New York and remove the evening's memory from my mind.

This perfect hell of immobility was cast on me as a punishment for trying to do what I have always done best...take the easy way out. My word was my command and it was obeyed. Now that I am crippled, and the hyenas smell death I have no further use for my voice.

In all of this, I am, as I expected I would be, alone.

- Erlyst Rae Atropos

‡

XIX

9/14/10

My final morning in Dublin has arrived; I woke easily, felt well rested, and commenced showering as a soft, dark-blue glow began to stripe the hostel's windowsill—dividing Dublin's day and night. In preparation for the worst, I set my first alarm for far earlier than needed. After leaving the room, I wandered through the café, and had a final cigarette on Aungier.

Though the sun rose lazily in the east, storm clouds provided a dense, opaque lens and the impossibly muted light resigned to paint the curvature of the gathering cloud armies in silver. My cigarette was gone before I was ready to relinquish the cool morning and light rain. So, I smoked another. The streetlights began, one by one, at times in pairs, to disappear into hibernation until dusk. Though Dublin was still painted in night, the lights' internal mechanisms recognized six am as day.

Aungier was awash in tiny rivulets. The stone sidewalk was a microcosmic Grand Canyon. The street, more modern, washed all opposition to the gutters and out to sea, to return, albeit soiled, to the cycle. The glassy Earth reflected the warm reds and browns of the buildings surrounding Avalon House. Framed by blue darkened sky, the colors of the silent and sleeping buildings seemed to be melting and pooling onto the street—rushing west, announcing the day. Sunlight streamed through the maelstrom in spotlights like arctic sunshine pressing through fissure-wracked ice. I hailed a cab and wished myself a rapid return.

9/14/2010
830AM

I'm through all the hoops now. The international gate is a dismal basement room, devoid of shopping, devoid of food and coffee stands, stark and sequestered. The only color in the room is an enormous mural depicting famous Irish Americans, from politicians, to musicians and writers. Top-notch propaganda for the returning American. Reminds me a little of Saddam's murals in the Baghdad airport depicting him riding a chariot with missiles into battle. (How American is that?)

Customs was annoying. Angry (or pretending to be angry) cop. Reminded me of some of my douche-bag football coaches in Texas. Dublin is pissing rain today, thank you Ireland.

‡

The warehouse had crawled further into filth and decline while Victor was in Europe. The trash heap in the corner of the main warehouse had grown by feet instead of inches and Victor felt certain a pest invasion of some form or another was in the offing.

Jem had run off to Texas with a guitarist from a touring gutterpunk band. They were a safety-pin-black-eye-kidney-punch-match-made-in-the-gutter. No one blamed her for running off, they just wondered what she was thinking, leaving the rave business to layabouts. The ranks of new tenants had swollen from three to nine and six of the new tenants had never started, nor intended to start, paying rent.

To make matters worse, the person left in charge was the person inviting the squatters in. Although most of the squatters were alright kids, all of them had 1-3 animals: large and medium-sized dogs, several cats, and who knows what else. The dogs were fond of urinating directly in front of Victor's door.

The air had become thick with animal dander and excrement, the constantly violated bathrooms off the main concert room were never cleaned, and several months of unchecked wrath had been unleashed on the already tenuous plumbing. The fragile, and frankly illegal, living situation was crumbling rapidly. It looked like Victor would be moving again soon, his sixth move in just five years. He had grown quite accustomed to living Downtown and loathed a return to Hollywood particularly and the rest of the city in general.

10/19/10

I've been home for a month now. Nothing is the same. I see through such altered lenses now. I feel that a certain self-imposed ennui has been staid. It may return, but now I know it can be combated. I long passionately to remove myself from the day-to-day turmoil. The duality of life and vocation is repellant and crushing simultaneously. Make no mistake, as we draw breath we struggle. It is not a magic curse brought on by sin or weakness, it is simply reality. With billions of humans all pursuing their unique experience how could everything always work out? It defies any honest sense of the world around us, further, it speaks to a willful ignorance, the kind of ignorance that begs for a myth—tell me a story about what a perfect world looks like, a world where no one ever infringes on their fellow human and everyone is eternally happy. I'll tell you a story...

We have seen the ravages of war, racism, and genocide; the graft, prevarication, and agonizing schisms that come with these stories; these myths of absolution from suffering for the chosen and none else. As a species we have over and over violently rejected the concept of the benevolent idealist dictator because we know that the myth always collapses. If we had the ability to see once and for all that there is no life after death, we would be forced to re-think our dedication to madmen and their myths of distant-yet-attainable perfection.

Universal peace doesn't look like a gigantic hippie orgy where disorder is subdued by inebriation and

> *positive vibes. It looks a little like competent, accountable people making decisions based on preserving human life rather than using it as kindling for massive altars to arrogance.*

‡

"What? Get the fuck out, you can stay with us." Ian slapped Victor on the back.

"Hey man, that's really incredible. Are you sure?" Victor began to give Ian an out.

"Certain." Ian took a long slug from his stout. "So, when's it happening?"

"I don't know; it's all fucking weird."

"Get the hell out of there. Grab your meager belongings and walk over to our place tonight. Done and done."

"Done and done," Victor smiled. "Thank you."

"Don't mention it."

Victor placed his backpack in the corner of the loft's cavernous main room, next to Ian's desk. Ian's '53 Olympia sat prominently on the back of the rough antique desk. Victor wanted to smash something poignant onto the white sheet of paper sitting silently in the typewriter. He depressed the l key with his index finger and watched the hammer slowly approach the ribbon; the Olympia was in stellar condition.

During the day Harper and Ian were at work. They spent their morning together drinking coffee while Harper prepared to leave. Ian was settling back into the construction industry with his ex-boss—construction management on contract, on the fly—and hit the streets by ten am.

Victor was engulfed in silence.

During the first days of solitude he was lost and wandering. Victor wasted large swaths of time on nothing, on simply combating the frustration of being penniless and free to do as one pleases. He accomplished nothing, he felt nothing, and he became a Dachshund awaiting one of the useful humans to return from their day.

§
LIII

The Exile was a no-show, and the peasants were at the proverbial castle walls armed with fire and pitchforks. Lawrence walked into Erlyst's chamber bent on cancelling the whole thing.

"Erlyst, please listen to me, this has to end now."

She lay silently in her bed. Her face was calm, and her eyes were lidded, as if in blissful sleep. Lawrence felt her cheek; she was cold. He checked for her pulse and cried out to the nurse, who entered the room in a blur of white.

"Oh my god, oh my god, oh my god," she shrieked as she checked Erlyst's vital signs. "She's dead. She's really dead."

Lawrence looked at the young nurse. "Don't you mean *'Oh no, she's dead'*?"

"If you say so, good riddance if you ask me. She hated my guts."

"You do realize that I am, was, Mrs. Atropos' attorney?"

"Wait, I didn't...she's old, she died in her sleep. I'm out of a job, why would I..."

"This could turn ugly rapidly. Do you have a good lawyer?"

The nurse began to cry.

"A jury can be easily swayed," Lawrence leered at the young nurse, "and so can I. This can all go away if you do me one small favor." Lawrence began walking toward the nurse and she looked away, disgusted at the compromise she faced.

"You'll help me?"

"Indeed." Lawrence sneered. "I'll call the police; it will look better if you're trying to revive her. Like we didn't wait and have this tiny, intimate chat. And my favor..."

"In front of a dead body? Not interested. Didn't you say it's best we call right away?"

"Yes." Lawrence grunted.

When the police arrived Lawrence and the nurse were having tea and cigarettes in the rooftop garden. The officer in charge interrupted their conversation.

"Mr. Robertson, I need to speak to you. Alone, please."

Lawrence complied and soon returned to the young nurse. "They suspect foul play. Apparently Erlyst suffered an arterial embolism and a subsequent stroke. I'm told this could have been caused by injecting air into an artery. With that in mind, they'd like to speak to you next. Do yourself a favor, get a lawyer; you're not smart enough to do this on your own."

"Wait, I thought you were going to... "

Lawrence walked into the stairwell without acknowledging the nurse.

The Police took the nurse into custody and Lawrence washed his hands of her. He needed to contact Wurtzel and see how things should play out. Melvin didn't hesitate; he threw around ideas of a public wake, a burial beneath Hollywood Boulevard on receiver screens worldwide.

"I need your help with something," Lawrence interrupted.

"Fire away."

"I need your confidence."

"Done. Get on with it Larry."

"The police think Erlyst was murdered, and they suspect the nurse. Honestly, I think she's too dim to pull it off, so I convinced them to keep it under wraps in hopes that the culprit re-surfaces. There must be no mention of this on the program."

"Come on Larry, you're fucking killing me. Murder is a godsend for the show." Lawrence feigned offense and Melvin held his hands up shrugging, "I'm just saying."

"The more likely suspect is The Exile. I told them that Erlyst left a sizeable amount of the estate to him. He may have caught wind and decided to rush things along. Erlyst, may she rest peacefully, never told us the man's name. You can appreciate our desire for secrecy at this time."

"Fine." Melvin couldn't pay people to write this caliber of apocalyptic drama. The final season would make more advertising money than the rest of them combined. This would play out for years in foreign markets and they may even get a movie or two out of the deal when all was said and done.

"Move forward as planned, celebrate Erlyst as she was, and we will intensify our search for The Exile." Lawrence concluded.

§

"You aren't afraid he'll refuse, are you?" Melvin suddenly wondered.

"Give me a break, who would refuse?"

"Someone who was concerned with something besides money."

Lawrence looked at Melvin as if an extra head had suddenly sprouted from his shoulder. "Show me a man who is not concerned with money and I'll accept that it is possible."

"Maybe Erlyst just did."

Lawrence's receiver buzzed and he bade Melvin farewell.

"Yes officer, I understand, and no, I was not aware, but I thank you." Lawrence ended the call, "That rotten little bitch."

According to the detective from the crime scene, the police commandeered (at the Nurse's request) the camera that Erlyst had installed in the wardrobe facing the southern post of her bed. She wasted no time advancing the digital recording to her discovery of Erlyst. The entire conversation, and the compromising offer of legal protection for a future rendezvous, were played out frame by frame as Erlyst's corpse looked on.

The nurse was far shrewder than Lawrence had anticipated. No matter, she wanted out of the situation as much as he did. He sat in his chair and played out every possible scenario. He would need to keep an eye on the investigation and keep counsel close at hand, until after The Exile surfaced.

The Audience mourned alongside the players in *Fallen Empire*. Faux-wakes and funerals were held worldwide, and social networking websites were rife with JPG homage to viewers' favorite characters from the show. Soon Irish flat caps sprung up all over America in honor of The Exile. Though it certainly made it more difficult to differentiate fans from the hunted, the Audience never thought their actions through. They stumbled through life, proud Americans, and smashed any fertile stab of beauty that penetrated their thick consumer armor. Over watercoolers and in chain bars, people wondered if The Exile would claim his share of the Atropos Empire. What would *they* do? The decision fascinated the country and through a vicarious parasitism they felt empowered by The Exile's ability to rule the world simply by appearing.

≈

LXXX

Winter ~ 2089

The Interrogator had long shaped the conscience of the Movement, but it had lately evolved further than his shepherd's vision had dared. The barbarity of the remaining RTVS citizens forced the Inter-Realists to bear arms once again, rather than wielding the light of reason. Preventing the decay of the RTVS from infecting the Outlands was paramount.

The Interrogator seated himself at a meager table across from two hooded, bound prisoners. He needed to know if the Fed was conspiring with the Sonshine Militia. Prisoner A wore smart, tailored clothing and his cuticles and fingernails were healthy and clean. Before the collapse he had been in sales, it didn't matter *what*, he could sell it. He turned that charisma into a high-ranking position among the christo-fascist elements preying on the remaining RTVS communities. Within the rapacious-consumer construct, the god-shaped hole seemed most firmly rooted by archaic, late twentieth century christ-worship, and the ghosts of Falwell's minions continued to haunt Federal soil.

To his left, Prisoner B was unkempt, his hands were scaly iron, and it was clear he hadn't slept in a bed, or through the night, in years. Before the collapse of the RTVS, he had been an ordinary Joe, a plumber until the Second Reformation. When the jobs dried up, he spent his time in the bar. Elements of the new ignorance were beginning to form over cheap pilsner and broken egos. Prisoner B thought *those guys* sounded a lot like him, like guys he'd have a beer with.

He looked around at their rallies and saw familiar, safe faces. Prisoner B knew his way around a hunting rifle and had received plenty of combat training during the A-PF occupation. When the beer hall revolutionaries called, Prisoner B took up arms.

After a long and disconcerting silence, the Interrogator smashed his hand on the table. Prisoner A jumped in his seat;

≈

Prisoner B remained unfazed. "Good, I like to know what I am working with," The Interrogator murmured. "Take their hoods off."

The Interrogator paced silently, adjusting his round, thin-framed glasses periodically and smoothing the black field uniform hanging awkwardly from his wiry frame.

"Where are we?" Prisoner A blurted.

"Safe."

"Inter-Realists..." Prisoner B growled.

The Interrogator motioned toward Prisoner B and a guard pistol-whipped the bound man. Prisoner B laughed quietly.

"I'm interested in uniting our, um...faiths. Your true enemy lies outside the walls of the RTVS. If our nation is to continue as a strong, pure State, under the one true god, the outsiders must be exterminated. Trampling over one another is counter-productive to say the least. I am releasing both of you. You will take a message to your leaders on my behalf. It is time to unite."

Neither prisoner spoke, they both seemed locked in a cocoon of silence. The Interrogator raised a long black cane and smashed it against the cheap table, "Do you understand?"

Both men remained silent.

"Take them away and bring me someone who is still on this planet..."

"Wait...wait." Prisoner A spoke up, "I'll deliver your message, just get me out of here...please."

"Excellent...you'll be processed today. Gentlemen, please take the other prisoner back to his cell so that we can go over this man's presentation..."

Prisoner A's neck perforated in tiny red droplets; he gripped the wound as blood rushed between his fingers. A whittled and burned piece of plastic bathed in Prisoner A's blood dropped to the floor. Prisoner B looked up from beneath his unkempt hair, "Traitors deserve death."

Prisoner A convulsed and splashed blood against the walls of the interrogation room. "I can appreciate your dedication, but that was a mistake. No one is being asked to betray the cause, quite the opposite."

"You ask for complicity, complicity is heresy. We are ordained by the almighty. Worldly groups covet power, and power belongs only to the Almighty."

The Interrogator laughed, "You were definitely chosen for your integrity, it's clear you're not the smartest...."

Prisoner B half-stood, pulling at his chains like a junkyard dog waiting to crush an intruder's windpipe.

"Sit down." The Interrogator leaned on the table sternly, "Now."

Prisoner B refused, growling his dissent.

The Interrogator turned his back. The guards entered the room on his signal and collected Prisoner B. The Interrogator stopped the guards at the door. "I want him placed in solitary confinement; he is not to speak to another human being."

"Yes sir, of course."

"And one last thing..." The Interrogator pulled a guard's revolver from his holster. "Hold him."

The guards stood at the prisoner's sides and held his shoulders and elbows steadily.

The Interrogator smiled tiredly. He never expected to last this long, he was amazed and beleaguered at each day's conclusion. "Joseph Ghālib, by the powers vested in me, I sentence you to execution."

Prisoner B's expression softened, and he looked up with thankful tears in his eyes. The Interrogator ceased smiling and pressed the revolver to the prisoner's forehead. "You are indeed a sick man. Martyrdom is what you have always wanted. Why? It's so cheap."

"I submit to god because it is my duty, I submit willingly, and I submit in whatever way god sees fit. I am honored to die for my god, undeserving though I may be." Prisoner B's eyes were adrift on a sea of dopamine as he, no doubt, patted himself on the metaphysical back and chalked a point into his tally of afterlife-deserving behaviors.

"That's my point son..." The Interrogator moved close to the prisoner's face, "you're taking the idiot hatch. Your god thought so little of you that he never made you useful. This was his plan for you. To your god you matter only in death."

"I do not have to explain myself to you, I answer to a higher power."

"Ah, yes, your higher power. You share this planet with a myriad of species you do not *answer to.* Conveniently, *All* answer to your god. Yet, you do not share this world with your god. You share it with me, with humanity, with animals and insects, with bacteria, viruses, supernovas, and collapsed stars. Yet you reject their authority in favor of a lie. Talk about living in denial. It's no surprise that questioning god's authority is heresy, what is left if you are wrong about god?"

"I have the Truth."

"Yes, then it is settled.

The guards removed the prisoner. The Interrogator sat at the empty table and stared at his hands. His ambulatory skeleton had moved beneath his skin. Raised flesh along the backs of his withered hands revealed the machine's long tendrils tracing his phalanges. The hands looked dead, weak, but he could still put a man down with them. In all of this, he had to ask himself the same question. *Why*?

There was a grasp for immortality in the prisoner's actions. After the Interrogator's death only vaporous traces of his masterwork would live on. No one will ever utter Prisoner B's name in worshipful reverence, but his deeds, forever scarring the soles of his god's feet, will cast the eternal spell of the *Martyr.*

They were biting the hand that fed them. They were bent on destruction, for destruction's sake. They did not fit into The Interrogator's perfect vision; their existence meant he had been wrong about something very important, something he was not certain he could correct.

Immortality—
evolutionary supremacy—
cultural authority—
dominance—
submission—
Mythology—
Control.

‡

XXIII

Spring – 2011

The first days of spring rain in Los Angeles blanketed the skies with threats of immersion. On a Friday morning Victor walked to Ian's desk as he sipped a cup of coffee, just a bit too hot to drink. The large chasm created by the four inner walls of Ian and Harper's building dropped fourteen floors to the sub-grade basement patios. Dense clouds blanketed the sky. "Feels like rain," he murmured quietly.

Transparent continents began to form on the massive panes of antique glass. Victor opened the bottom windowpane as the sky began to fall. He sat behind Ian's desk and replaced the paper in his typewriter. The smashing of key against pulp and the rain against glass carried him long into the evening. Victor continued typing until he heard a voice over his shoulder.

"Hey, get an idea?" Ian removed his overcoat and lit a cigarette as he walked in.

"Yes. Sorry, I hope you don't..."

"Don't even say it."

"Thank you."

"De nada. So, what's up, what are you working on?"

"The rain. Couldn't really help it, for whatever reason as soon as it started sprinkling this morning I sat down and kind of zoned out."

"Nice."

"How was work?"

"Same old shit, you know the drill. Get back to typing, I'll leave you alone."

"No, you don't have to..."

Ian had already walked into the kitchen and waved dismissively over his shoulder.

Victor continued until Harper came home. Shortly after they all sat down to eat. As Ian and Victor cleaned up, Harper called from Ian's desk. "This is really intense boyfriend, when did you write this?"

‡

"It's not mine, it's Victor's." Ian responded, soapy dish in hand.

"Oh, shit, sorry Victor."

"No, I left it out, you are welcome to read it. I think I'm going to write something that has a lot of rain in it."

"From the looks of it. I actually felt drenched by the time I reached the end."

Victor was careful from then on to remove his papers from Ian's typewriter. He considered it proper to return the machine and desk to its original state. Victor began to lead a separate life: short breaks and strolls through the neighborhood peppered his days, but ultimately, he lived behind the large wood desk looking out into the chasm and imagining a world devoured by a petulant storm.

In the evening he separated himself and lived amongst his roommates as they came and went. Without the occasional step into the neighborhood Ian would have accused Victor of being a recluse. He tried to lure Victor to the Library, especially in the rain, but Victor insisted on his schedule and insisted on being behind the desk during any chance of rainfall.

‡

The unbearable summer heat of the city rolled like a dense fog into Ian's loft. From the window, Victor could only see shadows in the chasm. The interior walls were littered with large, hinged factory windows open to let whatever trickle of cool air pass through that could. Victor needed to breathe.

He headed south on 110 past the monolithic cranes of the Los Angeles Port until it terminated in San Pedro. As the sodden, forgotten neighborhoods peeled away, Victor slowly approached the ocean. The air rushing through his open windows was playful and had the salty kink of the sea. He parked at Point Fermin and strolled along the short, ornate wall barring the casual walker from a one-hundred-foot drop.

Victor saw a long staircase leading down to the beach. He followed the curve of Paseo del Mar and walked down the steep incline to a small park area just above the beach. From there he descended a narrow, bent, and shuddering staircase haphazardly patched together with aluminum, scrap metal, and old rotted wood.

The day was clear and mild; from his perch on a large rock, he could see tiny white dots moving across the channel: summer boats in Avalon Bay. Beyond the peaks of Catalina Island, the Pacific seemed to rise into the sky. Victor watched the calm blue wall build into a tsunami, an unwell sea becoming death. As it engulfed the island and careened shoreward, his mind begged him to flee, but the rush of water was upon Victor immediately and the world lost all shape. Victor sank among the ruins of our drowned Los Angeles; above the flood, a bitter pestilence spread its tendrils throughout the city and slowly choked it into submission.

Victor's hand fell onto a full ashtray next to the typewriter and sent it across the room. The settling plastic cup jarred Victor from his vision and pulled him back into the real world. It had all been in his mind, but the sky remained grey as if a storm approached. A swift breeze lapped at his hair and the papers on his writing desk. The papers fell to the floor, slow as deceased oak leaves, and the wind was gone.

Victor rose from the desk and walked to the papers on the ground—his treatise to rain.

Ian placed his keys on the kitchen counter and began to pack bottles of beer into the refrigerator door.

"Ian," Victor spoke weakly from across the loft.

"Hold on brother, I can barely hear you." Ian cracked open two bottles and walked over to the desk where Victor sat with his head in his hands. "You alright man?"

"I think so. I think I need..."

"A beer?"

"Yes. Thank you. I'm moving out tomorrow."

"Oh," Ian was surprised. "So soon? You know you're totally welcome as long as you need..."

"I appreciate that, you have been more than gracious. I won't be far, only a block away. The Rosslyn is desperate for someone other than addicts to move in, so I got a spot for a song."

≈

"I'd offer to help you move, but I don't think you need it. What do you have, a backpack?"

"Some extra papers now. A few hundred."

"Really? Is this the rain piece?"

"Yes. It became a novel before I had a grip on the plot. But that's changed." Victor lit a cigarette.

"What happened?"

"In a vision, I sat at the rocky base of the Point Fermin cliffs and witnessed the conclusion. Felt it. Everything leading to this point is clear and I'm ready to finish."

Ian leaned in and set his beer on the desk. "Tell me what you saw..."

Victor took a corner apartment in the Rosalyn Hotel. The hotel had successfully gentrified: moneyed-hipsters and post-collegiate city employees occupied the top three floors. Victor's floor was still host to weekly tenants and the hopelessly addicted. As day faded into night and back again, Victor sat in a broken chair with a loaner typewriter on his lap that bucked like a rabid rodeo horse. Harper spied a desk being thrown out in South Los Angeles. She and Ian picked it up and delivered it. Victor was extremely grateful, but both Ian and Harper could tell he was anxious for them to leave.

≈

LXXXI

Winter ~ 2114

The long-Divided States lay in waste. Renewed European-style colonial fervor had the countries of the Asian-Pacific Federation treating the UK, France, Spain, and Germany to a taste of life under a foreign master's whip. With so much suffering to remind Europe of, the world's major players left the former United States to rot—*the Beast must never rise again.* The nation's resources, both natural and man-absconded, were over a century dead. The vast wild lands of America were pocked by war and the skyscrapers and subways of her proud gleaming cities formed massive indigent aviaries for frightened refugees.

The roving bands that survived outside of the militarized Inter-Realist communities swallowed proselytization whole. Some entered the fold out of sincere devotion to the ideas laid out passionately by the former Inter-Realists, and some entered because of desperate hunger and rampant vice. They organized under a banner of cooperation, their goal: nothing less than replacing a species' mythology of perpetual war with one of perpetual stability.

The movement was eventually canonized by the descendants of the Old Man's final council. The archetypes were woven carefully into the varying and often contradictory epistles of the Kanpotar, Inter-Realist, and post-Inter-Realist movements. Generations refined these lessons until children could sing the tenets and achievements of our heritage before bedtime.

An End. [34]

§

LIV

Fallen Empire - The Final Season

"Weeks have now passed, and The Exile shows no sign of making his big debut. Viewers are wondering..."

—Flash to newsreel—

"Who does this man think he is?" Representative Heisede from Kentucky asked a packed press conference.

We talked to people on the street ...

"What? That motherfucker is crazy! That old lady is richer than god! Where else he gonna find a better deal than that?"

Cut to brightly colored set with dozens of viewer screens flashing the corporate logo—

"Where indeed, ladies and gentlemen, welcome to...

P—O—V."

---

34 Apocrypha p. 315

§

—music—

"What man would walk away from taking care of himself and everyone he knows for the rest of their lives? What kind of selfish lunatic must he be to have run, to try to escape judgment? What gave him the right to shun the viewers and to walk out of the bright lights of justice and become nameless? Eric," the lanky host pointed dramatically at a retired general and the camera panned hard to catch his concealer-caked face.

"Well, to be frank, the Exile would not exist without his audience, he owes them an explanation, a public confession, and we will settle for nothing less. Judgment lays in the hands of the Audience."

"What do you think Shirley from Elko, Nevada?" The slick-haired host pointed into the sky to address a caller.

"What? Oh, oh my gawd, am I on the show? I love you and I love... "

"Let's hear from our best-selling author, non-fiction of course," the host skipped no beat.

"As I lay out in my new book, to be watched is to be exonerated of guilt, to be presumed innocent by the invitation of a watched life. The expiration of privacy is caused by our willingness to allow the court of public opinion to outweigh legal opinion."

"Let's throw our brain-doc in the mix, go!" The host swung his hands toward a young physician.

"Yes, well, whether this idea actually made any sense or not, escaped our scrutiny. It was simply a layer of reality woven into the fabric of our psyche for a century. For society to question the prime axiom (what one watches is what one lives) they would have to unplug for generations. Indeed, one day they may have no choice."

"Well that was depressing, right folks? Tell us what you think online @bestShowEver_period!"

The fraternal twin of our society's ignorance was impatience. Though this manhunt consumed American lives for the remainder of the season, sales became tepid, and the viscous puddles of public sympathy were coagulating. A wide dragnet began to slowly form downtown three weeks before the *Fallen Empire* season finale event. The City of Los Angeles barricaded traffic between Flower Street and Main, stretching from First Street to Ninth. Out of work men and women in putrid orange vests and carpenter pants were soon part of the Downtown landscape; as millions of cars and bodies filtered in and out of the downtown area, the orange vested worker ants erected long white and red barricades. They began on the perimeters of Pershing Square, dissecting the postmodernist park from the Downtown landscape. Next, subsequent blocks, including the opening to the Pershing Square Metro Station, were swallowed whole each morning by more barricades and legions of orange vests. The City authorities fashioned a slowly developing spiral that eventually created a "safe-zone" where journalists' tent cities, a murder of Lunch Trucks, and twenty-three catering companies, ran their operations. Several battalions of off-duty or retired LAPD officers were supplied to *Fallen Empire* with ample glee, by eager to please, eager to impress, Mayor Alamán.

Black and white posters papered the silent walkways of the Financial, Fashion, and Theater Districts—NOTICE OF FILMING; refuse blew down dry, angry streets. In the evenings the streetlights flickered on, in spite of the evacuation.

§

Ides of March ~ 2020

As late afternoon receded behind the shadows of skyscrapers, long black SUV limousines began choking downtown streets. The wealthy, famous, and morbidly powerful arrived at the Millennium Biltmore Hotel and emerged from petrol-guzzling beasts whose shiny black shells obscured the ground, giving the asphalt wasteland the appearance of life—whipping, cutting insect movement. Each finely clothed and pristinely bejeweled guest was personally escorted by uniformed staff past the lightning storm of paparazzi and into the hotel. The Biltmore's lobby, a monolithic testament to a past-time's reverence for beauty, was peppered with early guests. Tuxedoed wait-staff whispered calmly among the brash unapologetic conversations weaving between lips and rolling from pink, healthy tongues:

Chopard asked Ferragamo to please lower her voice—Bvlgari closed Manolo's account this afternoon, how long would it take for her to find out? (or did she already know?)—Blancpain pressed his nose lustily against the curve of Blahnik's neck—Constantin and his one and only Louboutin love, waited for their deaths in silence.

As the clock began striking seven post-meridian, uniformed hotel staff began to herd the crowd toward the hotel's bank of elevators. Groups of four were escorted into the waiting cars until the floor had cleared of guests.

"What a bunch of lousy human beings." Rafael, the concierge for the evening, grunted as he returned to the front desk.

"Right? Should'a started punchin' and seen what happened." Stanley added.

Stanley and Rafael's director spat hastily. "Shut your mouth. Feeding my kids is important to me, what about you?"

"Right Frank, we understand." Stanley lamented sincerely.

As the one hundred guests took their assigned seats in Erlyst's massive library, the room became stifling. The crush of *Fallen Empire* crew lining the walls, and the minimal, yet aggressive press photographers choking the foreground beneath Erlyst's Chippendale writing desk absorbed all available space. Lawrence E. Robertson seated himself at the antique pedestal desk beneath the pervasive floodlights and loosened his tie. Thirty feet above his glistening head, dark, English Regency-influenced Bibliothéques terminated against the curved mural-laden ceiling. The walls of archaic bound texts were painted in an unreal silence above the dense lights and the din of perspiring humans.

Beneath the penetrating glow the guests adjusted their finery and, perhaps for the first time in quite some time, felt uncomfortable. Several cell phones chirped forgotten alarms, the owners were kind enough to locate them and turn them off rapidly. There was a show to film after all.

The sun set precisely on cue; Melvin paced behind monitors on a lower floor. "Show me the cutey in the first row."

"Her?" His tech closed in on a provocatively attired kid's show host.

"No, you idiot, the emo kid. Didn't he put out a hit record recently?"

"Yes, that's..."

Melvin interrupted, "I don't care. Now, pan out, let's get a wide shot of the whole dog and pony show. Yes...that's it...perfect."

Nine o'clock passed; moreover, it had been another quarter-hour since it had. The restless guests were quite pleased when the Executor entered the study from a door on the southern wall.

"Good evening ladies and gentlemen. I am P. Anne Twardowski, I was named Executor of this last will and testament by Erlyst Rae Atropos, to be executed on this fifteenth day of March, two-thousand twenty. Please be seated and come to order." Mrs. Twardowski stood stoically on Lawrence's left side.

"I'm Lawrence E..."

"That's enough Larry." Mrs. Twardowski patted Lawrence on the shoulder. "I apologize to all in attendance for the delay, it is quite impossible to communicate the gravity of this moment for all of our esteemed and welcome guests."

The room erupted with applause. Those in attendance were quite pleased with themselves.

"Order please." The Executor waited for the audience to calm, then seated herself behind the stunning desk and opened a locked attaché containing Erlyst's last words.

In the control room, all the monitors went black. "What the fuck? What the fuck?" Melvin spun thrice shouting increasingly vile insults at his staff until the feed returned to the monitors. "If that happens again, you're all getting it with the strap-on from my girlfriend."

"Mr. Wurtzel..." a petrified assistant director squeaked.

"No lube," Melvin concluded. "What Schmitt?"

"Sir, Thalia's here." Schmitt pointed to a monitor showing the hotel's massive foyer.

§

"Nice. Wait, we lost her; do we have a hall camera on her?"

"No sir, she's out of sight. If she's still on the property, we'll find her."

"Schmitt, keep an eye on her, everyone else, back to the shenanigans."

Thalia walked slowly past the Biltmore's cavernous lobby. She knew she shouldn't have come. Her mother was dead, that entire life was dead. She was alive. Forgotten, but still alive. Thalia straightened her back and looked up into the breathtaking fleurs-de-lis shapes and lush hues along the immense ceilings and walls of the glamorous hotel. She turned around and walked toward Olive Street—back into the spring evening, as a light rain began to fall.

The Executor knew almost nothing about Erlyst. They had taken tea with one another in Erlyst's quarters each day until her passing. Though the Executor felt intense affection for the poor woman she did not understand why she had been summoned to her bedside.

"I will soon need someone to oversee something very important to me." Erlyst had said.

"I am flattered beyond words, but why have you chosen me Erlyst?"

Erlyst looked away. "I don't know you, we have only our afternoons together. You are the only person whom I can trust."

The Executor had thought her admission odd and at the very least dramatic. No matter, she assured herself, whatever this poised and important woman had in mind it would surely be of no harm. As the Executor sat before the gathered mob of moneyed miscreants, she understood how, in only a fortnight, Erlyst could recognize fealty and seek to cling to it.

"I'll now read from Erlyst's prepared statement: *To all in attendance, you have my dying gratitude. You have in some way touched my life, affected my view of the world, or influenced my happiness and peace. If the lovely woman before you would be so kind, I'd like her to read the contents of the red envelope silently.*"

Mrs. Twardowski set the statement down and tore the thick red envelope with a long platinum letter opener. The Executor's eyes darted through the enclosed text. Lawrence leaned closer to the Executor in an attempt to read over her shoulder and received the back of her hand instead.

The Executor placed the envelope in a small silver tray. She lit the corners of the thick red envelope with a crystal table lighter and continued to read Erlyst's statement as flames devoured the now secret missive.

"*If the Executor is reading this, she is about to see why I had to turn to a stranger to tie up my affairs.*" The audience muttered to one another. "*The envelope that was just destroyed contained the name of the man who saved my life; known to most of you as* The Exile. *It is clear now that he chose to remain anonymous rather than be here tonight. I wish him well wherever he is.*

Melvin smiled, Lawrence panicked, and the Audience prepared to change the channel.

"*Now that we are beyond that ugly business, we can get back to what is important, what you all came here to witness. My initial instinct was to simply disperse the family's money indiscriminately, choosing to let mathematics decide rather than dedicating a single moment of my short life to the thought. I watched all of you crush whoever stood in the way of your camera time. With each passing day, with each betrayal, with each sleight of hand and emergency loan, I hardened to the turmoil of those whom I would leave behind. It was my intent to burden our exiled friend with the Family Nightmare, but he appears to be more cunning than I expected.*"

The Executor continued, "*Instead, the execution of this testament converts Atropos International Re-Distribution Services Inc., LLC, GmbH into a State agency of the People's Republic of China.*" Men and women began to stand, shouting profanity, clutching the neck of decorum. Something flew past Lawrence's head.

"*It is my honor and privilege,*" the Executor continued above the escalating frenzy with an amused smile, "*to cede all assets to the PRC and the proud, courageous people of Mainland China.*"

A tsunami of cellular waves sparked insurrection in Melvin's beautifully manipulated scene. "Kill the wi-fi, block the signals. Do it now..."

The guests were panicked—no reception. The cameras had front row seats to a Great White feeding frenzy. Conspiracies erupted and heads merged, sinking into circles until movements of two-to-three persons began oozing toward

§

Lawrence and the Executor—they intended to slay the monster that threatened their comfort. Sergeant Jaime Pinkerton entered the shot unexpectedly, and with him the shining badges and black combat armor of the LAPD. The audience melted back into their assigned seats, under psychological detainment.

The Executor opened a large manila envelope and motioned to someone out of camera range. "Erlyst made several charitable donations as well. This suite, including the furniture and removable value will be compiled within a trust and given over to the Los Angeles Women's Rescue. Erlyst's liquid and non-liquid personal assets upon death will be consolidated and given to the Police Officer's Association of Los Angeles. The funding will help realize Mayor Alamán's vision of a task force to assist in Crowd Control and Maintenance Technology Training."[35] Sergeant Pinkerton smiled broadly and scanned the agitated crowd.

The Executor nodded to the waiting concierge. On his signal men in white coveralls wheeled bright-red dollies of document boxes into the room with hastily scratched cataloging numbers against their generic white sides. The ominous wall that began forming behind Lawrence and the Executor wrapped the audience in a blanket of silence. As soon as they had arrived, the workers and the concierge were gone.

The Executor broke the silence. "*The documents presented are hereby made public and will be entered into evidence by Sergeant Pinkerton at the conclusion of this statement. You are all, of course, welcome to peruse them under watch of the documents' new guardians.*" The Executor motioned to the standing wall of LAPD encircling the audience.

"*You see, I have some wonderful stories to tell. These precious volumes, and the multiple sets of copies I left under protective lock and key, tell our story. Kyrios, Thalia, all of us. Every transaction, every destination, every merger, every monopoly, every war crime, every filthy, rape-soaked cent is recorded. I spent my fleeting moments of mobility combing through this raw data and I assure you, no one in this room will be disappointed...or forgiven.*"

---

35 CCMTT (see-see-EM-teez): later used during Westside insurrections by Chief of Police Jaime Pinkerton and Mayor Escalada Alamán to subdue riots during Il Diluvio.

Lawrence stood and placed his hat in his hand. He bowed to the Executor and began to walk out of the study. Uniformed police officers refused to clear the doorway. Lawrence's desperate barking only made the Audience feel sorry for him, how embarrassing. The Sergeant walked across the long shot of the room, he stopped behind Lawrence and whispered in his ear, "You're under arrest, Larry." The uniforms took him into custody kicking and screaming.

The crowd was reeling. Ladies pulled tiny silver pillboxes from their brassieres and rubbed exotic chemicals on their collagen-swollen lips and beneath their heavily redacted noses. The Executor took her leave; the calm brought on by shock would not last, and arrests would soon have to be made.

Erlyst had sent Melvin and his crew off for a week, now he knew why. He had nothing to fear, so Melvin kept the cameras rolling long into the night. The occasional mental breakdown made the extra three hours of footage priceless. The demoralizing arrests of high-society movers and shakers were the stuff of dreams for the *Fallen Empire* audience.

A collective sigh of apathy escaped the Audience's lips. They watched in disbelief as the credits rolled. They turned to one another penetrated by confusion and awe, their loyal admiration and empathy lasted for an entire five and one-quarter seconds.

Next show, I guess. That was a good one, eh? Can't believe they ended it that way, what a waste. Let's see...what haven't we watched?

Another End.

‡

XXVI

November ~ 2011

"I don't know man, Goldflam says about the only thing they did was piss off the neighbors and completely fuck traffic." Melvin flipped his card at the bartender.

Ian took a stool at Hank's and tried to put his money on the bar.

Melvin pushed his hand away. "Stupid."

"I'm sure they did both, they also broke the cardinal rule of our society: they made the whole country discuss the previously verboten. People are complacent; they need to be shaken up a bit."

"You mean people like me," Melvin smiled.

"You do your best to harm no one as far as I can tell. What the NYPD did to the Occupy Wall Street encampment was criminal."

"Enough hippie bullshit for today. How's the wife-to-be?" Melvin giggled.

"Victor?"

"Oh, I didn't know you two tampered with the darkside, my son. You owe *me*, of all people, a poke." Melvin put his arm around Ian.

"No, I mean, look, it's Victor."

Melvin huffed, "Never met him. I feel like we were talking about something important."

Victor sat in the back of the room, hunched over a pint and a notebook. His flat cap was pulled down and his eyes never left the paper. His fierce beard was gone, Ian barely recognized him.

"I haven't seen him in months. Come on, it's a shame y'all haven't met." Ian took his pint with him and walked toward the back of the bar.

Victor looked up, stunned.

"Victor, good to see you too." Ian smiled; Victor still lacked social graces.

"I'm Melvin." Melvin shook Victor's hand. "If that's the last thing I say to you, don't take it personally."

Ian sat down. "How's tricks man? Long time no-see and shit."

"Right. I know. I've been really focused."

"There's a lot going on these days, right down the street."

"I know. It's hard to pay attention to it. The futility is disturbing."

"Have you been down there?"

"Nightly."

Ian sat back. "Of course you are."

"The process for decision making is frustrating and fascinating."

"You heard about New York?"

"I did." Victor responded. "The protest at City Hall's days are numbered too. Expect the same level of brutality and terror from LAPD."

"They seem to have a pretty good relationship with the Mayor." Ian was more optimistic.

"They do, but the Mayor has a better relationship with the Democratic Party, and in spite of its alleged liberalism, the Dems have marked all Occupy Wall Street copycats for violent dismantling."

"How long?"

"Couple of months, maybe. The Mayor has already started talking about what it will cost to replace the lawn at City Hall."

"Seriously?" Ian was disappointed.

"It ended up costing NYPD several hundred million to take Occupy Wall Street out—and that's just the last push to evict—so you can expect some creatively disingenuous arguments for the occupiers to go home."

"And the smell of shit. Don't forget all of the homeless addicts tagging along for fun." Melvin added.

"Safety in numbers, probably a lot more fun than skid row." Victor smiled.

"Touché," Melvin finally looked Victor in the eye. "You are both ridiculously boring. I could be at home, touching myself."

"Love you man, thanks for swinging by." Ian and Melvin hugged.

"Victor, I'd say it was nice to meet you, but honestly, it was a little stressful. We'll try again next time." Melvin shook Victor's hand.

"To next time," Victor offered.

"I need to hit the road in a bit, too. Have a smoke before I go?" Ian asked Victor.

"Absolutely,"

The men rose and walked toward the door.

Ian looked Victor up and down once they were outside. Just behind his glassy eyes was the terror of a small animal trapped in traffic.

"How's the writing?" Victor asked, to make sure Ian didn't ask him first.

"Shitty. And you?" Ian lit a cigarette.

"1300 pages so far."

Ian choked on smoke. "What?"

"I've been spending less time at City Hall, and that's helped."

"That's amazing man. Fuck, when do you think you'll be ready for extra eyes?"

"Hopefully before the unemployment runs out. I wanted to talk to you about that by the way. I think I'm almost done. So, I need a favor."

"Sure brother, of course."

"A big favor." Victor took a deep drag from his cigarette.

Ian smiled, "Okay, okay, what is it?"

"I need to be left alone for a little while."

"More than usual?" Ian laughed and leaned against the Stillwell Hotel.

"Yes, precisely."

Ian stopped laughing.

"I know it sounds peculiar, but I have only been successful in pulling this together when I am convinced of my own solitude."

"You mean impenetrable solitude."

"That would be ideal."

Ian stood silently smoking for a moment.

"So, what's this *thing* about?"

"Rain. The end. Hope for a *better* end. Hopefully."

"You have so much work, over a thousand pages, and...just rain?"

"What happens when it rains, what happens to people, places, lives; what might happen to our city if it rained forever. It's about lusting after something that rarely happens and suddenly never stops."

"The rain?"

"The rain is the catalyst. It is our first sign of weakness."

"Maybe you're not ready to address it outside of metaphor." Ian crushed out his cigarette.

"That's probably true." Victor crushed his out as well.

Il Diluvio

‡

XXVII

Autumn ~ 2012

Black clouds hung over the financial district but refused to rain. The rush of air from the great subway orifice under 7th street was bitter. Víctor descendió al abismo, el santo de las causas perdidas.

Everyone scanned the subway platform, but no one spoke. Victor noticed a tall woman, a wealthy east coast blue blood. She was dressed pristinely in a nineteen forties suit. The fabric was a muted teal, almost slate, and each stitch was tailored to her body. Her lustrous silver hair cascaded in long Lake curls down her back. She walked as if traversing universes, caught between the deepest peace and a tortured contemplation. She was in a trance, yet stern and stoic in the face of a mysterious immanence. Victor wondered what she was doing in a dingy downtown subway station, she looked like she'd never been east of Doheny or south of Wilshire. Then Victor realized she was not stopping.

"Ma'am." Victor began walking toward her, "Ma'am. Ma'am, there's a train coming."

She never looked back, never pulled her eyes from the cool concrete platform's vacillating streamers of grey and white. In Victor's mind he said, *to hell with her*, but his legs contracted, and he lunged. Victor's grip interrupted the woman's steps and she slammed to the platform, inches from her goal.

The woman glared at Victor, on the verge of tears. She reached for the train tracks as rivulets of blood formed on her face. Her broken body began to twitch, and the woman murmured a curse. The subway train rammed into the station, ignorant to her plight. Victor's fingers were wrapped tightly around her ankle; through the horrible grating sound of the train, he had never let go.

People rushed around the platform. A man gently removed Victor's fingers from the woman's ankle and helped him to his feet. She was no longer moving. A sanguine pool slowly formed around her face, fanning out as a crimson corona. Her proud silver mane shone a warm living red as her blood framed her in iconography.

A concerned citizen escorted Victor out of the subway.

"Are you doin' alright fella?" He asked while examining Victor for injury.

"Yes, quite alright. I'm just not sure my mind has come back to me yet."

"Don't worry someone called 911."

"Oh no, I wasn't hurt, I might have scraped something but..."

"You saved that lady's life is what you did."

"No, no I didn't."

"I watched it mister, you're a hero."

"She didn't want me too. I couldn't let go."

"What?"

"She didn't..."

"You're in shock buddy just have a seat, the paramedics will be here in a bit." He deposited Victor on a bus stop bench and rushed back into the subway.

In a callous act of self-preservation Victor stood and walked away, limped away, rightly paranoid about everyone who noticed. The police would certainly want to know why he didn't stick around. They'd get his photo from the surveillance cameras and show up on his front door soon. Better to deal with them down the road instead of just now, he had no desire to answer questions about saving a life someone was throwing away. The sun began to set over distant Santa Monica. Victor lit a cigarette; he had a lot to consider.

‡

Summer ~ 2013

By the time the rapacious June heat subdued the overcast spring, Ian's construction project had come to an end. He wondered how Victor was holding up. Ian carried a cold four pack of stout under his arm and whistled as he walked toward Fifth Street. Harper wanted to come along, but Ian insisted that if the old boy had gone kooky, it would be less traumatic for one person to attack at a time.

Ian slipped into the Rosalyn Hotel behind a man who had been using his trousers as a restroom for months. A guard sitting behind bulletproof glass ignored Ian and the Tinkle Master completely. Antique marble lent a bit of class to the lowlife-littered staircase leading to the second floor. Victor's hallway smelled of college kids and skid row addicts, a tingling bouquet of incense, burning glass, and neglect. Ian knocked on 301. He knocked a second and finally a third time. No one answered, no one inside stirred. Ian took a seat on the fire escape and opened a can of stout.

He caught a glimpse of Victor's typewriter on the meager desk they had found for him. Ian set his beer down and climbed onto the window ledge. The window opened after a heroic effort, and Ian climbed in.

"Victor, where are you, you fuckin' nutcase? Hello?"

Victor's apartment was empty. The walls were bare, as were the windows. A single coffee cup sat in the kitchen sink next to a single spoon, the assorted ashtrays were all half full, and his bed was perfectly made. At the edge of Victor's desk sat a large stack of typewritten pages, collecting dust. Ian brushed it away until tight black letters appeared: *Il Diluvio*. Victor had hand numbered the pages—the last, 2941.

A half-filled sheet hung from the back of Victor's typewriter. An unfinished sentence dangled beneath the silent keys, waiting patiently under its own pressure to be completed.

He hadn't finished. He was finally alone, and something interrupted him.

‡

Ian looked around the room from the desk. Victor was long gone.

He picked up a handful of pages and lit another cigarette. By the waning light Ian poured over the densely packed text and witnessed the sun set and rise through filthy windows.

The End.

Apocrypha

Missive to my dearest Sophia
LXXXII

Our People tired and our stamina began to weaken. Constant violent conflict with governments, foreign and domestic, had made clear the futility of fighting fire with fire. We kept to the borders and stopped the settlers from advancing. Knowing that every inch we lost would take centuries to regain. We melted into the shadows of the warscape and waited.

An Inter-Realist soldier, a confidant and emissary for their movement's Elder, moved beyond the Watched Society's border under cover of night and made camp near our outpost. By morning he sent warning of his presence via signal flare. Our Farmers approached the soldier, then sent word: he wanted an audience with a Kanpotar emissary.

I was chosen to represent our outpost and accepted the honor.

The soldier was courteous and wished our People prosperity. He came to his point rapidly and asked that the Kanpotar and the Inter-Realists come together against the Foreign Occupation and the government.

I explained. —We are wary of pacts with your society. It is not wise to take you at your word.

—We offer something more than our word. We know that someday the Watched Society will be no more. We, like you, seek that end now, and are prepared to shoulder the burden. We don't want your people to bleed in this war any longer, but when we are free, we ask for your help to evacuate those willing to leave, to a new life.

—A life built on our labor.

—A life built on your mercy. We are a military rebellion. We cannot manage the land.

—If the Watched Society comes to an end, what will become of the outlands?

—There will be no outlands; there should never be outlands. You have created a paradise that deserves to flourish without fear of reprisal. It is our hope that you will welcome those trapped in the Watched Society.

These were very impressive words, but they meant nothing without action. I asked, —How will you defeat the Occupation?

—We fight as mightily as we can, we daily increase the cost of their war, but we are against an immense rival and alone.

I shared our wisdom with him. —If you are prepared to suffer, then you must draw down. Your rebellion is for show. As you lay your weapons down, the Occupation will be forced to do the same.

—Forced, by whom?

—Wave a smirking white flag to the Audience. All power that flows through the Foreign Occupation flows from the Audience. When there is no enemy to attack, the Audience will punish the Occupation. The Audience fuels this fire, they must be distracted.

The soldier could not deny my wisdom, but it troubled him to accept it. He left pleased, pretending to be satisfied, but I saw the lust of the Occupier in his eyes. It is a dark omen that the Inter-Realist Elder has cast his poisoned light outside of the Watched Society.

Beware all, beware.

Sent with caution—but above all love,
Maat Nanuet

According to Salinan of the Chumash Valley LXXXII

The collapse of our Watched Society invited the deepest avarice from our Federal Government. Production companies, working on inside information, began to shutter their operations and the Fed moved in to arrest the studio heads and halt the drawdown. The Fed decreed that there would be no formal economic announcements regarding the death of the Watched Society. Though the transmission would be cut, the cameras spanning every usable inch of the Watched regions would remain in place. The citizenry was to continue performing, the Audience was a state of mind, and no longer needed to maintain control.

When the final collapse could no longer be hidden, the deluded kept up shop, kept up appearances, and kept the Potemkin villages intact until the patina of time pushed them from ruin to refugee. Deluded social Luddites waving the forty-nine-starred American flag, murdered families trying to flee the Watched Society. These ignorant hordes subsided on stripped copper from abandoned infrastructure and eked out a meager, proud existence burning rubbish in vacant apartment buildings and cannibalizing their youth.

On the frontiers of the Watched Society, those of us near the borderlands watched as immense vented obelisks in the Outlands began interrupting the sunset. Scrap metal from now useless tractor-trailer trucks was being used to create the girders and supports of hollow skyscrapers. Within two years the ominous scarecrow-like mysteries blossomed in full array of every currently edible plant. The Outland community began to barter with our Neighborhood. They taught us how to garden vertically and before long, domiciles from one story to one hundred began hosting their personal food requirements. We made ends meet by agreeing with other Neighbor communities to share crop.

Under the compassionate hand of the Kanpotar, the coastal plains were slowly becoming fragile yet feasible breeding and hunting grounds. Slowly, warily, species by species, the creatures that had survived, were returning.

In the vast lands outside of the Watched regions, hundreds of thousands of plastic post-millennium cars littered the borders of every state in the Entertainment Union. The shells of these cars became life-saving shelters and eventually homes.

Outland factions on the southwest coast began testing the tidal impressions of the moon's pull by attaching millions of tiny spidersilk-anchored buoys to piers. As the sea pushed the buoys in circles a volatile gel inside warmed with the friction of movement on all three axes. The energy produced by the friction was converted into electricity and either stored or amplified for distribution. Barring a disastrous alteration in our moon's orbit the Outlands could count on the satellite's gravitational water show for a steady and unshakable pulse *ad infinitum*.

What was left of the Federal Government attempted at various times to seize the Outlands' offshore generators, but the reluctant Kanpotar warriors fought them to a standstill. The Watched Society communities were permitted to sign compensatory contracts for use of energy. The Fed failed on all fronts to meet their responsibilities but the Kanpotar could not bring themselves to shut the power off when the children and families they would be murdering were not the ones refusing to pay.

I could no longer be part of my society's exploitation of the Kanpotar. I defected and was welcomed with open arms, educated, and shown a way of life worthy of human endeavor. I removed the markings of bondage from my skin, and committed myself to defending the provinces against tyranny, be it philosophical or in the flesh.

The efficiency of the Syndicalists' social organism gave birth to a legitimate alternative. As the Watched Society declined, it fed like a parasite on the foundations laid outside its walls. By engorging its rupturing belly on the resources wrenched from filth by the Kanpotar, the Watched Society propped its cadaver up for a final longing kiss to the cameras—though they were long gone.

as revealed by
Our Common Knowledge
LXXXIII

The Distant Elder called his trusted Inter-Realist lieutenant and a Kanpotar engineer to a modest room far above an abandoned storefront. All were seated beside The Elder at a short table. A large window, opaque with rushing rain, consumed the room. Thirteen floors below lay Old Main-Spring Street, deep within the charred Los Angeles Great Gardens.

"My friends, we must put our differences aside. Though a minority among us desires to antagonize and threaten chaos, we all have the same goal. I will be gone, sooner, rather than later. The movement, for all its faults, has remained true to its mission of granting differing ideas a common ground." The Elder looked around the table; he had his audience's rapt attention, as he had Alamán's, Calhoun's, and Fuentes', in their time.

"It appeared that what we hoped for was impossible. For far too long, people in this country could not muster the pride to wake up and rebel. After granting our people the freedom to live wide-awake, we will ultimately taste defeat as future generations forget how important our achievements are to humanity. Our young commanders have begun to mimic the old oppressors. The militarism necessary to defeat the Occupation has remained and is now being turned on the citizens of the fallen Watched Society. The love of power has been allowed to blossom, and the mistake of idolizing the victorious is upon us again." The Elder looked at his peers in turn.

Emma de Cleyre, our most gifted Kanpotar engineer, provided the first infrastructural proposals for the rapidly expanding, urban Syndicalist communities. Her vertical gardening schematics and alternating power generation schedules had defined the *maximum impact with minimal maintenance ethic that allowed the Kanpotar experiment to remain creative. In her time, she had been opposed by hardliners, hopelessly dedicated to industrial models, frightened by abstract thought and idle hands.*

Caroline Ascéndo, an Inter-Realist Lieutenant for the Western Front, had worked closely with The Elder to abate the infection caused by Inter-Realist commanders consolidating power centers. Throughout the A-PF occupation, Ascéndo had taken her fellow Inter-Realists to task when the temptation to glorify violence became too seductive for them to resist.

"The people are not the problem, they are vulnerable, and once they commit to comfort and relent, they submit to the old oppressions gladly." Ascéndo offered.

The Elder confirmed, "Making it that much harder to resist the imposition of control. Violence, empirically, is a strong motivator. Philosophy, to its detriment, takes time and consideration."

"Excuse me, why am I here? I don't feel like I belong in this conversation. I'm not a philosopher, and I'm certainly not an Inter-Realist."

"Utility is a philosophy, Emma. You belong here because you understand your people. When you shelter them, provide them with transportation by-ways, and mold their reality to function, you translate and define their essence. You create with an honesty that we must learn from." The Elder smiled.

"Well, then let me say that you're looking at it the wrong way." de Cleyre leaned in, convinced of her position at the table. "It isn't comfort, it's ignorance. In order to remake our society, we had to build a workforce, and to maintain that workforce against malignant opposition, work became life. But we are no longer nomadic and frightened tribes, we have worked toward a social organism that requires minimal maintenance. We yearn to create and to express ourselves, but my people, like yours, face resistance from a faction that claims any amendment to the model is a threat to the entire revolution. We are a young people; we have no first-hand memory of what life was like before the Occupation. As soon as a slick-tongued Syndicalist tells them they're in danger of losing everything, they allow charisma to supplant validation."

Ascéndo added, "The lingering masses within the Watched Society serve as an eternal enemy that Inter-Realist commanders can repel and vanquish."

"It is this ignorance that is plaguing our people and yours, Emma." The Elder completed the circle. "We teach our children to respect the good of the whole, but we have failed to give them a definition of what a complete society is."

"Universal concepts of morality are what failed us in past," de Cleyre urged. "They beg to be exploited."

"Morality is a tenuous contract, we need utility. Not right and wrong, but true and false. The first human tendencies toward religion were a veneration of animals and their knowledge. We saw the animal kingdom's seemingly effortless symbiosis with their environment and envied it. For all of our tools, art, and attempts at communication, we struggled against a mysterious and capricious environment. We reasoned that a show of respect for the power these animals held might grant us some of their knowledge. Emulation is the core of religious tendency—the imposition of a perfect example, and the plan for attaining that perfection. For any of this to take root, one must be convinced that one somehow *lacks* an attainable power."

"It has always been our way to empower, rather than impose." de Cleyre lowered her head, "It is sadly indicative of decline for persons to freely choose such a rigid model."

"That's why we need to provide our people with an alternative, an enduring compact," The Elder insisted. "The success of the Kanpotar project proved our people's resilience, now we must help them hold on to this precious knowledge and ensure that it survives the bloodlust and seduction of power."

"An archetypal system." Ascéndo offered.

"But we end up back at right/wrong, good/evil with archetypes." de Cleyre countered.

"Not right and wrong, true and false." Ascéndo reminded her.

"Tension, friction, and struggle—life ebbs and flows based on this interplay of events. We can provide a foundation upon which our two nations will build and adapt to their changing world."

"To codify is to court dogma." de Cleyre remained skeptical.

"Indeed," The Elder agreed, "and nullifying that danger is paramount."

"What you are proposing is very rational, but guidelines mistaken for rules have a tendency to become the means to an end."

"That is why we must appeal to our natural sense of wonder, the inner voice that compels us. Knowledge must again be a journey and a discipline, rather than an external construct one must fit into. By revering mystery, we allow evolution: if each generation produces a new set of dedicated seers, the ancient symbols will naturally invoke new, unique visions. The absence of dogma ensures that the seer's vision is not stifled by the past."—*The Elder's left eye rent, becoming two. His three Eyes now peering out with equal hate*—"We must symbolize the rational past absurdity. Reverse-engineer our natural ability to reason and separate the real from the fanciful. We can rebuild over and over, if necessary."

He spoke now from five mouths, each coercing in their way, each demanding their due.

But Our Kanpotar Architect could not be deceived.

"Whether fluid or rigid, your hunger for Control is a deadly current."

"Not control," The Elder answered spitefully. "We provide Order. We cannot separate a lasting peace from Order. And Order must be enforced."

"Soahc si Ymehpsalb." Ascéndo called eerily.

The Kanpotar Engineer closed her eyes and covered her ears: "We resist this Plague you summon. What you foresee is our Death."

The Elder's ancient chest heaved,
with each breath, he grew into a fearsome Beast
filling the room with the powerful arms of a storm.
Defiled names marred the Elder's flesh,
bending before all cardinal points,
Far beyond his control.

The Fork-tongued Elder's countenance ruptured.
And His Filth,
became one with the Air.

At long last, Concealed no more
From here, where Equity of hope
  Guides our actions

—Beatitudes Do harm no longer.

Acknowledgments

Deep-sea chasm-depths of gratitude for Spaceboy Books, Nate Ragolia, and Shaunn Grulkowski; thank you for publishing this *thing*, for it has always been more *thing* than book.

Undying gratitude and immense respect for the three people I am pleased to spend my days and nights with—Wife, Q, and Grey, I love you hooligans, you make me so proud.

Special thanks to Dr. Vincent James whose inspired insights meant so much to the final form of this work, and to Dean Moses, Scott Gilbertson, and Jordan Rothacker for their generous notes on earlier, far more chaotic versions of this manuscript.

Many thanks to Karen Armstrong for her work documenting the *Big Three* Monotheistic religions, and to the late David Graeber for providing refreshing critique of our sick society and suggesting saner methods of thought, community, and interaction.

About the Author

William considers coercive relationships the root of all oppression. Robbed of our ability to freely associate, humanity is enslaved. If there was ever a time to burn the whole fucking thing to the ground, that time is now. As a father, a husband, and an abused citizen of these United Snakes, I want every word in this manuscript to be treated as an open call to rebellion...because they are.

About the Publishing Team

Nate Ragolia was labeled as "weird" early in elementary school, and it stuck. He's a lifelong lover of science fiction, and a nerd/geek. In 2015 his first book, *There You Feel Free*, was published by 1888's Black Hill Press. He's also the author of *The Retroactivist*, published by Spaceboy Books. He founded and edits BONED, an online literary magazine, has created webcomics, and writes whenever he's not playing video games or petting dogs.

Shaunn Grulkowski has been compared to Warren Ellis and Phillip K. Dick and was once described as what a baby conceived by Kurt Vonnegut and Margaret Atwood would turn out to be. He's at least the fifth best Slavic-Latino-American sci-fi writer in the Baltimore metro area. He's the author of *Retcontinuum*, and the editor of *A Stalled Ox* and *The Goldfish*, among other.

www.ingramcontent.com/pod-product-compliance
Lightning Source LLC
Chambersburg PA
CBHW030416180626
46812CB00005B/2028

* 9 7 8 1 9 5 1 3 9 3 1 0 6 *